CW01216794

Terry Pratchett's
The Colour of Magic

ALSO BY TERRY PRATCHETT

THE CARPET PEOPLE
THE DARK SIDE OF THE SUN
STRATA
THE UNADULTERATED CAT (with Gray Jolliffe)
GOOD OMENS (with Neil Gaiman)
NATION

The Bromeliad
TRUCKERS
DIGGERS
WINGS

Johnny Maxwell
ONLY YOU CAN SAVE MANKIND
JOHNNY AND THE DEAD
JOHNNY AND THE BOMB

The Discworld® Series:
THE COLOUR OF MAGIC*
THE LIGHT FANTASTIC*
EQUAL RITES*
MORT*
SOURCERY
WYRD SISTERS
PYRAMIDS
GUARDS! GUARDS!
ERIC (with Josh Kirby)
MOVING PICTURES
REAPER MAN
WITCHES ABROAD
SMALL GODS
LORDS AND LADIES
MEN AT ARMS
SOUL MUSIC
INTERESTING TIMES
MASKERADE
FEET OF CLAY
HOGFATHER
JINGO
THE LAST CONTINENT
CARPE JUGULUM
THE FIFTH ELEPHANT
THE TRUTH
THE THIEF OF TIME
THE LAST HERO
NIGHT WATCH
MONSTROUS REGIMENT
GOING POSTAL
THUD!
MAKING MONEY

Discworld (children's)
THE AMAZING MAURICE AND HIS EDUCATED RODENTS
WEE FREE MEN
A HATFUL OF SKY
WINTERSMITH

Discworld non-fiction
MORT: A DISCWORLD BIG COMIC
(with Graham Higgins)
GUARDS! GUARDS! (with Graham Higgins)
THE PRATCHETT PORTFOLIO (with Paul Kidby)
THE DISCWORLD COMPANION
(with Stephen Briggs)
THE STREETS OF ANKH-MORPORK
(with Stephen Briggs)
THE DISCWORLD MAPP (with Stephen Briggs)
A TOURIST GUIDE TO LANCRE:
A DISCWORLD MAPP
(with Stephen Briggs and Paul Kidby)
DEATH'S DOMAIN (with Paul Kidby)
NANNY OGG'S COOKBOOK
THE DISCWORLD'S UNSEEN UNIVERSITY
DIARY 1998
(with Stephen Briggs and Paul Kidby)
THE WIT AND WISDOM OF DISCWORLD
(with Stephen Briggs)
THE FOLKLORE OF DISCWORLD
(with Jacqueline Simpson)
THE DISCWORLD'S ANKH-MORPORK
CITY WATCH DIARY 1999
(with Stephen Briggs and Paul Kidby)
THE DISCWORLD ASSASSINS' GUILD DIARY 2000
(with Stephen Briggs and Paul Kidby)
THE DISCWORLD FOOLS' GUILD
YEARBOOK AND DIARY 2001
(with Stephen Briggs and Paul Kidby)
THE DISCWORLD THIEVES' GUILD
YEARBOOK AND DIARY 2002
(with Stephen Briggs and Paul Kidby)
THE DISCWORLD (REFORMED)
VAMPYRE'S DIARY 2003
(with Stephen Briggs and Paul Kidby)
ANKH-MORPORK POST OFFICE HANDBOOK
DISCWORLD DIARY 2007
LU-TZE'S YEARBOOK OF ENLIGHTENMENT 2008
(with Stephen Briggs and Paul Kidby)
THE NEW DISCWORLD COMPANION
(with Stephen Briggs)
THE ART OF DISCWORLD

* ALSO AVAILABLE AS COMPACT EDITIONS

Terry Pratchett's
THE COLOUR OF MAGIC

The Illustrated Screenplay

Written by Vadim Jean
Mucked About by Terry Pratchett

Screenplay copyright © British Sky Broadcasting Ltd 2008
Film stills copyright © RHI Entertainment Distribution, LLC 2008
Unit stills taken by Bill Kaye
Cover Photography © Harry Borden 2008
Production storyboards, sketches and designs copyright © RHI Entertainment Distribution, LLC 2008
Production sketches and designs drawn by Ricky Eyres
Production storyboards drawn by David Allcock

Discworld ® is a trademark registered by Terry Pratchett
All rights reserved

The rights of British Sky Broadcasting Ltd, RHI Entertainment Distribution, LLC.
and The Mob Film Co. (TV) Ltd to be identified as copyright holders
have been asserted by them in accordance with the
Copyright, Designs and Patents Act 1988.

The Colour of Magic originally published in Great Britain by Colin Smythe Ltd
© Terry and Lynn Pratchett 1983.

The Light Fantastic originally published in Great Britain by Colin Smythe Ltd
© Terry and Lynn Pratchett 1986.

Terry Pratchett's The Colour of Magic is a Mob Film Co. (TV) Production
for Sky One/ RHI Entertainment

First published in Great Britain in 2008 by Gollancz
A subsidiary of the Orion Publishing Group
Orion House, 5 Upper St Martin's Lane, London WC2H 9EA
A CIP catalogue record for this book is available
from the British Library

ISBN 978 0 575 08045 4

1 3 5 7 9 10 8 6 4 2

Printed and bound in Italy.

www.orionbooks.co.uk

The Orion Publishing Group's policy is to use papers that are natural,
renewable and recyclable products and made from wood grown in sustainable forests.
The logging and manufacturing processes are expected to conform to the
environmental regulations of the country of origin.

Mixed Sources
Product group from well-managed
forests and other controlled sources
www.fsc.org Cert no. CQ-COC-000012
© 1996 Forest Stewardship Council
FSC

FOREWORD
By Vadim Jean

OH NO, the difficult second album. It is almost impossible not to let that thought enter your head when they let you do another one. With *Hogfather* having been pretty well received, there was bound to be expectation which is a worry; mainly because my best work always seems to have had pigs of some kind in the title.

Anyway if you're reading this I hope it means my adaptation of *The Colour of Magic* isn't too terrible and that it hasn't 'mucked up' the book where it all began.

If you've never read any of Terry's fantasytastic Discworld novels because you didn't think they were for you then hopefully the movie is why you're browsing this book; and if it's because you're thinking of buying this as a present for the friend everyone has who's read every single one, go on, have a sneaky read anyway . . .

For me the whole point of turning a book you like into a film is to make it like the book you loved in the first place, otherwise you might as well go and make any old humourless epic straight out of the same character arc, full of identical characters which these days floats on top of the flood of script editing courses which start with 'what does the protagonist want . . .' and ends with me screaming 'I want to run away!' just like Rincewind.

So I hope more than anything else that I have been faithful to the One where it all started. And hence Rincewind runs away. A lot.

The Colour of Magic was my first introduction to Discworld. It has for some time been a dream of mine to have the honour of bringing it to the screen, just as it has been a long-time desire of David Jason to play Rincewind, which he so wonderfully does in the finished film. I hope this care shows and that I haven't missed all your favourite moments – Bel Shamharoth and the giant spider, or the Wyrmberg and the Dragons? So many painful editorial choices to make. I know I won't have got it right for everyone but at least I hope I 'got it'.

Of course, one person really has 'mucked about' with the screenplay. Wonderfully . . . even sometimes urging me to be less faithful and more cinematic. People have asked me how that works and I tell them collaborating with Terry is like having the best Hollywood script doctor imaginable on tap, only a Klatchian mile better.

It was among Terry's many great suggestions, well before I even started writing, that we should also take *The Light Fantastic* and complete the Rincewind/Twoflower story. After all, we couldn't have left them falling off the Disc until next year. I'd hung Sir David upside down for quite long enough in the Wyrmberg, after all. So while Episode 1 is broadly *The Colour of Magic*, Episode 2 is mainly *The Light Fantastic*.

There are so many people to thank; so this book is for everyone who 'got it', from our incredible cast and crew who gave their all, to Johnny Brock who supports us all at The Mob, and especially my collaborators and producers, Rod Brown and Ian Sharples.

But most of all I have to thank Terry for letting me play with the Potent Voyager. Now that's what I call a train set.

Vadim Jean
December 2007

THE LUGGAGE.

TERRY PRATCHETT'S. THE COLOUR of MAGIC.

SIDE ELEVATION.

PLAN.

Episode 1

THE COLOUR OF MAGIC

EXTERIOR THE INTERSTELLAR GULF – NIGHT

Curling star mists . . .

> **NARRATOR (Voice Over)**
> In a distant and second-hand set of dimensions, through wavering star mists see . . .

The mists do indeed part to reveal . . .

> **NARRATOR (V.O.)**
> . . . The Great A'Tuin.

GREAT A'TUIN the turtle comes, swimming slowly, his huge and ancient shell pocked with meteor craters. Through sea-sized eyes he stares fixedly ahead. And then we see the ELEPHANTS . . .

> **NARRATOR (V.O.)**
> Drifting onwards through space atop the shell of the great turtle are four giant elephants, upon whose broad shoulders rests the Discworld.

And now the CAMERA cranes upwards to reveal: THE DISCWORLD.

> **NARRATOR (V.O.)**
> For the people on the disc the turtle was a mere hypothesis, until one day the island kingdom of Krull, whose rim-most mountains project over the Rimfall, lowered over the edge a brass vessel containing several astrozoologists.

And we . . .

> **DISSOLVE TO:**

. . . The same place on the rim, now in SEPIA TONES, SOME TIME EARLIER. A gantry and a quartz-windowed BRASS VESSEL hanging from it appear. From inside, through the window of the vessel, ASTROZOOLOGISTS peer through the mist veils. They are using viewing devices and take copious notes. There is much scratching of heads and shrugging of shoulders

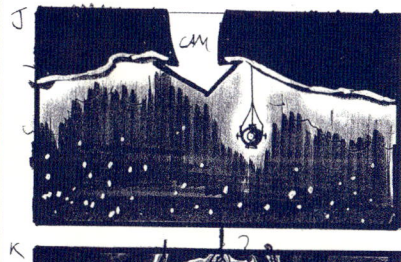

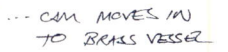

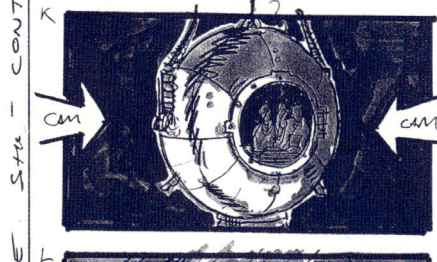

> **NARRATOR (V.O.)**
> Their mission did indeed prove the existence of the turtle. Unfortunately, owing to a minor malfunction,

The chain snaps and the brass vessel plummets out of shot

> **NARRATOR (V.O.)**
> . . . they were unable to answer an even more fundamental question . . .

as we . . .

> **DISSOLVE TO:**

EXT. AMPHITHEATRE/KRULL/ ARCH-ASTRONOMER'S TOWER - NIGHT

. . . a simple drawing of the vessel on a chalk board and the SEPIA TONES bleed back in to COLOUR and PRESENT DAY. As the CAMERA pulls back a pointer taps next to it.

> ASTROZOOLOGIST 1
> What is the sex of the turtle?

The Astrozoologist looks at the group of students in front of him.

> NARRATOR (V.O.)
> The remaining astrozoologists are never short of a question.

There is whispering and they point at the drawing.

> ASTROZOOLOGIST 2
> Why does it matter?

> DIM STUDENT ASTROZOOLOGIST
> So, we're gonna look at a turtle's bottom?

> ASTROZOOLOGIST 2
> That won't be very nice, will it?!

> DIM STUDENT ASTROZOOLOGIST
> No.

The students all look accusingly at the Astrozoologist who is exasperated.

> ASTROZOOLOGIST 1
> Since the failure of the last mission, this vital question cannot possibly be answered without sending a new expedition over the edge of the Disc . . . in this.

He holds up a model of the POTENT VOYAGER.

> DIM STUDENT ASTROZOOLOGIST
> It's a bit small.

> ASTROZOOLOGIST 1
> (sighing)
> It will be somewhat bigger.

There is muttering and murmuring among the students.

> DIM STUDENT ASTROZOOLOGIST
> Yeah, but . . . where in the world are you gonna find someone stupid enough to go in that?

Good point.

EXT. ANKH-MORPORK/RIVER - DAY

. . . TWOFLOWER, the tourist. He is wearing spectacles, trousers that are slightly too short and a baggy shirt with a large flower pattern all over it. As he cups his hand over his brow he smiles widely and we see that he is standing on the prow of a SHIP sailing up the river Ankh.

                NARRATOR (V.O.)
Several thousand miles hubwards from the rim in Ankh-Morpork, the Disc's oldest city, the ship arriving in its dock is carrying Twoflower.

Twoflower looks up to see the Unseen University's TOWER OF ART.

                NARRATOR (V.O.)
The Discworld's first tourist.

                NARRATOR (V.O.)
He is looking forward to all its sights . . . and smells. And of course no tour would be complete without a visit to the city's Unseen University for wizards and its famous Tower of Art.

EXT. UNSEEN UNIVERSITY/TOWER OF ART - DAY

The CAMERA flies towards the top of the tower where there's a swirl of OCTARINE BLUE through which appears . . . THE TITLE:

THE COLOUR OF MAGIC

INTERIOR UNSEEN UNIVERSITY/ TOWER OF ART STAIRS - DAY

A pair of massive wooden doors swing open

          NARRATOR (V.O.)
When our story begins, wizards are not very nice.

A wizard's STAFF sits on an OCTAGONAL funeral casket. Eight wizards are carrying it down the centre of the Great Hall in funereal procession.

          NARRATOR (V.O.)
Carrying the final remains of one of their number, the eight heads of the orders of wizardry have demonstrated great powers of survival . . .

We follow a pair of POINTY SHOES. The CAMERA jibs up to reveal that they are being worn by YMPER TRYMON, a rather neatly dressed wizard.

          NARRATOR (V.O.)
. . . because behind every wizard of the eighth rank there is at least one seventh rank wizard trying to bump him off.

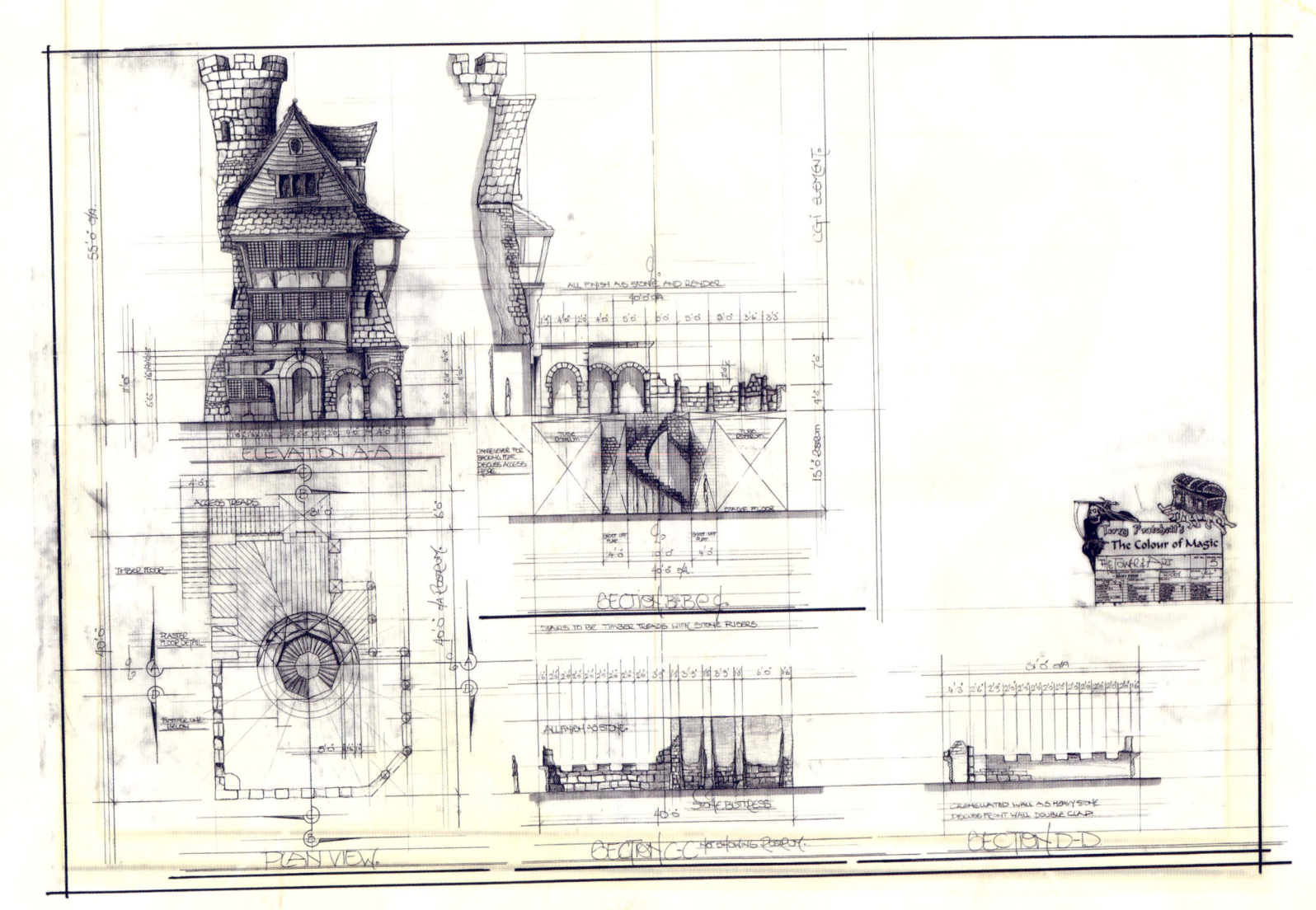

Trymon smiles. He is walking slightly
behind ARCHCHANCELLOR GALDER WEATHERWAX
who leads the procession.

          GALDER WEATHERWAX
  Old Runelet. He never saw it
  coming you know, Trymon?

          TRYMON
  Well you know what they say,
  Archchancellor: when a wizard is
  tired of looking for broken glass in
  his dinner he's tired of life.

Galder looks sideways at him.

          TRYMON
  I'm just speculating, obviously.

The cavalcade stops and they gather
round a large OCTOGRAM on the floor.
The Archchancellor steps forward.

          GALDER WEATHERWAX
  We are gathered here today to
  pay our respects to old Runelet, a
  wizard . . .

At that moment there is a commotion
from the back as the doors open again
and something forces its way through
the wizards.

          RINCEWIND
  Sorry.

          WIZARD
  Oh!

          RINCEWIND
  Sorry. Sorry.

A figure stumbles out of the gathering
breathlessly.

          WIZARD
  Oh!

He is wearing a dark red, hooded, very
frayed robe. Around his neck is a chain
bearing a BRONZE OCTAGON. On his head
is a particularly battered wizard's hat,
with a floppy brim and the word WIZZARD
embroidered on it in big silver letters.
RINCEWIND stands in front of Galder,
grinning.

          RINCEWIND
  I'm sorry. Ooh! Sorry. I'm not late,
  am I?

          GALDER WEATHERWAX
     (to Trymon)
  Who is that?

Trymon steps forward alongside Galder
and sighs.

          TRYMON
  Rincewind, Archchancellor.

          GALDER WEATHERWAX
  Rincewind!

TRYMON
He's the one who . . . (whispers to Archchancellor inaudibly).

GALDER WEATHERWAX
Oh! Have him sent to my office in ten minutes.

ASHBURN NARROWBOLT is creaking under the weight of the casket.

NARROWBOLT
Oh get on with it, Weatherwax! My back's killing me!

TRYMON
Run along, Rincewind.

RINCEWIND
Oh yes, sir. Yes, sir.

Rincewind backs up to scurry away, but just as he passes the creaking Narrowbolt bumps into the old wizard and treads on his foot. Narrowbolt bends over, and as he does . . .

NARROWBOLT
Oh!

RINCEWIND
Oh, sorry, Narrowbolt. Oh!

. . . a large metal sprung STAKE smashes out of the coffin just where Narrowbolt's head should have been. Rincewind looks back up to the Archchancellor to see . . .

. . . the furious face of Trymon staring back at him.

INT. UNSEEN UNIVERSITY/GALDER WEATHERWAX'S STUDY – DAY

Trymon shows the Archchancellor his notebook. Galder nods and then looks up at Rincewind.

> **GALDER WEATHERWAX**
> Mr Rincewind, there are as you know eight levels of wizardry to which the aspiring young . . .

The Archchancellor looks at Rincewind who hangs his head.

> **GALDER WEATHERWAX**
> . . . to which the student can aspire. In your not inconsiderable time here at the Unseen University you have failed to reach even level one.

> **RINCEWIND**
> Ah yes, but you see—

> **TRYMON**
> What the Archchancellor is trying to say, is that after decades of teaching you patience seems not so much a virtue as a life sentence!

> **RINCEWIND**
> Ah yes, but you—

> **TRYMON**
> There is simply no room for your kind of person in a modern university.

> **GALDER WEATHERWAX**
> I feel—

> **TRYMON**
> So you leave the Archchancellor no other course of action but to expel you!

Rincewind is left open-mouthed.

> **RINCEWIND**
> But it's only been forty years!

Trymon uses his quill to gesture ominously at Rincewind.

> **TRYMON**
> The hat!

Slowly and sadly Rincewind removes his hat and places it on the desk, one hand still resting on its crooked point.

> **TRYMON**
> Goodbye, Mr Rincewind.

Trymon marks a meticulous quill stroke neatly into his notebook, looks up, and smiles at Rincewind.

Rincewind glowers at him, pauses, turns and snatches his hat back from the Archchancellor's desk and RUNS AWAY.

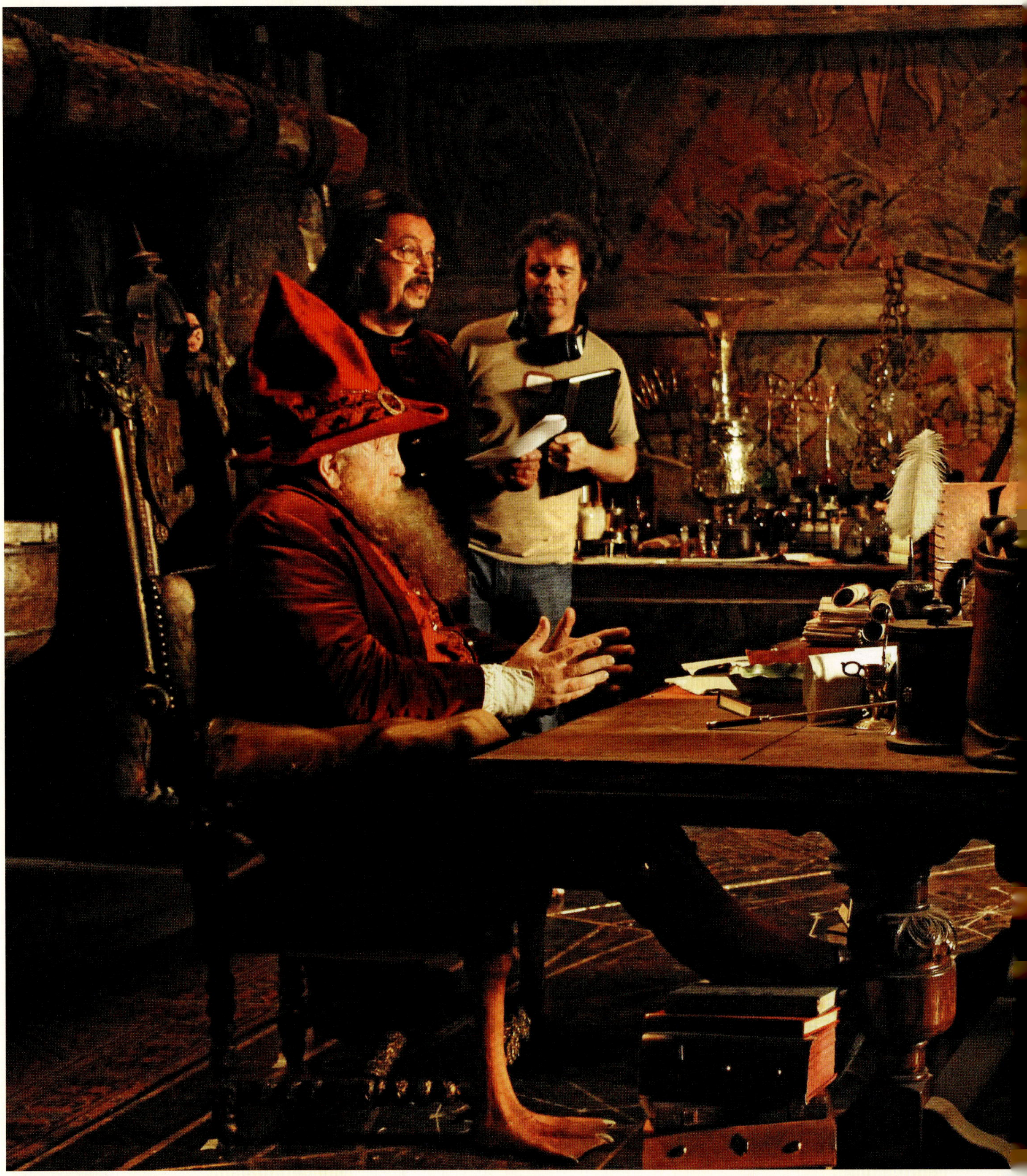

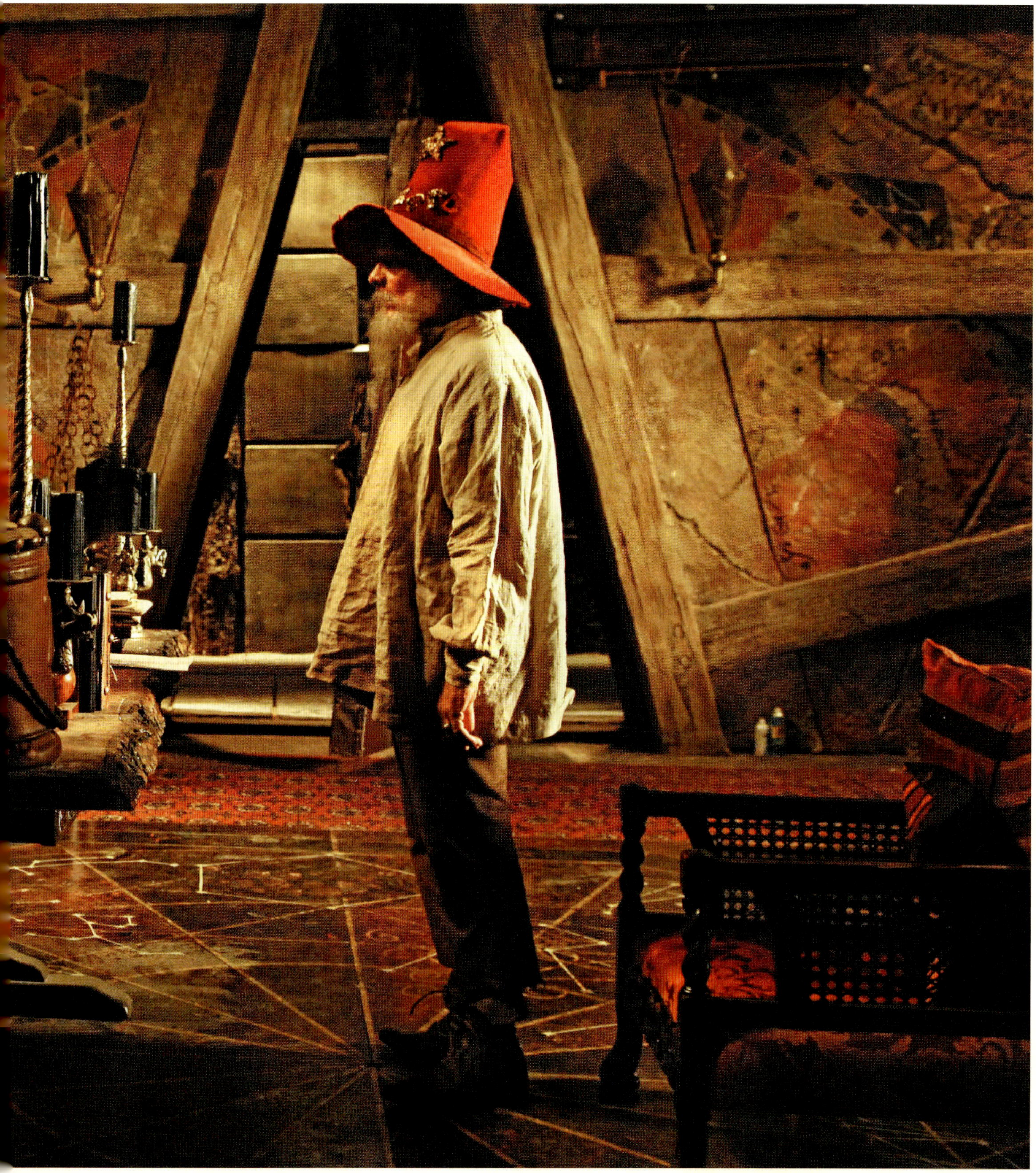

INT. UNSEEN UNIVERSITY/CELLARS - NIGHT

The POINTY-SHOED FEET of eighth level wizard ASHBURN NARROWBOLT walk slowly down the dark corridor.

          NARRATOR (V.O.)
    In the competitive world of
    wizardry, the way to the top is via
    a dead man's pointy shoes.

He becomes aware of footsteps behind him and stops. The other footsteps stop too. He listens, shrugs his shoulders and carries on walking. The other footsteps start up again.

          NARRATOR (V.O.)
    Even if you have to empty them
    yourself.

          VOICE (O.C.)
    Ashburn Narrowbolt.

Narrowbolt stops suddenly in his tracks, a pained expression on his face as he slumps to the floor with a knife in his back.

          NARROWBOLT
    Uh! Uh!

A pair of unknown feet step into Narrowbolt's POINTY SHOES, a hand picks up his WIZARDS HAT, and a wizard walks away down the corridor.

EXT. UNSEEN UNIVERSITY/MAIN GATE - DAY

The wicket gate in the big wooden gates opens and Rincewind is thrust out. He scuttles forward and stops.

          RINCEWIND
    Just . . . Ah!

          WIZARD
    And don't come back!

Then he turns and goes back to remonstrate.

          RINCEWIND
    Now let me tell you . . .

The door opens again and a bundle of his belongings comes flying out, knocking Rincewind down into the mud. As he lands in a pathetic heap, the wicket gate slams shut again.

          RINCEWIND
    Ah! Thank you very much. Ah! Ow!
    Ooh! Ah! Ooh!

Rincewind sighs, picks them up, and walks away

INT. UNSEEN UNIVERSITY/OCTAVO ROOM - DAY

The ancient spell book, the OCTAVO, rattles its chains.

> **NARRATOR (V.O.)**
> Deep in its very bowels, the departure of the Disc's worst wizard from the Unseen University has stirred magic.

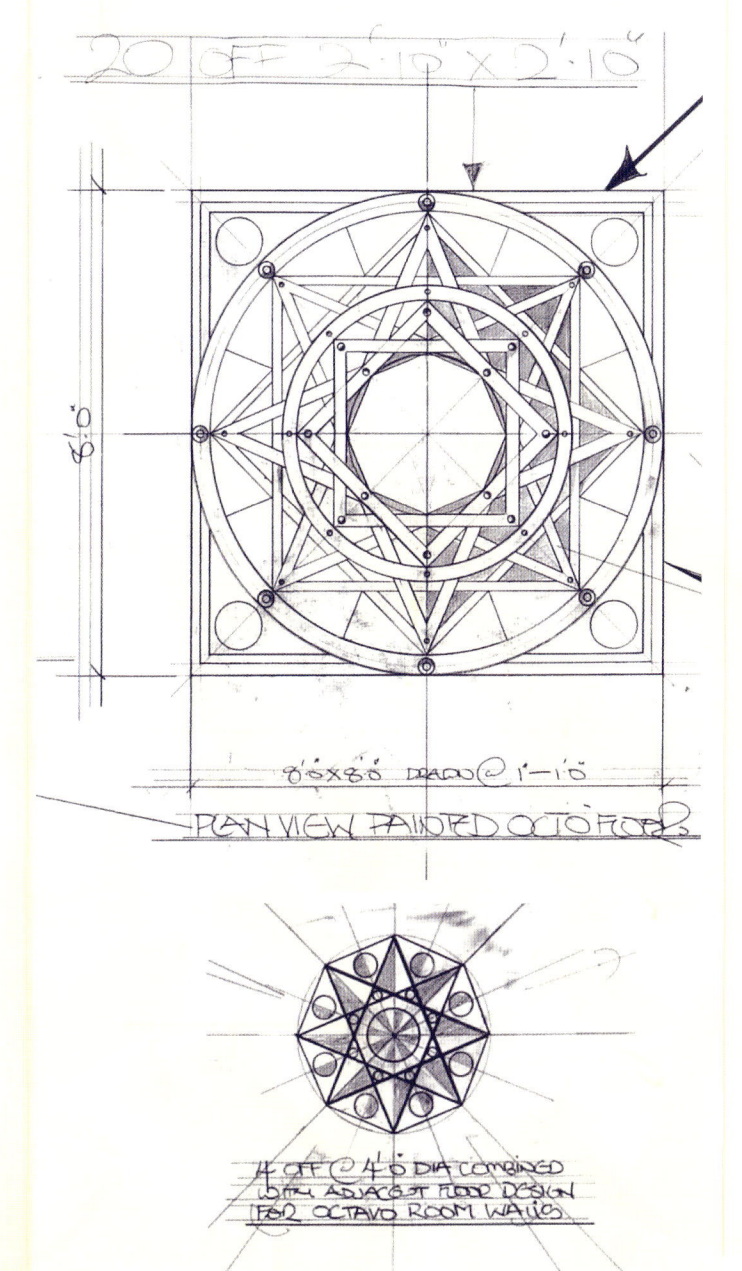

EXT. ANKH-MORPORK/DOCKS - DAY

A very nasty-looking beggar, BLIND HUGH, who has a sign around his neck reading

BLIND, PLEASE GIVE GENEROUSLY

is working the dock side stalls with his companion, CRIPPLE WA. WA's sign reads

LIKEWISE CRIPPLE (DEAF ALSO)

They make their way closer to a moored ship.

> **STALL HOLDER**
> On your way.

> **CRIPPLE WA**
> Oh!

TWOFLOWER steps off the ship onto the quayside. He is looking rather lost but excited as he watches several seamen carry a large, brass-bound WOODEN CHEST off the ship. Another man, obviously the CAPTAIN, is standing behind him.

The chest is deposited on the cobbles and Twoflower reaches into a pouch to pull out coin: GOLD.

Blind Hugh nudges Wa and sends him scurrying off down a nearby alley into the heart of the city.

EXT. ANKH-MORPORK/QUAYSIDE - DAY

The only person oblivious to the commotion is RINCEWIND who is standing on the quayside looking wistfully at his hat, bed roll and toothbrush.

He puts the toothbrush in his pocket, moves right to the edge of the quay and considers the drop into the dank river below.

EXT. ANKH-MORPORK/DOCKS - DAY

Blind Hugh snatches up his begging cup and makes his way across the street with an ingratiating leer.

> BLIND HUGH
> Good day to thee, sire.

> TWOFLOWER
> Right.

Twoflower reaches into the Luggage. The crowd gasps at the sight of so much gold.

EXT. ANKH-MORPORK/QUAYSIDE - DAY

Looking down, for the briefest of moments RUNES flicker in Rincewind's eyes.

His eyes close, he covers them with a hand and with a sigh he steps off the quayside . . .

> RINCEWIND
> Goodbye, world.

When Rincewind opens his eyes he looks down to see that he has stepped onto an EMPTY PALLET. It is swinging from the ship's boom, and lifts Rincewind over the quay wall.

A very tall, dark figure, dressed totally in black and carrying a scythe steps in to view.

> DEATH
> DISAPPOINTING.

EXT. ANKH-MORPORK/DOCKS - DAY

Twoflower has taken the book from the luggage and quickly thumbed through it.

> TWOFLOWER
> (over loud)
> Hello!

> BLIND HUGH
> Hello yourself.

Twoflower smiles and consults the book again.

> TWOFLOWER
> I wish to be directed to an 'otel, tavern, lodging house, inn, hospice.

Blind Hugh looks somewhat confused.

EXT. ANKH-MORPORK/QUAYSIDE - DAY

The EMPTY PALLET deposits RINCEWIND on the quay.

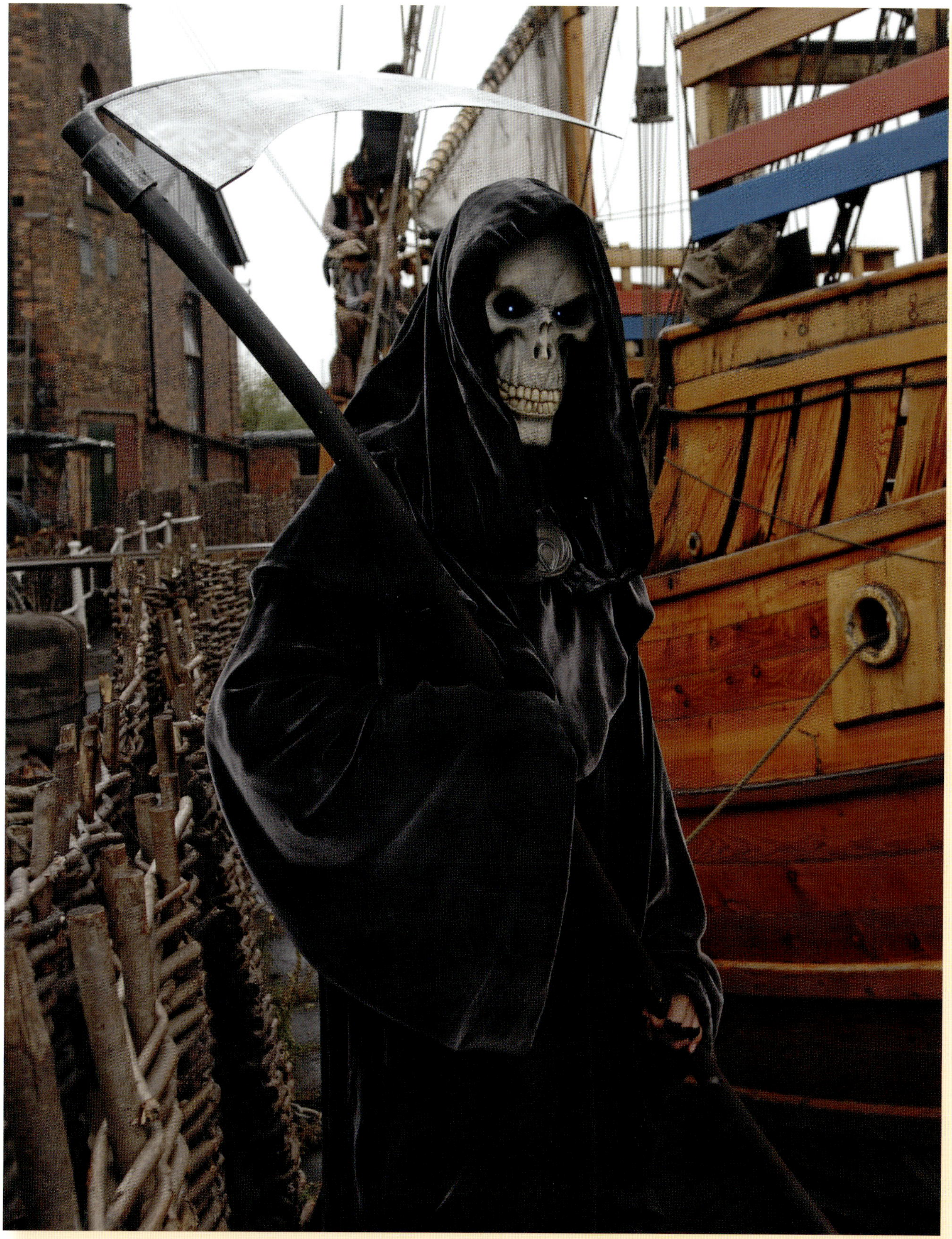

EXT. ANKH-MORPORK/DOCKS - DAY

As Twoflower continues to consult the book, it seems he is holding a large gold coin. Hugh's eyes pop as the crowd's murmur grows.

              TWOFLOWER
  I wish . . .

             BLIND HUGH
  I know a tavern.

Blind Hugh grabs the coin and, seeing a flash of gold, Rincewind finally notices the arrival of the Discworld's first tourist.

             BLIND HUGH
  This way.

He picks up one of the bundles and walks away quickly. Twoflower follows him with an expression of wonder.

Rincewind takes a closer look as . . .

. . . the large wooden chest lifts up off the ground by itself.

             RINCEWIND
  Ooh!

Sounds of astonishment from people in the market.

Rincewind looks closer still.

             RINCEWIND
  Sapient pearwood!

As the Luggage follows on its master's heels Rincewind can see it moves on lots and lots of little legs. Rincewind gives chase.

             MAN IN MARKET
  Well I never. I never seen anything like it.

EXT. BROKEN DRUM - DAY

Blind Hugh leads an excited Twoflower across the courtyard of the tavern followed by the Luggage.

             NARRATOR (V.O.)
  The tourist's Luggage is no ordinary suitcase: it has absolutely no brain, and a HOMICIDAL attitude towards anything that threatens its master, and would follow him anywhere.

INT. BROKEN DRUM - DAY

In the shadowy recesses of the tavern countless shady characters watch . . .

EXT. BROKEN DRUM - DAY

As Twoflower and the Luggage go up the tavern steps and disappear from view, Rincewind enters the frame and follows them in.

INT. BROKEN DRUM - DAY

. . . as Twoflower descends the stairs. The Luggage appears behind him and starts to lurch confidently down the steps.

BROADMAN the innkeeper looks up as the trio walk in.

Twoflower is already thumbing through his book.

> TWOFLOWER
> I wish for an accommodation, a room, lodgings, are your rooms clean, a room with a view, what is your rate for one night, what is for breakfast, where are the . . . bathrooms?

Broadman looks at Hugh. The beggar shrugs.

> BLIND HUGH
> (whispering to Broadman)
> He's got plenty money.

> BROADMAN
> Oh, it'll be um . . . two dollars then. Oh, and that thing has to stay in the stables.

> TWOFLOWER
> Hmm?

Broadman holds up two fingers and speaks very slowly.

BROADMAN
T-o-o-wah.

Twoflower hesitates for a moment then smiling broadly, holds up two fingers as a V sign as if it is a friendly response.

TWOFLOWER
T-o-o-wah?

Broadman growls and looks affronted until Blind Hugh reminds him about the money. Broadman turns Twoflower's hand the other way around.

BROADMAN
T-o-o-wah.

Twoflower looks at his fingers, thumbs through his book and laughs.

TWOFLOWER
Two. Oh. Mmm.

Broadman shakes his head grumpily and points to Twoflower's pouch. Twoflower's eyes light up and he reaches into his pouch. He puts two large GOLD PIECES into Broadman's palm.

Broadman stares at them.

TWOFLOWER
Two.

Twoflower tries another language to see if he can be understood.

All eyes in the room are watching the stranger . . .

. . . except for the pair belonging to RINCEWIND who is watching the Luggage. In disbelief.

RINCEWIND
(to himself)
It is! Sapient pearwood!

TWOFLOWER
(trying another language)
No. Um.

Twoflower smiles at Broadman.

Rincewind puts on his wizzard's hat very deliberately.
(tries another language)
Toilentries? Toilet. Toiletries . . .

RINCEWIND (O.C.)
May I be of assistance?

Broadman looks up to see Rincewind standing behind Twoflower.

BROADMAN
Ah, shove off, Rincewind!

Rincewind smiles politely at the stranger and speaks in Trob.

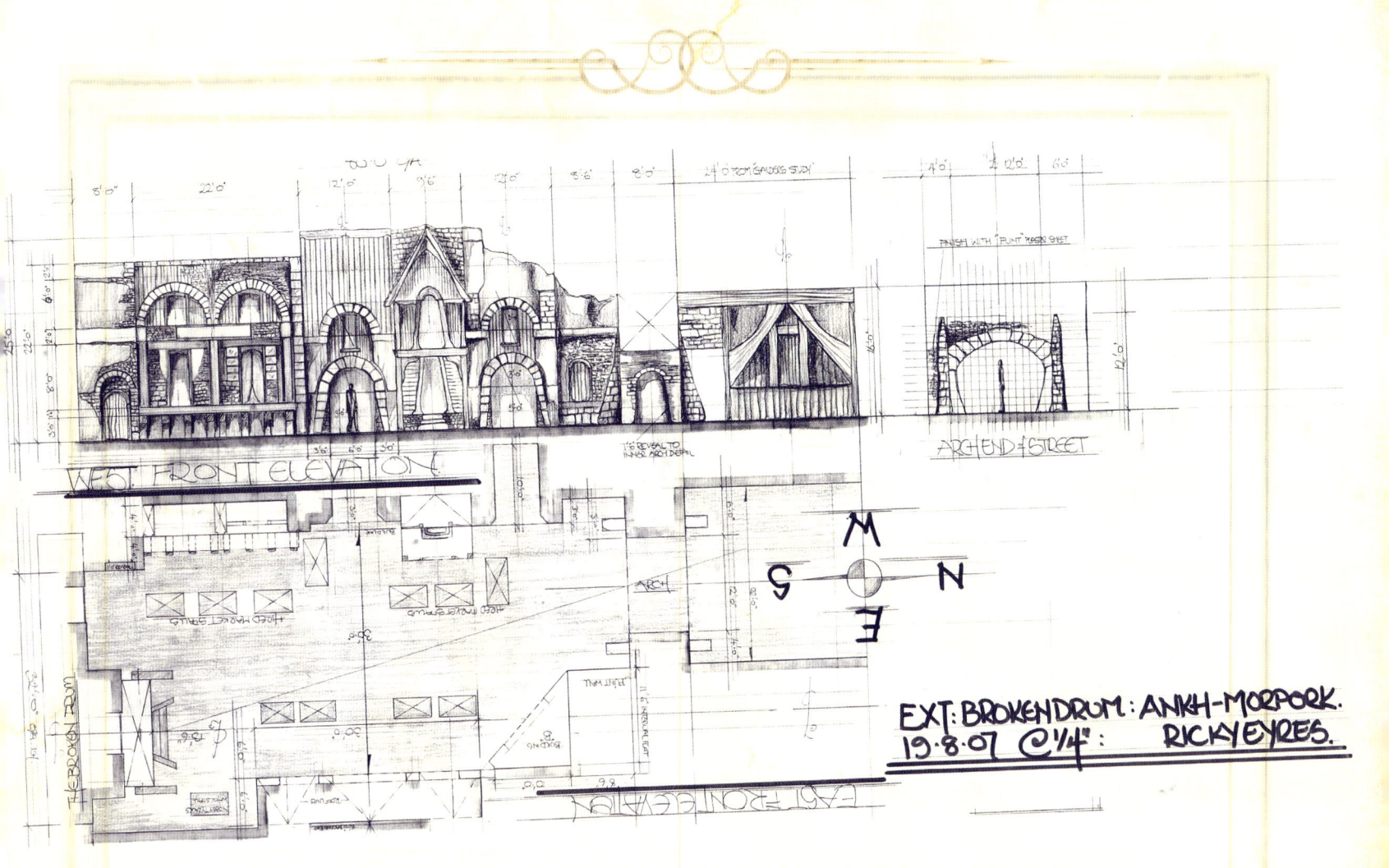

                RINCEWIND
                  (subtitled)
Good day, sir.

                BLIND HUGH
It won't work. It's the book you see, it tells him what to say. It's magic.

                RINCEWIND
Oh!

Twoflower's face splits into a delighted grin.

                TWOFLOWER
                  (subtitled)
You can speak Trob!

                RINCEWIND
Aye!

Rincewind takes him to one side and interrupts him quickly in Trob.

                RINCEWIND
                  (subtitled)
Stranger. If you stay here you will be knifed or poisoned by nightfall. But don't stop smiling, or so will I.

                TWOFLOWER
                  (subtitled)
No! But this looks like a delightful place. A genuine Morporkian tavern. I've heard so much about them, you know. And so reasonable, too. Hmm?

Rincewind glances around.

                RINCEWIND
Ah, Well I . . .

                TWOFLOWER
                  (subtitled)
My name is Twoflower.

Twoflower notices Rincewind's wizzard hat and gasps.

> **TWOFLOWER**
> Ah! So you're a wizard!

> **RINCEWIND**
> And you speak Ankh-Morporkian!

> **TWOFLOWER**
> Yes! I did a correspondence course.

> **RINCEWIND**
> Well what's all this about then?

Rincewind taps the book.

> **TWOFLOWER**
> Oh! Well, a tourist should always use his phrase book so that people will know you're one.

> **RINCEWIND**
> Aha! And, um . . .

Rincewind looks over at the box.

> **RINCEWIND**
> . . . is that really your Luggage?

> **TWOFLOWER**
> Yes! And . . . are you really a wizard? Hmm?

> **RINCEWIND**
> Oh! Well!

Twoflower mistakes his evasiveness for modesty.

> **TWOFLOWER**
> I hear the famous Unseen University is a must-see. I was hoping to visit it so that when I get back home I could say that you know I did that.

> **RINCEWIND**
> Ah, yeah, well it's closed. Yes, for, for, for . . . for the exams.

> **RINCEWIND**
> Ah.

> **TWOFLOWER**
> (subtitled)
> And I'm a tourist.

The stranger extends his hand. Instinctively, Rincewind looks down to see if there is a coin in it.

> **RINCEWIND**
> (subtitled)
> Ah. Oh. Pleased to meet you. I'm Rincewind.

> **TWOFLOWER**
> Ah!

Rincewind points Twoflower to an empty table, and they both sit.

> **TWOFLOWER**
> Oh.

                    TWOFLOWER
                (disappointed)
            Oh!

                    RINCEWIND
            Where is your home?

                    TWOFLOWER
            Ah, have you heard of Bes
            Pelargic? It's the major seaport of
            the Agatean Empire.

                    RINCEWIND
            That's the Counterweight
            Continent, isn't it?

                    TWOFLOWER
            Yes! We may be small, but we're
            equal in weight to all the major
            land masses of this hemicircle.

Rincewind nods sceptically.

                    RINCEWIND
                (dismissively)
            Well that's because the ancient
            legend says that it's made of gold.

                    TWOFLOWER
            Well it's not made of gold.

                    RINCEWIND
            No.

                    TWOFLOWER
            Gold is just a really common metal
            there.

Rincewind perks up a little and looks around for Broadman.

                    RINCEWIND
                (speaking quietly)
            You might like to keep that to
            ourselves.

But Broadman is standing right by them. He's heard every word and is open-mouthed.

                    RINCEWIND
            Hmm?

                    BROADMAN
            On the house.

He serves Twoflower beer.

          BROADMAN
        (to Rincewind)
Who is he?

          RINCEWIND
He says he's a 'tourist'.

          BROADMAN
Huh! Well, what's that mean then?

          RINCEWIND
I think it means 'idiot'.

Rincewind helps himself to a pint.

          TWOFLOWER
Urgh!

          RINCEWIND
Mmm.

          TWOFLOWER
    (speaks in another language)

          RINCEWIND
    (speaks in another language)

EXT. BROKEN DRUM - DAY

Broadman hurtles away from the Drum . . .

EXT. BACK STREET ALCHEMISTS - DAY

. . . and into a small shady-looking door.

INT. BACK STREET ALCHEMISTS - DAY

A few runny candles illuminate a DECREPIT ALCHEMIST at a shabby table covered with saucers and jam jars.

Broadman is peering over his shoulder impatiently.

The Alchemist is holding a rhinu in a pair of tongs. Something chemical is dripping off it.

          ALCHEMIST
Mmm, yes, you are correct in your surmise. This is technically false coinage.

          BROADMAN
I knew it! I knew it! I've got a nose for a dud'n. What do you mean technically?

          ALCHEMIST
Well you see our Ankh-Morpork coins contain rather less gold than a pint of seawater.

          BROADMAN
I knew it!

The angry innkeeper starts towards the door.

          ALCHEMIST
But this, my friend, is solid gold!

          BROADMAN
What?! What?! I— I've gotta get back!

BROADMAN runs out of the alchemist's like a bull, the sound of his footsteps disappearing into the dark.

The Alchemist turns the coin this way and that, looking very happy, and moves to put it into his pouch.

We hear the sound of running feet hurrying back, as Broadman returns to reclaim his coin.

          BROADMAN
    (clears throat)
Mmm!

He grins and runs . . .

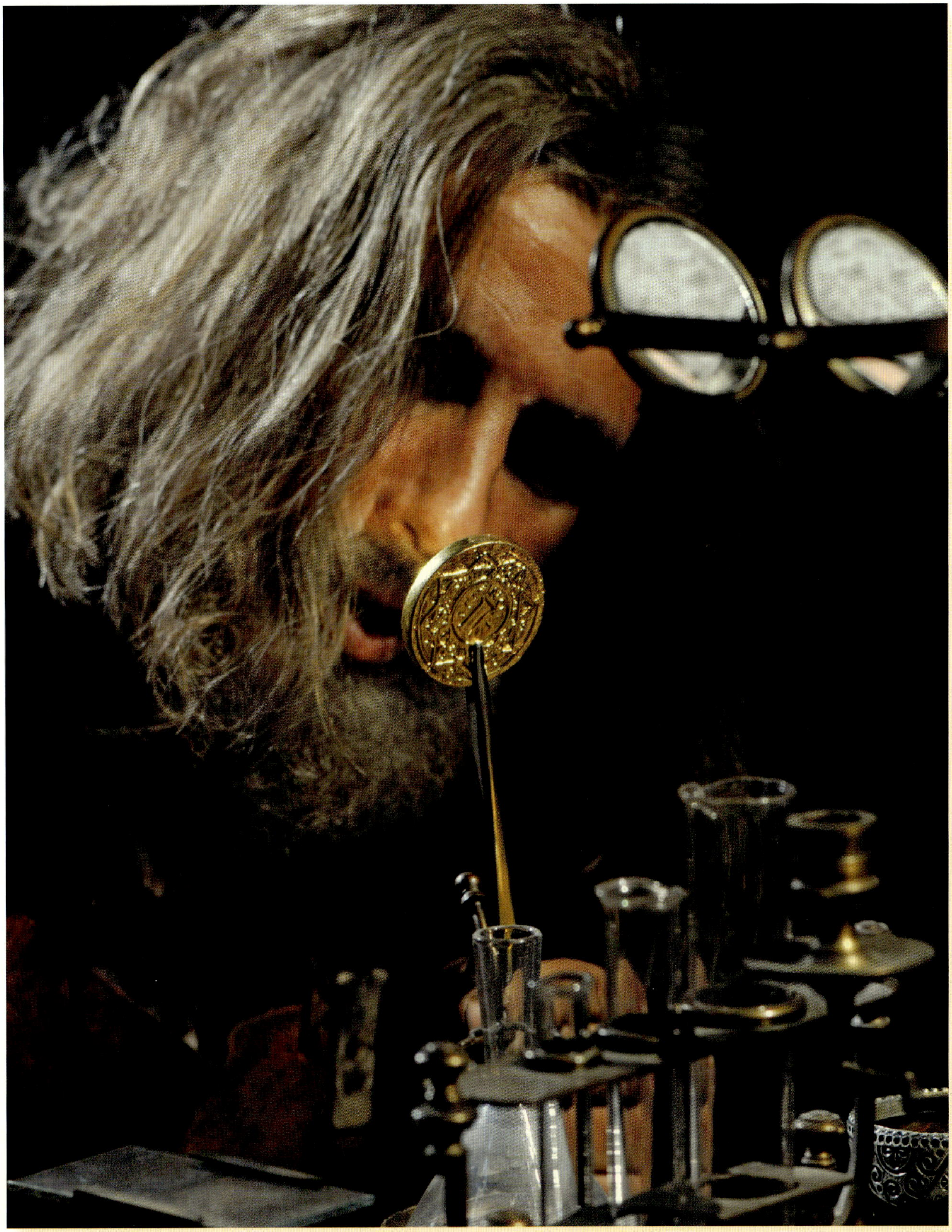

EXT. BACK STREET ALCHEMISTS - DAY

. . . right into Blind Hugh who has been listening at the door.

          BROADMAN
Oh.

Broadman sighs and whispers in his ear . . .

EXT. BROKEN DRUM - DAY

Blind Hugh whispers into Cripple Wa's ear . . .

EXT. BROKEN DRUM - DAY

Cripple Wa whispers into another dirty ear . . .

          NARRATOR (V.O.)
And so the leaders of a number of the many gangs, guilds and collections of other nefarious dirtbags of Ankh-Morpork were aware that someone had arrived in the city who appeared to have much treasure.

INT. YMOR'S HEADQUARTERS - DAY

In BIG CLOSE UP the owner of the dirty ear, STREN WITHEL, whispers into the ear belonging to the scar-crossed face of YMOR who smiles, nastily, and feeds the RAVEN by his side.

          NARRATOR (V.O.)
Including Ymor: its greatest thief.

INT. BROKEN DRUM - DAY

Rincewind has a large pile of food in front of him.

          RINCEWIND
So, no guards?

Rincewind starts to construct a sandwich from the food.

          TWOFLOWER
No, why? What do I have that's worth stealing?

          RINCEWIND
Well the trunk! I mean there can't be more than two very small wands made of sapient pearwood in all the cities of the Circle Sea, let alone a whole box!

Twoflower seems a little confused by this.

              RINCEWIND
That and . . . the gold.

              TWOFLOWER
Ah. Barely two thousand rhinu!

              RINCEWIND
Is a rhinu one of those big old
coins?

              TWOFLOWER
Yes!

Twoflower looks at the wizard over
his glasses, worried.

              TWOFLOWER
Do you think I paid the innkeeper
too much?

              RINCEWIND
I, I, I think he might have settled
for less.

              TWOFLOWER
Ah. Well I can see I've got a lot to
learn.

              RINCEWIND
Mmm.

              TWOFLOWER
Mmm.

              TWOFLOWER
An idea occurs to me. Rincewind,
would you perhaps consent to
be employed as a, um . . . well
perhaps the word guide would fit
the circumstances? I think I could
afford to pay you a . . . a rhinu a
day?

Rincewind is about to bite into a big
sandwich but his jaw drops. The contents
fall into his lap.

Twoflower blushes.

              TWOFLOWER
Oh dear, I've . . . I've offended you.
It was an impertinent request.
Doubtless you have works of high
magic to return to.

Rincewind is speechless.

              RINCEWIND
W . . . W . . . W . . . one of those a
day?!

              TWOFLOWER
Oh! Well er . . . two then?

Rincewind rallies magnificently with a
smile.

              RINCEWIND
                 (straight in)
What do you want to see?

              TWOFLOWER
Well I want to see everything! I
mean genuine Morporkian life.
You know I, I want to go to the, the
slave markets . . .

                    RINCEWIND
Yes.

                    TWOFLOWER
. . . and the Whore Pits, the Temple
of Small Gods . . .

                    RINCEWIND
Yeah, yeah.

                    TWOFLOWER
. . . and the Beggars' Guild and . . .

Rincewind looks at him as if he's mad.

                    TWOFLOWER
. . . and a genuine tavern brawl!

Rincewind looks at him suspiciously.

                    RINCEWIND
Ah. W . . . w . . . well . . .

                    TWOFLOWER
Oh no, no, no, I'm not suggesting
we get involved! I just wanna see
it, that's all.

                    RINCEWIND
Ah.

                    TWOFLOWER
        (gasps)
And some of your famous heroes
like Cohen the Barbarian. You do
know him?

                    RINCEWIND
Oh yes! Yes, of course! Yeah!

                    TWOFLOWER
Good. Well, so, it's agreed?

                    RINCEWIND
Agreed?

TWOFLOWER
Excellent! Be a good chap would you and see to it that the innkeeper shows my Luggage to the room and I insist that you take your first four days' wages . . . in advance.

Twoflower lays FOUR gold rhinu out before Rincewind then stacks them up neatly on the table. Rincewind nods.

RINCEWIND
Broadman! Luggage! Room!

The innkeeper steps forward and leads the way up the wooden steps behind the bar. The Luggage gets up and patters across the floor after him. As Twoflower looks for the rest of the coins he stares whimsically into the distance.

TWOFLOWER
And, and perhaps when the exams are finished . . .

BROADMAN
Come on!

As Twoflower lays out another four coins and stacks them neatly on the table by the others something in Rincewind's face says he's formulating a plan.

TWOFLOWER
. . . we can get a peek at the . . . Unseen University?

TWOFLOWER
This calls for a picture.

Rincewind looks down at the EIGHT COINS, smiles, grabs them and then . . .

. . . runs like hell.

RINCEWIND
All the best wizards have left! See ya, loser!

From the shadows, YMOR watches him go and indicates to STREN WITHEL, who moves across the room.

On the balcony of the landing which leads to the bedroom, the Luggage stops, it turns and runs directly towards, and out through, the door.

Withel makes as if to go after the chest.

          YMOR
Relax, Withel. The magic chest will come back for its owner, and with it the gold!

They laugh.

Ymor points to Twoflower.

Twoflower has pulled out a CAMERA and is trying to focus it.

        TWOFLOWER
Yes. Yes, yes. We'll just have a peek. Just look over here, Rincewind, and smile. Rincewind?

The camera comes in to focus on Withel. Withel leers a broken toothed smile.

Twoflower is somewhat surprised.

        TWOFLOWER
Hi.

EXT. THE CITY GATES - DAY

A HORSE carrying a dishevelled looking RINCEWIND belts through the city gates. Above the gates, two guards appear and one raises his crossbow and shoots a bolt.

          GUARD
Halt!

There is a neigh, and a thump.

        RINCEWIND
Argh! Bugger it!

INT. PATRICIAN'S PALACE/OFFICE – DAY

                    PATRICIAN
          The City Gates. Hmm. Attempting
          to leave.

                    NARRATOR (V.O.)
          The Patrician, the ruler of Ankh-
          Morpork, may not be particularly
          fair or even democratic, but
          at least for the first time in a
          thousand years the city works.
          This is largely because he knows
          where everyone is most of the time
          and which dissuasively vicious
          punishment to exact for whatever
          they are doing there.

Rincewind glances around, looking for an escape route.

The Patrician, holding a small dog, is reading a letter.

                    PATRICIAN
          Oath making. The theft of a horse.

                    RINCEWIND
          Oh no, my Lord Patrician, I didn't
          steal the horse. I paid for it fairly.

                    PATRICIAN
          Using false coinage, which is
          technically theft – offering false
          coinage.

Rincewind opens his mouth to speak, thinks better of it, and shuts it again.

                    PATRICIAN
          What are we going to do with you,
          you little scamp?

Rincewind wriggles uncomfortably.

                    PATRICIAN
          Mmm. Yes. It's the arena for you,
          Rincewind.

                    RINCEWIND
          What? Sorry!

                    PATRICIAN
          On top of these there is the moral
          obligatory attendant on the
          cowardly betrayal of a visitor
          to these shores. Shame on you,
          Rincewind! Will you be requiring a
          sword or a spear for the arena?

                    RINCEWIND
          (mutters incoherently in bewilderment)
          As...s...

Two guards seize Rincewind and frog-march him away.

                    PATRICIAN
          Of course... we could be merciful.

Rincewind looks back, insane hope on his face.

The Patrician addresses his dog.

                    PATRICIAN
          Do you think we should be
          merciful?

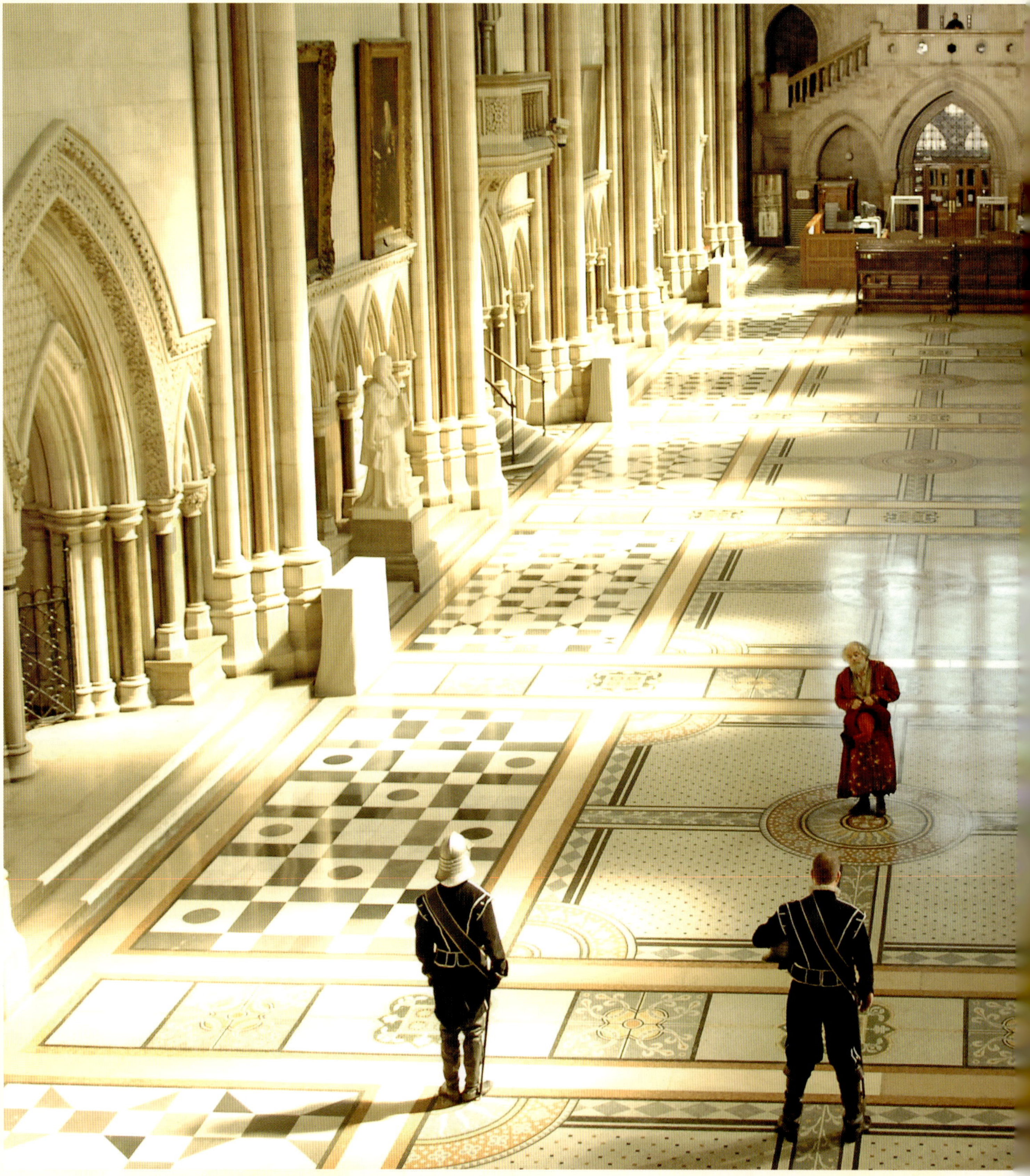

37

INT. BROKEN DRUM - DAY

Ymor is watching Twoflower who is talking to Broadman. Occasionally, Ymor feeds a raven scraps.

                BROADMAN
      Two rhinu.

               TWOFLOWER
      One polly-see.

Twoflower gives the innkeeper a piece of paper and Broadman gives the foreigner some coins. The innkeeper gets up.

The doors slam back on their hinges and thud into the wall.

                BROADMAN
      Oi! That's my door!

A short, black, dark arrow flies across the room and thunks into the woodwork.

                BROADMAN
      The door's fine.

                YMOR
      Why don't you join me, Zlorf? The
      Assassins' Guild are our friends!

ZLORF strolls down the stairs, followed by a number of assassins.

                ZLORF
      I've come for the tourist.

Two of the assassins step forward.

Stren is suddenly in front of them, his knife an inch from their throats.

Broadman rapidly ducks away from Twoflower's table.

YMOR
I thought we had an agreement: you don't rob and I don't kill?

Zlorf places his blowpipe on the table and sits down.

Zlorf and Ymor both look intently at Twoflower.

ZLORF
I'll kill him and then you can rob him.

The doors slam back on their hinge again as two crossbow-carrying DWARVES enter.

Broadman sighs heavily.

One fires a bolt into the pipes by Twoflower's head and Twoflower gasps.

The assassins and thieves jump to their feet and stare up at the short, fat, richly dressed figure on the threshold between the dwarves. RERPF gestures with a beringed hand.

RERPF
If anybody's going to kill him, they'll need to talk to me first.

BROADMAN
Get those dwarves out of 'ere!

One of the dwarves sends his axe whirling across the room into a beer keg.

Broadman gasps

TWOFLOWER
Oh!

BROADMAN
Oh.

ZLORF
Who the hell are you?!

RERPF
I am Rerpf, and I am here on behalf of the Guild of Merchants and Traders to protect our interests; meaning the little man.

He points at an excited Twoflower in the corner.

Ymor wrinkles his brow.

YMOR
And how long has this guild been in existence, may I ask?

RERPF
Since this afternoon. I am Vice Guild Master in charge of . . . Tourism.

Twoflower beams with excitement and rummages for his picture box.

YMOR
Oh! And what is this . . . tourism of which you speak?

RERPF
We're not quite sure.

YMOR
What's a tourist?

Twoflower raises the picture box to his eye. In his other hand he is holding a cage which appears to be full of sulking pink LIZARDS.

                    TWOFLOWER
          Smile!

The lizards stir. There is a flash of bright white light accompanied by screams of panic. Out of the moment of blindness . . .

SC. 1/25 BROKEN DRUM LIZARD FLASH

1. MEDIUM ON TWOFL. WITH PICTURE BOX. HE RAISES FLASHGUN

2. C/U DETAIL ON TOP OF OLD FASHIONED FLASH ON STICK — SEE LIZARDS IN TROUGH IN CAGE — TAILS QUIVER THEN . . .

3. THEY EXPLODE IN FLASH OF BRIGHT LIGHT

                    MAN
          It's magic!

. . . a full-on brawl ensues.

                    TWOFLOWER
          Ooh!

INT. PATRICIAN'S PALACE/OFFICE - DAY

The Patrician waves a hand and the guards move back.

                    PATRICIAN
                    (amiably)
          I want you to listen very carefully
          to what I have to say . . . otherwise
          you will die . . . in an interesting
          fashion . . . over a period. Please
          stop fidgeting like that.

Rincewind tries to stop, unsuccessfully.

The Patrician lifts a letter, which Rincewind tries to read over his shoulder.

                    PATRICIAN
          The Emperor of the Counterweight
          Continent has sent me a letter. It
          appears that one of his subjects has
          taken it into his head to visit our
          city. It appears he wishes to . . .
          look at it.

The Patrician puts the letter back down.

                    PATRICIAN
          You will continue to be a guide,
          Rincewind, to this, this looker, this,
          this . . . Twoflower. You will make
          sure that he returns home with a
          good report of our homeland. What
          do you say to that? You say yes!

                    RINCEWIND
          I say yes!

                    PATRICIAN
          Yes!

                    RINCEWIND
          Yes. Thank you, Lord. Thank you.
          Yeah.

                    PATRICIAN
          Because . . . it would be a tragedy
          should anything . . . untoward . . .
          happen to our visitor.

Rincewind raises his eyes to the heavens.

INT. BROKEN DRUM - DAY

As THIEVES stab ASSASSINS who attack DWARVES who throw AXES, Twoflower looks on, PICTURE BOX and LIZARD CAGE raised, in wonder and delight.

SC-1/25 BROKEN DRUM DWARVES VS. ASSASSINS

4
DWARF TURNS IN F/G
ZLORF FIRES BLOW DART IN B/G
PULL FOCUS TO ZLORF

5
REVERSE ANGLE
DWARF THROWS AXE

6A
TIGHTER ON ZLORF
TRACK IN TWDS HIM
ZLORF....
CAM
HE DIVES OUT THE WAY.
SHOT CONT'D...

41

INT. PATRICIAN'S PALACE/OFFICE - DAY

The Patrician continues to carefully explain the situation to Rincewind.

> PATRICIAN
> It would be dreadful if the tourist were to die, for example, because the Emperor looks after his own, and he could certainly extinguish us at a nod. Which would be dreadful for you, Rincewind, because I would hope when the Empire's huge mercenary fleet arrived that the avenging captains would find their anger somewhat tempered by the fact that my skilled operatives had just shown you the colour of your liver!

Rincewind nods slowly and starts to back away, cautiously.

> PATRICIAN
> I see by your face that understanding dawns.

> RINCEWIND
> Mmm.

The Patrician claps him on the back.

> PATRICIAN
> Hmm! Good luck.

> RINCEWIND
> Mmm.

> PATRICIAN
> Oh, there's one other thing.

> PATRICIAN
> I'm sure . . .

> RINCEWIND
> Mmm?

> PATRICIAN
> . . . you wouldn't dream of trying to escape from your obligations by say . . . running away?!

> RINCEWIND
> I assure you, Lord, that the thought never even crossed my mind!

> PATRICIAN
> Indeed. Then if I were you I would sue my face for slander.

Rincewind's face falls.

> PATRICIAN
> Don't let me detain you.

EXT. PATRICIAN'S PALACE - DAY

Rincewind runs like hell from the palace.

EXT. BROKEN DRUM - DAY

Rincewind runs towards the Drum. He pauses to catch his breath. He listens to the sounds of commotion from inside, sighs, takes a deep breath and steps forward just in time . . .

[Storyboard panels: 2A — CLOSE SIDE ANGLE BY ENTRANCE. RINCE LEANS IN NEAR DOOR LISTENING THEN SUDDENLY... 2B — SAME SHOT. WHAM! MAN COMES FLYING OUT SALOON DOORS WITH SPEAR IN HIM...]

. . . to see a man who comes out backwards, fast, on account of the spear in his chest, go sailing past him

              MAN FROM TAVERN
  Argh!

Sounds of a brawl.

Rincewind peers around the door frame, has a good look at the brawl, turns and runs.

EXT. BROKEN DRUM - DAY

Rincewind runs away from the Drum but . . .

. . . A SMALL LEG emerges from the shadows and trips him up.

              RINCEWIND
  Uh! Ah! Uh! Ah! Uh. Uh. Oh!

Rincewind lands flat on his face. He looks back.

It's the Luggage.

              RINCEWIND
  You! Oh.

The lid creaks open. The box moves forward slightly with an air of calculated menace.

Rincewind scrabbles up and tries to run again but finds that his robe is caught on something. Craning his neck he sees it's being gripped firmly by the lid.

              RINCEWIND
  Ah. All right! All right! All right! I give in!

INT. BROKEN DRUM - DAY

In the gloom no one appears to notice Rincewind making his way desperately from table to table as Twoflower takes pictures of the mêlée.

From beneath a table, Rincewind clubs the foot of a thief to clear his path to the next table, then barely avoids an assassin who is thrown on to the table he's hiding behind.

In a dash for Twoflower, Rincewind climbs over a number of fallen combatants . . .

              RINCEWIND
Excuse me. Thank you.

. . . and finally reaches Twoflower.

              TWOFLOWER
Rincewind, you came back!

              RINCEWIND
              (sullenly)
Oh, yeah!

              TWOFLOWER
I knew you would!

              RINCEWIND
I . . . I just had to!

              TWOFLOWER
Yeah. It's exciting, isn't it?! A genuine tavern brawl. It's better than anything I could have imagined.

Rincewind looks at him blankly.

              TWOFLOWER
Everybody say cheese!

Everyone in the room pauses mid-battle to pose, and hug, for the picture. At the sound of the picture box lever they resume the fight,

              TWOFLOWER
Wonderful! Do you think I should thank them or . . . Did you put them up to this?

Twoflower wags his finger at him.

              TWOFLOWER
That's where you were!

Rincewind considers for a moment.

              RINCEWIND
Yes, I . . . I didn't like to mention it. Ah!

              TWOFLOWER
Oh! Hey! Nice throw!

              RINCEWIND
We should be leaving!

INT. BROKEN DRUM – DAY

Rincewind drags Twoflower towards the door which is blocked by a thief with his back to them.

The thief turns. It is Withel. He draws a knife and menaces Rincewind with it.

          RINCEWIND
  Uh!

Stren Withel growls.

Rincewind looks around wildly, and then with wild improvisation draws himself up into a wizardly pose.

          RINCEWIND
  Ah! Ah-ha-ha-ha. Asoniti! Beazlebor!

Withel hesitates, his eyes flickering nervously as he waits for the magic and is then distracted by . . .

. . . Twoflower, who takes a picture.

          TWOFLOWER
  Smile!

Withel smiles and poses exactly as Rincewind kicks him sharply in the groin.

          STREN WITHEL
  Ooh!

And as the assassin's body clears his view Twoflower captures the thief's agonised grimace and Rincewind lurching as if he's just cast a spell.

          TWOFLOWER
  Magic!

Withel collapses in a heap.

          RINCEWIND
  Yes. It's a collapsing spell. Come along! We gotta go!

Rincewind and Twoflower run for the door as a thief runs into the Broken Drum. Outside there is a crescendo of running feet, the door smashes open, and the Luggage bursts in to the room.

> RINCEWIND
> Oh!

The Luggage shakes itself madly and then settles in the middle of the room.

Ymor looks up and points to Rincewind.

A RAVEN swoops down from its perch in the rafters and dives at the wizard. About halfway to its target the Luggage leaps from its bed of splinters, gapes briefly in mid-air, and snaps shut. It lands lightly.

> YMOR
> Argh!

> TWOFLOWER
> (proudly)
> That's my Luggage!

The Luggage snaps its lid ominously.

Suddenly the thieves, assassins, dwarves and merchants all realise at the same moment that they are in a room with something that is absolutely horrible. As one they make for the door, fast.

Twoflower raises the picture box.

> TWOFLOWER
> One more time!

Everyone freezes and smiles . . .

. . . and runs the second the picture has been taken.

A dwarf is left hanging from the candle wheel above the Luggage . . .

> MAN WITH BEARD
> Ooh. Ah! Argh!

. . . which jumps, snaps, and the dwarf is gone.

> TWOFLOWER
> Atta-boy!

EXT. BROKEN DRUM - DAY

The doorway is filled with bodies of people who tried to escape, but for whom it was was too late. Rincewind and Twoflower pick their way through them as they emerge from the Drum.

The Watch are piling up the bodies.

> RINCEWIND
> Ooh. Ooh. Oh!

Twoflower looks around eagerly.

> TWOFLOWER
> So, where's Cohen the Barbarian?

Rincewind takes a deep breath and looks at one of the Watchmen.

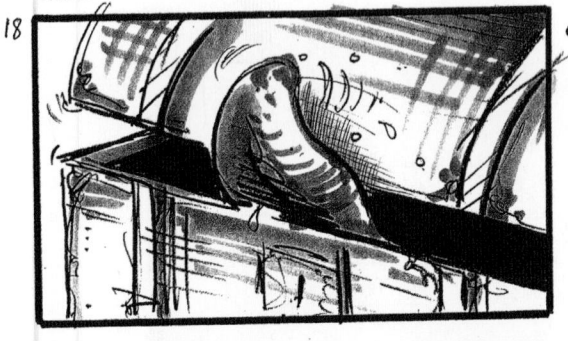

Sc.1/32 BROKEN DRUM

18 — CLOSE DETAIL ON LUGGAGE TONGUE ROLLING AROUND

19 — WIDE LOOKING BACK TO ENTRANCE - EVERYBODY RUNS OUT..

          RINCEWIND
    He's . . . right behind you!

Twoflower turns to look at the guard behind him.

          RINCEWIND
    Look, we really ought to be going!

          TWOFLOWER
    Ha, ha, Ha! Fantastic! No one at
    home is gonna believe this.

Twoflower beams, and fumbles with the picture box.

EXT. BROKEN DRUM - DAY

Close on the front of the big GLASS EYE on the box. The CAMERA pulls back to reveal Rincewind behind it

          TWOFLOWER (O.C.)
    All you do is rotate the lever and
    the iconograph does the rest.

          TWOFLOWER
      (to the Watchman)
    You wait here.

A door opens in the back of the box and almost hits Rincewind on the nose.

          RINCEWIND
    Oh!

A small, green, warty PICTURE IMP leans out and points at a colour-encrusted palette in one clawed hand.

          PICTURE IMP
    It's no good! I've run out of
    red, see! If you wanted red you
    shouldn't have took all those
    pictures of dwarves killing people,
    should you! It's monochrome from
    now on, friend! All right?

          RINCEWIND
    Yes.

In one dim corner of the little box he can just make out an EASEL and a TINY UNMADE BED. The imp shuts the door. Behind it there is the muffled sound of grumbling.

          RINCEWIND
    Ah!

          TWOFLOWER (O.C.)
    That's the Picture Imp.

Rincewind looks up at Twoflower.

          RINCEWIND
    Yes. Of course it is!

Twoflower is standing by two bewildered Watchmen.

          TWOFLOWER
    You know, Rincewind, I'd like to
    have you in the picture as well.

We see the group through the Iconograph lens, and there is a whirr from the box.

          TWOFLOWER
    Smile, please!

Rincewind nudges the Watchmen.

                    RINCEWIND
            Smile. Smile!

The shutter closes on the scene and opens on a monochrome iconograph of the ensemble.

                    TWOFLOWER (O.C.)
            What are we gonna see next?

We flick through a series of icons showing Rincewind and Twoflower's day including a fight, prison, the Patrician's palace, a brothel and an increasingly grumpy-looking Twoflower.

EXT. BROKEN DRUM - NIGHT

Rincewind is standing outside the Broken Drum playing with one of his rhinu.

                    TWOFLOWER
            What a great day!

Twoflower emerges from the Broken Drum.

                    TWOFLOWER
                       (sighs)
            Ah!

                    RINCEWIND
            Mmm?

Twoflower pulls a little glass portrait out of his shirt pocket and shows Rincewind.

                    TWOFLOWER
            Yes. That's my favourite, with
            Cohen.

INT. BROKEN DRUM/CELLAR - NIGHT

Broadman is humming a tune to himself as he stacks KINDLING up against a row of OIL BARRELS and then opens the stopcocks.

EXT. BROKEN DRUM - NIGHT

Rincewind is still laughing over the picture.

            RINCEWIND
    Ah! Oh what the . . .
          (sniffs)
    . . . Can you smell oil?

            TWOFLOWER
    I don't think so.

Rincewind shrugs and they walk away from the Drum.

INT. BROKEN DRUM/CELLAR - NIGHT

At the top of the cellar steps Broadman kneels down and fumbles in his tinderbox. It's damp and won't light.

            BROADMAN
       (growls)
    I'll kill that bloody cat!

A lit taper appears in mid-air, offered by a skeletal hand, right beside him.

            DEATH
    HERE, TAKE THIS.

            BROADMAN
    Oh! Thanks.

            DEATH
    DON'T MENTION IT.

Broadman lights his tinder and throws it down he steps. He burns his fingers as he does.

            BROADMAN
    Ooh!

EXT. BROKEN DRUM - NIGHT

Rincewind and Twoflower walk down the steps and away from the Drum.

>TWOFLOWER
>Tavern fights are pretty common around here, no?

>RINCEWIND
>Oh! Yeah, well it's practically a sport.

>TWOFLOWER
>Mmm. So innkeepers must need a lot of . . . well, in my language we call it inn-sewer-ants?

>RINCEWIND
>Inn-sewer-ants! That's a funny word. What does it mean?

INT. BROKEN DRUM/CELLAR - NIGHT

Broadman walks away up the steps with a smile. Then his smile falters and he turns, seeing a scythe and then the figure holding it . . .

>TWOFLOWER (V.O.)
>Well, say you have a tavern built of wood.

>RINCEWIND (V.O.)
>Mmm hmm.

EXT. BROKEN DRUM - NIGHT

Twoflower and Rincewind keep walking. Behind them, smoke begins to waft from the Drum.

>TWOFLOWER
>Well, it might burn down.

>RINCEWIND
>Mmm.

>TWOFLOWER
>Well you don't want that to happen so you take out an inn-sewer-ants polly-see, you see. And then I work out the odds against it burning down, and then add a bit, and then you pay me some money based on those odds.

INT. BROKEN DRUM/CELLAR - NIGHT

Broadman's taper illuminates the scythe . . . and the figure holding it. It's DEATH.

>BROADMAN
>Oh no!

>DEATH
>BUT YES!

EXT. BROKEN DRUM - NIGHT

Twoflower continues to talk authoritatively.

> TWOFLOWER
> Well, then if it does burn down I pay you the value of the tavern.

Someone emerges from the warm glow in the door of the Drum behind them ON FIRE and trying to beat off the flames.

> RINCEWIND
> Oh, it's a bit like a bet, right?

> TWOFLOWER
> A wager? Yes, I suppose it is!

Twoflower grins

> RINCEWIND
> (sniffs)
> Ah! Are you sure you can't smell oil?

Twoflower tips his head to one side.

> TWOFLOWER
> (sniffs)
> No. I can smell burning.

. . . as Rincewind and Twoflower turn to face it, the sullen glow in the doorway of the Broken Drum flickers, dims and then erupts into a roaring FIREBALL that carries burning embers a hundred feet into the air . . .

Rincewind and Twoflower land in a heap.

Flames are racing along the rooftops on either side of the street. All around them people are hurling their possessions from windows.

Rincewind groans. He looks back over his shoulder at the burning inn then suddenly stops and grabs Twoflower in astonishment.

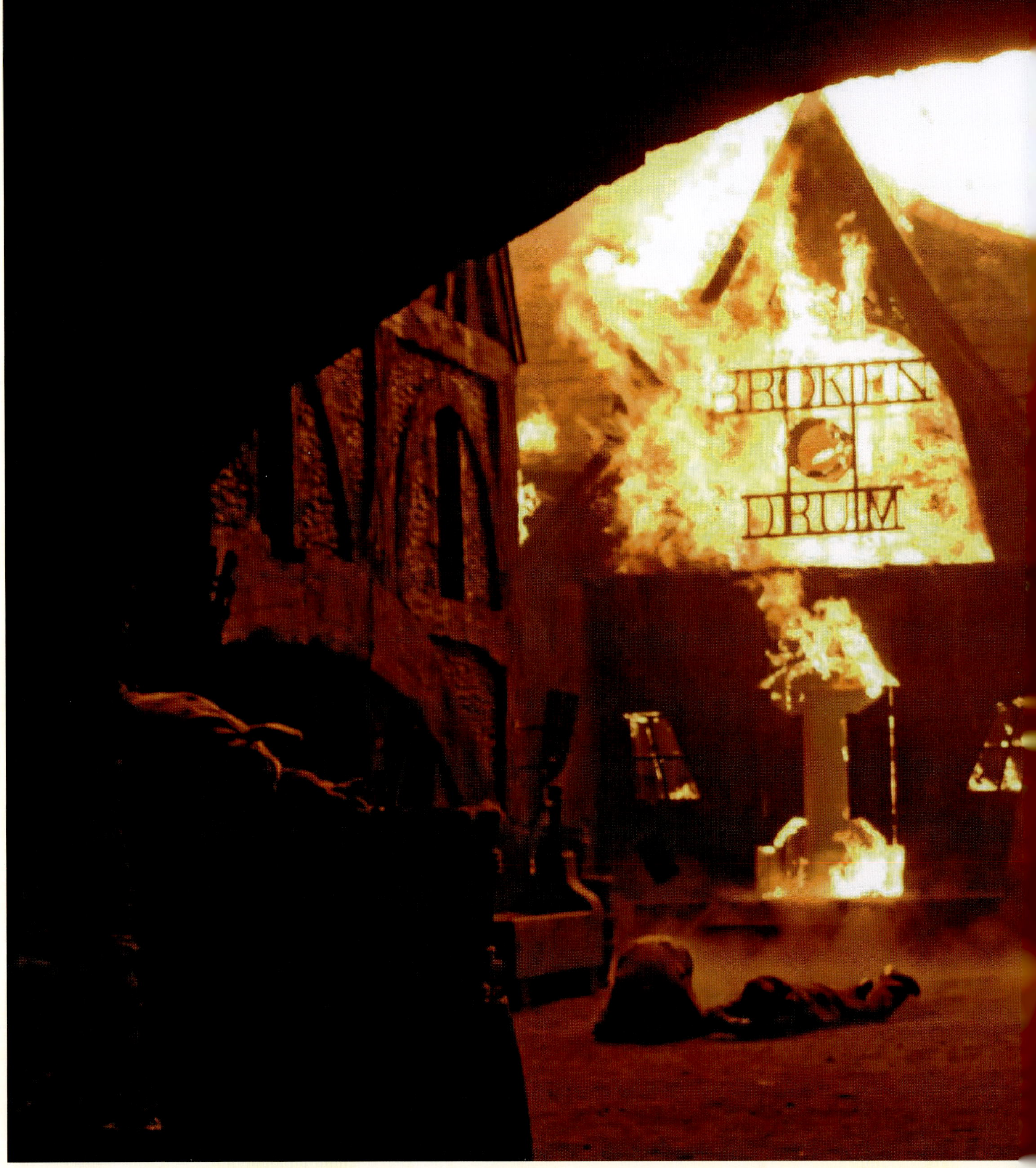
BROKEN
DRUM

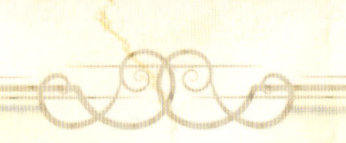

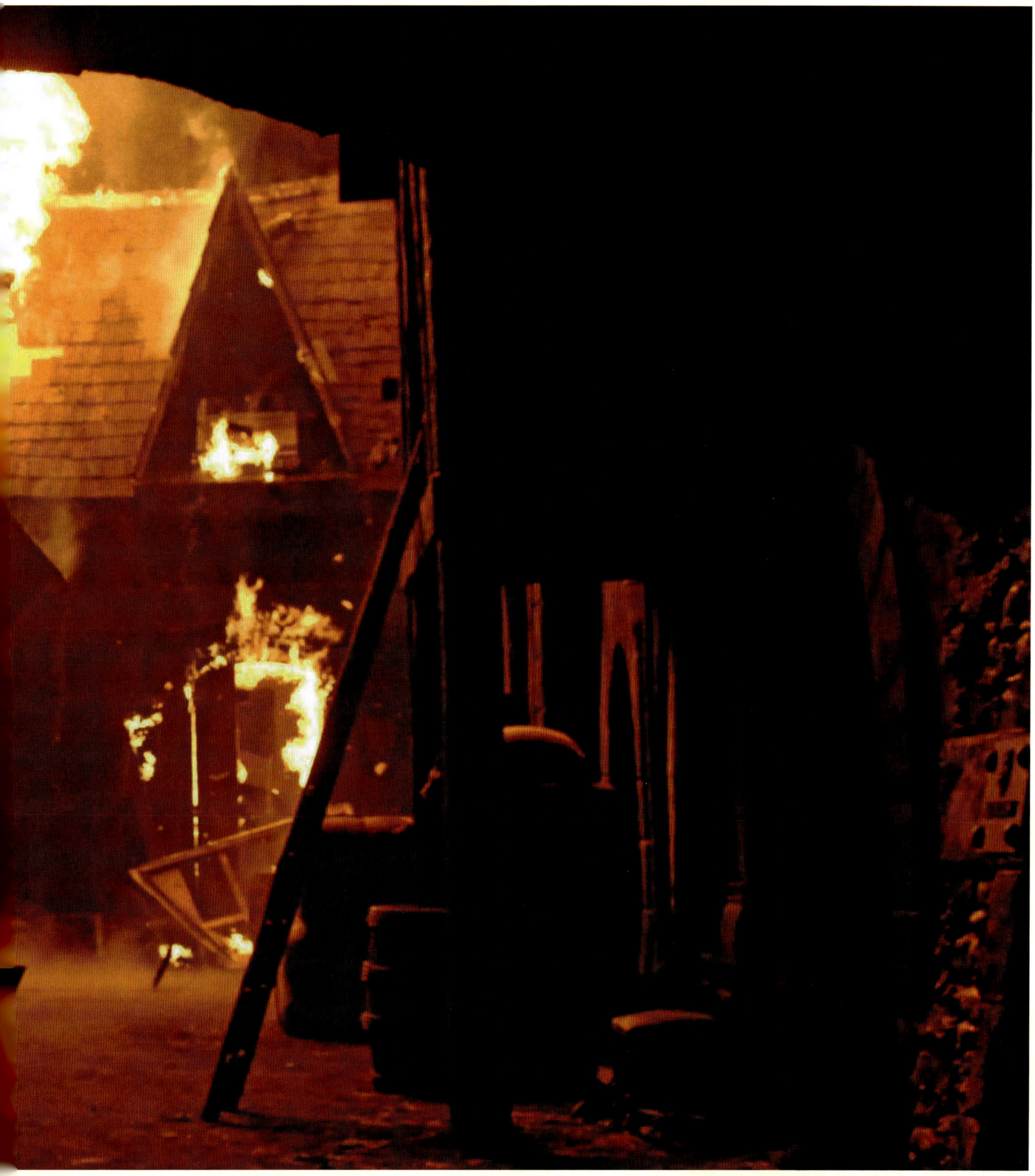

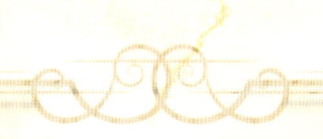

> RINCEWIND
> Did you inn-sewer the Drum?!

> TWOFLOWER
> Well, luckily for Broadman I still have the rhinu he paid as his first premium.

> RINCEWIND
> You bet Broadman that it wouldn't catch fire?

> TWOFLOWER
> Standard valuation 200 rhinu. Why? Why do you ask?

Rincewind indicates the flames.

> RINCEWIND
> That's why you, you . . .

Rincewind doesn't know the word in Trob.

> RINCEWIND
> . . . you, you, you dozy idiot!

A figure bumps into him, narrowly missing him with the SCYTHE BLADE over its shoulder.

> DEATH
> JUST CARRY ON AS IF I'M NOT HERE, RINCEWIND. YOUR APPOINTMENT IS LATER.

> RINCEWIND
> Who . . .?

> TWOFLOWER
> What's next?

Around them people are fleeing and dragging horses from smoking stables.

> RINCEWIND
> What's next?! We'll be hung, drawn and quartered if we stay here much longer!

> TWOFLOWER
> But why?

Rincewind points to the carnage around them.

> RINCEWIND
> What do you mean why? Why? Why?! Look! The whole of Ankh-Morpork is made of wood!

Rincewind runs after a stray horse. With a wistful look back, Twoflower follows him.

> TWOFLOWER
> What about my Luggage?

> RINCEWIND (O.C.)
> Bugger your Luggage!

EXT. HILLTOP OUTSIDE ANHK-MORPORK - DAWN

Twoflower signs heavily. He and Rincewind are standing by their horse looking down at Ankh-Morpork from the hilltop.

The whole of the downtown is alight. The smoke rises miles high, visible across the whole of the Discworld.

Another onlooker is also looking back over the city.

> ONLOOKER
> Tell you what: whoever started that fire, be wise for them to find a fast horse and make themselves very scarce.

He looks at Rincewind.

> RINCEWIND
> (quietly)
> Thank you very much, Twoflower!

Twoflower is consulting his book.

> TWOFLOWER
> It says that Chirm is lovely this time of year.

SC-1/39 HILLTOP OUTSIDE A·MORPORK

R+T + HORSE IN F/G LOOK OVER A·MORPORK SMOKE RISES HIGH INTO SKY

              RINCEWIND
   Yes, and very, very dangerous.

              TWOFLOWER
   Really?

              RINCEWIND
   Mmm.

              TWOFLOWER
   Hmm!

Twoflower puts his book back and tries, unsuccessfully, to get his foot into the stirrup.

There is an explosion in the city.

              TWOFLOWER
   Oh!

The horse starts to trot, Twoflower hopping alongside, until he climbs up into the WRONG STIRRUP so that, as the horse canters away, he is facing the tail.

55

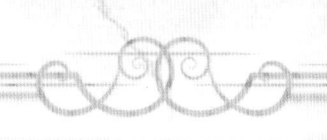

>   RINCEWIND
> That's the oil bond store going up.
>
>   TWOFLOWER
> Argh! Argh! How dangerous is
> Chirm? Rincewind! Whoa!
>
>   RINCEWIND
> Oops!
>
>   TWOFLOWER
> Whoa! Whoa!
>
>   RINCEWIND
> Oh no!

Rincewind groans and looks around to see Twoflower vanishing into the distance. He also sees the onlooker's horse tethered to a tree behind him.

>   RINCEWIND
> Look at that over there!

Rincewind sidles over to the horse and unties it.

>   ONLOOKER
> Oh, dear God, no!

By the time the onlooker looks over his shoulder . . .

. . . Rincewind is galloping into the distance in pursuit of Twoflower.

The onlooker grits his teeth and narrows his eyes.

>   ONLOOKER
> Oi! Oi you! Come back here! That's
> my 'orse! Come back!

On Rincewind's face as behind him the onlooker starts to run after him.

>   RINCEWIND/VOICE OF THE SPELL
>   (His voice echoes)
> Oi, Rincewind!

Rincewind looks around him, confused as to where the voice has come from.

EXT. UNSEEN UNIVERSITY/OCTAVO ROOM - DAWN

On a lectern of dark wood, carved into the shape of a winged thing, fastened to it by a heavy chain covered in padlocks, is a large, but not particularly impressive, BOOK. Metal CLASPS hold it shut. The OCTAVO. It is the book we have seen stirring earlier.

The lectern is the only furniture in a room where the walls are covered with OCCULT SYMBOLS. Most of the floor is taken up by the Eightfold Seal of Stasis. Black candles drip wax.

The Octavo stirs. A flicker of octarine blue spills from its pages. The padlocks rattle. The room sparkles with tiny flashes as dust motes incinerate in the flow of raw magic. The Seal of Stasis begins to glow.

Eyes peer in through the grille in the door.

>   NARRATOR (V.O.)
> The Octavo, greatest of all spell
> books, locked and chained deep
> in the cellars of the Unseen
> University. The spells imprisoned
> in its pages lead a secret life
> of their own, and Rincewind's
> departure from Ankh-Morpork has
> left them deeply troubled.

Galder Weatherwax's face is pressed against the grille.

>   HEAD LIBRARIAN
> I can't remember it being like this
> before.
>
>   GALDER WEATHERWAX
> No.

SC.1/37 OCTAVO ROOM

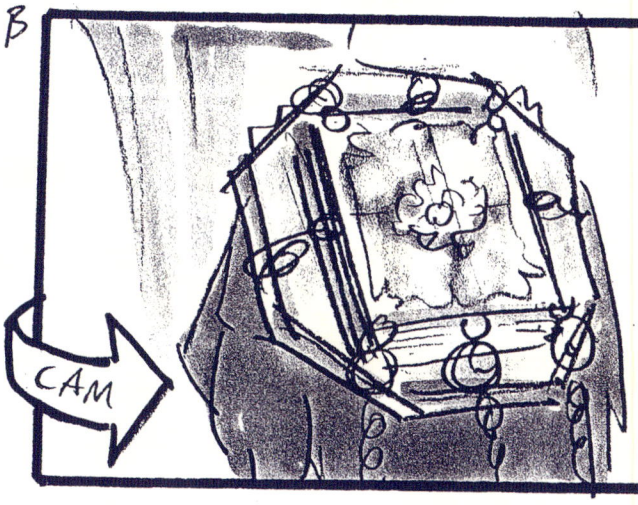

1.A

SAME SHOT

B

SAME SHOT

C

CAMERA TRACKS AROUND OCTAVO AND GETS CLOSER TO IT...

...FAVOURING THE PAGE - OPENING SIDE.

OCTARINE LIGHTS GLOWS OUT...

INT. UNSEEN UNIVERSITY/OUTSIDE OCTAVO ROOM DOOR – DAWN

Galder Weatherwax's face is pressed against the grille. He closes it and turns to the HEAD LIBRARIAN.

        GALDER WEATHERWAX
    Not since that time a young
    wizard . . .

The Archchancellor is deep in thought.

        GALDER WEATHERWAX
    Oh dear.

His jaw drops and he gasps as he remembers something.

        GALDER WEATHERWAX
    I've expelled him, haven't I?

INT. UNSEEN UNIVERSITY/GALDER'S STUDY – DAY

The Head Librarian is pacing in front of the Archchancellor.

        GALDER WEATHERWAX
    And nobody knows where he is,
    Librarian?

        HEAD LIBRARIAN
    Not even the Patrician's palace
    guard. Though they seem to think
    he'll turn up for some reason.

        GALDER WEATHERWAX
    Look, he's the only person in living
    memory who has actually touched
    the Octavo with his bare hands. We
    have no idea the effect it'll have on
    him in the outside world.

The Librarian doesn't looks so sure.

              GALDER WEATHERWAX
    At least when he was a student we
    knew where he was.

INT. UNSEEN UNIVERSITY/OUTSIDE GALDER'S STUDY - DAY

Trymon approaches Galder's study. Hearing a hushed conversation from behind the door he stops just outside. He quietly moves to the door and presses a LISTENING DEVICE to it.

INT. UNSEEN UNIVERSITY/GALDER'S STUDY - DAY

Galder starts to light his pipe.

          GALDER WEATHERWAX
    Perhaps I've been a bit hasty.

          GALDER WEATHERWAX (O.C.)
    Who else knows about this?

          HEAD LIBRARIAN
    Nobody, Archchancellor.

          GALDER WEATHERWAX
    Good. Let's keep it that way, shall we?

          HEAD LIBRARIAN
    Oh, apart from Greyhald Spold, of course.

Galder thinks about this for a moment and then shrugs.

          GALDER WEATHERWAX
    His days are probably numbered anyway. On the subject of which, I haven't seen old Narrowbolt around recently.

The Archchancellor finally fills his pipe.

          HEAD LIBRARIAN
    That's because he's dead, Archchancellor.

Galder raises his eyebrows, but only slightly.

INT. UNSEEN UNIVERSITY/OUTSIDE GALDER'S STUDY - DAY

Trymon opens the door hurriedly.

          HEAD LIBRARIAN (O.C.)
    I'm just glad nobody wants to be Head Librarian.

INT. UNSEEN UNIVERSITY/GALDER'S STUDY - DAY

Trymon enters the room and looks the Head Librarian directly in the eye.

          TRYMON
    Perish the thought, Horace . . .

There is a pause.

          TRYMON
    Oh, I am looking for a book!

Trymon smiles and turns to leave.

Galder tilts his head to look at Trymon's feet.

          GALDER WEATHERWAX
    New shoes . . .

Trymon leaves.

GALDER WEATHERWAX
And new hat...

Galder doesn't see Trymon's self-satisfied smile.

GALDER WEATHERWAX
...Mr Trymon.

INT. UNSEEN UNIVERSITY/LIBRARY – DAY

The Head Librarian hands Trymon a book.

Trymon puts the book on the table revealing the cover. Razor-sharp miniature KNIFE BLADES stick out around the title:

Room at the Top: How to Succeed in Wizardry

HEAD LIBRARIAN
Hmm!

TRYMON
(growls)
Ah!

Trymon starts to read.

TRYMON
Oh, how very neat and tidy! Did you know that in the event of the Archchancellor's sad demise he would be succeeded by Greyhald Spold?!

Trymon copies a drawing into his notebook.

HEAD LIBRARIAN
He's demonstrated remarkable powers of survival.

> **TRYMON**
> Up 'til now! I think it's very important to strive for perfection, don't you?

> **HEAD LIBRARIAN**
> Oh yes, sir. If you want to get to the very top, sir, yes.

He nervously goes back to tidying the books.

> **HEAD LIBRARIAN**
> The position of Head Librarian has never really appealed to you, sir?

> **TRYMON**
> No.

> **HEAD LIBRARIAN**
> Oh good.

> **TRYMON**
> It is quite possible that the next Archchancellor may well smile upon those who understand the importance of things being well-organised.

The Librarian looks at the book he is holding.

There is a low rattling sound from beneath the floor of the library.

> **TRYMON**
> Is everything in order down there?

> **HEAD LIBRARIAN**
> Oh absolutely. Everything is in . . . alphabetical order, in fact.

The unmistakable sounds of rattling chains and flaring magic come from the Octavo room.

Trymon fixes his gaze on the Librarian . . .

. . . who withers.

INT. UNSEEN UNIVERSITY/OUTSIDE OCTAVO ROOM DOOR – DAY

Trymon peers through the grille at the Octavo.

> **TRYMON**
> So, this is the famous Octavo?

> **HEAD LIBRARIAN**
> Famous and dangerous.

Trymon turns back to look through the grille at the restless book.

> **TRYMON**
> How long has it been like this?

> **HEAD LIBRARIAN**
> Well it's always been a bit strange as far back as I can remember. But for some reason it's got rather lively.

The Librarian peers through the grille and then closes it.

Trymon moves closer to the Librarian.

           TRYMON
  Why?

The Librarian shrugs.

      HEAD LIBRARIAN
  I don't know.

           TRYMON
  Who does?

Trymon is standing over him now.

The Librarian makes the mistake of catching Trymon's gaze again.

      HEAD LIBRARIAN
  Greyhald Spold.

The Librarian swallows but it's no good.

           TRYMON
  Hmm?

      HEAD LIBRARIAN
  Before my time.

Trymon marches away.

           TRYMON
  Greyhald Spold. How convenient!

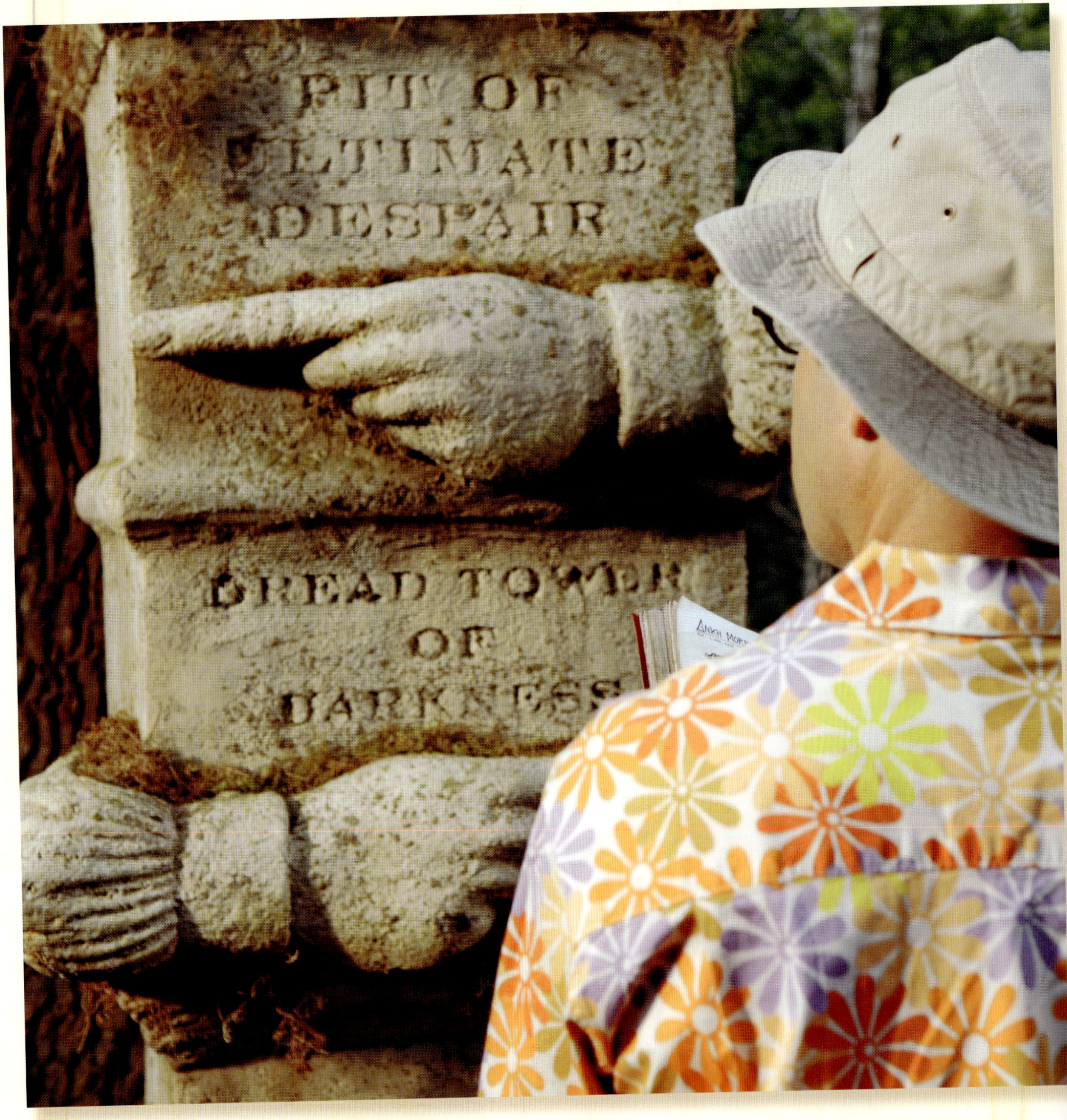
PIT OF ULTIMATE DESPAIR
DREAD TOWER OF DARKNESS

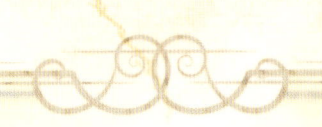

INT. UNSEN UNIVERSITY/OCTAVO ROOM - DAY

The Octavo continues to rattle and flare.

EXT. FOREST GLADE - DAY

Twoflower is lost. His horse trots down a path towards a forest.

    TWOFLOWER
 Rincewind!

EXT. FOREST GLADE - DAY

Rincewind's horse trots down another path . . .

    RINCEWIND
 Twoflower!

. . . and out of camera shot.

    RINCEWIND (O.C.)
 Twoflower!

After a pause, the horse trots back the other way again.

    RINCEWIND
 Twoflower!

EXT. FOREST GLADE - DAY

Twoflower has come to a sign post. It points to a number of destinations:

Pit of Ultimate Despair

    TWOFLOWER
 Pit of Ultimate Despair.

Dread Tower of Darkness
(ices and crèche)

    TWOFLOWER
 Dread Tower of Darkness.

He looks puzzled.

    TWOFLOWER
 Humph!

He consults a milestone. Looking down he notices a strange CARVING. There are runes carved below it:

    TWOFLOWER
 Traveller, the hospitable Temple
 of Bel-Shamharoth lies a thousand
 paces hubwards.

Twoflower straightens up.

    TWOFLOWER
 Hubwards.

He stands up and consults the next milestone.

    TWOFLOWER
 The Wyrmberg and Palace of The
 Dragon Lord lie a thousand paces
 Rimwards.

He looks rimwards.

> **TWOFLOWER**
> Huh! Dragons. I've always wanted to see dragons!

He sees an old track of sorts leading away between the trees. And then hears from the opposite direction, the sound of howling wolves.

> **TWOFLOWER**
> Dragons it is!

He nods decisively, unties his horse from a sapling and heads towards the track.

> **TWOFLOWER**
> Rincewind!

But there is no reply.

EXT. BEECH TREE - DAY

Rincewind is hanging by his hands from a high branch in a beech tree.

> **RINCEWIND**
> Uh!

The figure on the next branch turns towards him.

> **DEATH**
> YOUR LIFETIME IS UP, RINCEWIND. I CAN'T HANG AROUND ALL DAY.

> **RINCEWIND**
> I can!

He looks, hopelessly, for a way out.

> **RINCEWIND**
> (defiantly)
> What have you done with the tourist?

> **DEATH**
> NOTHING.

> **RINCEWIND**
> Uh!

> **DEATH**
> HE WAS LURED BY THE ATTRACTION OF THE WYRMBERG.

The CAMERA pans to a large SNAKE which has wound itself along the branch towards Rincewind.

> **RINCEWIND**
> Oh, so at least the Patrician won't be sending out his men to kill me just yet then, eh?

> **DEATH**
> THERE IS A DISTINCT POSSIBILITY THAT HE MAY NOT NEED TO.

Rincewind looks at the snake, at Death, and then down.

WOLVES are clustering around the base of the tree. They look up.

Rincewind groans.

                    RINCEWIND
          Ah! Ah!

                    RINCEWIND
               (to the snake)
          What are you grinning at, huh?!

                    DEATH
          OH I'M SORRY, I CAN'T HELP IT. NOW
          WOULD YOU BE SO KIND AS TO LET GO? IT
          WON'T HURT.

Rincewind's arms are in screaming agony.

                    RINCEWIND
          Being torn to pieces by wolves
          won't hurt!?

                    DEATH
          IT WILL BE OVER VERY QUICKLY. AND
          OF COURSE THEY ARE AN ENDANGERED
          SPECIES.

Rincewind notices a small branch further away from the snake. If he can just reach it . . .

He swings himself along, one hand outstretched.

The branch snaps and Rincewind drops . . .

. . . but it doesn't break completely, leaving the wizard hanging. Rincewind looks down. He is going to land right on the biggest wolf.

                    RINCEWIND
          Ah! Argh! He-elp!

The snake watches him thoughtfully.

Rincewind's grip slips slowly . . . and then holds. Relief begins to spread across the wizard's face. He hangs still for a moment.

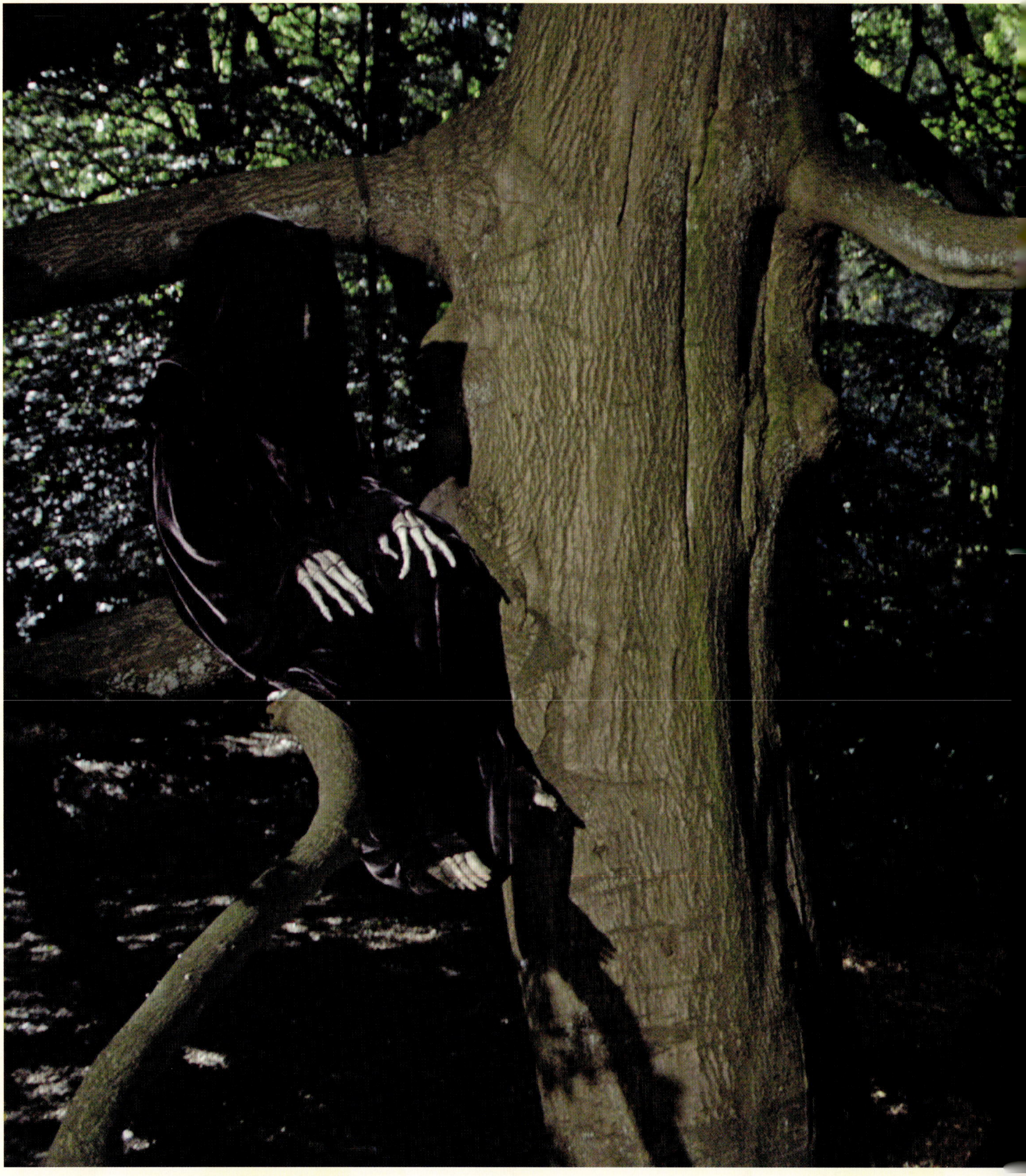

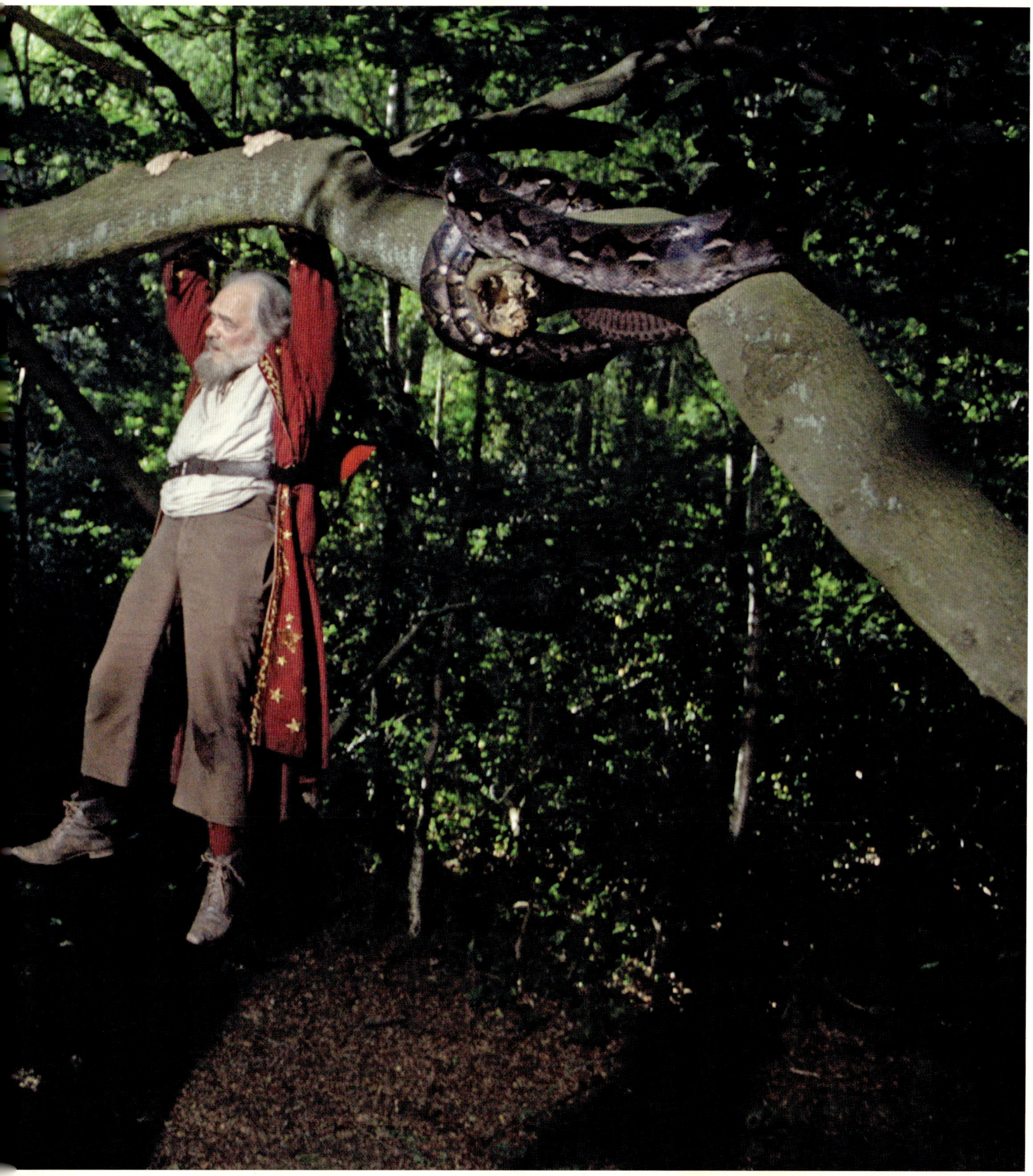

SC.1/49 — BEECH TREE.

23. *TOP SHOT DOWN ON 3x WOLVES SNARLING AND SNAPPING*

24. *C/U RINCEWIND — HE CLOSES HIS EYES TIGHT*

25. *ECU — OPENS EYES. THE RUNES FLICKER AND MAGIC GLOWS (RUNES BRIGHTER + MORE PROMINENT)*

26. *ECU WOLF SNARLING AND DROOLING + MAD EYES!*

RINCEWIND/VOICE OF THE SPELL
Ashoni!

His eyes slam open. The RUNES flicker and he sighs.

The wolves howl in expectation.

RINCEWIND
Who are you?

His grip slowly slips until . . .

RINCEWIND
Argh! Ooh!

. . . he falls . . .

There is a strange 'mattressy' sound . . .

The wolves whimper and run as we see Rincewind has landed inside the LUGGAGE. Laundry has cushioned his fall.

RINCEWIND
Oh, it's you!

He tries to scrabble out but sees that the Luggage is on the move.

DEATH
OH DEAR. I WONDER IF IT WAS SOMETHING I SAID.

Behind him in the tree, DEATH watches impassively.

Rincewind cautiously opens the Luggage lid and sits up.

RINCEWIND
Don't think I owe you a debt of gratitude! One of the consolations of being eaten by wolves was the fact that I would never have to have a near-death experience again thanks to your owner!

The Luggage starts to run faster and Rincewind falls back.

EXT. FOREST GLADE - DAY

Twoflower is leading his horse steadily in the direction of the Wyrmberg.

TWOFLOWER
737, 738, 739. Dragons. Dragons here and 741, 742, 743 . . .

EXT. FOREST GLADE - DAY

Rincewind bumps along on top of the Luggage. He looks down and sees the milestone with the runes and just catches sight of the words 𝔚𝔶𝔯𝔪𝔟𝔢𝔯𝔤, and 𝔓𝔞𝔩𝔞𝔠𝔢 𝔬𝔣 𝔱𝔥𝔢 𝔇𝔯𝔞𝔤𝔬𝔫 𝔏𝔬𝔯𝔡.

                   RINCEWIND
  Dragons! Huh! Nobody believes in
  them anymore!

He looks again and sees the word 𝔕𝔦𝔪𝔴𝔞𝔯𝔡𝔰 and groans.

The Luggage lurches onwards.

INT. UNSEEN UNIVERSITY/SPOLD'S ROOM - DAY

Spold enters his room, closes the door behind it and turns the massive lock which seals his room against the outside world. He removes the key and hangs it from a hook on the wall.

                GREYHALD SPOLD
  Ha!

He fails to spot TRYMON peering through the keyhole.

INT. UNSEEN UNIVERSITY/OUTSIDE SPOLD'S ROOM - DAY

Trymon looks down at his book and refers to the plan sketched in it. Then he takes a few paces down the corridor and places his hand on a book. He tips it forward gently.

The bookcase slides back to reveal a passage.

Trymon checks to see if anyone is looking and enters.

INT. UNSEEN UNIVERSITY/SPOLD'S ROOM - DAY

Spold is working at his desk. He leaves for a moment to collect another instrument, and as he turns back Trymon is sitting in his chair.

Spold almost jumps out of his skin.

> **GREYHALD SPOLD**
> (gasps)
> I, I never really wanted to be Archchancellor anyway. So, if you're here for—

> **TRYMON**
> For the Octavo, Mr Spold.

> **GREYHALD SPOLD**
> Ah. You're not here to . . . What about the Octavo?

> **TRYMON**
> It's rather . . . troubled at the moment, and it seems that you might be able to tell me why.

Spold seems almost relieved.

> **GREYHALD SPOLD**
> Well, it's not all there, you know.

> TRYMON
> As in mad?

Spold makes the mistake of looking directly at Trymon.

> GREYHALD SPOLD
> As in . . . one spell short of eight.

Trymon rises to his feet.

> TRYMON
> One of the eight spells is missing?!

Spold nods and taps his nose.

> TRYMON
> Well that's rather badly organised!

> GREYHALD SPOLD
> It's certainly extremely dangerous!

> TRYMON
> So where is it now?

Greyhald Spold sighs.

> TRYMON
> Do think very carefully, Mr Spold.

> GREYHALD SPOLD
> I . . . really wish I did know, Mr Trymon.

> TRYMON
> Mmm.

Trymon holds his gaze, and leaves. Spold goes up to the door, checks he's gone, then bars the door and gets back to work.

INT. UNSEEN UNIVERSITY/SPOLD'S ROOMS – NIGHT

The eightfold OCTOGRAM of withholding, surrounded by red and green candles, is in the centre of the room.

Spold goes to the door and sets the complicated clockwork of the lock and shuts the lid, after which he goes over to his bed, takes off his POINTY SHOES and lies down.

Through the keyhole an eye is peering.

INT. UNSEEN UNIVERSITY/OUTSIDE SPOLD'S ROOMS – NIGHT

Through the keyhole, someone's POINT OF VIEW is focused on the shoes.

Trymon takes his head away from the door and fills the keyhole with a piece of paste so that it is air tight.

He steps back. Every last crack in the door has been sealed.

> TRYMON
> Try breathing through this!

And he walks away down the corridor with a self-satisfied smile.

INT. UNSEEN UNIVERSITY/SPOLD'S ROOMS – NIGHT

Spold too has a satisfied smile on his face . . .

. . . as the candles begin to sputter and extinguish.

Spold wheezes more heavily than usual and right beside him, very close to his ear . . .

> DEATH
> DARK IN HERE, ISN'T IT?

EXT. GRASSY HOLLOW - DAY

Twoflower wakes up, the horse is tied up next to him.

> **TWOFLOWER**
> (sighs heavily)
> Oh God, the fire's gone out!

He stretches and gets up. He looks around him before starting up the grassy slope, collecting firewood as he goes.

As he reaches the top of the slope the CAMERA tracks to reveal . . .

EXT. THE WYRMBERG - DAY

The WYRMBERG, a mountain, huge, grey and UPSIDE DOWN rises above the green valley.

At its base it is a mere score of yards across, rising through cloud, curving outwards like an upturned trumpet and topped by a plateau fully a quarter of a mile across.

On top there is a tiny forest, its greenery cascading over the lip. There are buildings. There is even a small river, tumbling over the edge in a waterfall so wind-whipped that it reaches the ground as rain.

Twoflower's face is radiant with pleasure at the spectacular view. He angles his head to try to look at it upside down. As he does he hears a sound . . . of many small legs moving very fast. He smiles with delight and turns.

> **TWOFLOWER**
> Rincewind! Atta-boy! And you've brought the Luggage.

He looks down at the box.

> **RINCEWIND**
> No, it brought me. Ah! Oh!

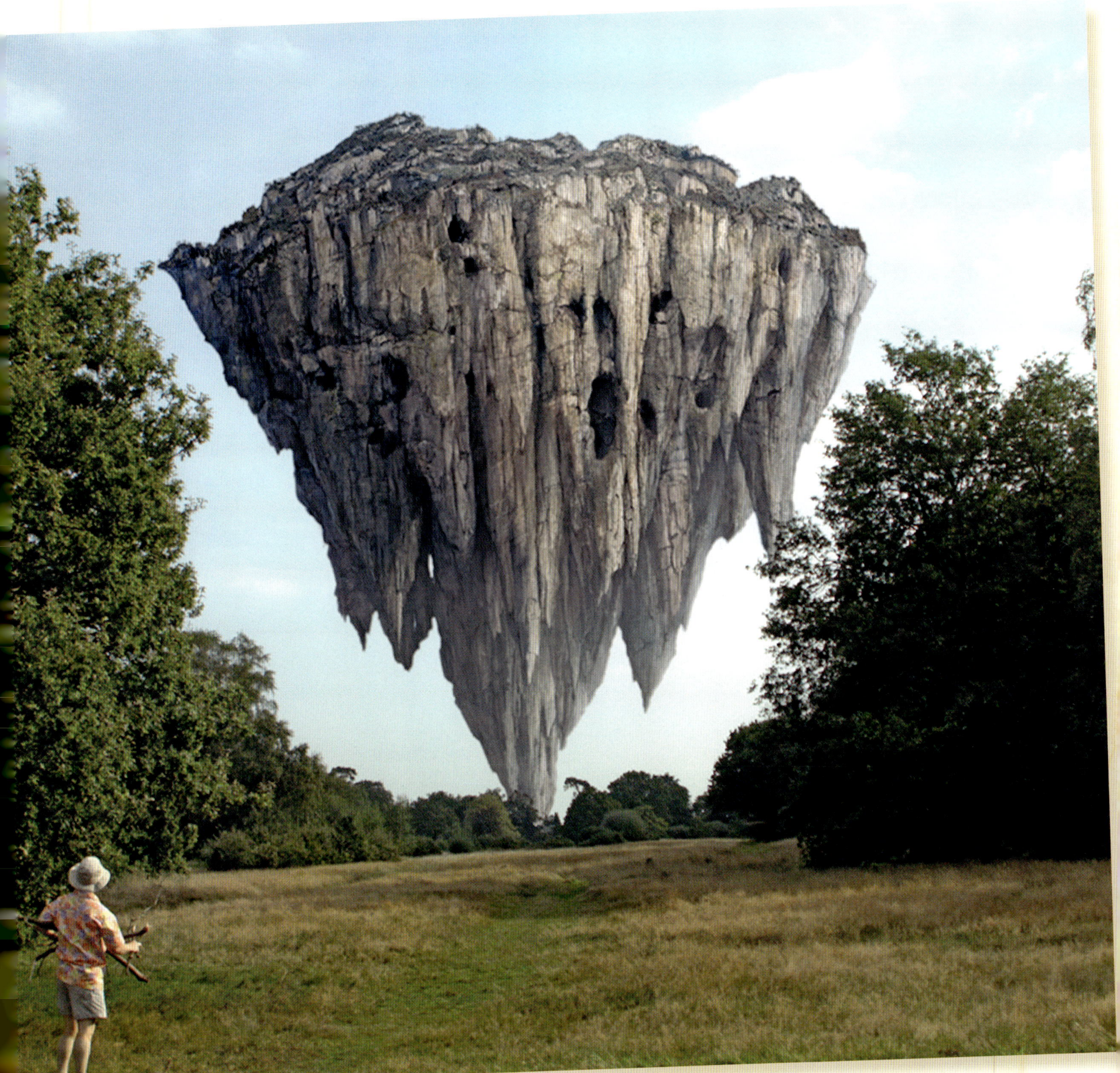

Rincewind gets off the Luggage and looks at it resentfully

>   TWOFLOWER
>   It's amazing, isn't it?

Rincewind looks at the view.

>   RINCEWIND
>   Yes, if you like the physically
>   impossible.

Rincewind looks over to where Twoflower's horse is tethered to a tree. Next to it Twoflower has set up a pig on a spit.

>   TWOFLOWER
>   Well, I think it's just amazin'. A bit
>   under-populated though. Listen, do
>   you think it could be the home of
>   the dragons?

Rincewind looks at the Wyrmberg . . .

>   RINCEWIND
>   Don't be ridiculous! Dragons don't
>   exist!

Rincewind starts to back off, pulling a resisting Twoflower away.

>   TWOFLOWER
>   All my life I've wanted to see
>   dragons.

A dragon roars in the distance.

There is a noise above them, like a strip of leather being slapped on a wet rock.

Rincewind doesn't look up as something glassy and indistinct passes over his head, throwing up a cloud of ashes from the fire as the pig carcase is ripped from the spit and rockets into the sky.

— BACK TO WIDE MASTER SHOT

— PIG ON SPIT IS SUDDENLY WHIPPED OUT OF FRAME

>   RINCEWIND
>   Huh?

The dragon roars again.

>   RINCEWIND
>   Uh!

He looks over to Twoflower just in time to see him shoot off his feet into the air.

>   TWOFLOWER
>   Uh!

>   RINCEWIND
>   I think that we . . . Wah! Ah!

Rincewind gulps and runs.

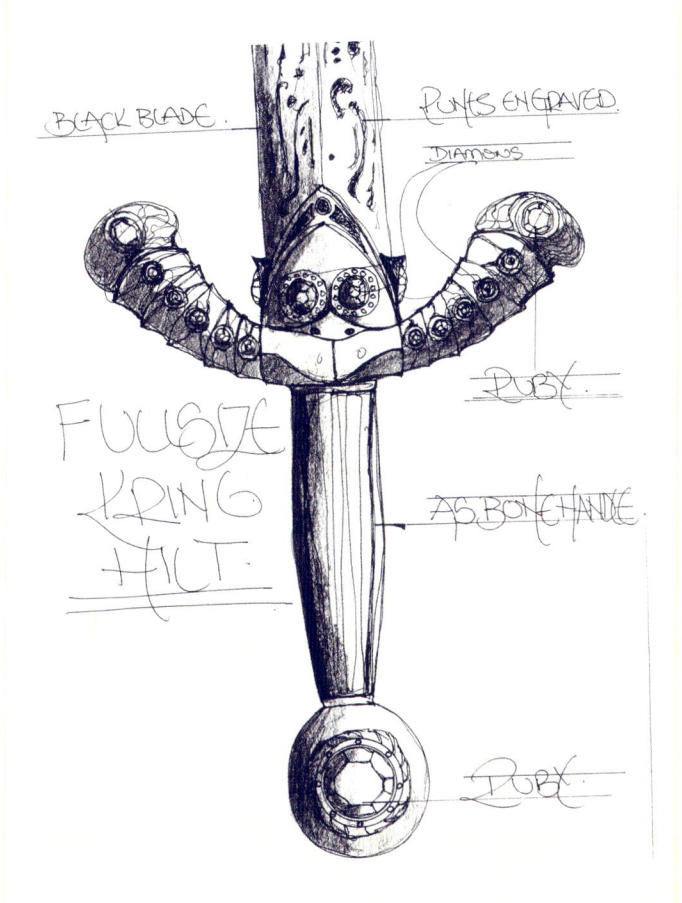

EXT. FIELDS BY WOODS - DAY

Rincewind is clinging onto the horse for dear life.

RINCEWIND
I don't believe in them! They don't exist!

Rincewind bends even lower over his horse's neck and groans.

He whips at his horse with the reins and stares at the wood ahead . . . He hears the clap of wings and kicks on.

He glances briefly over his shoulder and grimaces as we hear a sudden commotion behind him. As he looks forward . . .

RINCEWIND
Argh! Ooh!

. . . a dragon-shaped shadow passes over him and a LOW BRANCH knocks him from the saddle

RINCEWIND
Uh-ah!

The riderless horse trots by itself into the woods.

EXT. WOODS - DAY

The sun flickers between branches and leaves.

Rincewind is collapsed on the floor looking up at a tree which appears to speak.

KRING (O.C.)
Pst! Pst!

RINCEWIND
Uh-oh!

KRING
Pst!

RINCEWIND
No. Just dazed actually. Who said that?!

Rincewind lets his gaze slide sideways.

KRING
Well don't just lie there, pull me out!

A black sword is stuck in a stone by the side of the track.

                    RINCEWIND
What?

                    KRING
Come on, come on, pull me out!

Rincewind struggles to his feet.

                    RINCEWIND
You, you spoke!

                    KRING
I'm a magic sword. You, you
weren't born with a mysterious
birthmark in the shape of a crown,
were you?

                    RINCEWIND
No.

                    KRING
No? Oh, just asking. Were you with
the other fellow?

                    RINCEWIND
Might have been!

                    KRING
It's just the dragons got him. And
so I expect you'll be in a hurry to
slay the dragons and rescue him in
a fantastic feat of derring-do!

                    RINCEWIND
No, not really. No.

                    KRING
Come on!

Rincewind squints over at the sword. He
hesitates, unsure whether to go ahead
with this.

                    KRING
Come on!

Rincewind snaps out of it and scrambles
over to the stone. Kring is buried very
firmly in it. He grips the pommel . . .

                    KRING
Right! Take a firm grip. Ooh that's
good, that's good!

. . . and heaves.

                    RINCEWIND
Oh!

                    KRING
Could be worse; this could have
been an anvil!

                    RINCEWIND
Huh? Ah!

Rincewind sways backwards as the blade
slides free. It feels strangely light as
he topples and falls.

Back on the ground again . . .

                    KRING
Finally!

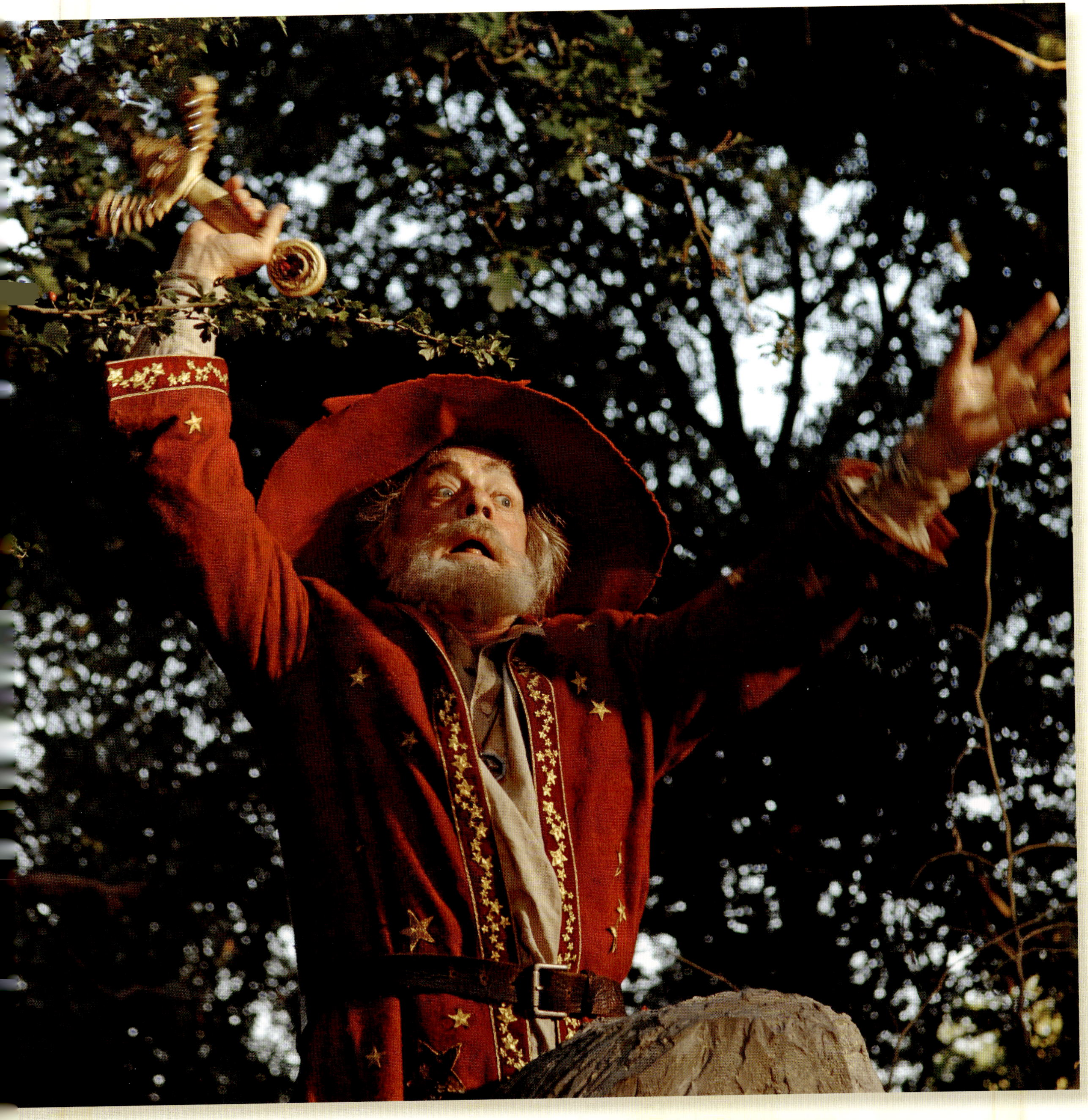

Rincewind is all but pulled back to his feet by the sword.

>   KRING
> The dragons headed hubwards!

>   RINCEWIND
> Even if they did exist, I'm not cut out for dragons!

>   KRING
> Nothing to it! I'll show you!

Kring drags Rincewind along for a few paces.

>   RINCEWIND
> Ah!

>   KRING
> Right, I suggest we start with the one in the trees. Over there.

Rincewind tries to run for it and comes up short as the sword refuses to go with him.

>   KRING
> No you don't!

Rincewind hears a leathery flapping and slowly and reluctantly peers out from behind his tree to take a look

>   RINCEWIND
> You see, there's nothing there!

The branch where something large and dragon-like might have just been sitting settles, as if something large and dragon-like might just have taken off.

>   KRING
> Oh. Well you can start with her instead! Okay?

In the tree . . . a WOMAN is sitting. LIESSA WYRMBIDDER is almost naked, except for a couple of scraps of the lightest leather armour, riding boots of iridescent dragonhide and a high-crested helmet.

SC. 1/60 WOODS - AFTER RINCEWIND FINDS KRING....

1. RINCEWIND IN THE WOODS TURNS TO LOOK

2. RINCE'S P.O.V - DRAGON AND LIESSA IN DISTANCE SLIGHTLY OBSCURED BY FOREGROUND FOLIAGE AND BRANCHES (DRAGON SEMI-TRANSPARENT?)

3. C/U RINCEWIND REACTIONS

>   KRING
> Okay?

>   RINCEWIND
> I don't know how to be a hero!

>   KRING
> No, obviously. But I propose to teach you.

Rincewind tries to pull away.

>   KRING
> Look, I'll be frank, I've worked with far better material than you. But it's either that . . . or I'll chop your head off!

Rincewind sees his own arm snap up until the shimmering blade is humming against his throat. He tries to force his fingers to let go. They won't.

KRING
I mean it!

RINCEWIND
All right. All right.

Rincewind pats the sword unconvincingly.

RINCEWIND
Good boy.

INT. UNSEEN UNIVERSITY/SPOLD'S ROOM - DAY

The keyhole is unblocked, revealing Galder's eye peering through.

The door opens and the Archchancellor walks in with the Head Librarian. They go over to Spold's dead body.

Galder turns to the Librarian.

GALDER WEATHERWAX
Mmm. There's an ambitious wizard on the loose. I think a certain degree of vigilance would be in order, especially if he's talked to Trymon.

EXT. WOODS NEAR FIELDS/CLEARING - DAY

LIESSA the dragonrider stands up and squints across the clearing.

RINCEWIND (O.C.)
Any suggestions?

KRING
Uh, well obviously you attack.

She summersaults down easily from the tree and lands lightly on the tussocky grass, drawing her sword.

RINCEWIND (O.C.)
Oh! Why didn't I think of that!

KRING
Because you're a defeatist.

Rincewind holds Kring in front of him at arm's length.

Liessa hefts her own sword and with a big grin, cartwheels towards him.

KRING
On your marks, get set, go!

The grin evaporates to shock as Rincewind's sword catches Liessa's blade and parries her blows repeatedly.

LIESSA DRAGONLADY
Sha!

KRING
Ha, ha, ha, ha! Got you! And again!

RINCEWIND
Ah!

LIESSA DRAGONLADY
Ah!

KRING
Have to be quicker than that!
Ha-ha!

Kring continues to parry her thrusts with ease.

[Storyboard panel labeled 7, A: "WHIP PAN FROM CLASHING SWORDS TO...." showing CLASH! B: "...TIGHT PROFILE ON LIESSA."]

RINCEWIND
Ah!

KRING
Hey!

LIESSA DRAGONLADY
Ah! Ah!

KRING
Ha-ha!

With a flourish, Kring jerks her sword out of her grip.

RINCEWIND
Uh, ha, ha, ha.

KRING
Did I ever tell you about the time I was thrown into a lake?

Liessa jumps back to avoid another thrust and falls full-length on the turf.

LIESSA DRAGONLADY
Ah!

KRING
Let's have a look at you, Madam!

The tip of the black sword is hovering over Liessa's throat. Rincewind appears to be struggling with it.

RINCEWIND
Where is the tourist?

LIESSA DRAGONLADY
He's been taken back to the Wyrmberg.

RINCEWIND
What is this Wyrmberg?

LIESSA DRAGONLADY
The Wyrmberg. It is dragon home.

RINCEWIND
(really unconvincingly)
They don't exist!

LIESSA DRAGONLADY
(leadingly)
But I suppose you'll be wanting to rescue your friend.

KRING
My point precisely.

RINCEWIND
He's not my friend! But I suppose you'd better take me to this Wyrmberg of yours.

Rincewind looks around desperately, and realises that this is something he is really going to have to go through with.

LIESSA DRAGONLADY
Leolith!

The dragon roars.

Rincewind turns to look and swallows.

SC. 1/61 — WOODS

15A — LOW ANGLE FROM BEHIND FALLEN LIESSA — LOOK UP TO RINCE WITH 2 HANDS ON SWORD.

B — ...SHADOW FALLS ON RINCE

16 — "LAOLITH!" — ANGLE DOWN ON LIESSA SHOUTING

THE COLOUR OF MAGIC

EXT. SKY ABOVE THE WYRMBERG – DAY

Rincewind is utterly terrified, riding on A DRAGON, holding on to Liessa around her waist. He makes the mistake of glancing downwards, and finds himself looking through the dragon to the treetops below. Far below.

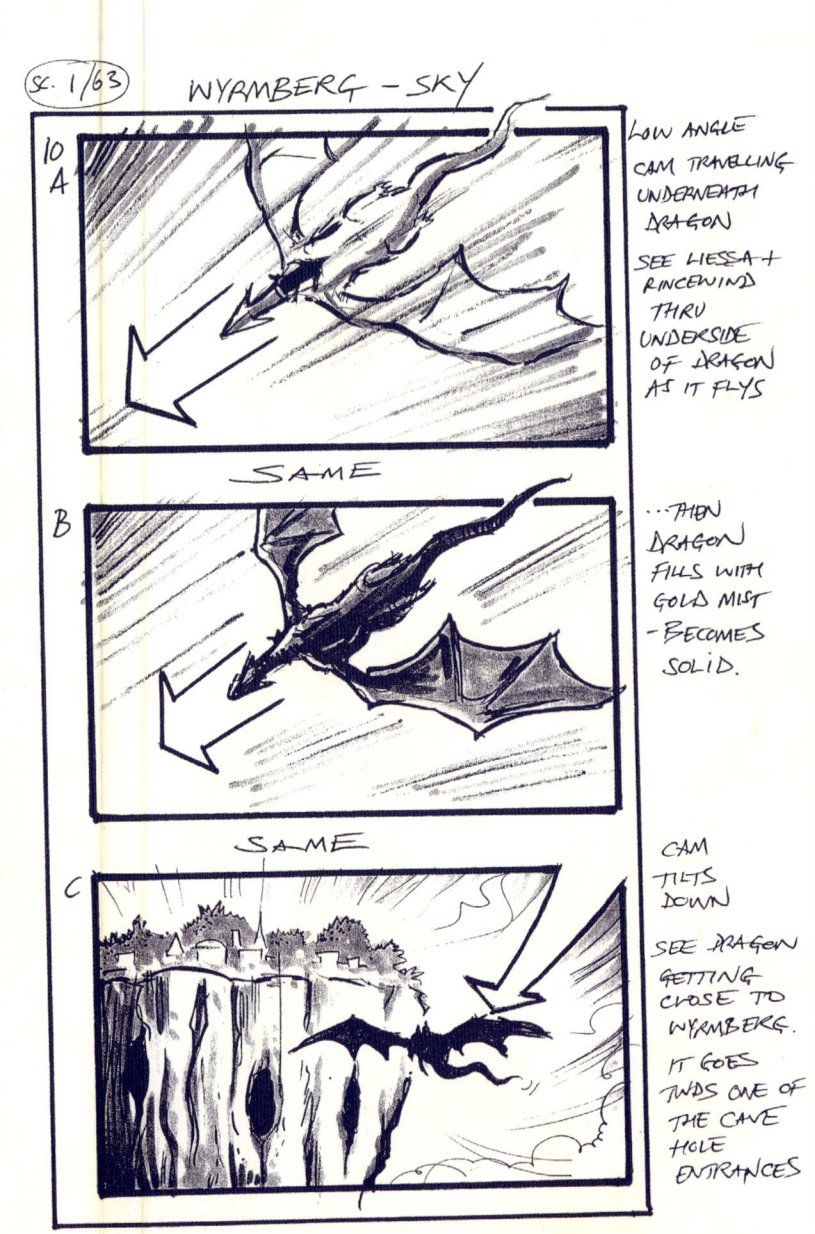

> RINCEWIND
> Uh! Uh! I didn't, I didn't know dragons were see-through!

He looks queasy and closes his eyes. Wind snatches at him.

> LIESSA DRAGONLADY
> (smiling falsely)
> Didn't you?

> RINCEWIND
> No!

> LIESSA DRAGONLADY
> Then watch him as we get closer to the Wyrmberg!

Rincewind's streaming eyes see the impossibly inverted mountain rearing out of the deep forested valley. Even at this distance he can make out the faint octarine glow.

> RINCEWIND
> Oh no!

He averts his eyes quickly. Now he can no longer see the ground through the dragon. As they glide towards the Wyrmberg it is taking more solid form, as if the creature's body is filling with a gold mist.

> RINCEWIND
> That at least is very marginally better.

By the time the Wyrmberg is in front of them, the dragon is as real as a rock.

The flared plateau of the upturned mountain drifts towards them. The dragon doesn't even slow. As the mountain looms over Rincewind he sees a cave mouth.

Laolith skims towards it, shoulder muscles pumping.

85

INT. WYRMBERG DRAGON CAVERN – DAY

Laolith emerges from the dark into . . . a huge cave. Rincewind looks terrified as it glides across its vast emptiness.

There are other dragons flapping across the sun-shafted air or perched on outcrops of rock.

Laolith rears in mid-air and alights on one of the large rings.

          LIESSA DRAGONLADY
Jump now!

          RINCEWIND
What?!

The dragonlady leaps from the creature's back to land on the platform, where she stands looking on at the wizard's discomfiture. Rincewind had also jumped, but missed the platform, and is now hanging over the edge.

There is the sound of a number of crossbows being cocked.

          LIESSA DRAGONLADY
Surrender!

Kring instantly settles against Rincewind's throat.

          KRING
Never.

                    RINCEWIND
                   (squeakily)
            Um, er, er never.

            LIESSA DRAGONLADY (O.C.)
            Of course not. He's a hero, isn't he?

                      KRING
            I taught him myself.

Liessa moves closer to him as Laolith
releases the ring and flies away.

                LIESSA DRAGONLADY
            And what is your name, hero?

                    RINCEWIND
            Um . . .

                LIESSA DRAGONLADY
            So that we know who you were.

                    RINCEWIND
            My name is . . . is er . . . Rincewind
            of Ankh.

                LIESSA DRAGONLADY
            And I am Liessa Dragonlady. You
            are to challenge me in mortal
            combat.

                    RINCEWIND
            Mmm! No! No, I ca-an't!

                LIESSA DRAGONLADY
            You are mistaken. Lio!rt, help our
            hero into a pair of hook boots. I am
            sure he is anxious to get started.

The dragonrider heaves the wizard onto
the platform and pushes him onto a seat.

                    RINCEWIND
            Ah! No. Really. I . . . Oh! Ah! Ow!

                    RINCEWIND
            If you are looking after my
            acquaintance . . .

                LIESSA DRAGONLADY
            You will see your friend soon
            enough; if you are religious,
            I mean. None who enter the
            Wyrmberg ever leave again, except
            metaphorically speaking, of course!

The dragonrider proceeds to strap
hookboots to Rincewind's feet.

INT. UNSEEN UNIVERSITY/OUTSIDE GALDER'S STUDY - DAY

Trymon closes the door carefully behind
him and walks away from the door with a
satisfied look on his face. As he walks
away down the passage . . .

. . . he meets Galder coming the other
way.

                GALDER WEATHERWAX
            Oh, Mr Trymon!

                    TRYMON
            Good day, Archchancellor.

Galder looks from Trymon's head to his feet.

          GALDER WEATHERWAX
     Oh! New, new shoes and hat, eh?!

He looks Trymon directly in the eye.

          GALDER WEATHERWAX
     Well, you came to see me?

          TRYMON
     Yes. I have taken the liberty of
     doing a little research.

          GALDER WEATHERWAX
     Ah, about the Octavo perhaps?

Just how much does Trymon know...?

          TRYMON
     Yes. It appears that one of the
     great spells is missing.

          GALDER WEATHERWAX
     Ah. And you were wondering,
     purely for administrative purposes,
     where it might have got to?

          TRYMON
     Well, yes! Do you know,
     Archchancellor?

          GALDER WEATHERWAX
     Well, if I did I think I've forgotten.

          TRYMON
     Oh.

The Archchancellor opens his door carefully, but pauses on the threshold.

          GALDER WEATHERWAX
     Oh! Old Spold, he...

Trymon looks directly at Galder.

          GALDER WEATHERWAX
     Oh no. No. Too late. He's already
     popped his pointy shoes, hasn't he?
     You know he always had difficult
     breathing, even before he managed
     to seal himself in his own room
     from the outside. Yes, great shame
     about Spold.

The Archchancellor goes in to his study and closes the door behind him.

The CAMERA pushes into the door. There is a clockwork noise, then a sickening crunch of metal against wood and then a thump as something heavy hits the floor.

          GALDER WEATHERWAX
     Argh!

As Trymon walks away with a vindictive smile.

INT. WYRMBERG/CELL - DAY

Twoflower grabs the bars and pulls himself up.

              TWOFLOWER
Just clouds.

He drops down and sits on the edge of one of the wooden beds that are the only furnishings in the cell.

              TWOFLOWER
Well, I expect this is all some sort of a misunderstanding. I expect they'll release me soon. They seem rather civilised. And when I get back I can tell people that I saw dragons. Imagine that.

He lies down and smiles.

              TWOFLOWER
               (sighs)
Dragons.

He begins to daydream. After a few moments there is the faintest of scrabblings in the darkness and a gout of FLAME rolls past his head and strikes the far wall. As the rocks flash into furnace heat he looks up.

              TWOFLOWER
Ah! Ah! Oh!

A DRAGON now occupies more than half the cell.

Twoflower's mouth is open as he looks at the dragon.

              NINEREEDS
I obey, Lord.

Twoflower looks at his own reflection in two enormous green eyes. Beyond them the dragon is multi-hued, horned, spiked and lithe. Its folded wings scrape the wall on both sides of the room.

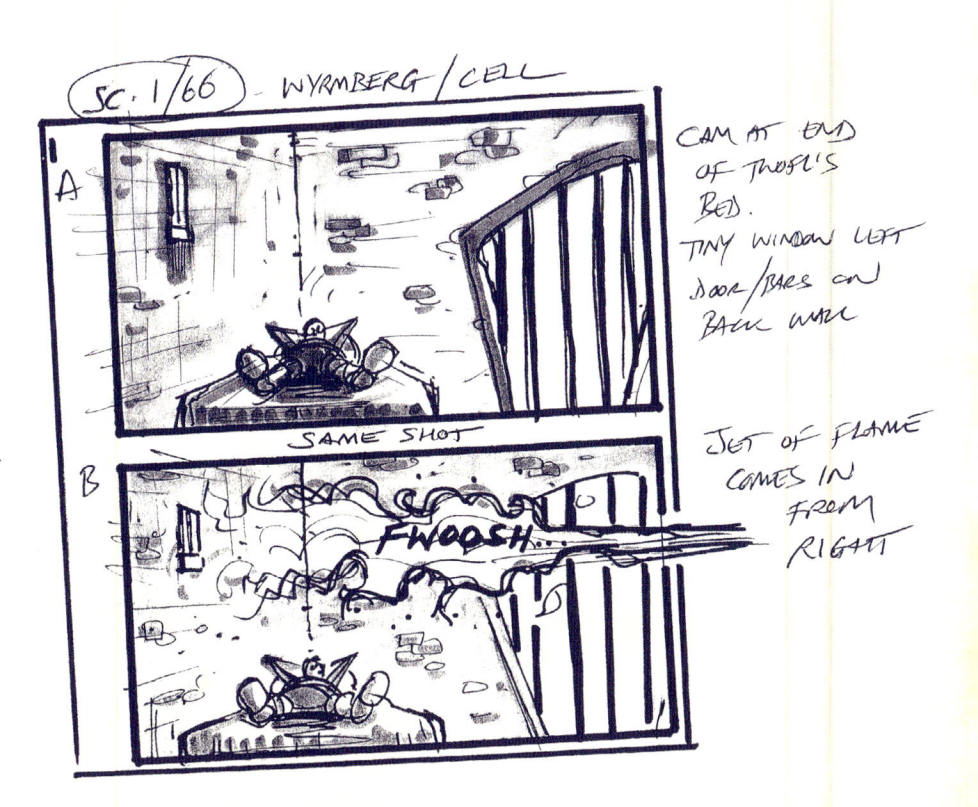

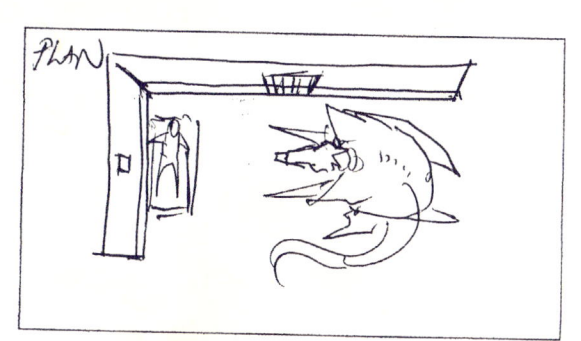

                    TWOFLOWER
          Obey?

His voice vibrates with terror and
delight.

                    NINEREEDS
          Of course, Lord.

The glow in the wall fades away.
Twoflower points a trembling finger to
the door.

                    TWOFLOWER
          Open it?

The dragon raises its huge head. The
ball of flame rolls, its colour fading
from orange to yellow, from yellow to
white, and finally to the faintest of
blues. Where it touches the door the
metal explodes into a shower of hot
droplets. Black shadows arc and jigger
over the walls. The metal bubbles and
the door falls into the passage beyond.

                    TWOFLOWER
          Ha! Ha-ha!

INT. UNSEEN UNIVERSITY/GALDER WEATHERWAX'S STUDY - DAY

Trymon opens the door to Galder's study.

                    TRYMON (O.C.)
          Archchancellor?

Trymon enters, cautiously, picking up
the Archchancellor's fallen hat.

                    TRYMON
          Archchancellor?

Trymon smiles, and is about to sit in
the Archchancellor's chair when . . .

. . . Galder suddenly appears from
behind something.

Trymon is shocked to see him.

                    GALDER WEATHERWAX
          Such a great shame.

Galder seizes his hat.

                    TRYMON
          About . . . Spold you mean? Yes.

Galder doesn't look up.

                    GALDER WEATHERWAX
          Is that all, Trymon?

                    TRYMON
          Yes, Archchancellor.

                    GALDER WEATHERWAX
          Very good.

As Trymon turns to leave . . .

                    GALDER WEATHERWAX
          Oh, Trymon . . . as you leave could
          you tidy the sprung heavy axe
          device some prankster student has
          rigged above my door? It seems to
          have . . . malfunctioned.

INT. WYRMBERG DRAGON CAVERN - DAY

Rincewind looks decidedly uncomfortable as the CAMERA pulls out and rotates to reveal that he is hanging upside down, robe tucked into his britches, Kring dangling from on hand.

              TRYMON
    I shall have it seen to,
    Archchancellor.

Trymon grits his teeth in a forced smile and growls to himself.

            GALDER WEATHERWAX
    Oh, and I, I do hope Spold's shoes
    are not too small for you.

              TRYMON
    Mmm hmm!

Trymon pulls the door away from the wall. A very large heavy axe is embedded in the wood at head level.

>   LIESSA DRAGONLADY
> We fight 'til the death!
>
>   RINCEWIND
> Ah.
>
>   LIESSA DRAGONLADY
> Yours.

Rincewind takes a deep breath.

>   RINCEWIND
> Ah!
>
>   RINCEWIND
> I suppose I ought to warn you that I have a magic sword.
>
>   KRING
> That's me!
>
>   LIESSA DRAGONLADY
> What a coincidence.

Liessa flourishes a jet-black blade. Runes glow on its surface.

>   LIESSA DRAGONLADY'S MAGIC SWORD
> Hello!
>
>   KRING
> Hello!
>
>   RINCEWIND
> Oh no!

Liessa lunges.

Rincewind goes rigid with fright but his arm swings out as Kring shoots forward.

Liessa swings herself backwards, her eyes narrowing.

The magical swords shout challenges at each other.

>   KRING
> Prepare to be defeated.
>
>   LIESSA DRAGONLADY'S MAGIC SWORD
> I don't think so.
>
>   KRING
> I've seen sharper butter knives!
>
>   LIESSA DRAGONLADY'S MAGIC SWORD
> Ha!
>
>   KRING
>   (to Rincewind)
> Going well, isn't it?
>
>   KRING
> Call yourself a magic sword, pah!
>
>   LIESSA DRAGONLADY'S MAGIC SWORD
> I don't actually.

With a growl Liessa launches herself at the wizard, boots clattering as she slides from ring to ring.

The swords meet again and, at the same time, Liessa brings her other hand down against Rincewind's head, jarring him so hard that . . .

. . . one of Rincewind's feet jerks out of its ring and flails desperately.

> RINCEWIND
> Ah! Argh!

Rincewind's one remaining ring, already overburdened, slides out of the rock with a nasty little metal sound.

He plunges down, swinging wildly, and ends up dangling with his hands gripping Liessa's arm so tightly that she screams.

> KRING
> Hang on, Rincewind! Hang on!

> LIESSA DRAGONLADY
> Let go, damn you! You're about to die!

> RINCEWIND
> That's easy for you to say! Ah!

Rincewind looks at his slipping hand

> RINCEWIND/VOICE OF THE SPELL
> Why don't you say me? What have you got to lose?

Rincewind is surprised and then realises something.

> RINCEWIND
> Is that you?!

And then . . .

> RINCEWIND
> Does that mean that I'm going to die?

> LIESSA DRAGONLADY
> Let go!

INT. WYRMBERG/CELL - DAY

Twoflower turns and looks up into the scaly face above him

> **TWOFLOWER**
> You're a fine looking dragon by the way, even if you did just turn up.

> **NINEREEDS**
> You summoned me, Master. You have the power.

> **TWOFLOWER**
> You mean I just thought of you and there you were?

> **NINEREEDS**
> Yes.

> **TWOFLOWER**
> But I've thought of dragons all my life!

> **NINEREEDS**
> The power only works near the Wyrmberg. As the dragons fly further away we begin to dwindle and fade.

Twoflower gapes.

> **NINEREEDS**
> All dragon lords have the power, as of course does the dragonlady Liessa, who, incidentally, is trying to hack your friend to pieces as we speak.

> **TWOFLOWER**
> What?!

INT. WYRMBERG/ROOSTING HALL - DAY

Liessa calls to the crossbowmen.

> **LIESSA DRAGONLADY**
> Shoot him!

Out of the corner of his eye Rincewind sees several crossbows levelled at his face.

Rincewind grimaces and lets go.

Then the wizard begins to tumble in the air as he drops to the distant, guano-speckled rocks. On his face . . .

> **RINCEWIND**
> Argh!

There is no reply. He hesitates for a moment, looks down and looks up in terror the look of someone with nothing to lose crosses his face and in the gathering slipstream he waves his hand.

RINCEWIND/VOICE OF THE SPELL
Ashoni!

His breath is knocked out of him
as . . . a dragon swoops beneath him and
catches him. He lands behind Twoflower.

RINCEWIND
Oh no, not you!

The dragon, curving gracefully at the
top of his flight, gives a lazy flip of
his wings and soars through a cave mouth
into the morning air.

Twoflower laughs triumphantly.

TWOFLOWER
Woo-hoo!

EXT. SKY ABOVE WOODLAND – EVENING

Rincewind clings desperately to
Twoflower's waist as the dragon circles
slowly. As they climb, the sun rises
over the edge of the Disc.

TWOFLOWER
Woo! How was that?! Are you all
right? What's the matter?

Rincewind tries shutting his eyes.

RINCEWIND
Aren't you scared of heights?

Twoflower looks down at the tiny
landscape mottled with cloud shadows.

TWOFLOWER
No, why should I be? You're just as
dead if you fall from forty feet as
from four thousand fathoms, that's
what I say. Oh!

RINCEWIND
It's not the actual falling, it's more
the hitting that worries me!

SC.1/76 SKY ABOVE WOODLAND

1. TIGHT FRONT 2-SHOT TWOFLOWER + RINCEWIND SITTING ON FLYING DRAGON

2. WIDE ANGLE ON DRAGON FLYING OVER TREETOPS RISING SUN IN DISTANCE

3. BACK TO 2-SHOT "DIALOGUE" + RINCE LOOKS DOWN AND GETS WOBBLY/SHUTS EYES

TWOFLOWER
Do you think dragons can fly all the
way to the stars, because now that
would be something?

Rincewind looks at the tourist.

RINCEWIND
I think you might be mad! Ah! Uh!
Uh!

Rincewind looks down, queasy. Twoflower
grabs him quickly and KRING falls from
Rincewind's hand . . .

				TWOFLOWER
Ha, ha, ha! That's where we camped. Oops!

				KRING
But I didn't tell you about the time I got stuck at the bottom of a lake for a hundred years!

				RINCEWIND
Oh, the sword. Oh.

				TWOFLOWER
You all right?

				RINCEWIND
Oh yeah. Uh. Oh-huh.

				TWOFLOWER
Come on now! Yah! Yah!

EXT. FOREST GLADE – EVENING

. . . and lands with a 'zing', quivering as it embeds in a STONE.

There is a silence and then a sigh.

				KRING
Hello!

There is no reply in the middle of the trees.

				KRING
Magic Sword here!

There is just the sound of the forest.

				KRING
If anyone can hear me out there what I could do with right now is someone who doesn't realise they're an orphan born in mysterious circumstances. Yow!

EXT. SKY ABOVE THE WYRMBERG – EVENING

Twoflower tries to pop his ears and looks down again.

There is a swarm of dragons rising from the Wyrmberg.

				RINCEWIND
Are you all right?

Twoflower wheezes with the chill thin air.

RINCEWIND
What's happening to the air?

Twoflower passes out.

RINCEWIND
We're flying too high!

The dragon vanishes . . .

RINCEWIND
Oh. Ah!

. . . for a few seconds they continue upwards. Twoflower and the wizard sitting one in front of the other astride something that isn't there . . .

. . . they drop

RINCEWIND
Dragons! Dragons. Think of dragons, yes. Uh! Think of dragons! Uh! Drag . . . Oh. Dragons. Dragons. Dragons. Drag . . . Oh!

He opens them . . . nothing.

DEATH rises into shot, to fall alongside Twoflower and Rincewind.

DEATH
IT WON'T WORK. YOU DON'T REALLY BELIEVE IN THEM.

              RINCEWIND
  Drag...

Rincewind opens his eyes and looks at DEATH, grinning at him.

The wizard looks down again in desperation and terror.

The cold waters of the Circle Sea roar up towards him . . .

              RINCEWIND
  Ah!

And they drop out of shot towards the Circle Sea.

EXT. AMPHITHEATRE/POTENT VOYAGER LAUNCH TOWER - DAY

CAMERA pans over the Krullian city and up to the Launch Tower. The Potent Voyager is in position.

              NARRATOR (V.O.)
  Meanwhile, at the very edge of the world, the Krullians have not given up on their quest to determine the sex of the turtle.

The ARCH-ASTRONOMER OF KRULL's throne is set down opposite the Potent Voyager. He gets out.

              ARCH-ASTRONOMER
  Are the chelonauts ready, Launch-Controller?

The MASTER LAUNCHCONTROLLER bustles forward.

              MASTER LAUNCHCONTROLLER
  Indeed, Arch-Astronomer.

              ARCH-ASTRONOMER
  How long to the doorway?

              MASTER LAUNCHCONTROLLER
              (carefully)
  The launch window, your Prominence.

              MASTER LAUNCHCONTROLLER
  Twelve hours when Great A'Tuin's tail will be in an unmatched position to determine its ... sex.

              ARCH-ASTRONOMER
  Then all that remains is to find an appropriate couple of sacrifices.

The Master Launchcontroller bows.

              MASTER LAUNCHCONTROLLER
  The ocean shall provide.

The old man smiles.

              ARCH-ASTRONOMER (O.C.)
  It always does.

As he looks out across the edge of the world we see DEBRIS collecting along the circumfence.

KRULL PALACE AMPITHEATRE.

12·4·07· RICKY EYRES

TOP OF POTENT VOYAGER LAUNCH TOWER 30·7·2007·

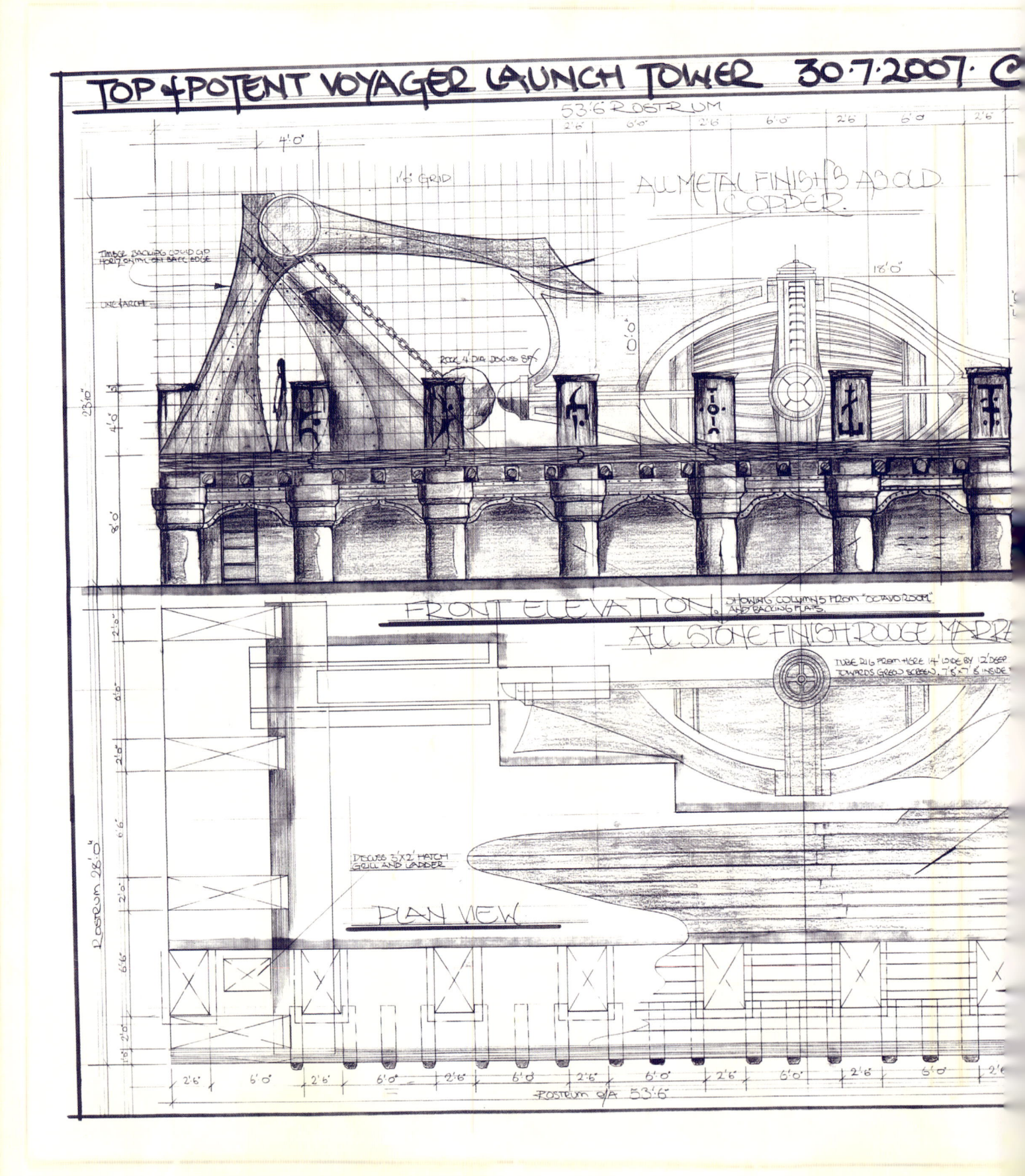

FRONT ELEVATION — showing columns from "OCTAVO/RSC" and backing flats.

PLAN VIEW

All metal finish as old copper.
All stone finish Rouge Marble.

Rostrum 53'6"
Rostrum O/A 53'6"
Rostrum 28'0"

RICKY EYRES.

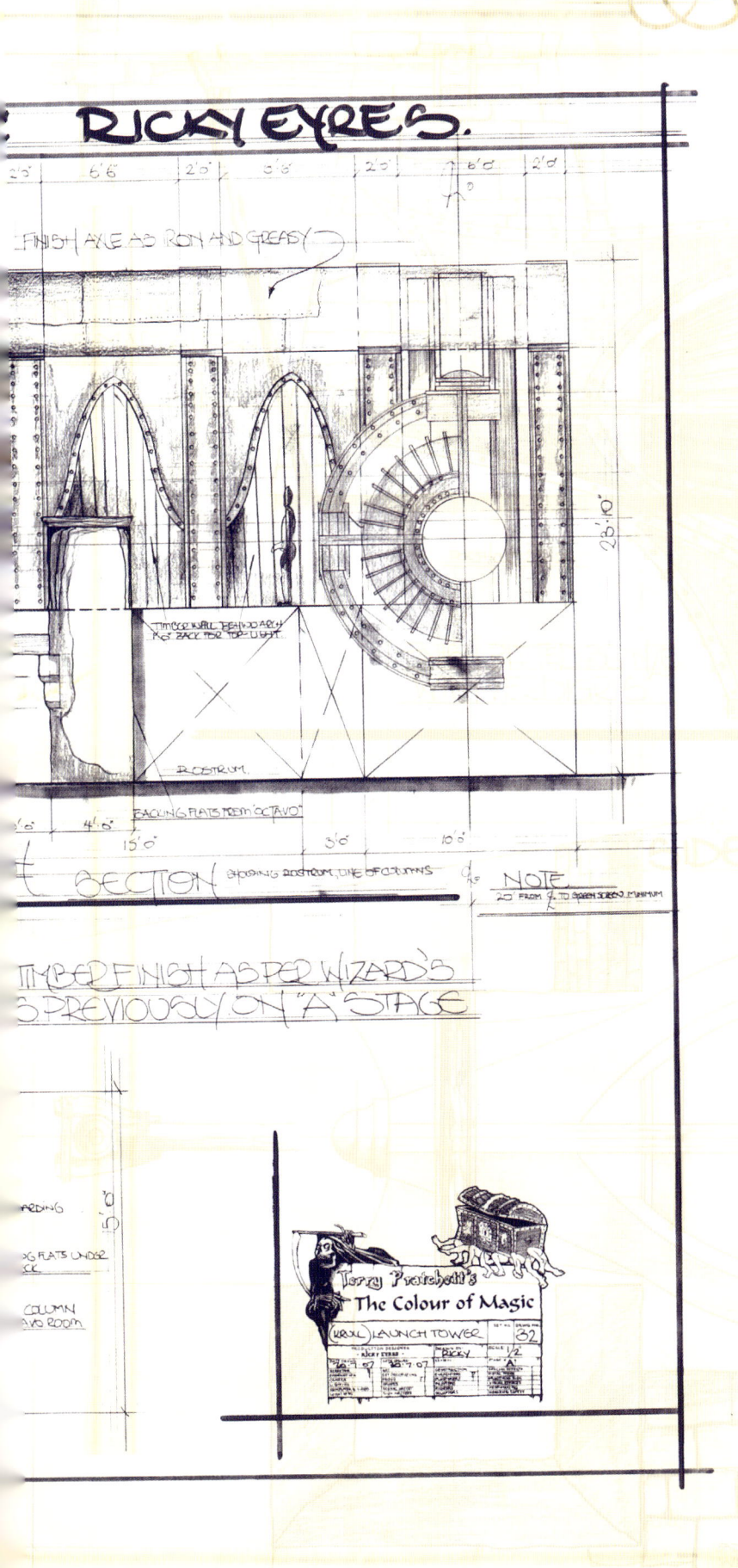

SECTION

Terry Pratchett's The Colour of Magic
KRULL LAUNCH TOWER

EXT. SEA AT THE RIM'S EDGE - DAY

A large floating log drifts into shot. Rincewind and Twoflower are clinging grimly onto it. Rincewind stares grumpily in the direction they are floating.

          RINCEWIND
      (monotone)
  Look at the horizon!

          TWOFLOWER
  It's all right!

Twoflower squints and looks for a while.

          TWOFLOWER
  Admittedly there seems to be a lot less than there usually is.

Rincewind looks accusingly at Twoflower and with ill-disguised panic in his voice.

          RINCEWIND
  We're being carried over the edge, you . . . ! Oh, no!

CAMERA shows the waterfall at the edge of the world . . . and then looks up to show Twoflower and Rincewind fast approaching it.

          RINCEWIND
  We're going to run out of world!

          TWOFLOWER
  We are?! Well I absolutely have to see that!

Twoflower starts to half crawl, half haul himself towards the front of the log.

          RINCEWIND
  Help!

There is a line of white on the foreshortened horizon and an audible but distant roaring.

TWOFLOWER
Rincewind! Rincewind!

RINCEWIND
Twoflower!

Then something hard and unyielding smacks into it. The trunk spins crazily and seems to hold its position so that surging water backs up behind it.

Twoflower almost falls off and a wash of cold sea foam cascades over them, not quite drowning out the SOUND OF A BELL ringing . . .

For a few seconds Rincewind is under several feet of boiling green water.

He surfaces.

DEATH is sitting on a deck chair on a rock on the edge, reading a book. He turns and looks at Rincewind.

DEATH
DON'T MIND ME, I'VE GOT A BOOK TO READ.

RINCEWIND
I don't want to leave this world!

Rincewind screams and then begins to drown.

NARRATOR (V.O.)
A prospect immensely troubling to the Octavo.

INT. UNSEEN UNIVERSITY/OCTAVO ROOM - DAY

The air thickens and swirls. The pages of the OCTAVO begin to crinkle in a horrible, deliberate way, and blue light spills out from between them. The padlocks begin to rattle.

INT. UNSEEN UNIVERSITY/OUTSIDE GALDER WEATHERWAX'S STUDY - DAY

As the Librarian walks along the corridor he sees Trymon coming out of the Archchancellor's study.

          HEAD LIBRARIAN
  Ah!

Trymon turns.

          TRYMON
  Oh! It's you.

The Librarian tries to get past him, but Trymon stands in front of the door.

          HEAD LIBRARIAN
  I just came to see Archchancellor Weatherwax.

          TRYMON
  Do you have an appointment?

          HEAD LIBRARIAN
  I've never needed an appointment before!

          TRYMON
  Well, the Archchancellor's never been organised before.

          HEAD LIBRARIAN
  It's just—

          TRYMON
  Look, the Archchancellor is going to have been very ill quite soon and mustn't be disturbed.

INT. UNSEEN UNIVERSITY/GALDER WEATHERWAX'S STUDY - DAY

The Archchancellor is asleep on his desk, with an anvil suspended precariously above him.

At the other end of a series of pulleys across the room a flame is burning through the rope holding it up.

INT. UNSEEN UNIVERSITY/OUTSIDE GALDER WEATHERWAX'S STUDY - DAY

> HEAD LIBRARIAN
> (sniffs)
> Can you smell burning?

Trymon sniffs the air.

INT. UNSEEN UNIVERSITY/GALDER WEATHERWAX'S STUDY - DAY

The Archchancellor sniffs in his sleep, wakes up, and sits up at his desk.

> GALDER WEATHERWAX
> Have I been smoking in my sleep?

He looks down in surprise at his bare, stockinged feet.

> GALDER WEATHERWAX
> Oh! I could have sworn I was wearing my shoes!

The flames start to burn through the last strands of rope.

INT. UNSEEN UNIVERSITY/OUTSIDE GALDER WEATHERWAX'S STUDY - DAY

Trymon puts and arm around the Librarian and tries to escort him away from the door.

> TRYMON
> Why don't you come with me instead? There's something I know you really want to show me.

INT. UNSEEN UNIVERSITY/GALDER WEATHERWAX'S STUDY - DAY

The Archchancellor looks around the room, and then up at the anvil, as the last strands of rope snap.

> GALDER WEATHERWAX
> Trymon! Oh dear.

The anvil plummets, and there is an ominous thud.

INT. UNSEEN UNIVERSITY/OUSIDE OCAVO ROOM DOOR - DAY

Through the grille Trymon watches the Octavo spit octarine violently. A key slides into the lock and the door opens.

INT. UNSEEN UNIVERSITY/OCTAVO ROOM - DAY

The door opens, pushing sand back behind it. As the Librarian backs away behind the door Trymon draws level with the lectern. He reaches out to touch the book but octarine fizzes from it like an electric shock.

> **HEAD LIBRARIAN**
> You'd better not monkey around with it or who knows what'll happen. The last person who went near it . . .

Trymon moves closer to the Head Librarian.

> **TRYMON**
> Yes?

> **HEAD LIBRARIAN**
> Well, it was a long time ago.

> **HEAD LIBRARIAN**
> All I'm saying is he never passed any exams after.

> **TRYMON**
> Ah!

The Librarian starts to usher him out.

> **TRYMON**
> As a matter of interest, after the last time, what exactly did they do to Rincewind?

Trymon leans in intimidatingly.

> **HEAD LIBRARIAN**
> (nervously)
> I never said anything about Rincewind!

> **TRYMON**
> Rincewind? Ah but . . . Did I say Rincewind? I meant whichever perpetual student wizard it was who monkeyed around with the Octavo.

The Head Librarian grimaces in a 'bugger, I gave it away' manner and shuffles nervously backwards.

Trymon turns to the Octavo.

> **TRYMON**
> (to Octavo)
> Rincewind!

Trymon moves menacingly towards the Librarian.

> **TRYMON**
> So, when the spell left the Octavo, where exactly did it go?

The Librarian swallows.

EXT. RIM'S EDGE/ROCK - DAY

A plume of sea water spumes out of Rincewind's choking mouth. The wizard swallows and the searing pain in his throat jerks him into full consciousness.

Twoflower is sitting on Rincewind's chest pumping it.

              RINCEWIND
Get off, will you!

              TWOFLOWER
Are you saying you want me to stop?

              RINCEWIND
Yes! Stop, will you!

Twoflower looks at him.

              TWOFLOWER
Stop saving your life?! It's actually twice now!

Rincewind picks himself up from the floor.

                    RINCEWIND
                    (quietly)
            Ooh. Oh, thank you.

His words are drowned under the roar of the Rimfall.

                    TWOFLOWER
            Say again?

                    RINCEWIND
                (reluctantly louder)
            I said thank you!

They are perched on a small ROCKY promontory and Twoflower is shaking Rincewind.

Twoflower blinks and engulfs him in a clumsy embrace.

                    RINCEWIND
            Ah! Stop that! Will you stop that! Look, a polite shake of the hand, having first checked for poisoned needles in the palm, in that old quaint Ankh-Morporkian tradition would be sufficient! Huh!

Rincewind eases himself from the embrace and grimaces. Twoflower is about to embrace him again when he pauses.

                    TWOFLOWER
            I'm on the edge of the world! Seeing things that most people can only dream of! On an adventure with visions and wonders unimaginable in one lifetime!

He looks at Rincewind.

                    TWOFLOWER
            It's all thanks to you, Rincewind.

                    RINCEWIND
            You forgot the near-Death experiences!

                    TWOFLOWER
            Well, I like to think of 'em as edge of life ones . . . with the best guide a little old inn-sewer-ants clerk from Bes Pelargic could ever hope for.

Twoflower checks his palm.

Rincewind hesitates, then checks his palm too. And they shake hands.

                    RINCEWIND
            Well, I would have been fine of course, even falling from the Wyrmberg, because, er . . . stop falling to certain death is only a level two spell.

Twoflower gets excited.

                    TWOFLOWER
            Actually I was sort of hoping that you could do some . . . you know.

                    RINCEWIND
            What, magic?

There is a flicker of panic on Twoflower's face.

                    RINCEWIND
                (carefully)
            Like what?

> TWOFLOWER
> In a fight you could turn people into worms.

> RINCEWIND
> Ah. No, no, no. Turning people into animals is an eighth level spell.

Twoflower takes off his hat and Rincewind pauses.

> TWOFLOWER
> Oh.

> RINCEWIND
> Look . . . the thing is I never really completed my training.

Rincewind can't look the tourist in the eye.

> RINCEWIND
> I only know one spell.

> RINCEWIND
> And even that I got by accident.

Twoflower, rather than being disappointed is excited.

> TWOFLOWER
> Well, what does it do?

> RINCEWIND
> Well, I dunno. I suppose it could do anything! But it's from the greatest spell book of all! The Octavo!

> TWOFLOWER
> The Octavo! Well . . . how did you learn it?

> RINCEWIND
> When I was a much younger student at the University I agreed to open the Octavo for a bet. A pint of beer, I think it was.

Rincewind takes a big breath and from his face we . . .

DISSOLVE TO:

INT. UNSEEN UNIVERSITY/OUTSIDE OCTAVO ROOM DOOR - NIGHT

. . . A YOUNGER-looking student Rincewind IN BLUE-TINGED MONOCHROME walking through the door of the room.

The door creaks as he passes through it.

> RINCEWIND (V.O.)
> It was as if it was waiting for me.

INT. UNSEEN UNIVERSITY/OCTAVO ROOM - NIGHT

The walls are covered in protective lead pentagrams.

The OCTAVO is placed on the OCTIRON PEDESTAL in the middle of the rune-strewn floor.

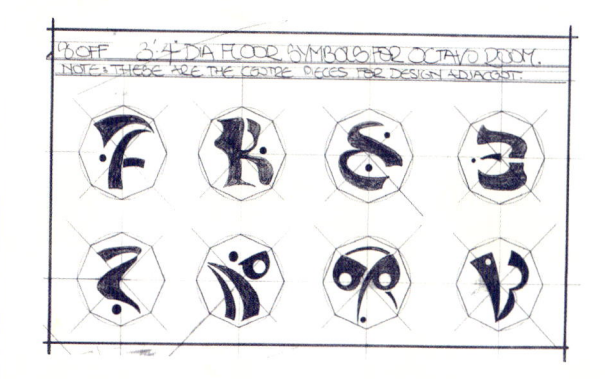

He gingerly opens the pages.

> RINCEWIND (V.O.)
> I only had a second before the spell leapt from the book and settled in my memory like a toad on a stone.

The One spell leaps from the crackling page in the form of RUNES OF LIGHTNING and enters his head through his eyes, lodging itself in the dark recesses of his brain.

The Octovo slowly closes itself again, and we . . .

DISSOLVE TO:

EXT. RIM'S EDGE/ROCK - DAY

PRESENT DAY and COLOUR on Rincewind's downcast face.

> **TWOFLOWER**
> Well, then what happened?

> **RINCEWIND**
> Well, they dragged me out and thrashed me, of course. I never did get the pint of beer.

> **TWOFLOWER**
> What did the spell say exactly?

Rincewind shakes his head.

> **RINCEWIND**
> It had vanished from the page, so nobody will know what it said until I say it. Or until I die of course, and then it'll sort of say itself.

> **TWOFLOWER**
> And nobody knows what it does?

INT. UNSEEN UNIVERSITY/OUTSIDE OCTAVO ROOM DOOR - DAY

> **TRYMON**
> ...what it does?

The Head Librarian closes the door behind Trymon.

> **HEAD LIBRARIAN**
> To know that you would need to be Archchancellor.

Trymon smiles as the key turns loudly in the lock, leaving the Octavo alone in the room once more.

> **TRYMON**
> Now you tell me!

EXT. RIM'S EDGE - DAY

Twoflower is peering over the edge.

> **RINCEWIND**
> Why didn't we go over the edge?

> **TWOFLOWER**
> Because our log hit that rope.

Rincewind points down.

Hubwards of the rock is a ROPE suspended a few feet above the surface of the water. It is stopping the log from going over the edge. As it surges against the rope a series of BELLS attached to it into the distance ring.

Twoflower pulls out his rather soggy book.

> **TWOFLOWER**
> I think it's called the circumfence. It runs around the edge of the world.

> **RINCEWIND**
> No, no, you mean the circumference. The circumference goes 'round the edge of things'. Mmm.

> **TWOFLOWER**
> So does the circumfence.

Rincewind turns back to Twoflower.

But he is looking down.

The CAMERA pulls slowly back to reveal that just below the lip of the endless Rimfall where Rincewind and Twoflower are standing on the rock, the RIMBOW is forming and rising.

> **TWOFLOWER**
> (beatifically)
> I suppose that's the rimbow. It's just so beautiful!

                    RINCEWIND
            Great. It's a nice view before we
            die.

It hangs in the mists a few lengths
beyond the edge of the world. Close into
the lip of the Rimfall are the seven
lesser colours, sparkling and dancing
in the spray. Floating beyond them is a
wider band of colour . . . OCTARINE.

                    RINCEWIND
            Do you see the eighth colour?

He points.

                    RINCEWIND
            That's the colour of magic.

Rincewind's eyes turn slowly downwards, drawn by some irresistible fascination.

A glittering curtain of water hurtles towards infinity on its way to the long fall.

Rincewind steadies himself to stop himself falling and leans back.

Twoflower casually peers over the edge.

Rincewind leans even further back

                    TWOFLOWER
            I bet you there are a lot of other
            worlds down there.

                    RINCEWIND
          Yes, quite a number. Look, there's
          one.

Twoflower looks up and sees a RED STAR.

                    TWOFLOWER
          Oh. Hey, that star's new! Perhaps
          we should name it.

                    RINCEWIND
          What's the point?! Who will we
          tell?! We're never gonna get off
          this rock.

Twoflower is lost in the view.

                    TWOFLOWER
          Unless we get in the boat!

                    RINCEWIND
          Well, unless we get in the . . . What
          boat?

                    TWOFLOWER
          That boat!

A bell rings on the circumfence in an odd jerky rhythm. Rincewind looks towards the sound and sees a boat with a railway engineer-style self-propelling mechanism.

Twoflower looks out across the extraordinary view and takes a big breath of fresh air.

                    TWOFLOWER
          'Course, I could stay here forever.
          I mean . . .

                    RINCEWIND
          On balance I know I should be very
          suspicious of that boat, but I do like
          the idea of getting back to dry land.

                    TWOFLOWER
          Mmm . . . er. Are you sure?

A big bloom of spray crashes onto the rock into Rincewind's face.

                    RINCEWIND
          I'm sure!

                    TWOFLOWER
                      (sighs)
          Well.

Twoflower steps off the rock and into the boat.

EXT. PLAINS - DAY

The Luggage can be seen running rimwards, presumably in pursuit of its master.

EXT. CIRCUMFENCE - DAY

Twoflower and Rincewind have taken a handle each and bob alternately up and down as the boat cranks along the fence, approaching Krull along the very lip of the Rimfall.

It is a large island, quite mountainous and heavily wooded, with pleasant white buildings visible here and there among the trees. The land slopes gradually up towards the rim, so that the highest point lightly overhangs the Edge. Perched on top is the city of Krull.

Entire ships have been morticed together and converted into buildings. The city rises tier on tier between the blue-green colours of the Disc and the soft cloud sea of the Edge, the eight colours of the Rimbow reflecting in every window.

                RINCEWIND
  Civilisation.

INT. UNSEEN UNIVERSITY/GALDER'S ROOM – DAY

Trymon is at the door, his face expressionless.

Galder Weatherwax is stripped to the waist and wearing a large apron. He brings a hammer down with surgical precision on a SILVER ARROW. The magic squeals and writhes in the tongs.

Galder doesn't even turn. At the faint indrawing of breath behind him a flicker of satisfaction crosses his face.

                TRYMON
  Lovely to see you're still here, Archchancellor.

Galder hangs up his apron, reaches down and picks up an ancient book.

GALDER WEATHERWAX
Do you know what happens when a
wizard dies?

TRYMON
All the spells that he has
memorised say themselves. It's one
of the first things we learn.

GALDER WEATHERWAX
Mmm. It's not quite true with the
eight great spells. A great spell will
simply find refuge in the nearest
mind ready and open to receive it.

Trymon's face twitches.

TRYMON
Mmm!

Galder picks up a LONGBOW from the rack
and shuffles across to the forge to
collect the arrow.

GALDER WEATHERWAX
Amorarate. Non multus, tamen
amorarate!
(subtitled)
*You'll like it, not a lot, but
you'll like it*

Galder stands in front of a mirror.
He makes a few passes in front of the
glass, which clouds over and then clears
to show an aerial view of the rock at
the RIM'S EDGE and RINCEWIND in the
BOAT.

GALDER WEATHERWAX
There you are . . .

Trymon's eyes light up.

TRYMON
You are going to recapture the
spell from its host!

Galder just looks at the mirror intently while holding the bow with the arrow pointing vaguely at Rincewind.

> GALDER WEATHERWAX
> And now for wind speed, say three knots . . .

Galder alters the angle of the bow slightly

> GALDER WEATHERWAX
> . . . adjust for temperature . . .

And then, with a rather disappointing movement, releases the arrow.

With a *spang!* the arrow vanishes.

Galder throws the bow aside and grins.

> GALDER WEATHERWAX
> There. Of course it'll take a while to get there and kill Rincewind. Then the spell will immediately return along the ionised path back here to me.

> TRYMON
> Remarkable . . . if, dare I say, a little old-fashioned.

Trymon looks down at the cluttered workbench, where a long and very sharp KNIFE catches his eye. He picks it up.

> GALDER WEATHERWAX
> It's what happens when all eight spells are spoken together that might interest a wizard now, is it not?

Galder looks over to Trymon and then down at his feet. He is wearing GALDER'S OWN SHOES now.

> GALDER WEATHERWAX
> Especially when they aspire to wear the biggest shoes of all?

> TRYMON
> Oh, becoming your second has always been the limit of my ambition.

> GALDER WEATHERWAX
> Yes, of course it has.

> TRYMON
> I wish only to acquire knowledge, master.

He taps the knife against his back.

> GALDER WEATHERWAX
> Which, as we know, is power.

> TRYMON
> Ah. And so, for the furtherance of my knowledge, master, when the eight spells are said together—

Galder laughs.

> GALDER WEATHERWAX
> Oh to receive that ultimate nugget you'll have to do much better than that, young man.

Galder gets up from his seat.

                    TRYMON
          Oh, I congratulate you, master.
          I can see that we must all get up
          very early in the morning if we are
          to get the better of you!

                    GALDER WEATHERWAX
                    (pleasantly)
          Early in the morning. My dear lad,
          you will have to stay up all night.

Galder leans across the table, and Trymon is in the very act of stabbing him when . . .

. . . there is a knock at the door.

                    GALDER WEATHERWAX
          Come.

The Head Librarian enters.

                    HEAD LIBRARIAN
          Galder, it's the Octavo! It's
          going . . . really ape!

INT. UNSEEN UNIVERSITY/OCTAVO ROOM - DAY

Through the little grille in the door half a dozen WIZARDS are taking turns to peer in.

                    GALDER WEATHERWAX (O.C.)
          Right, what's going on here?

Octarine and purple sparks glitter on the spine of the book. A thin curl of smoke is beginning to rise from the lectern, and the heavy metal clasps that hold the book shut are beginning to look strained.

                    JIGLAD WERT
          Why are the spells so restless?

Galder looks closer.

                    GALDER WEATHERWAX
          The key.

                    HEAD LIBRARIAN
          Oh.

A look of worried resolve appears on Galder's face.

                    GALDER WEATHERWAX
          Oh-ho!

EXT. KRULL - DAY

Galder's SILVER ARROW flies like a missile over the landscape.

EXT. KRULL/GANTRIES - DAY

The parapet along the edgewise cliff is dotted with gantries. The boat glides towards one and docks with it. Water splashes up onto the dock.

Rincewind and Twoflower climb onto the dock.

                    TWOFLOWER
          Ah, so we're back in civilisation!

There is a jingle and clank of armour and suddenly they are surrounded by spears.

                    RINCEWIND
          Yes, it looks like civilisation to me!

They are surrounded by grim-faced guards.

A hooded woman with moonlight hair and a nightblack face appears behind the guards.

                    MARCHESA
          Welcome to Krull. My name is
          Marchesa.

Twoflower sees two slave-style tunics hanging on hooks. Draped over the hooks are manacles.

Twoflower turns to Rincewind and swallows.

> TWOFLOWER
> I hope you're not proposing to enslave us?

Marchesa holds up her hands reassuringly.

> MARCHESA
> Certainly not!

> RINCEWIND
> Oh, good!

> MARCHESA
> You will in fact be sacrificed.

> RINCEWIND
> Thank you for another fine mess, Twoflower!

> RINCEWIND
> Yah!

Rincewind kicks the nearest guard in the groin and drags the startled tourist down the gantries and through a door into the palace of Krull.

EXT. CLIFFS - DAY

Still in pursuit of Twoflower, the Luggage runs along the cliff edge and then jumps off, into the sea, and begins to swim . . .

INT. KRULLIAN PALACE/PASSAGE - DAY

Rincewind and Twoflower hurry down the corridor.

Rincewind stops at a door he can see no way of opening. Trapped, he looks wildly back in the direction they came from.

> RINCEWIND
> Oh, here we are completely trapped in a palace on an island we have no hope of leaving! And what's more we . . . Eh? Oh!

Twoflower pulls a chain and the door opens.

> RINCEWIND
> Ah! Ah-ah!

Twoflower is staring around the room because . . .

. . . it contains the whole Universe.

Twoflower looks at it in wonder.

Rincewind grunts and moans unhappily as the door closes behind them.

Twoflower turns to a complicated astrolabe, in the centre of which is the entire Great A'Tuin-Elephant-Disc system wrought in brass and picked out with tiny jewels. Around it stars and planets wheel on fine silver wires.

                    TWOFLOWER
          Look at all those worlds.

On the walls around him constellations
made of tiny phosphorescent seed pearls
have been picked out on vast tapestries
made of jet-black velvet. Various easels
hold huge sketches of Great A'Tuin.

Twoflower stares about him with a
faraway look in his eyes.

                    TWOFLOWER
          It's fantastic!

Rincewind looks deeply troubled.

Behind him are two SUITS that hang from
supports in the centre of the room.
Rincewind looks at Twoflower. He is
looking through a big brass TELESCOPE
lying on a table, as does the CAMERA,
and has also caught sight of the suits.

                    TWOFLOWER (O.C.)
          Huh! I wonder who's gonna be
          wearing those suits.

They are made of white leather, hung
about with straps and brass nozzles.
The leggings end in high, thick-soled
boots, and the arms are shoved into big
gauntlets. There are big copper helmets
designed to fit on heavy collars around
the neck of the suits. In the front
of each helmet there are little glass
windows and on top, a crest of white
feathers.

                    RINCEWIND
          Someone who isn't going to be
          sacrificed, that's who.

Rincewind takes one of the helmets from
the rack.

There is a sound from the corridor
outside. Rincewind and Twoflower flatten
themselves against the wall to either
side of the door

                    RINCEWIND
          Oh! Ah!

Two husky young CHELONAUTS step into the
room. All they are wearing is a pair
of woollen pants apiece. One of them is
still towelling himself briskly.

Rincewind raises the helmet and . . .
brings it down on the man's head as hard
as he possibly can. The chelonaut falls
forward with a soft grunt.

                    RINCEWIND
          Er-ah!

The other man takes one startled step
before Twoflower hits him with the
telescope. He crumples on top of his
colleague.

                    TWOFLOWER
          Ah!

                    CHELONAUT
          Uh!

                    TWOFLOWER
          Ha!

                    RINCEWIND
          Ha!

Rincewind and Twoflower look at each
other over the carnage.

EXT. AMPITHEATRE/KRULL/ ARCH-ASTRONOMER'S TOWER - EVENING

The large semicircular amphitheatre overlooks the cloud sea that boils up from the Rimfall, far below. Crowds of restive people fill the arena.

The POTENT VOYAGER rests in is cradle on top of a wooden tower in the centre of the arena. In front of it a railway runs down towards the Edge, where for the space of a few yards it turns suddenly upwards.

There is a fanfare of trumpets at the edge of the arena.

The Arch-Astronomer stands in his box of honour and raises his hand to silence the crowd.

> **ARCH-ASTRONOMER**
> In the annals of the exploration of our cosmos, many have been the valiant efforts of our cosmo-chelonians and astrozoologists in their quest for knowledge of the Great A'Tuin.

The crowd cheers.

INT. KRULL/AMPHITHEATRE ENTRANCE TUNNEL - EVENING

Dressed in the suits, Twoflower and Rincewind are making their way out of the city, towards a door opening on to the amphitheatre.

> **TWOFLOWER**
> And you said we had no way of escaping!

> **RINCEWIND**
> Just keep walking. They'll never know it's us. But I wasn't expecting an audience.

EXT. AMPHITHEATRE/KRULL - EVENING

The white-suited explorers step out into the light to a tumultuous roar. The crowd rises to its feet.

> **RINCEWIND**
> Ah! Ah!

Rincewind tries to make a dash for it, but is stopped by the closing door.

> **RINCEWIND**
> As soon as we get a chance we make a run for it, okay?

SIDE ELEVATION.

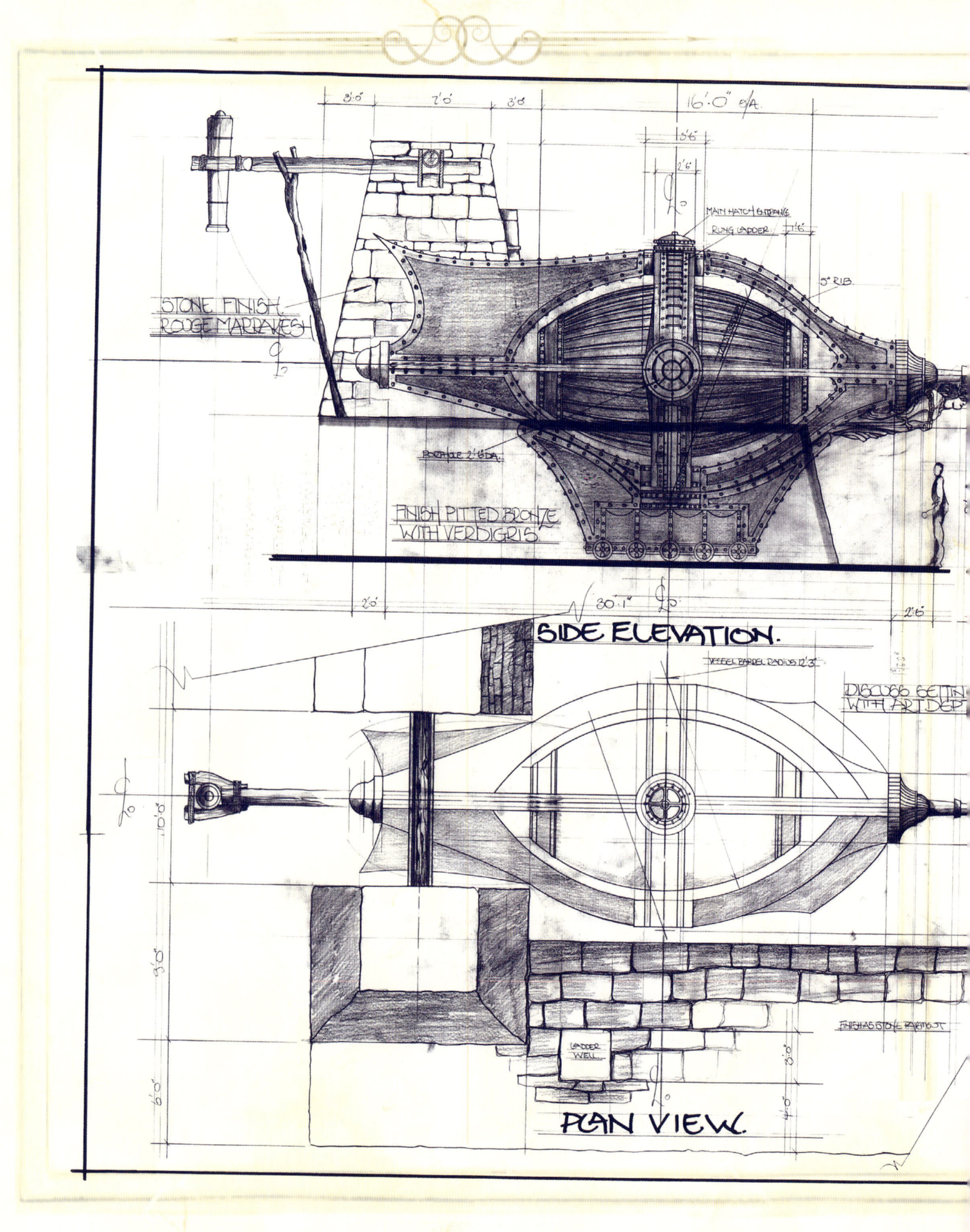

PLAN VIEW.

STONE FINISH
ROUGE MARRAKESH

FINISH PITTED BRONZE
WITH VERDIGRIS

MAIN HATCH ENTRANCE
RUNG LADDER

5" RIB

VESSEL BARREL RADIUS 12'3"

DISCUSS SETTING
WITH ART DEPT

FINISH AS STONE PAVEMENT

LADDER WELL

FRONT ELEVATION.

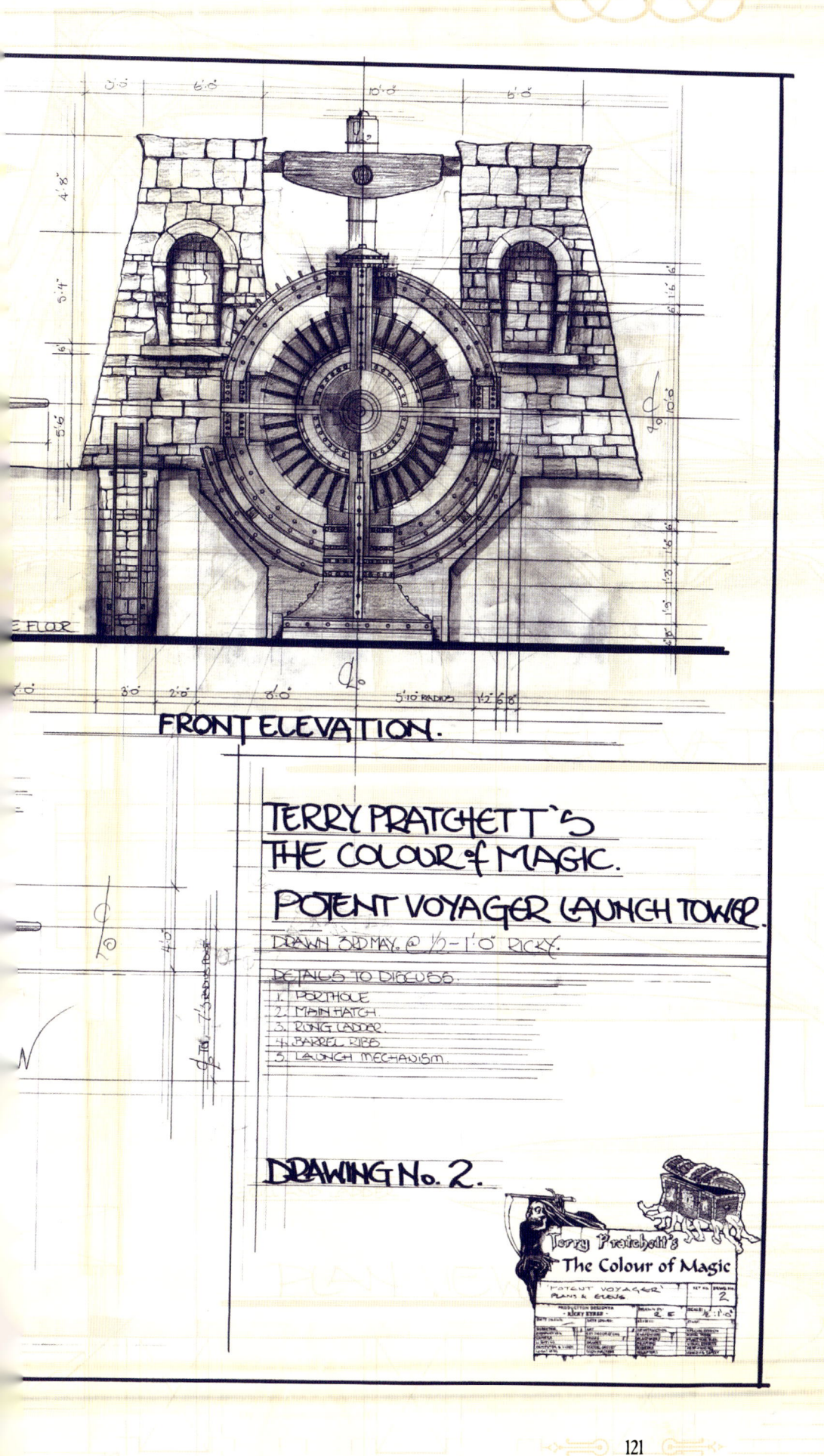

TERRY PRATCHETT'S THE COLOUR of MAGIC.

POTENT VOYAGER LAUNCH TOWER.

DRAWN 3RD MAY. @ ½"–1'0" RICKY.

DETAILS TO DISCUSS.
1. PORTHOLE
2. MAIN HATCH
3. RUNG LADDER
4. BARREL RIBS
5. LAUNCH MECHANISM.

DRAWING No. 2.

EXT. AMPITHEATRE/KRULL/ARCH-ASTRONOMER'S TOWER – EVENING

The Arch-Astronomer raises his arms.

> ARCH-ASTRONOMER
> But never has the bravery of those who laid down their lives before in the pursuit of the answer to the ultimate question of the sex of the turtle been more valid by those who today venture forth . . . to certain deat—

> MASTER LAUNCHCONTROLLER
> Depths!

> ARCH-ASTRONOMER
> –ps. Depths! These two specially trained, highly skilled chelonauts will be honoured by the chronicles of Krull!

EXT. AMPHITHEATRE/KRULL – EVENING

The two chelonauts wave heroically.

> RINCEWIND
> Is there a toilet in this suit?

> TWOFLOWER
> I don't think so!

> RINCEWIND
> It's just that I think I need to boldly go.

EXT. AMPITHEATRE/KRULL/ARCH-ASTRONOMER'S TOWER – EVENING

> ARCH-ASTRONOMER
> I give you heroes, not just of Krull but of the galaxy!

Rincewind trips and stumbles.

EXT. AMPITHEATRE/KRULL/ARCH-ASTRONOMER'S TOWER – EVENING

The Arch-Astronomer leans forward to look a little closer. Concern flickers across his face.

One of the chelonauts is definitely waddling.

EXT. AMPHITHEATRE/POTENT VOYAGER LAUNCH TOWER – EVENING

The roar of the assembled people of Krull is deafening as the chelonauts cross the great area to the ladder . . .

> RINCEWIND
> On the count of three we make a run for it that way.

EXT. AMPHITHEATRE/POTENT VOYAGER LAUNCH TOWER – EVENING

. . . the expression on the Arch-Astronomer's face reveals that he has decided something.

> ARCH-ASTRONOMER
> I don't think it's them.

EXT. AMPHITHEATRE/POTENT VOYAGER LAUNCH TOWER – EVENING

Rincewind and Twoflower are standing at the base of the tower.

> TWOFLOWER
> Well you don't think anyone's realised, do you?

EXT. AMPITHEATRE/KRULL/ARCH-ASTRONOMER'S TOWER - EVENING

    MASTER LAUNCHCONTROLLER
  Guards! Guards!

Soldiers are beginning to appear at the edge of the arena.

EXT. AMPHITHEATRE/POTENT VOYAGER LAUNCH TOWER - EVENING

Rincewind looks over and groans.

    TWOFLOWER
  To the top of the ship. They won't dare shoot at that!

    RINCEWIND
  I'm not. Not for me, I'm off!

A spear arcs out of the sky and trembles to a halt in the woodwork by the wizard's ear. He screams briefly and scrambles up the ladder after Twoflower.

    RINCEWIND
  Ah! Perhaps you're right.

INT. UNSEEN UNIVERSITY/OCTAVO ROOM - DAY

The wizards are gathered around the snarling, octarine-spitting Octavo.

SC. 1/103 OCTAVO ROOM

PAN UP WITH THICK COLUMN OF SPITTING LIGHT AS IT SHOOTS UP INTO CEILING FROM THE BOOK. WIZARDS RECOIL

As they watch a thick column of spitting light springs up from the book and a glowing fireball forms within it, rises, hits the ceiling in a splash of flame, and disappears.

Galder stares up at the hole. He points dramatically.

          GALDER WEATHERWAX
  To the library!

          JIGLAD WERT
  Quick!

They bound up the stone stairs followed by the other wizards falling over one another in their eagerness to be last . . .

INT. UNSEEN UNIVERSITY/LIBRARY ABOVE OCTAVO ROOM - DAY

The wizards enter just in time to see a series of fireballs of occult potentiality disappear into the ceiling of the room above.

The small sad ORANG-UTANG sitting in the middle of it all looks very much like the HEAD LIBRARIAN.

          GALDER WEATHERWAX
  Head Librarian?

The Orang-Utan waves.

          HEAD LIBRARIAN
  Ook.

Galder stares upwards.

                GALDER WEATHERWAX
        To the Great Hall!

He wades through custard to the next flight of stairs.

EXT. AMPHITHEATRE/POTENT VOYAGER LAUNCH TOWER – EVENING

Twoflower is nearing the top of the ladder.

Several muscular men including the two CHELONAUTS dressed just in their woolly pants have reached the bottom of the tower. The chelonauts begin to climb.

Twoflower walks out onto the platform on which the POTENT VOYAGER stands.

                TWOFLOWER
        I wonder if they're gonna send the
        ship over the edge.

Behind him, Rincewind has emerged onto the platform, and has closed the hatch behind them.

Guards shout behind him.

                GUARD (O.C.)
        Move around, now!

                GUARD (O.C.)
        Follow me. This way.

                GUARD (O.C.)
        Follow me.

                GUARD (O.C.)
        Surrender!

                GUARD (O.C.)
        Stop, now!

                    RINCEWIND
          This time I'm definitely going to die!

Twoflower leads the way, as they come
out onto the narrow catwalk that leads
along the spine of the Potent Voyager.

On top the centre of the ship is a
round BRONZE HATCH with hasps around
it. Twoflower kneels and starts to open
them.

                    GUARD (O.C.)
          Right, surround them! Go! Go! Go!

                    RINCEWIND
          Now listen, we'll tell them that
          we'll damage the thing unless they
          let us go, right? And that's, that's
          all we're gonna do, right?

Twoflower finishes undoing a wing nut
and starts to climb down the ladder.

                    TWOFLOWER
          Yeah. That's it! They won't lift off
          now.

INT. POTENT VOYAGER - NIGHT

Twoflower's foot kicks a mechanism
inside the Potent Voyager. Fine sand
begins to trickle into a carefully
designed cup at the top of an elaborate
mechanism.

EXT. AMPHITHEATRE/POTENT VOYAGER LAUNCH TOWER - EVENING

Rincewind hears the noise of the clonk.

                    TWOFLOWER
          Oh!

                    RINCEWIND
          What was that?

                    TWOFLOWER
          What was what?

                    RINCEWIND
          I thought I heard something.

From inside the Potent Voyager, a
countdown begins.

                    COUNTDOWN
          Twelve . . .

Rincewind looks horrified as he
sees . . .

. . . Twoflower disappearing down the
ladder into the Potent Voyager.

                    RINCEWIND
          That's good; make it look like
          you're damaging it!

                    COUNTDOWN
          . . . eleven, ten . . .

INT. POTENT VOYAGER – NIGHT

The sand cup is filled to exactly the right level to tip the balance, but the arm pointing to the countdown is stuck.

Cogs struggle to move against each other.

EXT. AMPHITHEATRE/POTENT VOYAGER LAUNCH TOWER – EVENING

> TWOFLOWER (O.C.)
> I think it's stuck!

> COUNTDOWN
> ...nine...

> RINCEWIND
> What is?

> COUNTDOWN
> ...nine...

> RINCEWIND
> You're not messing about with anything there, are you?

> COUNTDOWN
> ...nine...

> TWOFLOWER
> No, of course not!

> COUNTDOWN
> ...nine...

Rincewind takes a few steps up the ladder.

> RINCEWIND
> Oh good!

> COUNTDOWN
> ...nine.

INT. UNSEEN UNIVERSITY/OCTAVO ROOM – DAY

The Octovo shakes and roars against its restraints.

INT. UNSEEN UNIVERSITY/GREAT HALL – DAY

Panting and custard-covered, the fitter wizards arrive to find the fireball is hanging motionless, except for the occasional small prominence that arches and splutters across its surface, in the middle of the hall. Something is taking shape inside the fireball.

Galder shields his eyes and peers at the shape forming.

There is no mistaking it . . . it is the UNIVERSE. The tiny universe inside the fireball is uncannily real. There is no colour. It is all in translucent misty white. There is GREAT A'TUIN, and the four ELEPHANTS, and the DISC itself.

                    GALDER WEATHERWAX
                 What is the Octavo doing?

Gently, but with the unstoppable force
of an explosion, the shape expands,
white mist heading through the walls.

                    GALDER WEATHERWAX
                      To the roof!

He points a shaking finger skywards
and runs through the continents flowing
smoothly through the solid stone,
followed by the wizards with enough
breath left to run.

EXT. ANKH-MORPORK - EVENING

The sky is tinted with the promise of
night. A crescent MOON is just rising.

Across the city a pale tide streams through
the streets, noticed only by . . .

EXT. UNSEEN UNIVERSITY/GATE PARAPET ROOF TOP - EVENING

. . . the wizards, who from their
vantage point, watch the white tide foam
across the distant fields

Galder strains to see out across the city in the mist-swirled, dust-filled air. He looks up.

Looming high over the University is the grim and ancient TOWER OF ART.

> GALDER WEATHERWAX
> To the Tower of Art!

Galder points upwards and hurries over to a door at the base of the tower.

INT. UNSEEN UNIVERSITY/TOWER OF ART – NIGHT

The door opens. Galder enters and looks up.

The famous SPIRAL STAIRCASE rises erratically upwards into a seeming infinite distance.

SC.1/114 INT. TOWER OF ART

1. GALDER BY DOOR – LOOKS UP.

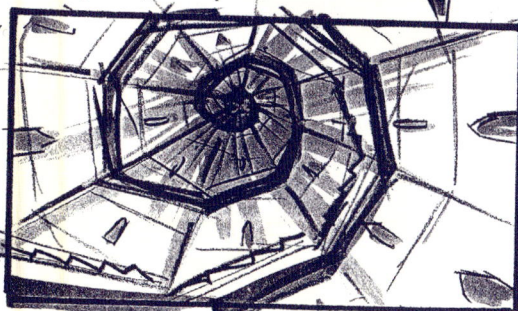

2. GALDER'S POV – VIEW UP SPIRAL STAIRCASE WITHIN TOWER OF ART... ...GOES ON FOREVER (NEED DESIGN) + CGI EXTENSION

> GALDER WEATHERWAX
> How many steps are there?

GANMACK arrives breathlessly behind the Archchancellor.

> GANMACK TREEHALLET
> Eight thousand, eight hundred . . .

GANMACK wheezes.

> TRYMON
> And eighty-eight!

The wizards begin to climb.

EXT. POTENT VOYAGER – NIGHT

The chelonauts have arrived at the top of the tower and are fumbling with the hatch.

> COUNTDOWN
> Nine, nine . . .

> RINCEWIND
> Ah!

> TWOFLOWER
> Ah!

> COUNTDOWN
> . . . nine . . .

Rincewind's brave face is wiped off as a vigorous banging starts from within the Potent Voyager. There is a clunk.

> RINCEWIND
> What was that?

> TWOFLOWER (O.C.)
> It doesn't seem to wanna go!

> RINCEWIND
> What?

Cogs begin to turn smoothly, as does the pointer controlling the countdown.

EXT. AMPHITHEATRE/POTENT VOYAGER LAUNCH TOWER - NIGHT

The hatch finally opens and the chelonauts burst through.

INT. POTENT VOYAGER - NIGHT

The pointer continues its countdown.

> COUNTDOWN
> ...two, one...lift off.

There is a *ping*, a pin flies out of the mechanism and a weight begins to move.

EXT. AMPHITHEATRE/POTENT VOYAGER LAUNCH TOWER - EVENING

The weight touches the back of the Potent Voyager and the ship lurches. Then, with infinite slowness, it begins to move along the rails.

One of the chelonauts seizes a corner of the Potent Voyager and tries, uselessly, to stop it.

EXT. AMPITHEATRE/KRULL/ARCH-ASTRONOMER'S TOWER - EVENING

The Arch-Astronomer looks on in horror.

> ARCH-ASTRONOMER
> No!

EXT. POTENT VOYAGER - NIGHT

> TWOFLOWER
> Stars! Worlds! The whole damn sky full of worlds! Places no one's ever gonna see except us!

> RINCEWIND
> Ah, ah! Oh!

> COUNTDOWN
> nine, eight, seven...

Twoflower's head emerges from the Potent Voyager.

> TWOFLOWER
> That's it! I've fixed it!

Rincewind jerks back.

> COUNTDOWN
> ...six...

> RINCEWIND
> Fixed what?

> COUNTDOWN
> ...five, four, three...

> RINCEWIND
> We gotta get off this thing!

Rincewind tries to keep his balance as the ship begins to speed up. He turns as one of the chelonauts tries to leap the gap between the Potent Voyager and the tower.

EXT. AMPITHEATRE/KRULL/ARCH-ASTRONOMER'S TOWER - NIGHT

The Arch-Astronomer looks increasingly horrified. He glances down on the arena as the soldiers start to run towards the tower, fleeing from Twoflower's Luggage.

EXT. POTENT VOYAGER - NIGHT

The Potent Voyager is travelling quite fast now as it tips over the top of the rails and begins the journey down, picking up speed.

          TWOFLOWER
Oh!

Twoflower loses his grip on the ladder and falls into the cabin.

          RINCEWIND
Oh!

          TWOFLOWER
Oh!

The hatch slams down and the catches snap into place.

          RINCEWIND
Oh no!

Rincewind dives forward and scrabbles at them, whimpering.

EXT. AMPITHEATRE/KRULL/ARCH-ASTRONOMER'S TOWER - NIGHT

The Arch-Astronomer and his entourage lean forward to see.

EXT. POTENT VOYAGER - NIGHT

The cloud sea is much nearer now. The Edge itself, a rocky perimeter to the arena, is startlingly close.

          RINCEWIND
  Oh no!

Rincewind is in a blind panic just as . . .

. . . the ship flies up, into the sky, and OVER THE EDGE.

It climbs upwards and then both it and Rincewind fall away down into space.

          RINCEWIND
  Oh, waaah!

Moments later . . .

Where Rincewind has just been Galder's SILVER ARROW shoots over the rim and slows as if 'looking' for him and then curves sharply BACK TOWARDS THE HUB . . .

The Luggage leaps over the edge of the Rim to follow its master.

EXT. DISCWORLD - NIGHT

The white mist now covers the whole of the Disc.

EXT. UNSEEN UNIVERSITY/ TOWER OF ART – NIGHT

Galder stares at the vertiginous view.

Among the star-filled sky one RED STAR stands out

              TRYMON
I've not seen that one before!

There is a crackling of dry twigs behind Galder. He turns to see TRYMON, then turns back and grips the parapet.

         GALDER WEATHERWAX
I don't know the significance of the star, but *that*, that mist, is important.

The whole of the visible Disc is now covered with a shimmering white skin that fits it perfectly.

              TRYMON
So, what's happening?

         GALDER WEATHERWAX
I fear . . . the only way to find out exactly is to perform the Rite of Ash-Kente.

Trymon makes a mental note.

Galder raises his arms and shuts his eyes.

Trymon watches him and tenses, his fingers curling around the knife in his hand.

              TRYMON
Thank you, Archchancellor.

And Galder opens one eye, nods at him and sends a sideways BLAST of power that picks the younger man up and sends him sprawling against the wall of the tower.

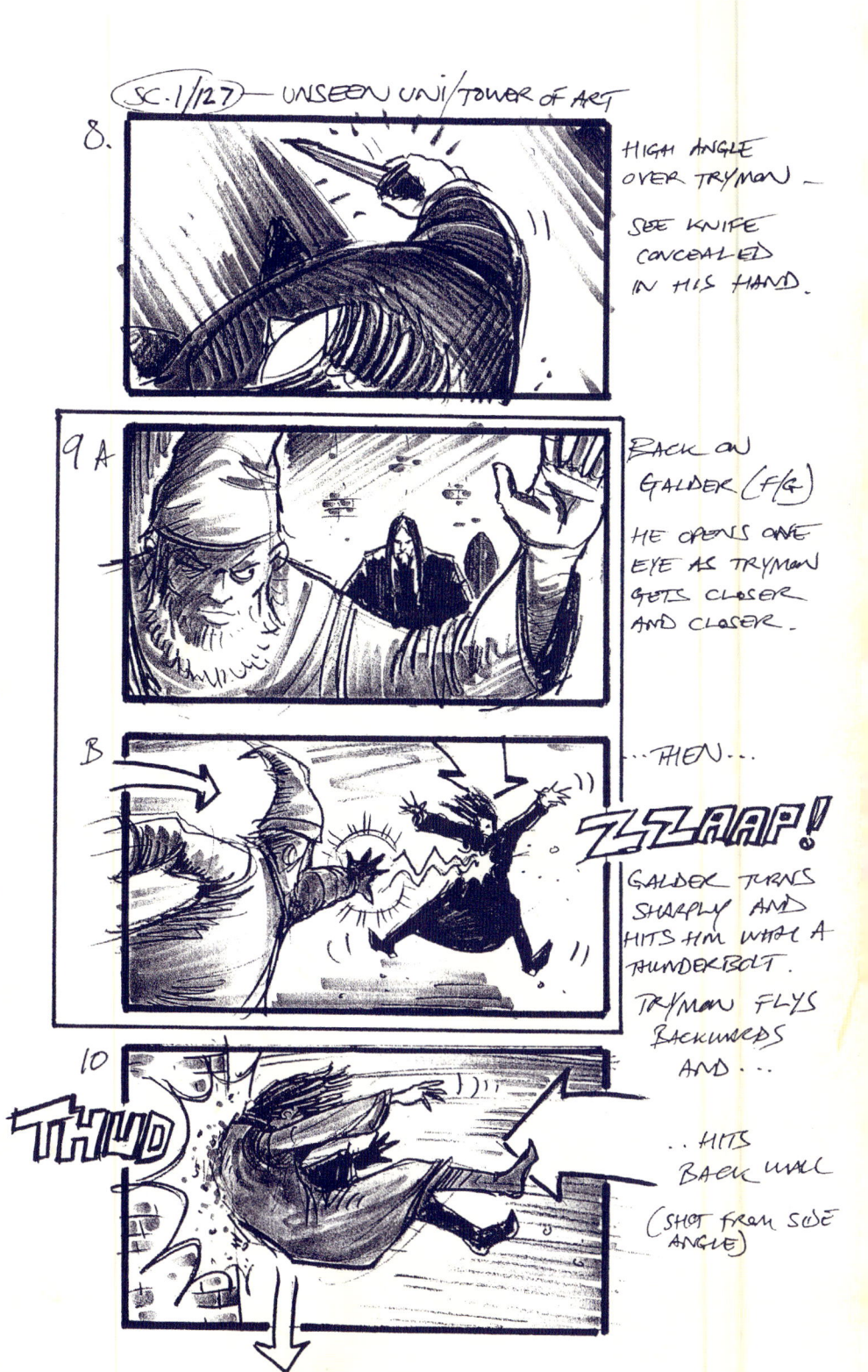

SC.1/127 – UNSEEN UNI/TOWER OF ART

11.A — BACK ON GALDER — FACING FRONT AGAIN (COLLAPSED GALDER OUT OF SHOT)

11.B — SAME SHOT. TRYMON RISES INTO FRAME IN THE BACKGROUND.

12.A — MEDIUM SINGLE ON GALDER OVER BY WALL. QUICKLY WITHDRAWS ARM AND...

12.B — SAME SHOT. ...THROWS KNIFE...

TRYMON
Argh!

Trymon picks himself up. His arm flashes from behind his back.

The knife leaves Trymon's hand at such speed that it appears to grow shorter and a little more massive as it plunges, with unerring aim, towards Galder's neck.

TRYMON
Ah-ah-ah.

But before it can get there it swerves to one side and begins an orbit of Galder's neck so fast that he appears suddenly to be wearing a metal collar. Galder turns around.

To Trymon he seems to have suddenly grown several feet taller and much more powerful.

The knife breaks away and stabs into the ground at Trymon's feet.

GALDER WEATHERWAX
Nice try. That mist is a change spell created by the Octavo.

Galder turns and looks out at the white skin over the city.

GALDER WEATHERWAX
The whole world is changing.

Galder raises his arms again. He is about to speak when there is a thunderclap, an implosion of light. Trymon hears a sharp intake of breath and then Galder's SILVER ARROW chooses this moment to return, puncturing Galder's hat and distracting his attention.

Trymon smiles and steps forward. It's a vicious smile.

TRYMON
For the better I think.

And he pushes the Archchancellor off the top of the tower.

GALDER WEATHERWAX
Oh! Argh!

TRYMON
Mmm.

EXT. OVER THE EDGE - SPACE

In the porthole of the Potent Voyager a beaming Twoflower stares beatifically into space.

> **TWOFLOWER**
> Ah!

A strange red light illuminates his face.

> **TWOFLOWER**
> Ah. Ah! That's so pretty! Ah. I really should name it.

EXT. UNSEEN UNIVERSITY/ TOWER OF ART - NIGHT

The ANGRY RED STAR looms in the sky.

Puffing and wheezing, the wizards arrive at the top of the stairs where Trymon looks up quickly from over the edge to the red dot.

> **JIGLAD WERT**
> Has anybody seen the Archchancellor?

Trymon turns to face them.

> **TRYMON**
> Yes.

He pointedly puts on Galder's POINTED HAT.

> **TRYMON**
> And how can I help you?

The wizards are stunned.

EXT. OVER THE EDGE - SPACE

Rincewind opens his eyes and shivers. He is lying belly-down in the rushing air, staring down into space . . .

> **RINCEWIND**
> He-el-lp! Uh-oh!

. . . he looks ahead.

> **RINCEWIND**
> Uh.

Right in his eye-line is the RED STAR.

> **RINCEWIND**
> I'll give it a name, Goodbye World!

EXT. GREAT A'TUIN - SPACE

The two tiny dots are falling off the edge of the Discworld. Light flares at the edge of the screen, followed by a massive, deep, roaring sound as the BIG RED STAR passes the camera ominously heading DIRECTLY TOWARDS the Discworld . . .

END OF EPISODE 1.

THE LUGGAGE.

TERRY PRATCHETT'S. THE COLOUR of MAGIC.

SIDE ELEVATION.

PLAN.

Episode 2

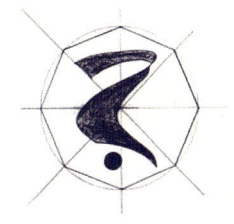

THE COLOUR OF MAGIC

EXT. DISCWORLD – DAWN

The Great A'Tuin comes into view, travelling through space.

The CAMERA tracks fast towards a SMALL OBJECT falling below the Disc.

> NARRATOR (V.O.)
> Currently Twoflower, the Discworld's first tourist, is rapidly leaving it in an attempt to escape Krull.

We are close enough to see that the small object is TWOFLOWER in the POTENT VOYAGER.

> NARRATOR (V.O.)
> This attempt has been one thousand per cent successful; although this means he may also be the Disc's last tourist, he is enjoying the view.

Twoflower looks out of the porthole in awe.

> NARRATOR (V.O.)
> Meanwhile, some way above Twoflower, Rincewind isn't enjoying the view at all.

The CAMERA pans up to see RINCEWIND plummeting through space.

> NARRATOR (V.O.)
> Only Great A'Tuin the world turtle knows why it's heading towards the star, but those on the Disc are due to find out in about two days, and then they're really going to worry.

Rincewind turns in space to see the giant red star in the distance.

INT. UNSEEN UNIVERSITY/OCTAVO ROOM – DAWN

The OCTAVO thrashes against its chains.

> NARRATOR (V.O.)
> The Octavo, the greatest spell book of all, is so worried about all this that it must take action of its own.

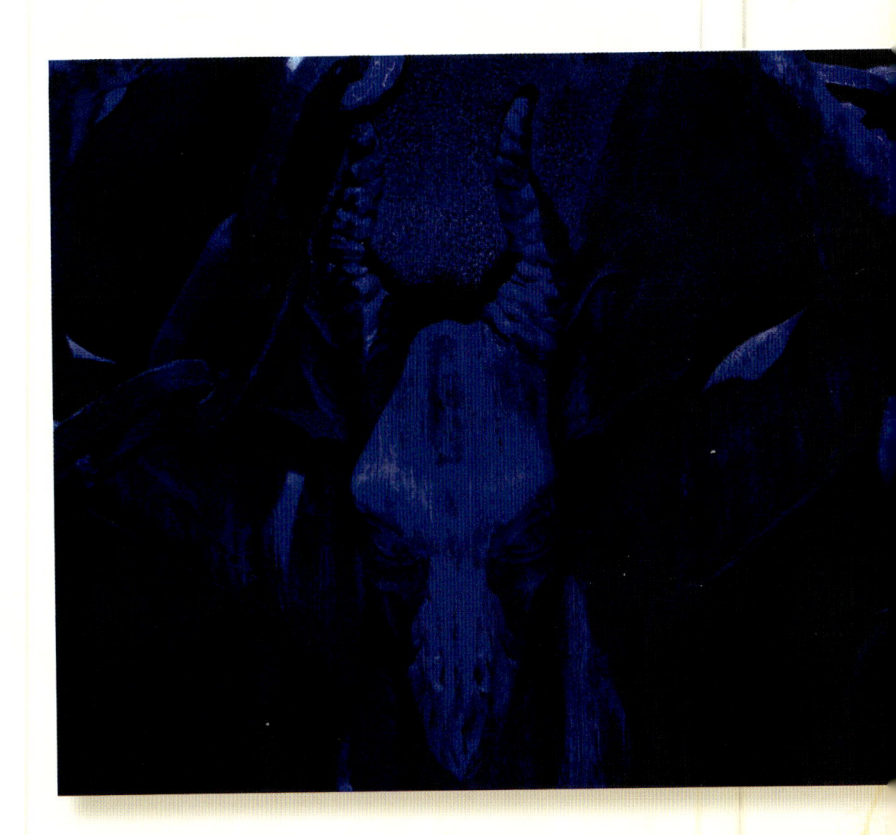

INT. UNSEEN UNIVERSITY/GREAT HALL – NIGHT

The white mist universe begins to TILT . . . Great A'Tuin is sinking through the floor level.

EXT. DISCWORLD – DAWN

The actual Great A'Tuin also tilts and is dropping at an alarmingly great speed through space. As is Rincewind.

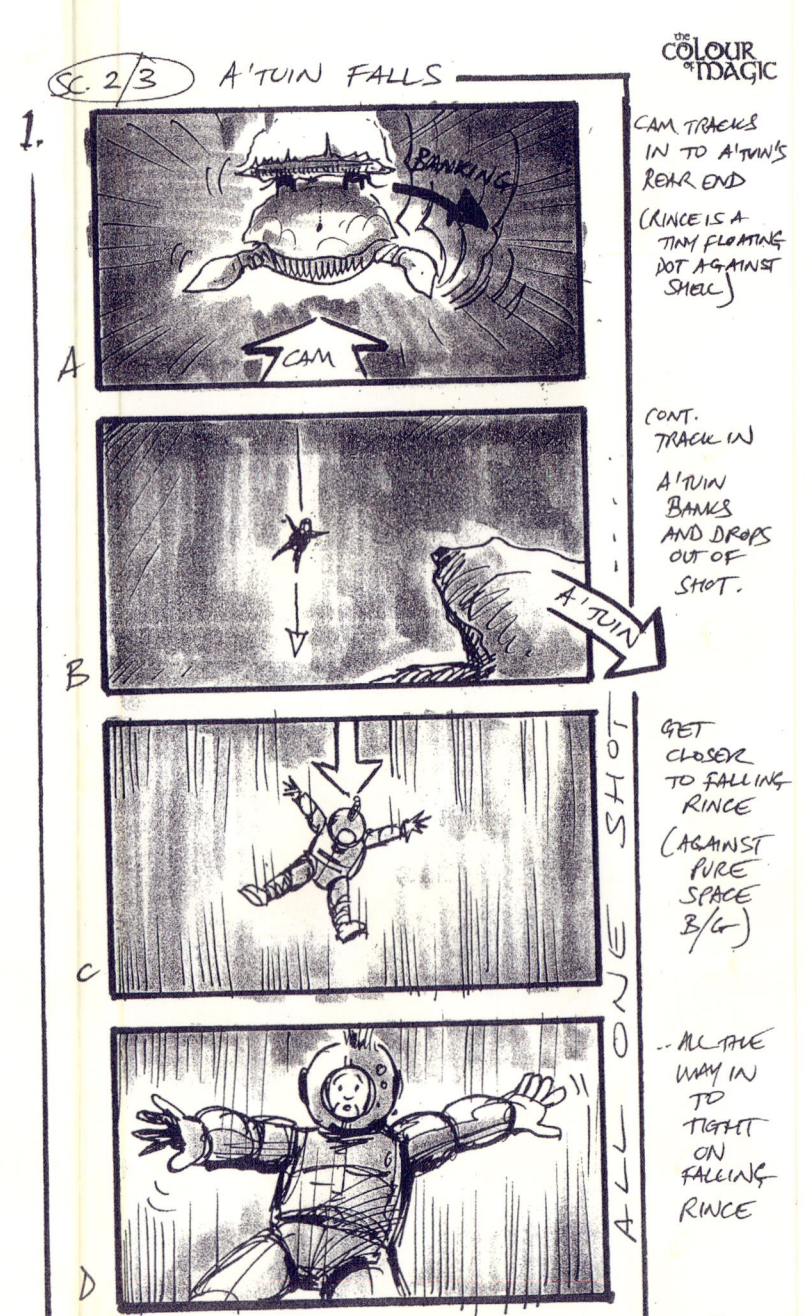

The CAMERA tips down to see him plunge towards the Disc WHICH IS NOW BELOW HIM AGAIN. He is rapidly catching it up. And its dark surface is suddenly washed with sunlight.

> **RINCEWIND**
> Oh great, the ground is gonna break my fall. Aaaaaargh!

EXT. PINE FOREST - DAY

Rincewind plummets uncontrollably towards the ground.

INT. UNSEEN UNIVERSITY/OCTAVO ROOM - DAY

The Octavo stirs on its lectern. The eye of the AVIAN creature beneath it snaps open.

EXT. PINE FOREST - DAY

Rincewind falls to earth with an almighty thump.

EXT. UNSEEN UNIVERSITY/TOWER OF ART - DAY

The CAMERA flies towards the top of the tower where there's a swirl of OCTARINE BLUE through which appears . . . THE TITLE: The Colour of Magic

EXT. PINE FOREST - DAY

The bushes Rincewind landed in rustle.

Rincewind staggers to his feet and pulls off his helmet, tossing it aside.

> **RINCEWIND**
> Did I just leave the world only to land back on it again?

Out of Rincewind's eyes RUNES of the eighth spell flicker out for a moment and then rush back into his head.

> RINCEWIND/VOICE OF THE SPELL
> Yes you did.

Rincewind grabs hold of his head.

> RINCEWIND
> Oh why, why, why?

> RINCEWIND/VOICE OF THE SPELL
> We're not going anywhere. Look at that.

His head suddenly jerks upwards as if forced to by the spell and he finds himself looking at the horrible RED STAR.

> RINCEWIND
> Is that me or is that getting bigger?

EXT. UNSEEN UNIVERSITY - DAY

Sounds of a crowd rise across the Unseen University as the light of the Disc's sun and the red star shine down on its roofs and gargoyles. Down below, crowds of people are gathering and pointing up to the RED STAR.

A tall thin man steps forward and addresses the crowd.

> RABBLE-ROUSER
> Is the turtle flying straight towards it, I ask you?

They look up.

> RABBLE-ROUSER
> The wizards say we always miss the stars . . . but has anyone seen one get this close before? Where are the wizards when we need them?

> CROWD
> Wizards out, wizards out, wizards out . . .

The chanting of the crowd rises up to where . . .

INT. UNSEEN UNIVERSITY/GREAT HALL - DAY

The battered ARCHCHANCELLOR'S HAT with a circle of octarine round its crown, is lifted from its velvet cushion in a round leather box, and placed on Trymon's head.

> TRYMON
> One small step for a wizard into the unseen. One giant leap for the Unseen University.

> JIGLAD WERT
> Would the student body please acknowledge the three hundred and fifth Archchancellor.

The student body and the faculty behind him on the knock their staffs against the floor and bow.

> TRYMON
> Let it be known that although limited personnel alterations have been made, one or two other significant things will be changing for the tidier . . .

The wizards look worried by this.

> TRYMON
> As none of us have received guidance as to the events of this morning . . . and . . . there seems to be a degree of quite unnecessary anxiety amongst the populous about the star . . .

There is a murmur among the wizards.

Trymon rises to his feet and accepts his staff.

> TRYMON
> (dramatically)
> . . . I propose that we perform the rite of Ash-Kente.

There is a general mutter of approval.

INT. UNSEEN UNIVERSITY/OCTAVO ROOM – NIGHT

The Octavo stirs on its lectern. The eyes of the AVIAN creature beneath it blink.

EXT. HORSE PEOPLE'S YURT – NIGHT

The glow of a fire can be seen from within the yurt.

> NARRATOR (V.O.)
> After its own space odyssey, many miles from Ankh-Morpork in the Vortex Plains, the Luggage has plans of its own.

INT. HORSE PEOPLE'S YURT – NIGHT

A group of nomadic barbarian horsemen sit around a horse turd fire.

The chieftain is turned respectfully to a bald-headed man whose face we do not see.

> BARBARIAN CHIEFTAIN
> I said, our guest whose name is legend must tell us truly, what is it that a man may call the greatest things in life?

> BARBARIAN 1
> The crisp horizon of the steppe. The wind in your hair, a fresh horse underneath you.

The chieftain nods.

> BARBARIAN CHIEFTAIN
> Or is it the sight of your enemy slain, the humiliation of his tribe and the lamentation of his women?

There is a general murmur of whiskery approval at this. The warriors lean closer. This should be worth hearing.

And we reveal COHEN THE BARBARIAN. He is trying unsuccessfully to light a roll-up and carefully warming his chilblains by the fire. Finally he speaks.

            COHEN THE BARBARIAN
  What you shay?

. . . revealing his toothlessness. He is a very old man with a totally bald head, a beard almost down to his knees, and a pair of matchstick legs with varicose veins. One eye is covered by a black patch. His thin body is a network of scars. He wears only a studded leather holdall and a pair of very large boots.

            BARBARIAN CHIEFTAIN
  I said, our guest whose name is legend must tell us truly—

            COHEN THE BARBARIAN
  Ah yesh.

Cohen raises his hand, thinks long and hard and then with deliberation . . .

            COHEN THE BARBARIAN
  Hot water. Good . . . dentishtry . . . and shoft lavatory paper.

There is silence from the barbarians. They mutter amongst themselves and go back to tearing meat with their hands.

But Cohen has seen something in the door of the yurt. Something that looks like a roll of WHITE PAPER. He cranes a little closer.

There is a box with hundreds of legs. It turns, and the roll of paper slowly unravels as it tiptoes into the forest.

Cohen gets up and puts the cigarette into his mouth with determination.

EXT. PINE FOREST - NIGHT

The Luggage makes its way through the forest. Behind it, COHEN follows, sword in one hand and leading his horse with the other.

EXT. UNSEEN UNIVERSITY/TOWER OF ART - NIGHT

The RED STAR can be seen looming ominously over the Tower of Art. TRYMON (O.C.) chants the rite of Ashe-Kente.

INT. UNSEEN UNIVERSITY/GREAT HALL - NIGHT

RAMS' HORNS, SKULLS, BAROQUE METALWORK and HEAVY CANDLES are heaped around the octogram which is in turn surrounded by wizards.

Trymon chants the final words of the spell. Runes fill the air.

> TRYMON
> Ash-Kente. Rise up, oh creature of earth and darkness.

They hang in front of him for a moment before dissolving.

The air in the centre of the octogram shimmers and thickens, and suddenly contains a tall, DARK FIGURE, DEATH. He holds his SCYTHE in one bony hand. The other skeletal hand holds small cubes of CHEESE and PINEAPPLE on a stick.

He catches the wizards' gaze, and glances down at the stick.

> TRYMON
> We do charge thee to abjure for—

> DEATH
> (reproachfully)
> I WAS AT A PARTY, YOU KNOW.

> TRYMON
> It is said that you can see both the past and the future.

> DEATH
> CORRECT.

> TRYMON
> Then perhaps you can tell us, why is the red star getting bigger?

> DEATH
> BECAUSE THE TURTLE IS FLYING TOWARDS IT.

> TRYMON
> Why?

> DEATH
> FOR A PURPOSE THAT HAS NOTHING TO DO WITH ME.

> TRYMON
> Then ... perhaps you can tell us what exactly happened this morning?

DEATH
I UNDERSTAND THAT THE OCTAVO WAS ANXIOUS NOT TO LOSE THE EIGHTH SPELL.

TRYMON
Hold on.

DEATH
IT WAS DROPPING OFF THE DISC, APPARENTLY.

TRYMON
Hold on. Are we talking about the spell that is inside the head of Rincewind?

DEATH
THAT HE'S BEEN CARRYING AROUND ALL THESE YEARS, YES.

Trymon frowns.

TRYMON
Any idea why?

DEATH
ALL I KNOW IS THAT ALL THE SPELLS HAD TO BE SAID TOGETHER AT SOLSTICE, OR MANY WORLDS *WILL* BE DESTROYED.

He stops.

TRYMON
Destroyed?

DEATH
IT'S AN ANCIENT PROPHECY WRITTEN ON THE INNER WALLS OF THE GREAT PYRAMID OF TSORT.

Trymon makes a mental note.

> **TRYMON**
> Can you tell us where Rincewind is now?

Death shrugs.

> **DEATH**
> THE FOREST OF SCUND, RIMWARDS OF THE RAMTOP MOUNTAINS.

EXT. PINE FOREST - NIGHT

Rincewind is walking through the dark forest.

> **DEATH (O.C.)**
> FEELING VERY SORRY FOR HIMSELF.

In the distance behind him he hears something in the undergrowth.

> **RINCEWIND**
> Hello? Anybody out there?

Rincewind stops and listens. He shakes his head and carries on walking. The sound in the undergrowth starts again, a little closer now.

> **RINCEWIND**
> Twoflower?

INT. UNSEEN UNIVERSITY/GREAT HALL - NIGHT

Trymon frowns.

> **TRYMON**
> Oh.

> **DEATH**
> NOW, MAY I GO?

Trymon nods distractedly.

> **TRYMON**
> Oh, yes. I hope it's a good party.

> **DEATH**
> I THINK IT MIGHT GO DOWNHILL AT MIDNIGHT.

> **TRYMON**
> Why?

> **DEATH**
> THAT'S WHEN THEY'LL BE TAKING MY MASK OFF.

> **TRYMON**
> Hmm.

He vanishes, leaving only the cocktail stick and a short paper streamer behind.

TRYMON has something on his mind.

INT. UNSEEN UNIVERSITY/LIBRARY – NIGHT

The Head Librarian is sitting on top of his desk, quietly peeling an orange. He glances up when Trymon enters.

          TRYMON
Evening. I am looking for anything we've got on the Pyramid of Tsort.

          HEAD LIBRARIAN
Oook.

He takes a banana out of his pocket.

          TRYMON
Yes.

The Librarian reaches for it but Trymon holds it just out of reach.

          TRYMON
No, no.

The Head Librarian looks at it and flops down heavily on the floor. His hand takes Trymon's and leads the way between the bookshelves. Trymon waves the banana encouragingly.

He stops by a soaring stack of musty books and swings himself up into the darkness. There is a sound of rustling paper, and a cloud of dust floats down to Trymon.

Quickly the Librarian is back, a slim volume in his hands, which he thrusts at Trymon.

          HEAD LIBRARIAN
Oook.

          TRYMON
Ah.

Trymon takes it gingerly, leans in and on the scratched, very dog-eared cover can just make out . . .

Jyt gryet Teymple hyte Tsort, Y Hiystory Myistical.

          TRYMON
Thank you.

Trymon turns the pages cautiously. There are whole pages covered with meaningful hieroglyphs.

The Librarian is peering over his shoulder at the same time.

          TRYMON
Whoever says all the spells together when the Disc is in danger . . .

          HEAD LIBRARIAN
Oook! Oook! Oook!

Trymon looks up to the Librarian, who is pointing upwards.

> **TRYMON**
> Yes, yes, the star, I know . . .

Trymon looks back down at the book.

> **TRYMON**
> . . . will gain after much power . . .

Trymon looks up, avarice on his face.

The Librarian taps the page.

> **HEAD LIBRARIAN**
> Ook. Ook.

Trymon looks down and reads what the Librarian is indicating.

> **TRYMON**
> 'To save the worlds', yes, and that.

Trymon turns to the Librarian.

> **TRYMON**
> Now listen, if you were to *ook* this to any members of the faculty, you will be disciplined.

Trymon looks sideways at him.

> **TRYMON**
> It's not as if bananas grow on trees.

The Librarian nods.

Trymon gives him the banana.

> **TRYMON**
> As much as it pains me to say this, Rincewind must not die . . . at least, not until we bring him back here . . . and empty his head.

EXT. PINE FOREST – DAWN

Rincewind is moving slowly in the half light.

> **MUFFLED VOICE (O.C.)**
> 'Incewind.

Rincewind grabs his head.

> **RINCEWIND**
> Go away. Go away.

> **MUFFLED VOICE (O.C.)**
> 'Incewind!

> **RINCEWIND**
> I'm not listening. I'm not listening.

> **TWOFLOWER (O.C.)**
> It's me, Twoflower.

Rincewind groans and holds his head.

> **RINCEWIND**
> He's dead and he's inside my head. Oh why me? Why me? Why . . .

He falls to his knees and throws his head back in desperation.

Hanging in the branches of the tree is a figure in a chelonaut's suit.

It waves at him.

Rincewind smiles uncertainly.

> **RINCEWIND**
> Twoflower?

The chelonaut gives him a thumbs-up.

> **TWOFLOWER**
> Isn't it an amazing thing that we ended up back on the world?

> **RINCEWIND**
> I must have done something really bad to have got stuck with you.

Twoflower manages to remove his helmet.

Twoflower looks a little hurt for a moment.

A flicker of guilt flickers across Rincewind's face.

> **RINCEWIND**
> The turtle must've caught us somehow.

> **TWOFLOWER**
> Why would it do that?

> **RINCEWIND**
> I don't know, do I? Anyway, where are we?

Twoflower moves to see that through the trees there is a STONE CIRCLE in the forest . . . and in the process falls out of the tree.

Light streams across the circle to reveal that it is full of RAM'S SKULLS on poles topped with MISTLETOE, and BANNERS embroidered with twisted snakes.

INT. UNSEEN UNIVERSITY/GREAT HALL - NIGHT

Trymon has the Temple of Tsort book in his hands.

> **JIGLAD WERT**
> Alive or dead?

> **TRYMON**
> Well, since we need him to say the spell in order to save the worlds, I suspect alive might be better.

> **JIGLAD WERT**
> Save the worlds? What does that mean?

> **TRYMON**
> I don't know . . . but as long as one of the worlds he saves is ours, I shall consider it a most satisfactory outcome.

The wizards turn and hurry away, muttering to each other.

EXT. FOREST NEAR DRUIDS' CIRCLE - DAWN

A WHITE CHARGER gallops through the forest. Its rider suddenly stops. By the side of the track is the Luggage. Its top opens invitingly, displaying much gold.

Cohen climbs somewhat slowly off his horse to approach it. As he does it sprouts legs and trots off into the forest at great speed. Cohen seizes his horse's bridle and follows the Luggage . . .

EXT. DRUIDS' CIRCLE - DAWN

Twoflower is no longer wearing his chelonaut suit. Rincewind pulls him away from the circle and back into the forest.

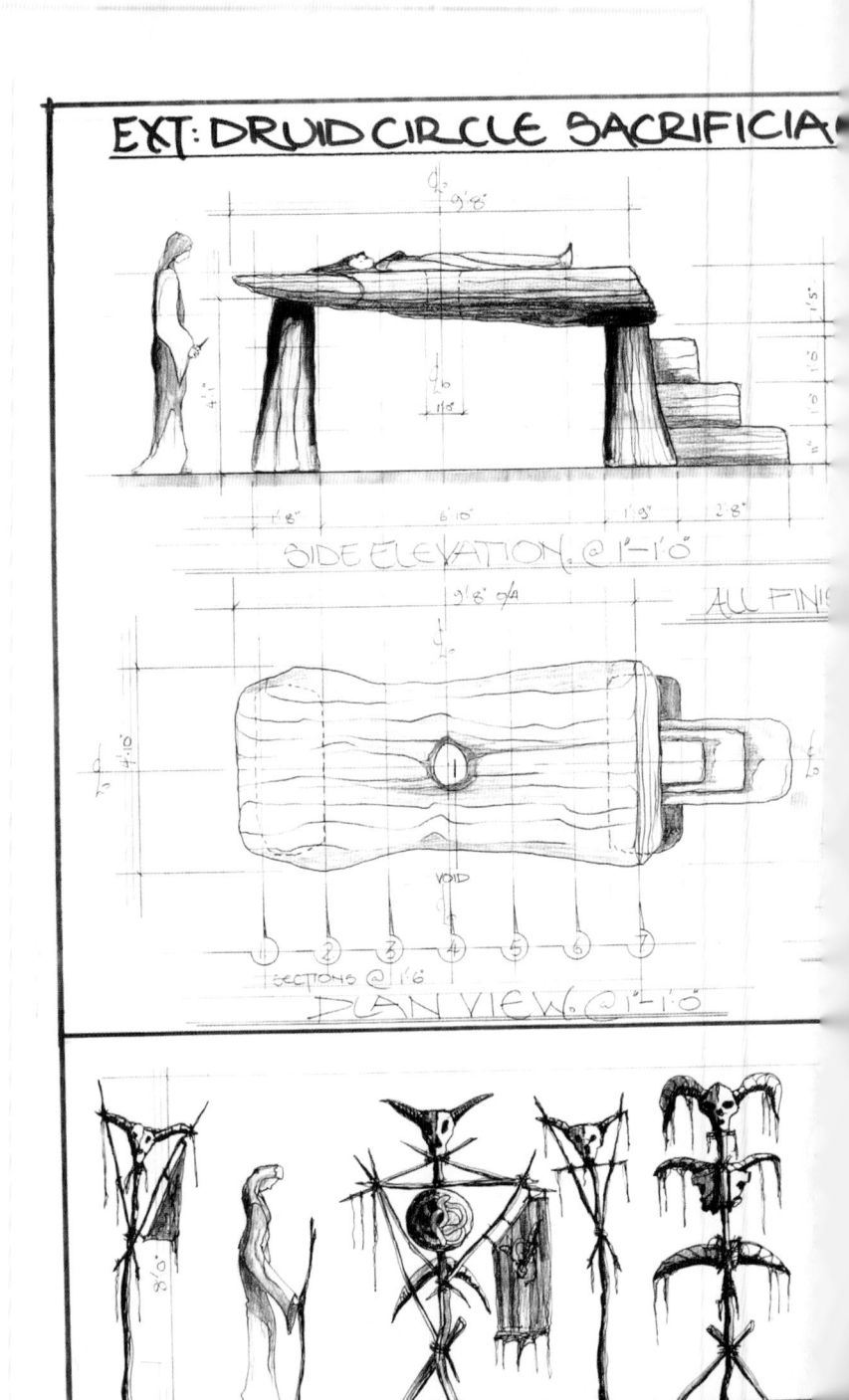

> **TWOFLOWER**
> It's extraordinary. It looks like they're gonna have a ceremony, ancient and traditional ritual probably dating back thousands of years, to celebrate the, um . . . the . . .

> **RINCEWIND**
> Look, all that golden bow and cycle of nature stuff . . . just boils down to sex and violence, usually both at the same time.

> From the far side of the stones there is a loud blarting of trumpets.

> **RINCEWIND**
> Think we ought to be going.

                TWOFLOWER
        Oh.

Rincewind stops and then pulls Twoflower into the bushes. From their cover they peer over at the stone circle.

                RINCEWIND
        Come on, let's go.

At the far side of the outer circle some sort of procession is forming up. Rincewind and Twoflower hide behind a tree. There is a band of bronze trumpets and a line of druids marches slowly past, their long sickles hung with sprays of mistletoe

              TWOFLOWER (O.C.)
        If only I had my picture box.

As Rincewind turns to look for an escape route there is a commotion in the undergrowth. The Luggage, with Cohen still pursuing it, heads towards the Druids' Circle. Rincewind groans.

                TWOFLOWER
        Oh, there you are. It's very loyal.

                RINCEWIND
        Yes, if loyalty is what you look for
        in a suitcase.

Twoflower turns in delight and comes over. He opens the lid and rummages until he finds the picture box.

                RINCEWIND
        Now come on, look, we ought to
        leave.

But Twoflower isn't listening. He is lost in the spectacle.

As the druids spread out around a great flat stone that dominates the centre of the circle Rincewind notices the attractive if rather pale YOUNG LADY in their midst. She wears a long white robe, a gold torc around her neck, and an expression of vague apprehension.

> TWOFLOWER
> Is she a druidess?

> RINCEWIND
> I don't think so.

The druids begin to chant, an ominously building chant.

Rincewind's eyes narrow. He's had an idea.

> RINCEWIND
> (manipulatively)
> Look, you're not going to like this next bit, I promise you.

> TWOFLOWER
> No, no, I want to stay. I think ceremonies like this hark back to a primitive simplicity which—

> RINCEWIND
> If you must know, they're going to sacrifice her.

The young lady climbs up to the central stone.

Twoflower looks at him in astonishment.

> TWOFLOWER
> What, kill her?

The young lady is now lying on the central stone.

> RINCEWIND
> Well it wouldn't be much of a sacrifice if they didn't, would it?

Rincewind starts to creep away, beckoning Twoflower.

Twoflower is opening and shutting his mouth.

> TWOFLOWER
> Couldn't they just use flowers and berries and things, you know, sort of symbolic?

Rincewind sighs and stops.

> RINCEWIND
> Look, no self-respecting high priest is going to go through all the business of trumpets and processions and then shove his knife in a daffodil and a couple of plums, is he?

To his amazement Twoflower's lip is trembling.

The chant is rising inexorably to a climax. The head druid is testing the edge of his sickle and all eyes are turned to the finger of stone on the hills beyond the circle.

> RINCEWIND
> Get out of here, come on.

But Rincewind is talking to himself.

> TWOFLOWER
> Really, honestly, please.

EXT. OUTSIDE DRUIDS' CIRCLE – DAWN

From the cover of a handy fallen stone is the small and solitary figure of COHEN THE BARBARIAN, watching . . .

EXT. DRUIDS' CIRCLE - DAWN

. . . the druids circling and chanting as . . . the chief druid raises his sickle and . . .

          TWOFLOWER (O.C.)
I say there, yes, I say, may I have a word there sir? I'm sorry to intrude, I don't mean to be a bother but I was just there and I saw what looks to be a lovely enterprise you have here but the purpose, I just wonder if you'd reconsider for a moment the idea of sacrifice . . .

EXT. DRUIDS' CIRCLE - DAWN

Rincewind looks back into the circle.

Twoflower is standing by the altar stone with one finger in the air and an attitude of polite determination.

The druids are looking at him in astonishment.

Fingers like a bunch of straws clamp onto the wizard's shoulder and a sword pinks his Adam's apple.

          COHEN THE BARBARIAN
Tell me what that other idiot ish doing or you ish a dead man.

Rincewind strains to hear what he is saying

          TWOFLOWER
You see I can't really go back, you see, with the blood in the way . . .

The knife squeezes his throat.

          RINCEWIND
His name is Twoflower and he's not from these parts.

          COHEN THE BARBARIAN
Doeshn't look like it. Now, what I'm looking for ish the boxsh full of treashure with the legsh.

          TWOFLOWER
The, you know, more symbolism, less blood, nobody actually does—

One of the druids finally moves to shut Twoflower up.

          TWOFLOWER
Oh, hello.

The druids are all looking up through a mountain valley which lines up perfectly with the circle's holist stone.

And at that moment the sun rises above the mountain line . . . behind them.

The druids all turn to look at it, confused. And then turn back as . . .

. . . where they were expecting the sun . . . peeking through ragged clouds, is the glaring RED STAR.

The druids all look down from it in unison. It is hanging exactly over the circle's holiest stone. A cry of horror goes up from the assembled priests.

          RINCEWIND
           (muffled)
    Look, it's getting bigger.

A big knife slips into Rincewind's hand.

      COHEN THE BARBARIAN
    Have you ever done this sort of thing before?

          RINCEWIND
    What sort of thing?

      COHEN THE BARBARIAN
    Rushed into a temple, killed the priesthts, shtolen the gold and reshcued the girl?

          RINCEWIND
    Um, not in so many words, no.

      COHEN THE BARBARIAN
    You do it like thish.

Cohen rushes past him towards the druids.

The two druids closest to him exchange glances and heft their sickles. There is a brief blur and they collapse into tight balls of agony, making rattling noises.

Rincewind sidles along towards the altar stone.

Behind him the druids attempt to discuss the subject of sacrilege with Cohen, whose fists are flying in response.

Twoflower is watching the fight with interest. Rincewind grabs him by the shoulder.

          RINCEWIND
    Let's go.

Twoflower takes Rincewind's knife and hurries up to the altar stone.

          TWOFLOWER
    It's all right—

BETHAN sits up . . .

          BETHAN
    Bloody well isn't!

. . . and bursts into tears

          BETHAN
    Why do people always go and spoil things?

She climbs down from the altar stone.

Twoflower looks down at her in embarrassment.

> **TWOFLOWER**
> You've just been saved from absolutely certain death.

She speaks wretchedly.

> **BETHAN**
> It's not easy around here, you know. I mean, keeping yourself, I mean staying, I mean not letting yourself . . . oh! Not losing your qualifications.

> **TWOFLOWER**
> Qualifications?

The girl's eyes narrow.

> **BETHAN**
> I could have been up there with the moon goddess by now, drinking mead out of a silver bowl. Eight years of staying home on Saturday night just . . . right down the drain.

She looks up at Twoflower and scowls . . .

> **TWOFLOWER**
> Oh. Well . . .

. . . and then turns and runs off.

Rincewind crawls out from his hiding place beneath the altar just in time to trip ARCHDRUID ZAKRIAH, rushing to strike with a sickle.

Rincewind topples over into a foetal position on the ground.

The Archdruid can't stop and falls over him. As he does Rincewind cautiously opens his eyes. He rubs the side of his head. The last thing we see from his POV is . . .

. . . the Archdruid slowly standing up to reveal the sickle impaled in his front. As he reaches for it there is a nasty fleshy sound and he falls forward. Behind the druid Cohen pulls his sword from the body and wipes it.

. . . and then Rincewind's eyes flicker and close.

INT. THE OCTAVO - DAY

When they open again . . . the world has vanished and he is in darkness. There is the sound of paper rustling.

>   RINCEWIND
>   Where am I now?

Rincewind stares hard at the darkness.

>   SPELL 1 (V.O.)
>   You're dreaming.

>   RINCEWIND
>   Can I wake up please?

>   SPELL 2 (V.O.)
>   No.

>   SPELL 3 (V.O.)
>   You have a very important task
>   ahead of you.

>   RINCEWIND
>   Oh good.

EXT. DRUIDS' CIRCLE - DAY

With the battle over, Twoflower and Cohen are trying to wake Rincewind up. The druids have all gone.

>   TWOFLOWER
>   Rincewind. Rincewind? Are you in there?

>   COHEN THE BARBARIAN
>   There's not even a flesh wound.

>   TWOFLOWER
>   Rincewind. Can you hear me, Rincewind?

>   COHEN THE BARBARIAN
>   What's up with the girl?

>   TWOFLOWER
>   She won't let us rescue her.

Bethan scowls.

>   COHEN THE BARBARIAN
>   Bugger that.

And with one movement he picks her up . . .

>   BETHAN
>   No!

. . . staggers a little, screams at his arthritis and falls over. He pauses, prone, Bethan on top of him.

>   COHEN THE BARBARIAN
>   Don't just lie there, you daft cow, help me up.

To her own amazement, she does.

>   TWOFLOWER
>   Are you sure you can't hear me in there, Rincewind? Rincewind? Rincewind?

INT. THE OCTAVO - DAY

Rincewind is straining to see in the darkness. Scratchy lines are slowly becoming visible in front of him. The voice is like the rustle of old pages.

          SPELL 3 (V.O.)
Many years ago, we arranged for one of our number to hide in your head.

          RINCEWIND
Who are we exactly?

          SPELL 1 (V.O.)
We are the Seven Spells and our task is to see that nothing dreadful happens to the eighth, Rincewind.

          SPELL 2 (V.O.)
It is most important that you don't let the wizards take the Spell from you.

          SPELL 1 (V.O.)
All eight Spells must be said at the right time or terrible things will happen.

          SPELL 2 (V.O.)
And they mustn't be said by the wrong people.

          RINCEWIND
The wizards.

          SPELL 1 (V.O.)
Precisely.

Rincewind squints harder in front of him.

From his POV it becomes clear that what he can see ahead of him is WRITING on a page, seen from underneath.

          RINCEWIND
Am I in the Octavo?

          SPELL 3 (V.O.)
In certain metaphysical respects, yes.

He can hear the dry rustling right in front of his nose . . .

          RINCEWIND
Aaaarrrghhh!

          SPELL 2 (V.O.)
Why are you screaming?

          SPELL 3 (V.O.)
Yes, why are you screaming?

>   RINCEWIND
>   (shouting)
>   I'm inside a bloody book, talking to
>   voices I can't see, and you ask me
>   why I'm screaming?

There is a papery sigh.

>   SPELL 1 (V.O.)
>   Look, it is very important you
>   safeguard the spell in your head
>   and bring it back to us at the
>   University in time for the solstice,
>   so when the moment is precisely
>   right, we can be said.

Rincewind hesitates.

>   RINCEWIND
>   Why should anyone want to say
>   you?

>   SPELL 3 (V.O.)
>   It's the star. You see, the turtle is
>   heading towards it because . . .

>   RINCEWIND
>   No, no, no, stop, stop, stop, stop,
>   stop, stop. You've totally ruined
>   my life, you do realise that, don't
>   you? I could've really made it as
>   a wizard if you hadn't used me
>   as a portable spell book. I can't
>   remember any other spells because
>   they're all too frightened to be in
>   the same head as you.

>   SPELL 1 (V.O.)
>   (brightens)
>   Look at it like this then – as soon
>   as the spell is said, you'll be rid of
>   it.

>   SPELL 2 (V.O.)
>   And us.

>   SPELL 3 (V.O.)
>   Forever.

Rincewind closes his eyes and concentrates really hard.

EXT. DRUIDS' CIRCLE – DAY

Rincewind sits bolt upright.

>   RINCEWIND
>   When's the solstice?

>   TWOFLOWER
>   Hey. Oh, er . . . two days' time, I
>   think.

>   RINCEWIND
>   Huh, drat. We've got to go right
>   now.

He gets up and pulls Twoflower away from Cohen and Bethan.

>   TWOFLOWER
>   (serious)
>   Well, won't the druids be
>   celebrating the solstice here?

Rincewind glances down at the bodies strewn around the floor as he steps over them.

>   RINCEWIND
>   Probably not.

>   TWOFLOWER
>   Are you sure? 'Cause I'd really like
>   to stay here.

Rincewind's thinking fast.

>   RINCEWIND
>   Yes. But Ankh-Morpork is *the* place
>   to be on the solstice.

>   TWOFLOWER
>   Oh Rincewind, if we're not gonna be
>   here—

>   RINCEWIND
>   Oh to feel the cobbles under your
>   feet and the old familiar smell of
>   the cesspits. They're at their very
>   best this time of year.

                    TWOFLOWER
          Well the place that I feel I really
          need to see is—

A tear almost springs in Rincewind's
eye.

                    RINCEWIND
          I want to take you home, home to
          the potatoes they sell at the fried
          fish store at the junction of the
          Street of Cunning Artificers and
          Midden Street.

                    TWOFLOWER
          Yeah, potatoes, Rincewind . . . this
          was a lovely fight but what I really
          wanna see is the temple at Bel-
          Shamharoth.

                    RINCEWIND
               (relishing the thought)
          'Tatoes, I hear you calling. What
          did you say?

                    TWOFLOWER
          I want to see the temple of Bel-
          Shamharoth.

                    RINCEWIND
          Not the home of the giant terrifying
          spider from which no one has ever
          returned alive?

                    TWOFLOWER
          That's the one.

Rincewind hesitates.

                    RINCEWIND
          Oh. Right. Ah, of course. The River
          Snarl runs right past it.

His eyes narrow as a plan begins to form
in his mind and he leads Twoflower on
again by the arm.

                    TWOFLOWER
          Well that settles it then.

Twoflower beams.

                    RINCEWIND
          On our way to the solstice
          celebrations at Ankh-Morpork.

                    TWOFLOWER
          I can hear the potatoes calling.

                    RINCEWIND
          Ah, hahaha.

Rincewind holds out his palm . . .

                    TWOFLOWER
          Oh . . .

. . . Twoflower does likewise, they
inspect them, and shake hands.

                    RINCEWIND
          Right.

They walk away from the Druids' Circle
with determination until . . .

          BROTHER OF THE ORDER OF MIDNIGHT
                         (O.C.)
          Sham?

Rincewind stops.

                    RINCEWIND
          I don't like the sound of that.

160

Rincewind and Twoflower hear movement in the forest.

                TWOFLOWER
    What shall we do?

                RINCEWIND
    Panic?

    BROTHER OF THE ORDER OF MIDNIGHT
                 (O.C.)
    Oh, that's him.

Rincewind listens and then turns.

A wizard's head pokes up from the undergrowth.

                TWOFLOWER
    Wizards.

                RINCEWIND
    Panic.

And Rincewind pulls Twoflower back towards the stone circle in a panic.

                TWOFLOWER
    Did they come to celebrate the solstice?

Rincewind and Twoflower jump a fallen druid and head towards the altar. Rincewind points to an opening in it.

                RINCEWIND
    Quick, in there!

EXT. FOREST AROUND DRUIDS' CIRCLE - DAY

Wizards emerge from the forest undergrowth, prepared to follow Rincewind.

EXT. DRUIDS' CIRCLE/SACRIFICIAL SLAB - DAY

Rincewind and Twoflower are hiding under the sacrificial slab with their backs to one end of an upright stone.

          WIZARD LEADER (O. C.)
    Rincewind!

          TWOFLOWER
          (smiling)
    Hey, they know you!

Rincewind shakes his head in disbelief.

EXT. OUTSIDE DRUIDS' CIRCLE - DAY

The wizards surround the circle. The Wizard Leader cups his hands around his mouth and shouts.

          WIZARD LEADER
    We've got you surrounded. You come back with us to see Archchancellor Trymon . . . and everything will be all right. You have his word.

EXT. DRUIDS' CIRCLE/SACRIFICIAL SLAB - DAY

Twoflower beams with excitement.

>TWOFLOWER
>It's nice they want you back.

>RINCEWIND
>No it isn't. Even by wizards' standard, Trymon is a nasty piece of work.

Rincewind looks glum.

EXT. OUTSIDE DRUIDS' CIRCLE - DAY

The Wizard Leader signals to the other wizards to ready themselves.

>WIZARD LEADER
>Now we can do this the easy way . . . or we can do this a very easy way.

EXT. DRUIDS' CIRCLE/SACRIFICIAL SLAB - DAY

Rincewind twists around to shout back.

>RINCEWIND
>What's the easy way?

EXT. OUTSIDE DRUIDS' CIRCLE - DAY

The Wizard Leader brandishes his wand.

>WIZARD LEADER
>You come out not covered in burning leaf mould.

EXT. DRUIDS' CIRCLE/SACRIFICIAL SLAB - DAY

Rincewind and Twoflower exchange a worried look.

EXT. OUTSIDE DRUIDS' CIRCLE - DAY

>RINCEWIND (O.C.)
>What's the very easy way?

>WIZARD LEADER
>We set fire to the sacrificial pyre . . . with you in it.

EXT. DRUIDS' CIRCLE/SACRIFICIAL SLAB - DAY

Rincewind bends a little to peek out through the piled up pyre wood. He see the RED STAR.

>TWOFLOWER
>How do you think it will end?

>RINCEWIND
>(sarcastic)
>Well . . . if that star is an omen, looks like we're all going to die.

Rincewind turns back in while Twoflower bends round to look.

> TWOFLOWER
> We should name it now then.

> RINCEWIND
> (gloomily)
> Might as well.

> TWOFLOWER
> How 'bout . . . the 'Death Star'?

> RINCEWIND
> Well don't be daft, what sort of name is that? The Death Star.

They look at each other as the horrible irony sinks in.

A stray spell explodes right by their side.

Rincewind looks at him in disbelief.

EXT. OUTSIDE DRUIDS' CIRCLE - DAY

The Wizard Leader narrows his eyes and glares at the other wizards.

> WIZARD LEADER
> Who cast a spell?

The wizards all point at the sheepish-looking young wizard, who holds up his hand and then hides behind a tree.

The Wizard Leader glares at him.

EXT. DRUIDS' CIRCLE/SACRIFICIAL SLAB - DAY

Rincewind picks up two gun-shaped branches and tests their weight.

Twoflower steadies the picture box in his hands.

                    TWOFLOWER
You didn't see that Trymon out
there, did you?

                    RINCEWIND
Trymon? No, why?

                    TWOFLOWER
Well . . . for a minute there, I
thought we were in trouble.

                    RINCEWIND
Huh.

They nod to each other and in one movement they leap out from under the slab . . .

EXT. DRUIDS' CIRCLE - DAY

. . . straight into SLOW MOTION, scattering the funeral pyre branches as they emerge. As they run towards CAMERA they are engulfed in a volley of spells. Magic begins to fly like a match in a box of fireworks.

Rincewind raises his branches, Twoflower gets the picture box into position and starts to take pictures.

As one particularly pointy spell heads directly for Rincewind . . .

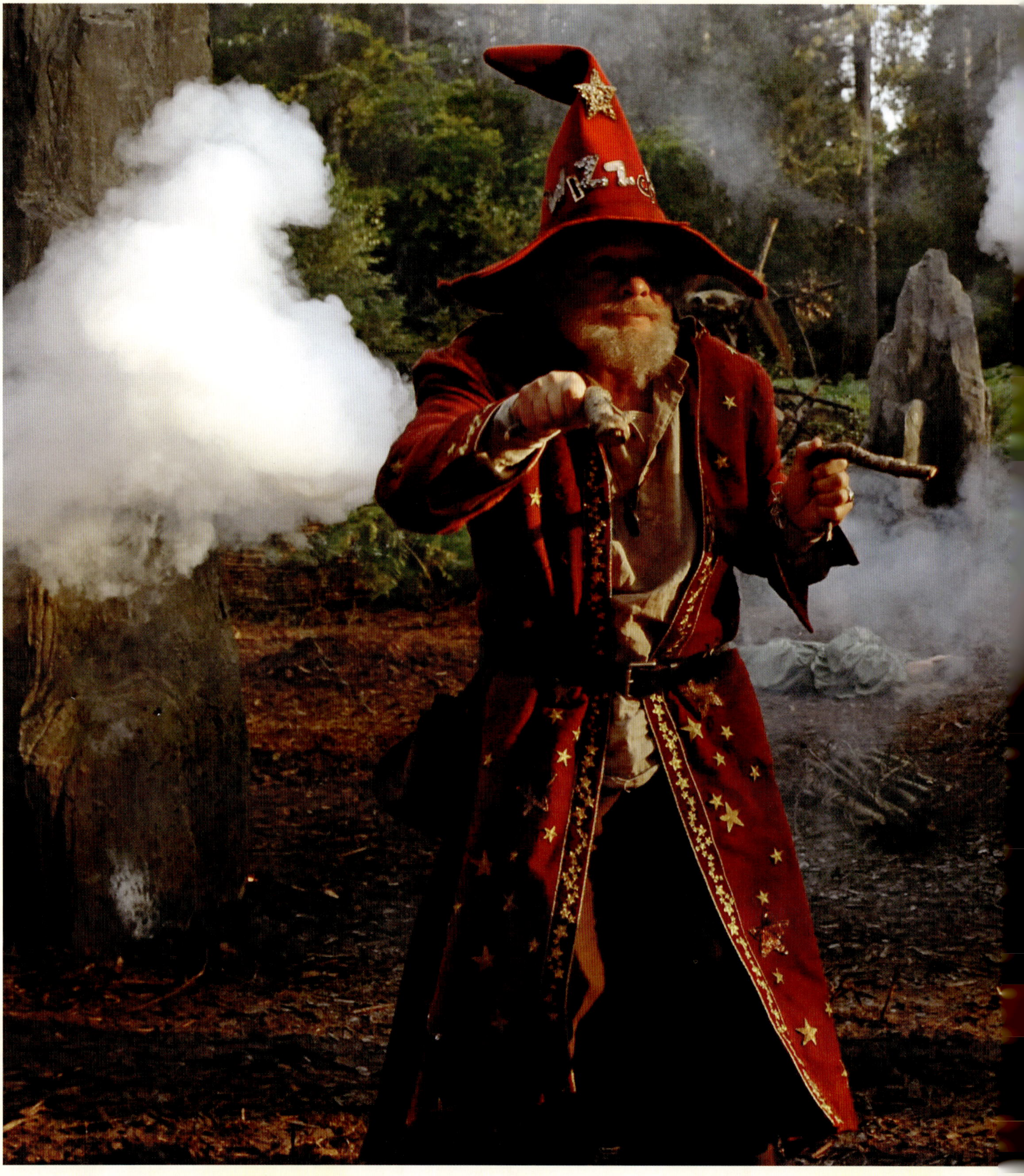

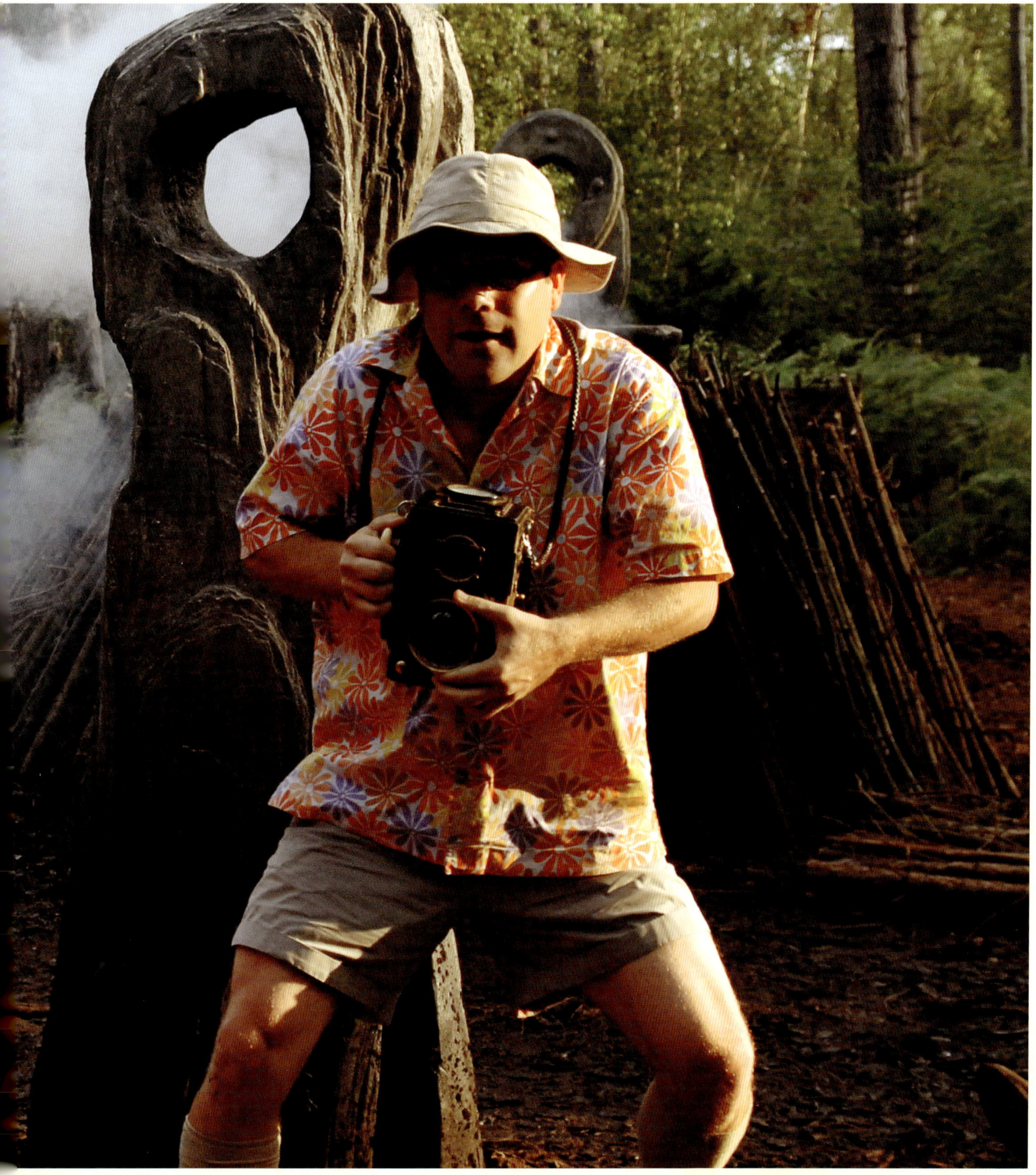

TWOFLOWER
Rincewind, look out!

. . . Twoflower leaps in front of the wizard with a beaming smile and 'takes one' for his friend. He takes a picture too, and with the flash the action freezes.

Then it unfreezes. The spell glances off the side of Twoflower's head as Rincewind curls up into a terrified ball and disappears from view in a cloud of flames and smoke . . .

The wizards bombard the circle with spells until they themselves are completely engulfed in smoke. The fizzing sounds of spells stop and are replaced by the swishing sound of sharp metal through air and the repetitive slamming of wood against wood.

The smoke clears to reveal a wizard-free zone. Cohen wipes the blade of his sword. A pair of POINTY-SHOED FEET disappear into the Luggage and a large RED TONGUE lifts the lid before closing with a snap.

RINCEWIND looks up from his curled-up position.

RINCEWIND
A little bit earlier would've been nice.

He crawls over to Twoflower.

RINCEWIND
Twoflower. Twoflower!

EXT. UNSEEN UNIVERSITY/GATES – DAY

There are crowds banging on the gates and shouting demands. Several large bonfires have been lit.

> RABBLE-ROUSER
> If the wizards can't get rid of the star, they should cease all magic...

EXT. UNSEEN UNIVERSITY/GATE PARAPET ROOFTOP – DAY

The Heads of the Orders are peering down at the crowds.

> RABBLE-ROUSER (O.C.)
> ...and commit suicide in good order.

Trymon looks down and sees that one of the gutters leading to a gargoyle is blocked with an old BIRD'S NEST. Rain water is backed up behind it.

He thrusts his staff into the nest.

Water suddenly shoots out of the GARGOYLE'S MOUTH...

EXT. UNSEEN UNIVERSITY/GATES – DAY

...as the Rabble-rouser punches the air a plume of water drenches him.

EXT. UNSEEN UNIVERSITY/GATE PARAPET ROOF TOP – DAY

The Heads of the Orders are peering down over the parapet.

          TRYMON
   If they're going to be like that, personally I'd let them burn.

Trymon steps forward.

          TRYMON
   The fact is . . . the star is getting bigger and without Rincewind's spell, there's nothing we can do about it.

          JIGLAD WERT
   I've looked into the mirror of oversight.

          GANMACK TREEHALLET
   Last night, I sought to make the runes from horn.

          LUMUEL PANTER
   May I make it clear that I tried both the runes and the mirror and the entrails of a manicrach.

          JIGLAD WERT
   Any good—?

          TRYMON
   So nobody knows where he is now.

          LUMUEL PANTER
   No.

          TRYMON
   In times of crisis, one must be wise . . . and wise men do what the times demand.

Trymon turns away from them.

EXT. DRUIDS' CIRCLE – DAY

Rincewind is bent over Twoflower, trying to wake him up.

          RINCEWIND
   Twoflower, Twoflower, come on, wake up, we've got to go.

He stands up. Twoflower has a faintly worried smile. His breathing is shallow and strange.

          RINCEWIND
   All right, if that's the way you want it.

Rincewind drags Twoflower out of shot.

EXT. GULLY - DAY

Rincewind puts Twoflower by a tree. A large white horse is tethered in the background. It has a HAEMORRHOID RING attached to the saddle.

Rincewind settles Twoflower down by a tree and starts to examine his eyes.

        COHEN THE BARBARIAN
    Let me resht me back.

            RINCEWIND
    Twoflower.

Rincewind shakes Twoflower's head from side to side.

            RINCEWIND
    Wakey, wakey, come along now, are you in there?

        COHEN THE BARBARIAN
    There'sh shome liniment shtuff in the shaddle bag if you wouldn't mind . . .

Bethan gets up and begins to hunt for it in the saddle bag.

Rincewind turns and looks at Cohen.

            RINCEWIND
    Who are you?

Cohen's star-bright eye looks over to him.

        COHEN THE BARBARIAN
    Cohen ish me name.

Bethan's hands stop moving.

            BETHAN
    Cohen the Barbarian?

    COHEN THE BARBARIAN
  The very shame.

Rincewind stops looking at Twoflower but is still holding his face.

    RINCEWIND
  Oh hang on, hang on. Cohen is a great big chap, neck like a bull, chest muscles like a sack full of footballs.

Bethan eases closer to Cohen in awe, drinking in the sight of him.

    RINCEWIND
  He's the Disc's greatest warrior. I mean, he's a legend in his own lifetime. My grandfather used to tell me . . .

He falters under the gimlet gaze.

    COHEN THE BARBARIAN
  Yesh.

Cohen sighs.

    COHEN THE BARBARIAN
  That's right, boy. I'm a lifetime in me own legend.

    BETHAN
  You were the greatest. Bards still sing songs about you.

    COHEN THE BARBARIAN
  I never get any royaltiesh. That'sh the shaga of my life. Eighty yearsh in the bushiness and what have I got to show for it? Back ache, pilesh, bad digeshtion and a hundred different recipes for shoop. Shoop, I hate shoop.

Bethan's forehead wrinkles.

    BETHAN
  Shoop?

    RINCEWIND
  Soup.

    COHEN THE BARBARIAN
     (miserably)
  It'sh me teeths, you shee. No one takes you sheriously when you've got no teeths. They shay 'Shit by the fire, granddad, and have shome shoop—'

Rincewind laughs.

Cohen looks sharply at Rincewind.

Rincewind's laugh becomes a cough.

    COHEN THE BARBARIAN
  That'sh a nasty cough you've got there mate.

    RINCEWIND
  Yes, yes, I know, I'm sorry, I'm sorry, it's just that . . .

Unable to look Bethan in the face, Rincewind turns back to tending Twoflower. He slaps him around the face.

    RINCEWIND
  . . . wake up.

    COHEN THE BARBARIAN
  He'sh gone.

    RINCEWIND
  What, he's dead?

    COHEN THE BARBARIAN
  Well . . .

    RINCEWIND
     (panicking)
  I've got to get him back to Ankh-Morpork.

    COHEN THE BARBARIAN
  Well, he'sh not exshactly dead.

    RINCEWIND
  He can't die.

Rincewind tries to hide his concern.

                    RINCEWIND
          The Patrician will kill me.

               COHEN THE BARBARIAN
          He's just – gone.

                    RINCEWIND
          He's gone? Where? Can't I get him
          back?

               COHEN THE BARBARIAN
          I don't know, but I think I know
          shomeone who might have a map.

INT. HORSE PEOPLE'S YURT - NIGHT

Rincewind, Twoflower, Cohen and Bethan are sitting around a fire opposite the HORSE CHIEFTAIN and other Horse people.

                    RINCEWIND
              A necromancer!

The old woman, who is the CHIEFTAIN'S GRANDMOTHER, shrugs and pulls a pack of greasy cards from some unseen pocket.

Bethan leans sideways to Rincewind.

                    BETHAN
          What's neck romance?

                   RINCEWIND
          No, necromancy is talking to the
          dead.

                    BETHAN
                  (disappointed)
          Oh.

The chieftain's grandmother nods at
Rincewind and spreads the cards in front
of her.

                   RINCEWIND
          Course, I don't believe in Caroc
          cards. I mean, all that stuff about
          it being dissolved wisdom from the
          universe . . . lot of old rubbish.

The first card, smoke-yellowed and age-
crinkled, is . . .

              CHIEFTAIN'S GRANDMOTHER
          The Star . . .

Instead of the usual image of a star, it
is a tiny RED DOT.

Rincewind spits out his beer.

The old woman mutters and scratches at
the card with a fingernail, then looks
sharply at Rincewind.

                   RINCEWIND
          It's nothing to do with me.

She turns up some more cards, including
the Four of Elephants. The Ace of
Turtles . . .

              CHIEFTAIN'S GRANDMOTHER
          Four of Elephants. The Ace of
          Turtles.

and . . .

                   RINCEWIND
          Death.

Rincewind looks down at it and starts a
little.

Behind Death on his white horse, the sky
is red-lit.

Rincewind looks across the tent to the
pale Twoflower.

                   RINCEWIND
          Oh. Is he really dead?

He tries to hide his face.

                   RINCEWIND
          Oh.

The old woman shakes her head and
rummages about until she finds a tiny
BROWN BOTTLE which she tips into
Rincewind's beer.

He looks at it suspiciously.

              COHEN THE BARBARIAN
          She shays it's a short of medicine,
          sho if you want to shee your friend
          in thish world again, I should drink
          it if I were you.

>   RINCEWIND
> Well if you're sure it's okay. Can't
> make the beer taste any worse, can
> it?

He lifts up the glass and hesitates.

>   RINCEWIND
> Well, he did take a spell for me
> so ... here goes.

He takes a big breath and a swig, aware of all eyes on him

>   RINCEWIND
> Well actually it doesn't taste too
> bad.

Something picks him up and throws him into the air. Except that he is also still sitting by the fire. He can see himself there, a dwindling figure in the circle of firelight that is rapidly becoming smaller. The toy figures around it are looking intently at his body. Except for the old woman. She is looking right up at him, and grinning

>   RINCEWIND
> Oh, where am I going?

>   CHIEFTAIN'S GRANDMOTHER
> Don't look back.

>   RINCEWIND
> But where am I going?

EXT. DEATH'S HOUSE/OUT OF RINCEWIND'S BODY – NIGHT

DEATH is standing on his front lawn sharpening his SCYTHE on an enormous whetstone. Sparks fly.

He stands upright and tests the sharpness of the blade. Satisfied, he picks up two LIFETIMERS. One has TWOFLOWER written on it, and the other says RINCEWIND.

Death turns and walks away into the house.

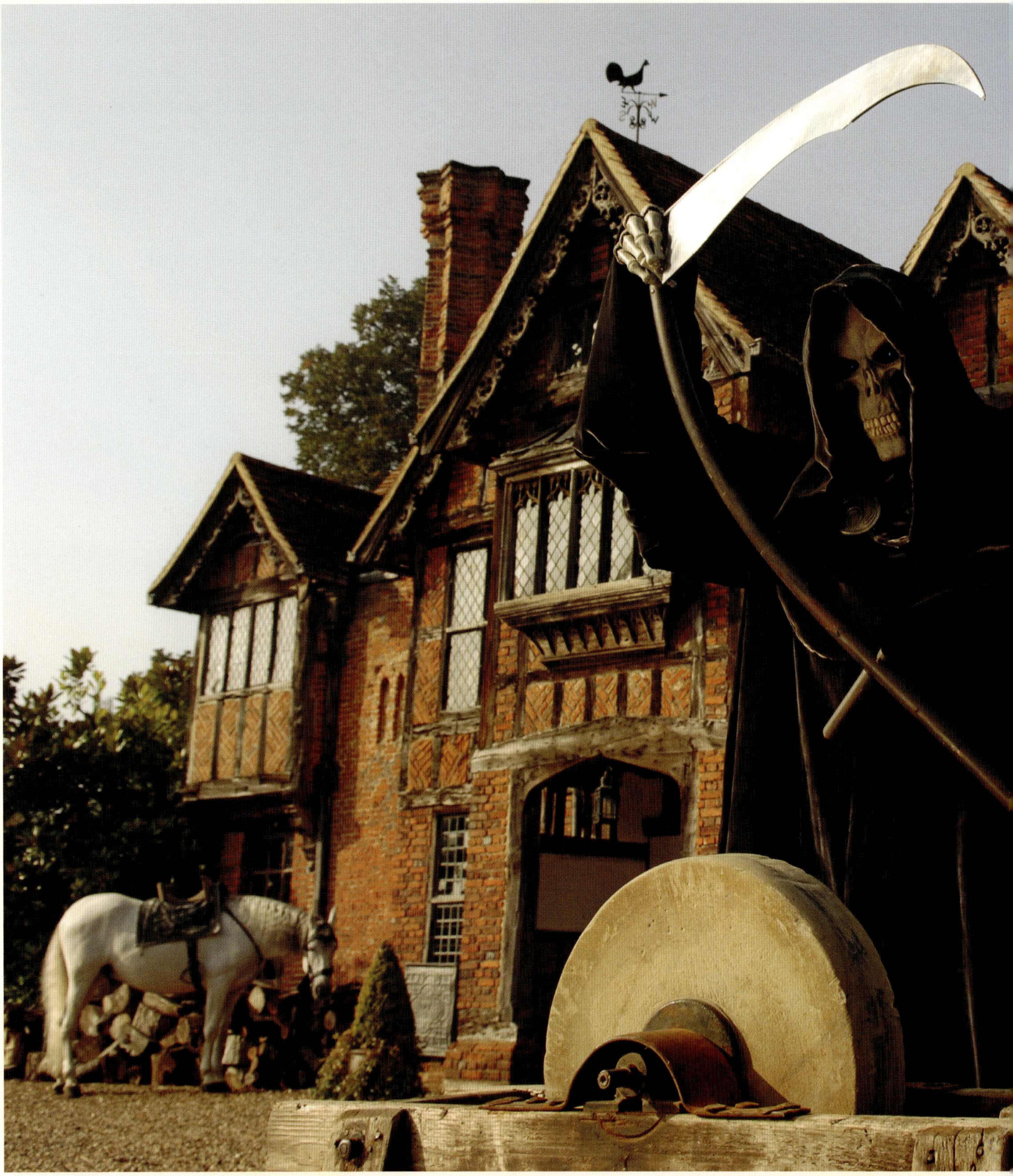

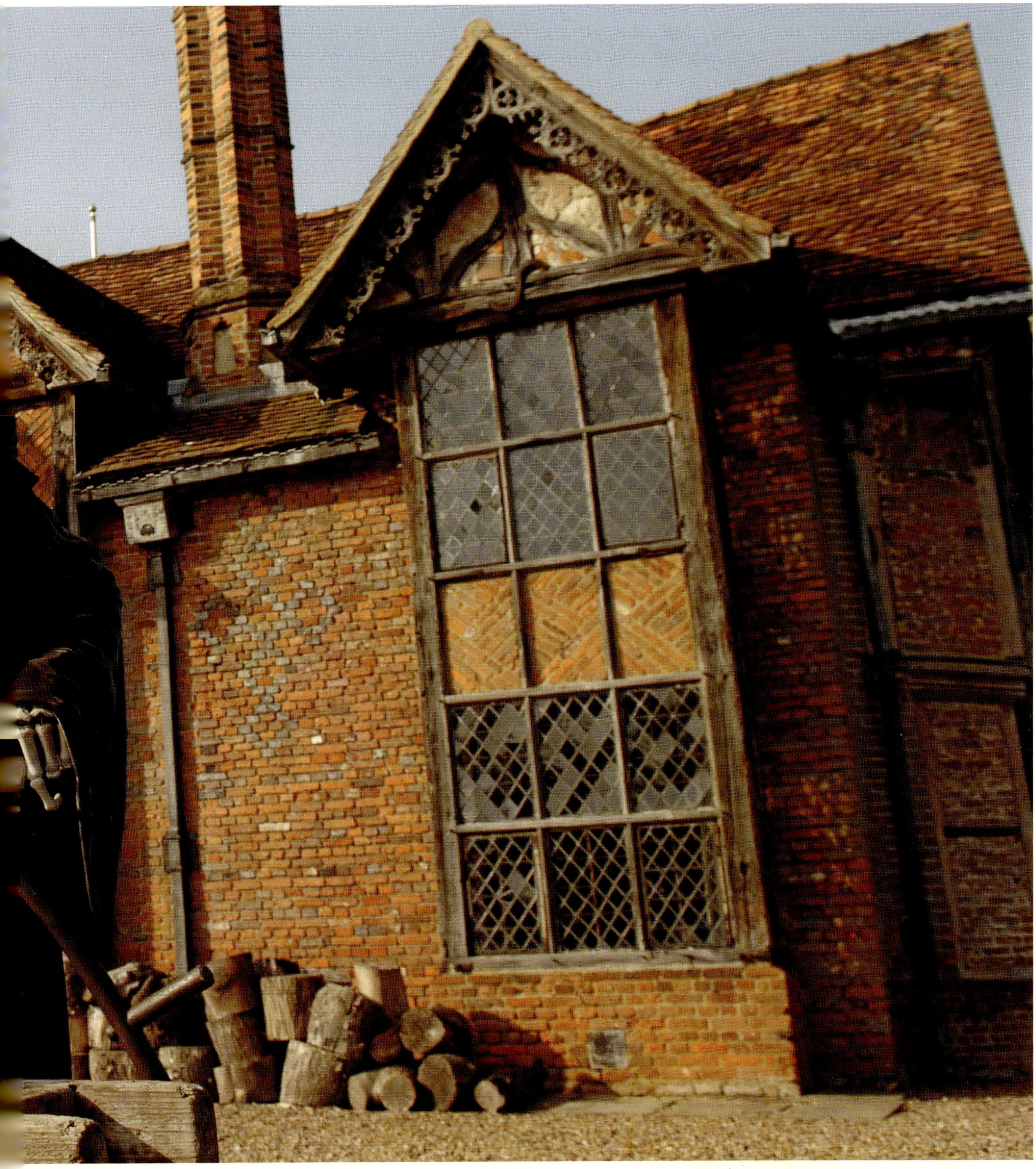

EXT. DEATH'S HOUSE/OUT OF RINCEWIND'S BODY - NIGHT

Rincewind is rising up a long, thin, vertical shaft, over the edge, and onto an area of flat land at the top.

A little path leads up to a garden, with orchards and flower-beds, and a quite small black COTTAGE. And there, walking cheerfully into the house is . . .

> **RINCEWIND**
> Oh no. Twoflower!

Rincewind pursues the tourist.

The garden on the outcrop is well kept and full of huge deep purple, night-black, or shroud-white LILIES. There is a SUNDIAL without a gnomon on the freshly scythed lawn.

> **RINCEWIND**
> Twoflower! Twoflower!

INT. DEATH'S HOUSE/HALLWAY - NIGHT

Rincewind creeps into a stone-flagged passageway, which in turn opens out into a wide entrance hall. He moves forward with his back pressed tightly against a wall.

The hall itself is considerably larger than the whole cottage appears from the outside. The décor, which is Early Crypt, runs heavily to black drapes.

There is a very big CLOCK in the space between two curving wooden staircases covered with strange carvings. The clock has a long pendulum which swings with a slow tick-tock. The weight on the end of the pendulum is knife-edged and razor-sharp . . .

. . . and Twoflower is walking slowly towards it.

> **RINCEWIND**
> Twoflower. There you are.

> **TWOFLOWER**
> What an amazing clock. Rincewind, where are we exactly?

> **RINCEWIND**
> Well we're sort of . . . informally dead.

> **TWOFLOWER**
> Oh.

Twoflower lifts the picture box up to his eye.

> **RINCEWIND**
> Come along, look, we haven't got time to take pictures. Let's go.

> **TWOFLOWER**
> Won't take very long.

Twoflower looks at him with some bemusement and raps on the side of the box. A tiny door flies open and the imp pokes his head out and squints. Rincewind dashes off.

            PICTURE IMP
Poor light. Three bloody years at F8, if you ask me.

            TWOFLOWER
Do your best.

He slams the door shut. A second later there is the tiny scraping noise of his stool being dragged up to his easel.

Rincewind come dashing back, teeth gritted.

            RINCEWIND
Look, what do you want to take pictures for? Can't you just remember it?

            TWOFLOWER
Well, in years to come, when I'm sitting by the fire, I—

            RINCEWIND
Oh you, you'll be sitting by the fire permanently if we don't get out of here. Quick, come on.

            DEATH (O.C.)
OH, I DO HOPE YOU'RE NOT GOING. I SO SELDOM HAVE COMPANY.

They both turn.

Death is standing in the archway.

            RINCEWIND
We, we really mustn't keep you. Get ready to run.

Rincewind grabs Twoflower and tries to shuffle imperceptibly towards the door.

            TWOFLOWER
Oh, but . . . I've never been at Death's door before.

And the wizard, with great deliberation, hits Twoflower smartly on the chin.

            RINCEWIND
Right, now run.

EXT. DEATH'S HOUSE/GARDEN – NIGHT

Rincewind and Twoflower run out of the cottage and through the garden towards the shaft.

> RINCEWIND
> (to himself)
> Don't look back. Don't look back, I mustn't look back.

DEATH, mounted on BINKY, follows them, scythe in hand.

> DEATH
> THERE ARE WORSE THINGS THAN BEING DEAD, YOU KNOW.

Rincewind pauses for a moment at the edge of the shaft.

> RINCEWIND
> (muttering)
> Name two.

Rincewind and Twoflower jump.

Moments later DEATH arrives. When he reaches the edge of the rock he doesn't stop but simply rides into the air and reins BINKY in over the nothingness.

> DEATH
> THAT ALWAYS ANNOYS ME. I MIGHT AS WELL INSTALL A REVOLVING DOOR . . .

Death looks up at the new star . . .

> DEATH
> (a trifle uncertainly)
> . . . IF I'VE GOT TIME.

INT. HORSE PEOPLE'S YURT – NIGHT

On Rincewind's face. Bethan waves her hand in front of his face.

              BETHAN
Rincewind.

              RINCEWIND
Oh!

Rincewind snaps out of it.

              BETHAN
Oh.

              RINCEWIND
Oh.

              BETHAN
Hello.

              RINCEWIND
Hello. Did I move at all?

              BETHAN
No, you just looked at the fire as if you'd seen a ghost.

There is a groan behind them.

Twoflower is sitting up, holding his head in his hands.

              RINCEWIND
              (excited)
Oh you're alive . . .

He looks at the others then turns back to Twoflower.

              RINCEWIND
Ah. But no thanks to yourself, Mr 'would you like some berries while you stick your sickle in my head?'

Twoflower reaches out and hugs Rincewind.

              RINCEWIND
Hey, ah, no hugging. I do not hug. Oh.

              TWOFLOWER
Oh, my head.

Twoflower rubs his head where the spell struck.

              RINCEWIND
You've been ill. You've been . . . hallucinating.

Twoflower looks down at the picture box.

              TWOFLOWER
Mmm. Well, if I've been hallucinating, bet I took some great pictures.

Rincewind seizes the box from him.

              RINCEWIND
Ah. No. No, no, no, you can't. No pictureography. The horse people are very superstitious. I'll put this in the Luggage for you.

He takes the picture box and dashes away.

INT. HORSE PEOPLE'S YURT - NIGHT

Rincewind is about to put the picture box back into the Luggage when he knocks instead. The picture imp opens his hatch.

> **PICTURE IMP**
> You'd better not be going somewhere next where we need too much black.

The ratchet of the picture box begins to click.

Very slowly, the box extrudes the last picture.

Rincewind snatches the picture. We DO NOT SEE what is on it, only the horror on Rincewind's face.

> **RINCEWIND**
> (softly)
> It wasn't like that. It was a little cottage and everyth—

> **PICTURE IMP**
> You see what you see, I paint what I see and I only see what's really there, see?

The hatch slams shut.

> **RINCEWIND**
> Oh.

Rincewind jumps back a little and quickly stows the picture box.

INT. UNSEEN UNIVERSITY/GALDER WEATHERWAX'S STUDY - NIGHT

The star is still hanging ominously over the university.

The six surviving heads of the Eight Orders are sitting at the long, shiny, new table. They look sidelong at one another and Trymon sits down at the head of the table and shuffles through some papers.

On the wall is a sign painted with the words:

> There is no 'U' in team.

> **GANMACK TREEHALLET**
> What happened to old Galder's chair, the one with lion arms and the duck's feet?

> **TRYMON**
> Oh that. I had it burnt.

Trymon treats the wizards to a fleeting smile.

> **JIGLAD WERT**
> But it was a priceless magical artefact, a genuine piece of—

Trymon taps his glass to call the meeting to order.

> **TRYMON**
> Now . . . may I draw your attention to the agenda?

Jiglad waves the document in front of him.

              LUMUEL PANTER
What does a genda do?

              TRYMON
It's simply a list of things that we need to discuss . . . top of which is the matter of Rincewind.

              JIGLAD WERT
And the star. People are agitating, you know.

              TRYMON
That is item number two on the agenda. Item number one is the fact that you have failed to find him.

The wizards look at one another, embarrassed.

              JIGLAD WERT
So what are you suggesting we do about it?

              TRYMON
I'm not suggesting anything.

Trymon looks along the table.

              TRYMON
I've sent someone to find him.

The wizards turn in unison.

              JIGLAD WERT
Who?

> TRYMON
> A hero.

The wizards look at Trymon, open-mouthed.

> JIGLAD WERT
> On whose authority?

Trymon turns his grey eyes on him.

> TRYMON
> Mine. I need no other.

> JIGLAD WERT
> You've hired a bloodthirsty idiot who can't walk and think at the same time?

EXT. VORTEX PLAINS - DAY

The CAMERA flies towards the plains where far, far below, a small dot of travelling dust is evident.

> LUMUEL PANTER (O.C.)
> How can you take anyone seriously...

As we get closer the dot is becoming clear as a hero on a galloping horse.

> NARRATOR (V.O.)
> The hero, even at this moment galloping towards the Vortex Plains, doesn't get involved in trading insults with wizards, not just because they don't take it seriously, but because this particular hero is in fact... a heroine named Herrena.

HERRENA is dressed in light chain-mail, soft leather boots, and a short sword.

Riding with her are a number of swarthy men. And they are heading towards the bare Trollbane Mountains.

INT. HORSE PEOPLE'S YURT - NGHT

Rincewind rejoins the group.

> COHEN THE BARBARIAN
> The horshe people have deshided—

Bethan jumps to her feet beside him.

> BETHAN
> (proudly)
> They hold Cohen in the highest regard—

Twoflower's mouth gapes.

> TWOFLOWER
> Cohen the Barbarian?

And then his expression changes as he turns to Rincewind.

> RINCEWIND
> I was going to mention that.

> TWOFLOWER
> But back in Ankh-Morpork, you said that—

> RINCEWIND
> I lied.

Rincewind looks quickly to Cohen.

> COHEN THE BARBARIAN
> The horshe people have deshided to give you mountsh and direcshuns to the River Shnarl where you can catch a ferry back to the Shircle Shea.

> TWOFLOWER
> You lied?

Rincewind brightens a little and hurriedly heads over to Cohen.

> RINCEWIND
> Yeah, ah, well, I would . . . like to thank you very much because you've been most helpful and it will be very . . . different without you.

> COHEN THE BARBARIAN
> You don't wish ush to accompany you?

> RINCEWIND
> No, no, we'll be fine.

Cohen takes Rincewind to one side and out of Twoflower's earshot.

Bethan heads over to Twoflower and they whisper together.

> COHEN THE BARBARIAN
> Theshe are dangeroush timesh.

> RINCEWIND
> Yes I know, but . . . I'm beginning to cope very well with these near death experiences.

> TWOFLOWER
> (to Bethan)
> I just can't believe it's Cohen the Barbarian.

Twoflower is beaming with awe.

> COHEN THE BARBARIAN
> Ish he perhapsh being sharcashtic?

> RINCEWIND
> No, no, he's always like that.

Cohen turns.

Twoflower beams at him, and waves proudly.

Cohen turns back, and grunts.

> **COHEN THE BARBARIAN**
> He's got eyesh, hashn't he?

> **RINCEWIND**
> Yes, but . . . he doesn't see things as other people do. See, take this Yurt for example, it's . . . well, it's dark and greasy and smells like a very ill horse.

> **COHEN THE BARBARIAN**
> Yesh.

> **RINCEWIND**
> Yes, but he would say that it smells like the curious and rare resins plundered by lean-eyed warriors from the edge of civilisation, you know, and so on and so on.

Cohen turns again.

Twoflower is talking to Bethan.

> **TWOFLOWER**
> . . . well he single handedly defeated the . . . snake warriors of the . . . .

A weird smile forms among the wrinkles of Cohen's face.

> **RINCEWIND**
> I could tell him to shut up.

> **COHEN THE BARBARIAN**
> No, I . . . I like his eyesh. They can shee for fifty years.

Cohen turns to Rincewind.

> **COHEN THE BARBARIAN**
> I shall accompany you for the reason that if anything should happen to you, the legend would be beshmirched . . .

Cohen shivers.

> **COHEN THE BARBARIAN**
> . . . but . . . also on account of me chillblainsh.

> **BETHAN**
> I'm coming too . . . in case Cohen needs anything . . . rubbed.

She looks admiringly at her hero.

EXT. PLAINS - DAY

Rincewind, Cohen and Bethan are riding in single file across a field, looking up at the Red Star in the sky. Twoflower is on a DONKEY.

> **COHEN THE BARBARIAN**
> It's even brighter now. What is it?

He looks hard at Rincewind, who rcddens.

> **RINCEWIND**
> Why does everybody look at me? I don't know what it is. It . . . it's probably a comet or something.

> **BETHAN**
> I wonder if it's a sign.

She looks up at it again.

> **TWOFLOWER**
> Will we be burned up?

> **RINCEWIND**
> Well, how the hell would I know? I've never been hit by a comet before, have I?

They ride on.

> **RINCEWIND**
> Walk on.

Rincewind takes a closer look at Cohen.

> **RINCEWIND**
> Have you combed your beard?

> **COHEN THE BARBARIAN**
> Eh?

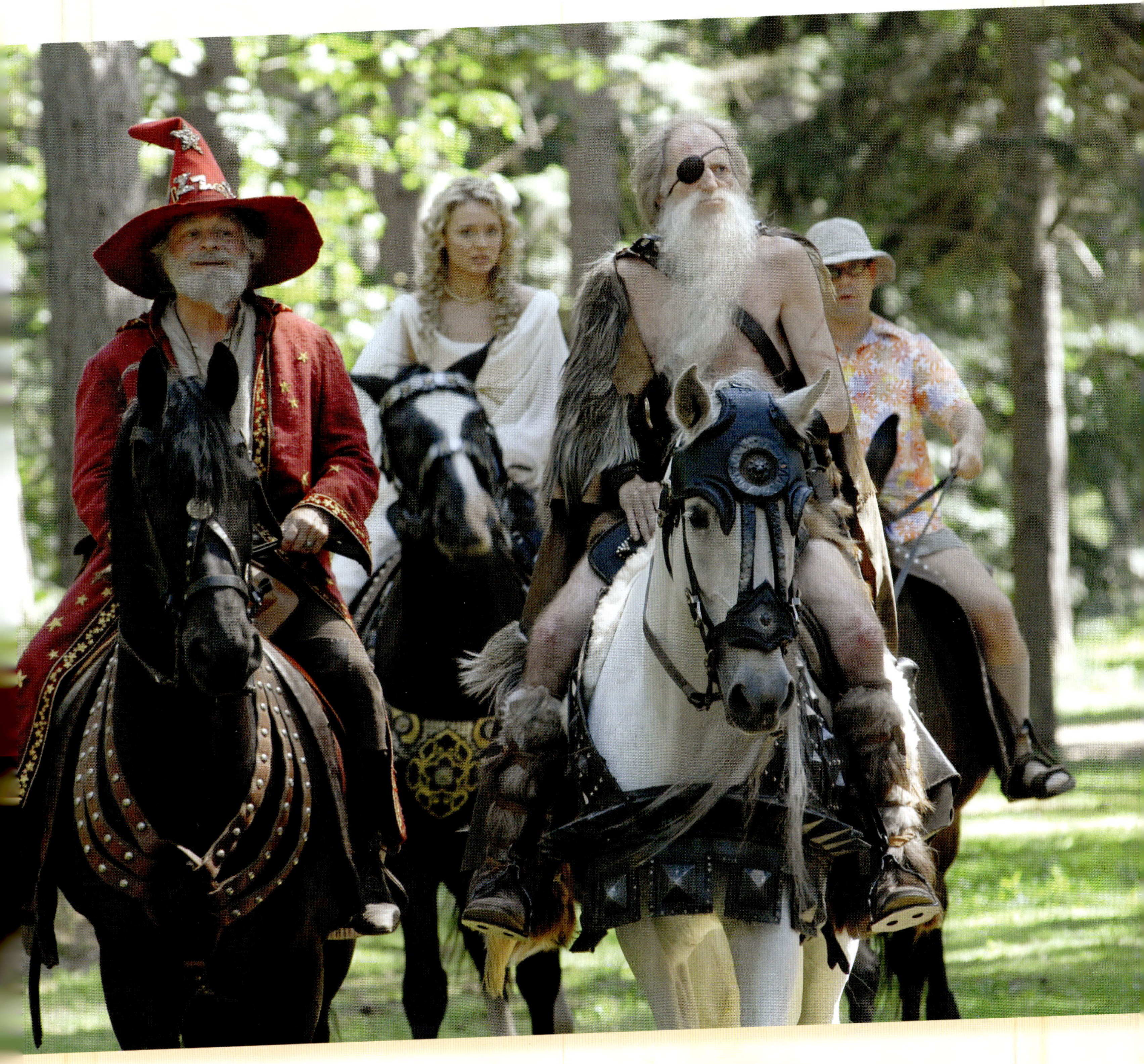

Cohen appears not to have heard and
Rincewind smiles.

                    RINCEWIND
          I think she's taken a bit of a shine
          to you.

Rincewind taps the side of his nose and
grins.

                    COHEN THE BARBARIAN
                         (wistfully)
          If I wash twenty yearsh
          younger . . .

                    RINCEWIND
          Yes?

                    COHEN THE BARBARIAN
          . . . I'd be shixty-sheven.

                    TWOFLOWER
          Me, riding with Cohen the
          Barbarian. Who could possibly
          attack us now?

A hundred yards behind them, in the
undergrowth, the Luggage is following.

EXT. MOUNTAINS - DAY

A line of barbarian horsemen break a ridge. Herrena's horse walks forward and she surveys the landscape before her.

> NARRATOR (V.O.)
> It is indeed a hundred miles rimwards to the River Snarl, across the high plains and down to the grey pine forest that lies rather closer than is comfortable to the Trollbone Mountains. The clue is in the title.

Tiny dots in the far distance kick up dust.

EXT. PLAINS - DAY

The little procession of horses winds across the plains . . .

DISSOLVE TO:

EXT. MOUNTAINS - EVENING

. . . to the foot of the mountains.

EXT. CAMP FIRE - EVENING

Twoflower tends the camp fire. Rincewind is pacing.

> RINCEWIND
> Did we really have to stop here? The River Snarl can't be that far away.

> COHEN THE BARBARIAN
> The ferryman doeshn't work at night sho we might ash well get shome resht. Beshidesh, my feet are killing me.

Bethan is seeing to Cohen's chilblains.

> BETHAN
> You'd have quite nice feet if only you looked after them.

> COHEN THE BARBARIAN
> (sheepishly)
> You don't get to meet very many chiropodishts in my line of work. I've met any amount of shnake prieshtsh, mad godsh, warlordsh, never any chiropodishts. I shupposhe it wouldn't look right really, Cohen Against the Chiropodishts.

> BETHAN
> Or Cohen and the Chiropractors of Doom.

Cohen cackles.

> TWOFLOWER
> (laughing)
> Or Cohen and the Mad Dentists.

Cohen's mouth snaps shut.

                    COHEN THE BARBARIAN
                What'sh funny about that?

Twoflower swallows.

                    TWOFLOWER
                Oh, uh . . . nothing in particular.

Cohen glares at him. Then he sags,
looking small and old.

                    COHEN THE BARBARIAN
                No, I don't blame you. It'sh hard
                being a hero when you've got no
                teeths. Don't matter what elsh
                you lose, you can get by with one
                eye even, but show 'em a mouthful
                of gumsh and no one hash any
                reshpect.

                          BETHAN
                         (loyally)
                I do.

                    TWOFLOWER
                Why don't you have a new pair
                made for yourself?

Cohen looks confused.

                    COHEN THE BARBARIAN
                Well . . . I do have trouble
                mashticating.

                    RINCEWIND
                Huh? I beg your pardon?

                    COHEN THE BARBARIAN
                You know, chewing.

                    RINCEWIND
                Oh, yeah, chewing.

                    TWOFLOWER
                They're called den-tures.

                    COHEN THE BARBARIAN
                Din-chewersh?

                    RINCEWIND
                Dentures.

                    TWOFLOWER
                Lots of people wear them where I'm
                from.

                    COHEN THE BARBARIAN
                What, and, and they don't jusht
                have to eat shoop?

                    TWOFLOWER
                No—

THWACK. And somebody hits him.

INT. OLD GRANDAD - NIGHT

Cohen tugs ineffectually at his bonds.

Twoflower peers at him muzzily and rubs the back of his head against Rincewind's who is tied back-to-back with him.

The Luggage is still and silent under its net in the corner.

Herrena stands over them with some sort of gang around the fire in the cave mouth.

        HERRENA
That has to rank as the most pathetically easy ambush in swordswoman history. I've no idea why you're so important.

        RINCEWIND
Important? To who?

        HERRENA
The wizards.

        RINCEWIND
The wizards.

        HERRENA
At the Unseen University. For some reason, they want me to take you back.

Rincewind's head slumps.

        HERRENA
It's a short ride hubwards to the ferry at the River Snarl. From there, we'll be at Ankh-Morpork by morning.

Herrena starts to walk away.

        TWOFLOWER
Excuse me.

She stops and turns.

        HERRENA
Yes?

        TWOFLOWER
Well, do you think we could drop by the temple of Bel-Shamharoth on the way?

        HERRENA
Only if you want to ride a thousand miles Rimwards in the wrong direction.

Rincewind shakes his head sadly.

Twoflower turns and looks firmly at Rincewind.

        TWOFLOWER
You mean you can't reach the temple of Bel-Shamharoth by the River Snarl?

        HERRENA
No, of course not.

        TWOFLOWER
    (trying not to be hurt)
Oh.

Herrena shrugs her shoulders and walks away.

Twoflower turns to Rincewind and looks at him testily.

                    TWOFLOWER
                  (pointedly)
          Well at least we'll be in Ankh-
          Morpork for the special solstice
          celebrations then.

Rincewind looks away.

                    RINCEWIND
          Oh yes.

Bethan and Cohen are also tied together.

                    BETHAN
                  (brightly)
          What special solstice celebrations?

                    COHEN THE BARBARIAN
          Never heard of them.

Twoflower lets him stew.

                    TWOFLOWER
          So my guide wasn't gonna take me
          to Bel-Shamharoth at all, was he?

                    RINCEWIND
          No. It was too dangerous.

Twoflower is a little choked.

                    RINCEWIND
          Do you want half your money back?
          Do you want all your money back?

                    TWOFLOWER
          Look, it's not about money. We're
          supposed to be friends. We shook
          on it.

                    RINCEWIND
                  (blurting)
          Look, if you must know the truth,
          I only agreed to be your guide
          because the Patrician of Ankh-
          Morpork said he'd do unspeakable
          things to me if I didn't. So there
          you have it.

Twoflower is genuinely hurt.

                    TWOFLOWER
          Thank you for being honest.

He sniffs.

                    RINCEWIND
          Well...

                    TWOFLOWER
          They don't even celebrate the
          solstice in Ankh-Morpork, do they?

                    RINCEWIND
          No...

Twoflower sighs.

                    RINCEWIND
          ...and I'm probably the worst
          wizard this side of the Circle Sea.

                    TWOFLOWER
          And I thought everything was going
          so well.

                    RINCEWIND
          Well you thought wrong.

They turn their backs on each other.

Rincewind looks away in a huff. But something catches his eye. He stares at a bulbous stalactite shape in the ceiling at the back of the cave and a look of realisation crosses his face.

          RINCEWIND
Ah, ah, ah! You're in great danger, you've got to put the fire out.

Herrena turns.

          HERRENA
Oh no, *you're* in great danger and the fire stays. Don't try to distract me.

          RINCEWIND
No, it . . . you've obviously never heard of the legend of Old Grandad. I knew he was around here somewhere. When a troll gets older . . .

          TWOFLOWER
There are trolls?

          RINCEWIND
He gets bigger and bigger, and this is a very old troll.

          HERRENA
Everyone knows trolls keep away from fire.

          RINCEWIND
          (desperately)
But this specific troll . . . can't.

          TWOFLOWER
Can't?

          HERRENA
Can't?

          RINCEWIND
No, because you've lit the fire on his tongue!

Then the floor moves as OLD GRANDAD awakes very slowly from his centuries-old slumber.

EXT. OLD GRANDAD - NIGHT

Trees topple, turf slips, as OLD GRANDAD stirs.

INT. OLD GRANDAD/MOUTH - DAWN

As Old Grandad lurches, Herrena and her gang stumble and fall towards the mouth of the cave . . .

> **TWOFLOWER**
> Is it an earthquake?

> **BETHAN**
> Cohen!

EXT. FOOT OF OLD GRANDAD - DAWN

. . . and out falling through the air.

FINGERS the size of ships unfold and grip the ground.

INT. OLD GRANDAD/MOUTH - DAWN

Rincewind and Twoflower, still tied together, struggle towards the opening.

> **RINCEWIND**
> (to Cohen and Bethan)
> Come on, you two.

Moments later, Rincewind and Twoflower jump out, still tied together.

> **BETHAN**
> Cohen!

> **COHEN THE BARBARIAN**
> Get up you silly cow.

The Luggage struggles beneath its net as Cohen and Bethan make it to their feet and head for the exit.

OPTIONAL

SC. 2/63 OLD GRANDAD AWAKES

A — CLOSE ON ROCKY RECESS

THE EARTH QUIVERS

ROCKS CRUMBLE

SAME SHOT

B — .. AND A GIANT EYE POPS OPEN AMONGST THE RUBBLE

CLOSE ON
GIANT
ROCKY
FINGERS
LIFTING
OUT
OF THE
GROUND.

195

OPTIONAL
SC. 2/63
OLD GRANDAD AWAKES

THE GIANT MOUNTAIN TROLL RISES FROM HIS SLUMBER WITHIN THE HILLS PULLING HIMSELF FREE FROM THE EARTH

EXT. OLD GRANDAD/MOUTH – DAWN

Like a fat man trying to do press-ups Old Grandad pushes himself upwards.

Two enormous rock-slides high on his cliff-face mark the opening of eyes like great crusted opals as the whole dark landscape shakes itself slowly, then begins to rise impossibly . . . and turn into the BIGGEST TROLL YOU'VE EVER SEEN.

EXT. ROCKY HOLLOW – DAWN

Scattering in many directions, Herrena's gang flees for their lives as behind them the giant troll lumbers forward.

There is a flurry of activity in the trees and Rincewind emerges. When he turns we see that Twoflower is still tied to him back to back.

They run in the opposite direction away from the troll like a strange crab-like creature, until, out of breath, they stop and watch it stride with footfalls like an earthquake after Herrena's gang.

Twoflower looks over his shoulder and points upwards.

The troll has stopped and is slowly turning towards Rincewind and Twoflower.

          RINCEWIND
  Come on, run!

They try, but fall over each other into a heap.

A dark shadow looms over them and they look up slowly. Rincewind cowers in horror as the troll raises its fist and brings it down towards them, closer and closer . . .

RINCEWIND
I think we're going home in an envelope.

. . . and then suddenly stops as . . .

. . . DAY comes with a silent explosion of light. The huge terrifying bulk of Old Grandad is a breakwater of shadow as the daylight streams past. There is a brief grinding noise and then silence. A few birds start singing.

Old Grandad has turned back to stone.

EXT. VORTEX PLAINS - DAWN

Sunlight roars silently across the land like golden surf.

EXT. ROCKY HOLLOW - DAWN

Rincewind and Twoflower lie in the grass, panting.

TWOFLOWER
Wow!

RINCEWIND
If complete and utter chaos was lightning, then being tied to you is like standing on a hilltop in a thunderstorm wearing a wet copper armour and shouting, 'All gods are bastards'.

TWOFLOWER
Thank you.

RINCEWIND
It wasn't a compliment.

                    TWOFLOWER
            Oh.

Twoflower tries to stand up.

                    RINCEWIND
            Come on, let's stand up.

                    TWOFLOWER
            Well . . . I'm off to see Bel-
            Shamharoth.

                    RINCEWIND
            Good luck, and I hope the spider
            eats you. Sod the Patrician. I'm
            going home to Ankh-Morpork.

                    TWOFLOWER
            Fine.

                    RINCEWIND
            Fine.

Twoflower starts to move in one
direction, pulling Rincewind with him.

Rincewind starts to go in the opposite
direction, so that they are like a human
Pushmepullyou.

EXT. HILL ABOVE THE RIVER SNARL - DAY

On Rincewind, grumpy.

                    RINCEWIND
            Ow.

                    TWOFLOWER (O.C.)
            Happy now?

                    RINCEWIND
            I don't want to talk about it.

                    TWOFLOWER
            We're going to Ankh-Morpork . . .

There is a thug to either side of
Twoflower . . .

                    RINCEWIND
            This isn't exactly what I had in
            mind.

And we CUT WIDE to reveal that . . .

Rincewind has his hands tied behind his
back, and walks ahead of Twoflower, also
restrained. Beside Twoflower are two of
Herrena's men.

Herrena herself follows them as they
head towards the river.

A few wisps of early mist wreathe the
banks of the River Snarl below.

EXT. OLD GRANDAD - DAY

High up on the face of Old Grandad a
hole breaks though. The Luggage plummets
through to the ground . . .

EXT. UNSEEN UNIVERSITY/GATE PARAPET ROOFTOP - NIGHT

The six surviving heads of the Eight Orders are huddled together, looking down over the parapet.

Below them some of the crowd place a BIG RED STAR on the University wall.

Jiglad leans over to look.

>   JIGLAD WERT
> Is it just me, or does that look
> rather like a very large target?

The wizards look up to the even larger star, alarmed.

Beneath them the Rabble-rouser is leading the chanting.

>   RABBLE-ROUSER
> Let the star destroy the false
> wizards!

He has the crowd in the palm of his hands.

>   CROWD
> Destroy all wizards! Destroy all
> wizards! Destroy all wizards!

The wizards huddle closer together.

>   LUMUEL PANTER
> The trouble is, the Archchancellor
> is just not a team player.

>   JIGLAD WERT
> There is, of course, the tradition of
> dead men's pointy shoes.

               LUMUEL PANTER
          You mean . . . create a vacancy in
          the Archchancellor's department
          sort of thing . . . ?

               JIGLAD WERT
          Very well. We need a volunteer.
          Anyone?

     He looks around. No one moves.

               JIGLAD WERT
          Anyone?

     Jiglad sighs.

               JIGLAD WERT
          Everyone then.

               HEAD LIBRARIAN
          Ook!

     He holds up a banana.

     They all look down at the banana, and
     have the same idea.

INT. UNSEEN UNIVERSITY/OUTSIDE GALDER'S STUDY - DAY

Trymon steps out of the room but before his foot falls he looks down, and avoids stepping on a BANANNA SKIN on the floor. His foot falls solidly onto the flagstone next to it which depresses slightly. There is a hissing sound.

SC. 2/64 — OUTSIDE GALDER'S STUDY

1. MEDIUM SHOT ON TRYMON AS HE EXITS GALDER'S STUDY.

2. CUT TO LOW ANGLE CU AS HE STOPS IN DOORWAY. LOOKS DOWN...

3A. ..TRYMON'S P.O.V. HIS FOOT HOVERS OVER....

SHOT CONT'D...

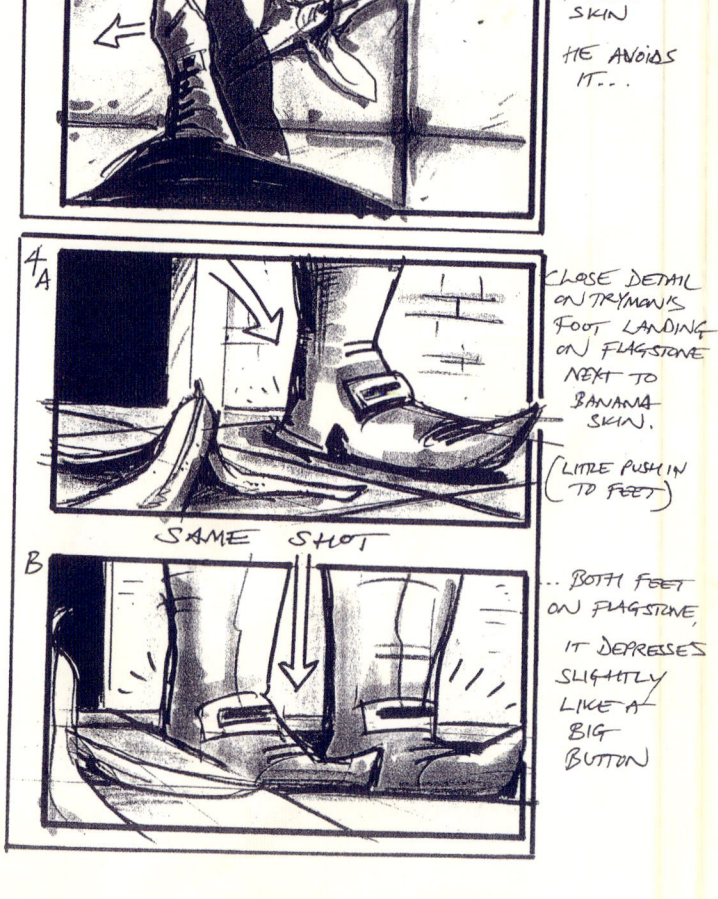

SC. 2/64 — OUTSIDE GALDER'S STUDY

3B. ....A BANANA SKIN. HE AVOIDS IT...

4A. CLOSE DETAIL ON TRYMON'S FOOT LANDING ON FLAGSTONE NEXT TO BANANA SKIN. (LITTLE PUSH IN TO FEET)

SAME SHOT

4B. ..BOTH FEET ON FLAGSTONE, IT DEPRESSES SLIGHTLY LIKE A BIG BUTTON

Trymon looks down and picks up the banana skin.

He tries to move his foot but his pointy shoe seems to be stuck to the floor.

He looks up.

Above him a hatch slides back directly above his head and LIQUID CEMENT pours from it.

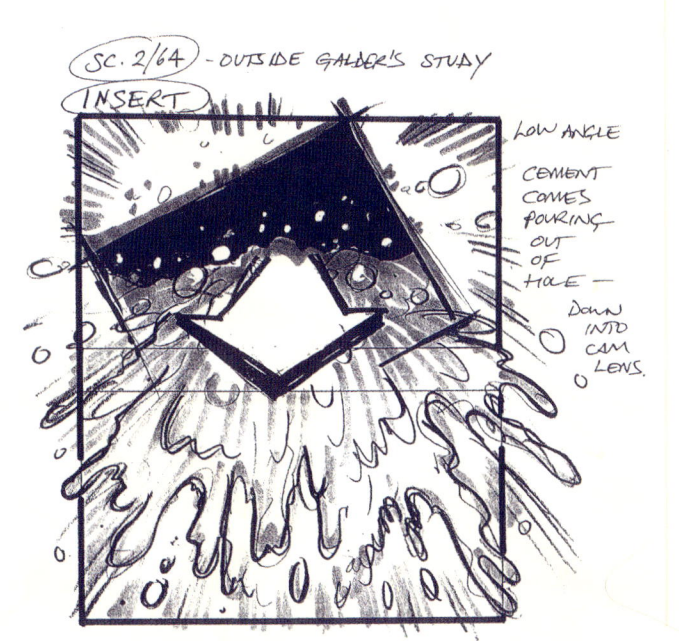

SC. 2/64 - OUTSIDE GALDER'S STUDY
INSERT

LOW ANGLE
CEMENT COMES POURING OUT OF HOLE — DOWN INTO CAM LENS.

Trymon yells and the wall spatters with concrete.

CAMERA pans down on a sticky person-sized cement pile, complete with protruding pointy shoes, exactly where Trymon would have been.

SC. 2/64 - OUTSIDE GALDER'S STUDY

12A — BACK TO WIDE ANGLE SEE PILE OF CEMENT WITH POINTY SHOES STICKING OUT.

B — THEN TRYMON POPS HIS HEAD OUT FROM BEHIND CEMENT AND...

...STEPS INTO THE OPEN IN HIS SOCKS.

He brushes himself down and glares at the banana skin. Then, in a moment of uncontrolled rage, he throws it on the floor and stamps on it viciously over and over again.

EXT. RIVER SNARL JETTY - DAY

Herrena and her captives arrive by the jetty.

> **HERRENA**
> Wait.

At the crude jetty is a big bronze gong. Weems picks up the hammer and hits it.

A cloaked figure on the ferry stirs and then pulls the ferry over.

Herrena strides out to meet him as Rincewind jiggles, trying to see what's going on.

The cloaked figure steps down onto the jetty to Herrena.

> **HERRENA**
> You're not the usual ferryman. I've been here before. The usual man is a big fellow.

The figure neither moves nor speaks

> **HERRENA**
> Okay.

Herrena returns to the others.

> **HERRENA**
> Two of you, grab him.

> **COHEN THE BARBARIAN**
> Daft cow.

There is a pause.

The two men nearest to the bowed figure look at each other, shrug and each take a shoulder. The ferryman is about half their size.

> **HERRENA**
> You, shut up. Let's see what's under that robe.

Cohen throws back his hood and his fists smack into the guards to either side. He punches Herrena, who staggers away.

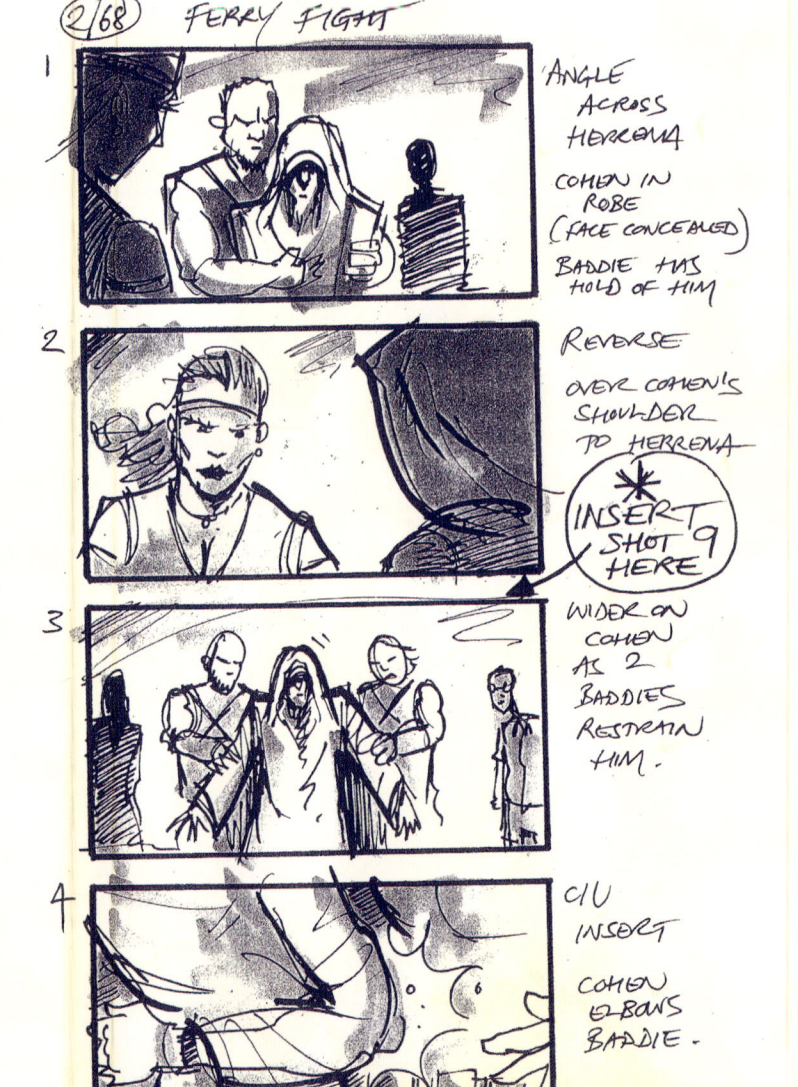

2/68 FERRY FIGHT

1. ANGLE ACROSS HERRENA — COHEN IN ROBE (FACE CONCEALED) BADDIE HAS HOLD OF HIM
2. REVERSE OVER COHEN'S SHOULDER TO HERRENA — *INSERT SHOT 9 HERE*
3. WIDER ON COHEN AS 2 BADDIES RESTRAIN HIM.
4. C/U INSERT COHEN ELBOWS BADDIE.

2/68 FERRY FIGHT

5. CRACK CRACK — COHEN BACKHANDS BOTH BADDIES
6. C/U INSERT COHEN FIST IN ONE BADDIE'S FACE

TWOFLOWER
(delighted)
Hey.

Cohen curses as he struggles to untangle his sword from his robe while hopping crabwise towards Herrena.

With a cry of triumph Cohen manages to free his sword and waves it triumphantly, severely wounding a man creeping up behind him.

HERRENA
Kill them both. I'll deal with this old fool.

Rincewind groans, grits his teeth and jerks his head backwards hard. There is a scream from the guard behind him and Rincewind falls forward, landing heavily in the mud.

Herrena lunges at Cohen, who . . .

. . . parries the thrust and grunts as his arm twinges.

The blades clang wetly.

Rincewind manages to get up just as Weems' hand drops onto his shoulder and a fist slams into his head. Rincewind goes down again.

There is a creak and the sound of scurrying feet from the bushes as the Luggage surges towards them, knocking over one guard and heading for Weems. Weems stares at it in horror, turns and runs.

Herrena is forced to back away as a cunning upward sweep from Cohen nearly disarms her.

Rincewind staggers towards Twoflower and tugs at him ineffectually.

RINCEWIND
Time to get going. Come on.

Herrena's sword spins out of her hand and stands quivering in the dirt.

TWOFLOWER
I say, well done. Excellent, sir.

With a snort of satisfaction Cohen brings his own sword back, goes momentarily cross-eyed, gives a little yelp of pain and stands absolutely motionless.

COHEN THE BARBARIAN
Ooh the back. Oh. Ooh. Ooh. Ooh.

Herrena looks at him, puzzled. She makes an experimental move in the direction of her own sword and when nothing happens, grabs it, tests its balance, and stares at Cohen.

Only his agonised eyes move to follow her as she circles him cautiously.

HERRENA
I don't know who you are or where you're from and there's nothing personal about this, you understand.

She raises the blade in both hands.

There is a sudden movement in the mists and the dull thud of a heavy piece of wood hitting a head.

Herrena looks bewildered for a second and then falls forward.

Bethan drops the branch she has been holding and looks at Cohen. Then she grabs him by the shoulders, sticks her knee in the small of his back, gives a businesslike twist and lets him go.

An expression of bliss passes across his face. He gives an experimental bend

BETHAN
Are you okay?

COHEN THE BARBARIAN
Oh, ish . . . that ish . . . ish cured.

Twoflower turns to Rincewind.

TWOFLOWER
My father used to recommend hanging from a door.

RINCEWIND
Hmm.

EXT. FERRY/BANK OF THE RIVER SNARL – DAY

The star is a lurking glow on the horizon. Cohen is having his back massaged. He watches the Luggage settle down.

RINCEWIND
We really ought to be going.

COHEN THE BARBARIAN
I don't shuppose you'd be intereshted in shelling the Luggage?

Twoflower shakes his head.

TWOFLOWER
No, I couldn't possibly do that.

COHEN THE BARBARIAN
I wash looking for a preshent for Bethan, you shee. We're getting married.

                    TWOFLOWER
          That's great.

                    BETHAN
          We thought you ought to be the
          first to know.

          She blushes.

                    RINCEWIND
          That's very . . . mmm . . .

                    TWOFLOWER
          This is cause for celebration. I am
          pretty sure that I have some travel
          biscuits and water in my Luggage.

          Twoflower starts to look in the Luggage.

          Rincewind pulls Cohen to one side.

                    RINCEWIND
          You . . . you serious about getting
          married?

                    COHEN THE BARBARIAN
          Any objectionsh?

                    RINCEWIND
          Oh no, no, no, no. No, I was just
          thinking, you know, that she's . . .
          in her twenties and you . . . are of
          the elderly persuasion.

                    COHEN THE BARBARIAN
          Time to settle down, you mean?

Rincewind gropes for words.

              RINCEWIND
No, I was thinking more of the . . . physically, the age difference about, um—

           COHEN THE BARBARIAN
I shee what you mean. The shtrain. Yeah, I hadn't looked at it like that.

             RINCEWIND
I hope I haven't upset anything.

Rincewind straightens up.

           COHEN THE BARBARIAN
Oh no, no, no, don't apologise 'cause you're right to point it out.

He gets to his feet.

           COHEN THE BARBARIAN
You know, shometimes you jusht have to take rishks. Now don't be offended, but I think we'll go ahead with the wedding anyway and, well . . . just have to hope she'sh strong enough.

             RINCEWIND
Will we get to Ankh-Morpork by dawn?

           COHEN THE BARBARIAN
Absolutely.

Cohen turns to the others.

           COHEN THE BARBARIAN
Right. Who wants to learn how to row a ferry to Ankh-Morpork?

Twoflower raises his hand.

INT. UNSEEN UNIVERSITY/OCTAVO ROOM - DAY

The eyes of the carved creature in the lectern supporting the Octavo blink as the Octavo rages above it.

SC.2/77 OCTAVO ROOM

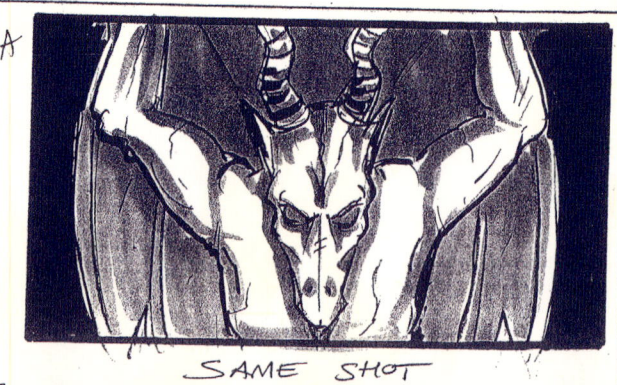

CLOSE ON OCTAVO LECTERN SCULPTURE

SAME SHOT

. . . IT'S EYES FLASH OPEN!

Through the grille in the door TRYMON'S greedy EYES peer.

INT. UNSEEN UNIVERSITY/OUTSIDE OCTAVO ROOM DOOR - DAY

Trymon turns, agitated and paces purposefully away. From his robe he produces the BANANA SKIN . . .

INT. UNSEEN UNIVERSITY/GALDER WEATHERWAX'S STUDY – DAY

Trymon is standing with his arms braced at the head of the table addressing the nervous-looking Heads of the Orders.

          TRYMON
The reason that I have gathered you here today is to announce that there will be a meeting . . . with an agenda . . . with just one item on it.

          GANMACK TREEHALLET
An agendum.

          TRYMON
I'm sorry?

Ganmack shrinks back from Trymon.

          JIGLAD WERT
We're assuming that this must be to do with the news that your hero has failed to capture Rincewind.

The wizards murmur in timid agreement.

          TRYMON
            (shouting)
I don't recall you being minuted to talk.

He slams the banana skin down.

The Heads of the Orders stop talking and stare at it.

          TRYMON
There will be a meeting . . . to consult the Octavo.

. . . and then look at each other, worried.

          LUMUEL PANTER
With only seven spells?

          JIGLAD WERT
Are you sure that's wise, Archchancellor?

          TRYMON
We have gone beyond wisdom.

EXT. ANKH-MORPORK/DOCKS - DAY

The star is bigger than the Disc's own sun and the city is soaked in red light.

Rincewind, Twoflower, Cohen and Bethan step off the ferry looking decidedly dishevelled and tired.

> **RINCEWIND**
> Ankh-Morpork. Pearl among Cities.

Rincewind peers along the quayside, radiantly happy.

> **RINCEWIND**
> There's no city in the multiverse which can rival Ankh-Morpork for its smell.

He sniffs the air.

> **RINCEWIND**
> Look, come on.

EXT. ANKH-MORPORK/JEWELLER'S - DAY

They walk into the city. There is a lot of traffic going the other way.

Twoflower sees a merchant painting a RED STAR on to his sign.

> **TWOFLOWER**
> What's he doing?

Cohen peers at merchant's signs until . . .

> **COHEN THE BARBARIAN**
> Thish ish what I've been looking for. We'll join you shortly.

> **RINCEWIND**
> What, a jeweller's?

> **COHEN THE BARBARIAN**
> It's a shurprishe.

Cohen goes over to the shop.

> **COHEN THE BARBARIAN**
> You wait here, Bethan.

Cohen goes into the shop.

Twoflower stops one of the people heading out of the city.

> **TWOFLOWER**
> Excuse me . . . why's everyone leaving?

The refugee grabs him tightly.

> **BIG STAR MAN**
> The star's gonna crash into the Disc. We're all gonna burn up and die.

The man stares manically into Twoflower's eyes and then runs away.

Rincewind is still.

> **RINCEWIND/VOICE OF THE SPELL**
> The star is life, not death.

> **TWOFLOWER**
> What?

> **RINCEWIND**
> What, what?

Twoflower points an accusing finger.

> **TWOFLOWER**
> Your voice, it just went all crackly, it didn't sound like you.

> **RINCEWIND**
> It's the Spell, it's trying to take me over. It knows what's going to happen.

Twoflower looks around him.

Almost every door is painted with a large RED STAR.

> **TWOFLOWER**
> But why are they painting all the stars? They think it will ward it off or something?

> **RINCEWIND**
> No, that's not gonna work but I think I know what will. Come on.

Rincewind strides away again. Twoflower follows.

EXT. ANKH-MORPORK/JEWELLER'S - DAY

LACKJAW, the dwarf jeweller, shows Cohen out of his shop. He walks over to Bethan with enormous pride.

> **LACKJAW**
> Strangest thing I've ever made but practical, I'll give you that. What did you say they were called again?

When Cohen opens his mouth to smile at Bethan little pinpoints of bright light illuminate all the shadows.

> **COHEN THE BARBARIAN**
> Dentures made from trolls' teeth.

Bethan smiles with delight.

Cohen gestures to Bethan.

          COHEN THE BARBARIAN
This is Bethan, my betrothed. Is there anywhere round here where I can get a wedding dress?

          BETHAN
Ah!

Cohen pauses lovingly, savouring the words.

          COHEN THE BARBARIAN
...and a steak?

EXT. ANKH-MORPORK/BONFIRE STREET - DAY

Rincewind and Twoflower turn a corner . . .

. . . and see a bonfire of BOOKS in the middle of the street. A woman throwing books into it turns around and scowls at the newcomers. She has a red star painted on her forehead.

Rincewind points to the bonfire.

> RINCEWIND
> What, what are you . . . what are you doing?

The star woman gazes intently at Rincewind's left ear.

> BOOK BURNER WOMAN
> Ridding the Disc of Wickedness.

Rincewind pulls his hat off quickly and hides it from view.

He sees the heavy book the woman is holding. Its cover is crusted with strange red and black stones.

> RINCEWIND
> That's the Necrotelecomicon.

> BOOK BURNER WOMAN
> Yes. Wizards use it to contact the dead. How did you know that?

> RINCEWIND
> Oh, I just, you know, just, just guessed.

A big man with a STAR on his head steps forward.

> BIG STAR MAN
> You've got the big box on legs. He looks like a wizard.

A circle of grey-faced, red star-painted, solemn people stare at the wizard.

Rincewind looks terrified.

INT. UNSEEN UNIVERSITY/OCTAVO ROOM - DAY

The door opens and the wizards enter tentatively.

> TRYMON
> Gentlemen . . . the light fantastic.

The wizards behind him look extremely worried.

> JIGLAD WERT
> We're safe so long as we don't touch the book.

He slumps.

      TWOFLOWER
 What?

Twoflower grabs his shoulders and looks at him.

      TWOFLOWER
 When I look at you, all I see is a wizard.

      RINCEWIND
 Wizard?

      TWOFLOWER
 Yes, you're a wizard, now act like it. Put your hat on.

      TRYMON
 Let's see.

Trymon holds up a scroll, unfurls it, and reads aloud.

      TRYMON
 To appease It, the thynge that is the Guardian. Be silenced and return to the darkness.

The light retreats into the Octavo.

EXT. ANKH-MORPORK/BONFIRE STREET - DAY

The group of star people advance menacingly towards Rincewind and Twoflower.

Rincewind takes a deep breath.

He raises his hands in the classic wizard's pose . . . and then brings them down again.

      RINCEWIND
 Argh! Oh, what am I talking about? I can't do magic.

RINCEWIND
            Act like it.

                    TWOFLOWER
            Yeah.

He looks at Twoflower, who smiles, and
then at the advancing crowd. He raises
his hands again.

                    RINCEWIND
            Yeah, yeah. All right. Stand back or
            I'll fill you full of magic.

                    STAR REFUGEE
            All the magic's gone. Star has
            taken it away.

                    RINCEWIND
            I mean it.

In his eyes, RUNES begin to take shape.

His arms rise of their own volition. His
mouth opens and shuts and a voice that
isn't his, old and dry, comes out.

                    RINCEWIND
            Asoniti! Kyorucha! Beazleblor!

Octarine fire flashes from under his
fingernails.

An octarine mist weaves from Rincewind
out to the man, and pokes him in the
chest. He is thrown backwards.

                    RINCEWIND
            Oh, oh.

Rincewind stares at his hand in
horror . . . and faints.

Twoflower catches him.

There is a pattering of feet from
several alleyways ad suddenly a dozen
STAR PEOPLE are advancing on them.

Twoflower grabs Rincewind's limp hand
and holds it up threateningly.

                    TWOFLOWER
            Right, that's far enough. We're
            heavily armed—

Rincewind whispers something to him.

                    RINCEWIND
            (groggy loud whisper)
            Where's the Luggage?

Twoflower looks around. The Luggage is
missing.

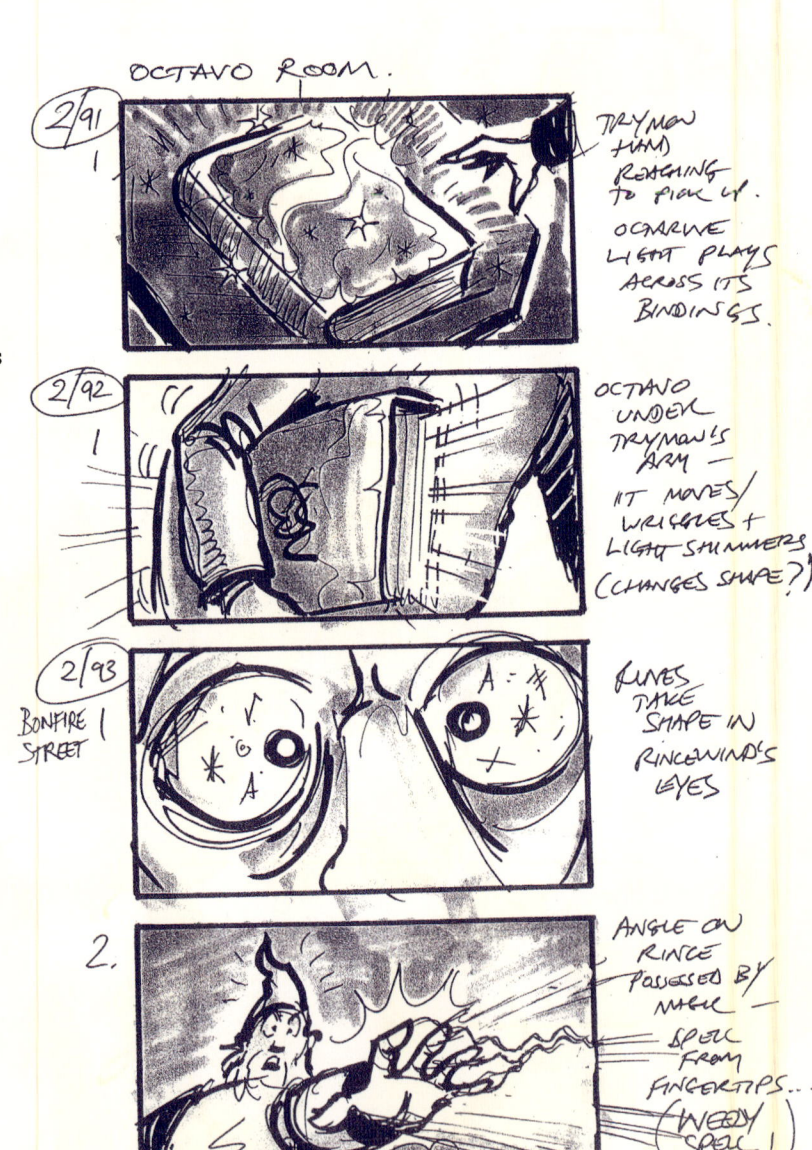

                TWOFLOWER
    What?

                RINCEWIND
    Where is the Luggage? Where's
    your Luggage?

                TWOFLOWER
    Well I often don't know where my
    Luggage is, that's what being a
    tourist is all about.

                RINCEWIND
    Ah.

Twoflower turns back to the advancing crowd.

                TWOFLOWER
    Right. I have a wizard and I'm not
    afraid to use him.

Twoflower spins Rincewind around by his arm. He looks at the crowd, waves Rincewind vigorously at them, and just as they back off a few steps, runs like hell.

As the crowd advances, the Luggage emerges from an alley and stares them down.

INT. UNSEEN UNIVERSITY/OCTAVO ROOM - DAY

The eight wizards insert their keys into the locks of the Octavo and, with worried glances at one another, turn them. There is a faint little snicking sound as the locks open.

The Octavo is unchained. A faint octarine light plays across its bindings.

Trymon reaches out and picks it up.

The other wizards gasp open-mouthed.

He turns towards the door.

                TRYMON
    To the Great Hall, gentlemen.

He reaches the door with the book tucked under his arm.

The others are halfway across the dungeon by the time he is through the door but as he crosses the threshold he turns, grips the handle and slams it. The KEY turns in the lock.

INT. UNSEEN UNIVERSITY/OUTSIDE OCTAVO ROOM DOOR - DAY

Trymon pockets the key.

He walks easily back along the corridor, ignoring the enraged screams of the wizards.

The Octavo squirms under his arm, but Trymon holds it tightly, and smiles the smile of imminent power.

EXT. DISCWORLD/GREAT A'TUIN - EVENING

Great A'Tuin slows. With flippers the size of continents the sky turtle fights the pull of the star and waits.

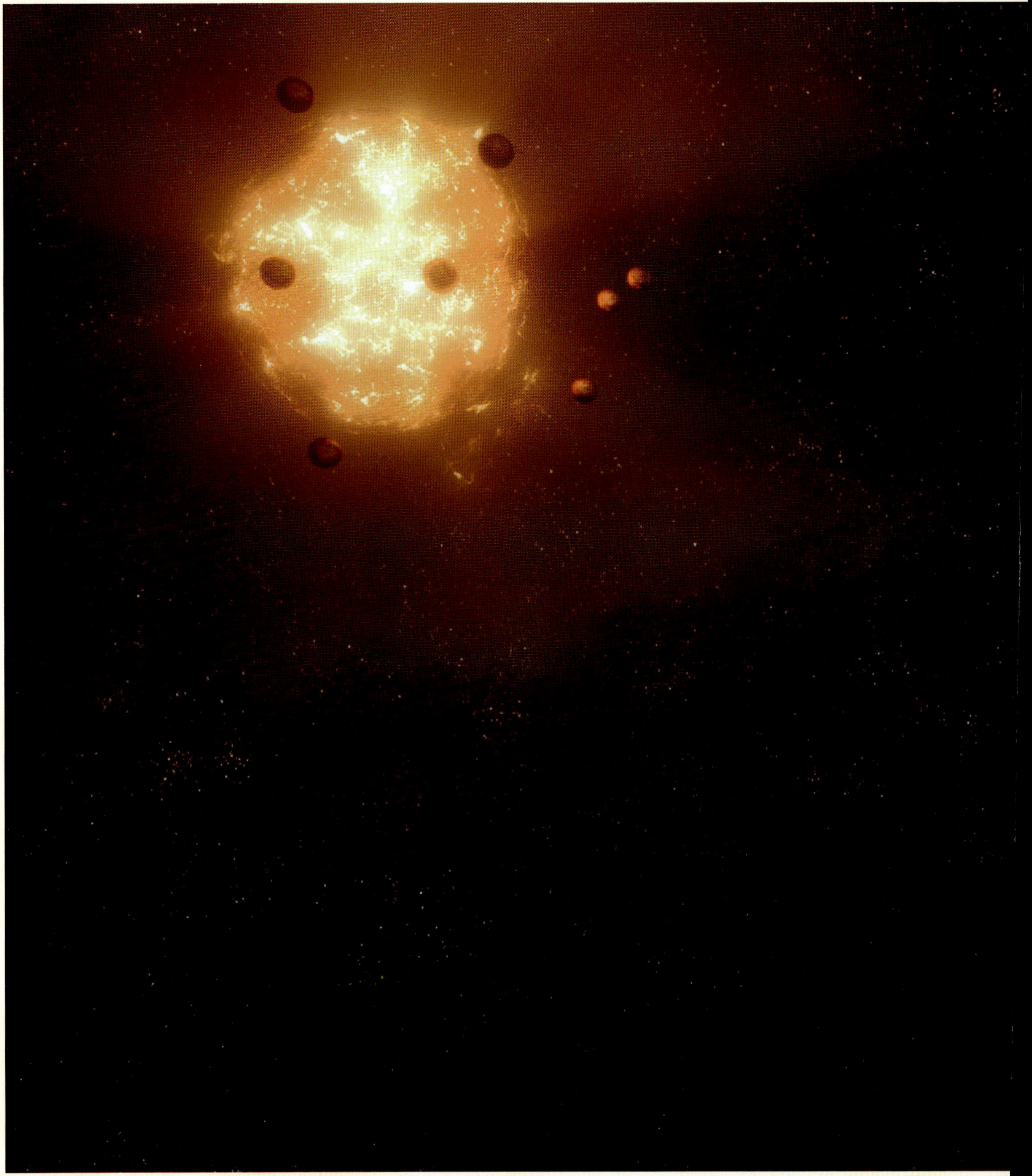

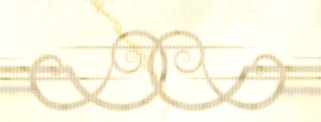

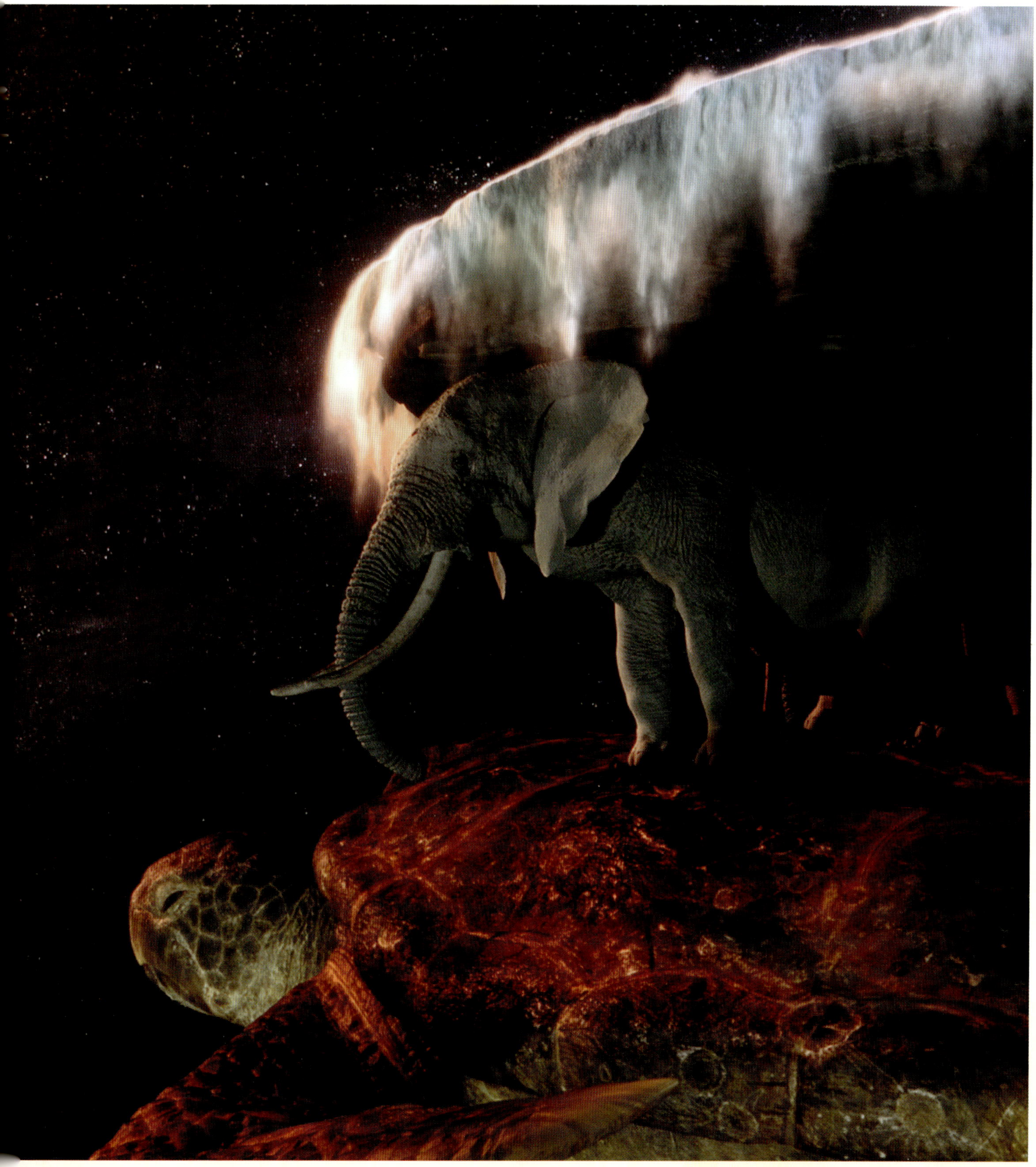

EXT. ANKH-MORPORK TUNNELS – EVENING

Twoflower stops. They can hear a distant chanting and the stamping of many feet.

Twoflower looks up.

The star is rising. As the Disc's own sun dips below the horizon the STAR climbs slowly into the sky until the whole of it is several degrees above the edge of the world.

> TWOFLOWER
> The star has spots on, look.

> RINCEWIND
> No, no, they're not spots, they're, they're, they are, they're things, things, things that go round the, round the star like the sun goes round, round the Disc. I mean, they're closer because...

> RINCEWIND/VOICE OF THE SPELL
> ...because...

Rincewind pauses, his face a mask of pain. He puts his hand to his ears and groans.

> TWOFLOWER
> They're definitely spots, yeah?

Just then the lead marchers come around the corner behind a ragged white banner with an eight-pointed star on it.

Twoflower pulls Rincewind into the safety of a doorway. Rincewind snatches off his hat.

The crowd hardly notice them, but run on, terrified.

Rincewind pulls Twoflower into the crowd, which sweeps them up in its passage.

> RINCEWIND
> All right. Come on, let's go.

> CROWD
> False wizards must die! False wizards must die! False wizards must die! False wizards must die! False wizards must die! False wizards must die!

Twoflower grabs a fur and wraps Rincewind up in it as they run with the crowd until they can duck into a side street.

INT. UNSEEN UNIVERSITY/GREAT HALL - EVENING

Rincewind sidles into the Great Hall. There are a few torches burning and it looks as though it has been set up for some sort of magical work. But the ceremonial candlesticks have been overturned and the complex octograms chalked on the floor are scuffed.

There is a distant crash, and a lot of shouting.

> **RINCEWIND**
> Come on. The lower cellars are this way.

He sets off through an arch, takes a torch from its bracket on the wall and starts down the steps.

INT. UNSEEN UNIVERSITY/CELLARS - EVENING

They hurry along the dripping passages, following the screamed curses and deep, hacking coughs.

> **TWOFLOWER**
> Anything that wheezes like that can't possibly be dangerous.

> **RINCEWIND**
> Don't look back.

INT. UNSEEN UNIVERSITY/OUSIDE OCTAVO ROOM DOOR - EVENING

The arrive at a door. There is a tiny grille.

           JIGLAD WERT (O.C.)
        Is anyone out there?

There is a sudden silence.

          LUMUEL PANTER (O.C.)
        Please.

Rincewind is suddenly like a terrified school boy.

              RINCEWIND
           (squeaking)
        Hello?

          LUMUEL PANTER (O.C.)
        Who's there?

              RINCEWIND
        Ah, ah, argh!

He sees Twoflower looking at him and coughs.

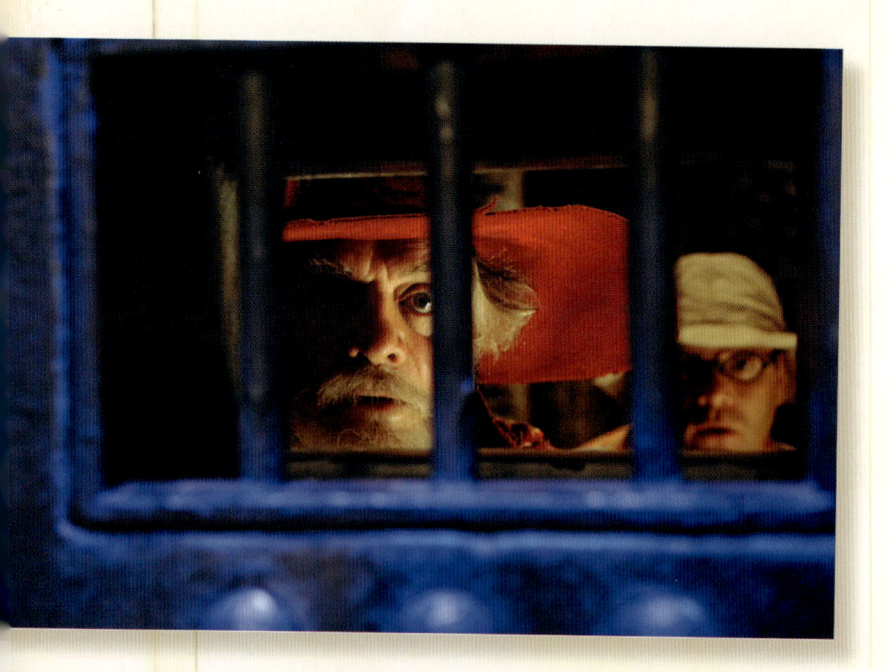

          JIGLAD WERT (O.C.)
        It's Rincewind.

              RINCEWIND
        (as deep as he can)
        Yes. That's right, it's Rincewind.

There is heated whispering on the other side of the door.

          LUMUEL PANTER (O.C.)
        Rincewind!

          JIGLAD WERT (O.C.)
        Did you bring the spell?

              RINCEWIND
        Er . . . yeah, who's in there?

          LUMUEL PANTER (O.C.)
           (haughtily)
        The Masters of Wizardry.

              RINCEWIND
        The Masters . . . why are you in there?

          LUMUEL PANTER (O.C.)
        We got locked in.

              RINCEWIND
        What, with the Octavo?

Whisper, whisper.

          LUMUEL PANTER (O.C.)
           (slowly)
        The Octavo, in fact is . . . not here.

Rincewind looks at the door . . . the very strong, heavy door.

              RINCEWIND
        Oh. Oh, okay.

          LUMUEL PANTER (O.C.)
        Now look, this is going to need a bit of magic so be a good fellow, run along and find a wizard, would you?

                    RINCEWIND
          Run along and find a . . . all right.

Rincewind looks affronted. He takes a
deep breath.

                    RINCEWIND
          Stand back. Find something to hide
          behind.

His voice is shaking only slightly.

               LUMUEL PANTER (O.C.)
          What for?

                    TWOFLOWER
          Oh, he means it. When you see that
          vein bulging in his forehead, he's
          serious.

                    RINCEWIND
          Will you shut up? Right.

               LUMUEL PANTER (O.C.)
          Oh very well.

Rincewind raises his arms and points
them at the door.

There is a flicker of runes in his eyes
as he looks at . . .

. . . the metal of the lock. Nothing
happens.

He concentrates harder. His face
scrunches up with concentration, and
Rincewind begins to moan with effort. An
octarine glow begins around his fingers
and slowly winds its way to, and into,
the lock.

There is a tiny grinding noise, and a
click.

Rincewind's face is a mask. Perspiration
drips off his chin. There is another
click, and the grinding of spindles.

INT. DOOR LOCK MECHANISM – EVENING

Metal rods flex in pitted grooves, give
in, push levers. Levers click, notches
engage.

INT. UNSEEN UNIVERSITY/OUTSIDE OCTAVO ROOM DOOR – EVENING

There is a long-drawn-out grinding noise
that leaves Rincewind on his knees.

The door swings open on pained hinges.
The wizards sidle out cautiously.

                    JIGLAD WERT
          Did you see Trymon on the way
          down here?

                    RINCEWIND
          No, why?

                    JIGLAD WERT
          Because he's stolen the Octavo.

Rincewind's head jerks up. His eyes focus.

               RINCEWIND
    Oh, *him*.

              JIGLAD WERT
    I always said he'd go a long way.

             LUMUEL PANTER
    And he'll go a lot further if he opens that book.

              TWOFLOWER
    Why? What will happen?

The wizards look at one another.

              JIGLAD WERT
    Well . . . one mind can't hold all the spells. It'll break down and leave a hole.

              TWOFLOWER
    In his head?

              JIGLAD WERT
    Um, no . . . in the fabric of the universe. He might think he can control it by himself but . . .

             LUMUEL PANTER
    But he hasn't got the spell in your head so we—

The sound starts off as a slow vibration then rises suddenly to a knife-edge whine like a human voice singing, or chanting, or screaming.

The wizards go pale. Then they turn and run up the steps.

               RINCEWIND
    Come on!

EXT. UNSEEN UNIVERSITY – NIGHT

There are crowds outside the building. Some people are holding torches. Everyone is staring at the Tower of Art.

The wizards push their way through and turn to look up.

The sky is full of moons. Each one is three times bigger than the Disc's own moon, and each is in shadow except for a pink crescent where it catches the light of the star.

[Storyboard panel annotated: UNSEEN UNI / 2/105 / 1. / Low angle tower (flames at top). Big star – sky full of moons.]

But in front of everything the top of the Tower of Art is an incandescent fury with shapes dimly formed within it.

Some of the wizards sink to their knees.

              JIGLAD WERT
    He's done it. He's opened the pathway.

              TWOFLOWER
    Are those things demons?

              JIGLAD WERT
    Demons would be a picnic compared to what's trying to come through up there.

              TWOFLOWER
    What do you propose to do about it?

They all turn to look at him.

Twoflower is glaring at them, arms folded.

> **RINCEWIND**
> Oh, it's all over, you see. You can't put the spells back in the book, you can't un-say what has been said.

> **TWOFLOWER**
> You can try.

Rincewind sighs and turns to the other wizards. When he turns back . . .

. . . Twoflower isn't there.

A sword is snatched from one of the star people.

Rincewind's eyes turn inevitably towards the base of the Tower of Art . . . just in time to see the tourist, sword inexpertly in hand, as he disappears into a door . . .

Rincewind sighs, and runs towards the door.

> **RINCEWIND**
> Oh, get out of my way.

The wizards try to avoid one another's eyes. There's mumbling. Then they all look at each other.

INT. UNSEEN UNIVERSITY/TOWER OF ART STAIRS – NIGHT

Twoflower is already several turns up the stairs.

Twoflower turns to see Rincewind catching up with him. He flourishes his looted sword.

Rincewind hops after him, keeping close to the wall.

> **RINCEWIND (O.C.)**
> Listen . . . you don't understand. There are unimaginable horrors up there.

Twoflower stops.

> **TWOFLOWER**
> I've always wanted to do something like this. I mean, this is an adventure, isn't it?

Rincewind opens and shuts his mouth until . . .

> **RINCEWIND**
> You are definitely mad.

The wizards reach them, coughing horribly and fighting for breath.

The light above them goes out. The terrible noises die as if strangled. Silence fills the tower.

> **RINCEWIND**
> It's stopped.

> **TWOFLOWER**
> Huh.

Something moves, high up against the circle of red sky. It falls slowly, turning over and over and drifting from side to side. It hits the stairs a turn above them.

It is the OCTAVO. But it lies on the stone as limp and lifeless as any other book, its pages fluttering in the breeze that blows up the tower.

It slides to a stop beneath Twoflower's foot, and he cautiously opens the book.

> **TWOFLOWER**
> (whispering)
> They're blank. They're all completely blank.

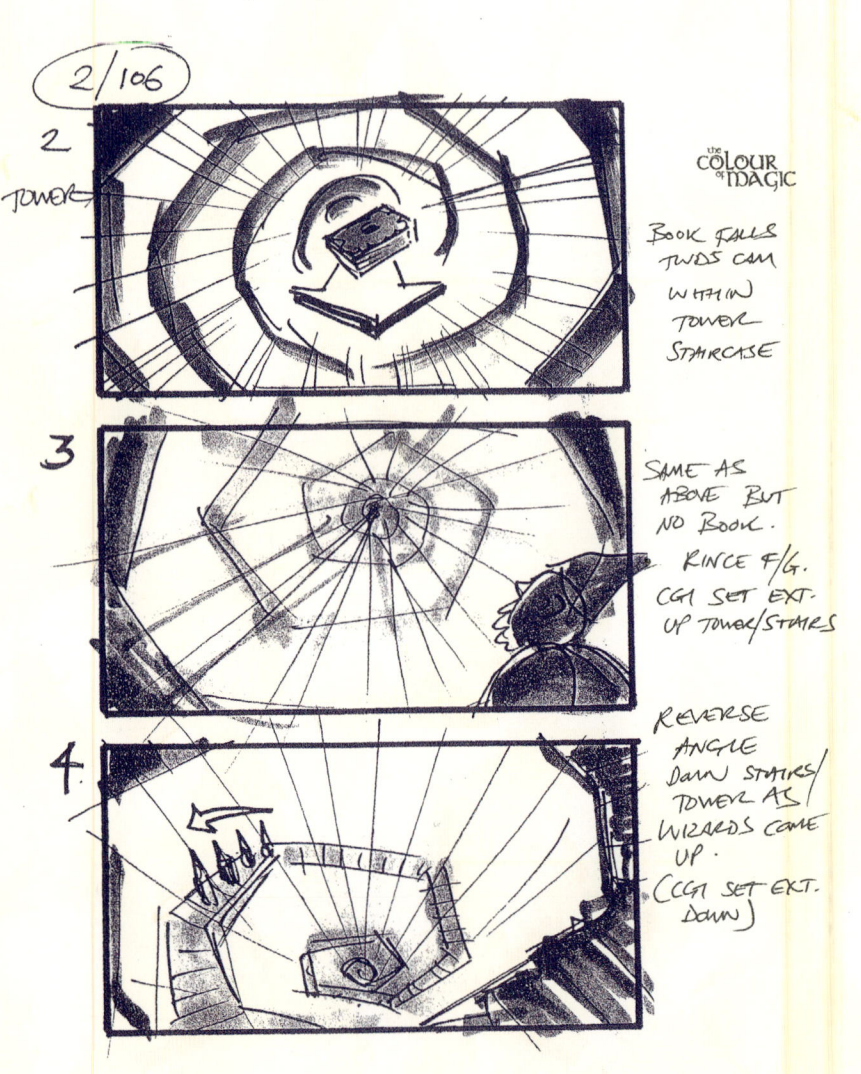

(2/106)

2 TOWER — BOOK FALLS TWDS CAM WITHIN TOWER STAIRCASE

3 — SAME AS ABOVE BUT NO BOOK. RINCE F/G. CGI SET EXT. UP TOWER/STAIRS

4 — REVERSE ANGLE DOWN STAIRS/TOWER AS WIZARDS COME UP. (CGI SET EXT. DOWN)

The Colour of Magic

                JIGLAD WERT
Then he did it. He's read the spells.

           GANMACK TREEHALLET
                Successfully too.

Instinctively they look up. There is no sound. Nothing moves against the circle of light.

                JIGLAD WERT
      I think we should go up and . . .
            congratulate him.

                RINCEWIND
          Congratulate him?

The wizards exchange knowing looks.

They set off up the spiral leaving Rincewind behind, scowling at the darkness.

             LUMUEL PANTER
      When you are advanced in the
      craft lad, you'll find there are
      times when the important thing is
      success.

Twoflower puts a hand on his shoulder. He is holding the Octavo.

                TWOFLOWER
      Well, that's no way to treat a book.
      The spine's bent right back.

He looks at the book, takes it from Twoflower and staggers off up the steps.

                RINCEWIND
      Right, give me that. A lad, am I?
      I've advanced in the craft, eh?
      I've already been walking around
      for years with one of the greatest
      spells in my head and didn't go
      totally insane, did I?

He considers the last question as he climbs.

                RINCEWIND
          No, you didn't.

EXT. UNSEEN UNIVERSITY/TOP OF TOWER OF ART – NIGHT

Rincewind's hat emerges at the top of the tower.

                TWOFLOWER
      Where are the other wizards?

                TRYMON
      Ah, Rincewind. Join us, won't you?

Rincewind and Twoflower make their way up the last of the steps, Rincewind holding the Octavo before him like a shield.

Trymon turns.

He looks up and into Trymon's eyes. It is everything he can do not to run in terror or be violently sick because . . .

. . . Trymon's eyes are EMPTY and GREY.

IRYMON [POSSESSED]
12-7-07

- EYES ARE HOLLOW SOCKETS
- GLOW FROM WITHIN SOCKETS
- RED FLAMES/SMOKE CURL FROM SOCKETS?

> TRYMON
> The Eighth Spell . . . give it to me.

Trymon blinks and his eyes revert to normal.

Rincewind backs away. He looks at the other wizards. They are immobile, like statues.

> TRYMON
> Give . . . me . . . the spell.

> RINCEWIND
> No, you'll have to try and take it . . . and I don't think you can.

Rincewind backs away.

> TRYMON
> Oh. But I only have to kill you . . . and it is mine.

Trymon sends a spell-blast shooting past Rincewind.

Rincewind runs towards the wizard statues.

EXT. UNSEEN UNIVERSITY/TOWER OF ART – NIGHT

The Head Librarian looks around to make sure he's not being watched. He has a BANANA in his mouth and starts to climb the tower.

He scuttles quickly upwards towards the very top . . .

EXT. UNSEEN UNIVERSITY/TOP OF TOWER OF ART – NIGHT

Trymon pursues Twoflower and Rincewind menacingly and slowly.

> TWOFLOWER
> These statues look like wizards.

> RINCEWIND
> They are the wizards.

Trymon turns and sends two big bolts from his eyes straight for Rincewind, who jumps behind one of the statues to avoid it. The bolt takes its head off.

SC. 2/107 TRYMON vs. RINCEWIND.

14 — WIDE ANGLE ON RINCEWIND

15 — REVERSE ON TRYMON — ARMS OUTSTRETCHED

16 — EX. ANGLE (SPLIT DIOPTER?) TRYMON DEEP F/G. TWOFL. BEHIND. TWOFL. CREEPS UP WITH SWORD.

17 — BACK TO SAME SHOT AS 15. TRYMON RAISES ARMS FOR SPELL...

TWOFLOWER
They are?

Rincewind's head appears cautiously behind the statue where the head should be. He ducks as another bolt flies past him.

RINCEWIND
They were.

Trymon advances on him.

TRYMON
There are worse things. I could clothe your body with ants. I have the power.

TWOFLOWER (O.C.)
I have a sword, you know.

Rincewind raises his head.

Twoflower is standing behind Trymon, holding a sword in exactly the wrong way. As Trymon turns to look at him he freezes at the sight of his grey sockets.

Trymon laughs and flexes his
fingers. For a moment his attention
is diverted.

Rincewind stands up and tries a
spell. Not a very dramatic-looking
spell.

A rather small BOLT OF LIGHTNING
flies towards Trymon, who turns just
in time to raise his hands so that
the spell slows right down and he
can absorb its power harmlessly.

              TRYMON
  Pathetic.

            RINCEWIND
  Pathetic? I'll show you
  pathetic.

Rincewind springs, striking Trymon
in the stomach with his head and
flinging his arms around him in
desperation.

Twoflower is knocked aside as they
slide along the stones.

Rincewind's wildly flailing elbow
catches Trymon in the neck. He
fights with a great deal of
whirlwind effort. Meanwhile
Twoflower is searching for his
sword.

           TWOFLOWER
  Hello?

Trymon manages to get several blows
in with his hands, which Rincewind
is far too high on rage
to notice . . .

Rincewind uses knees, feet, and
teeth as well and he is, in fact,
winning . . . which comes as a
shock to him as he kneels on
Trymon's chest hitting him
repeatedly about the head.

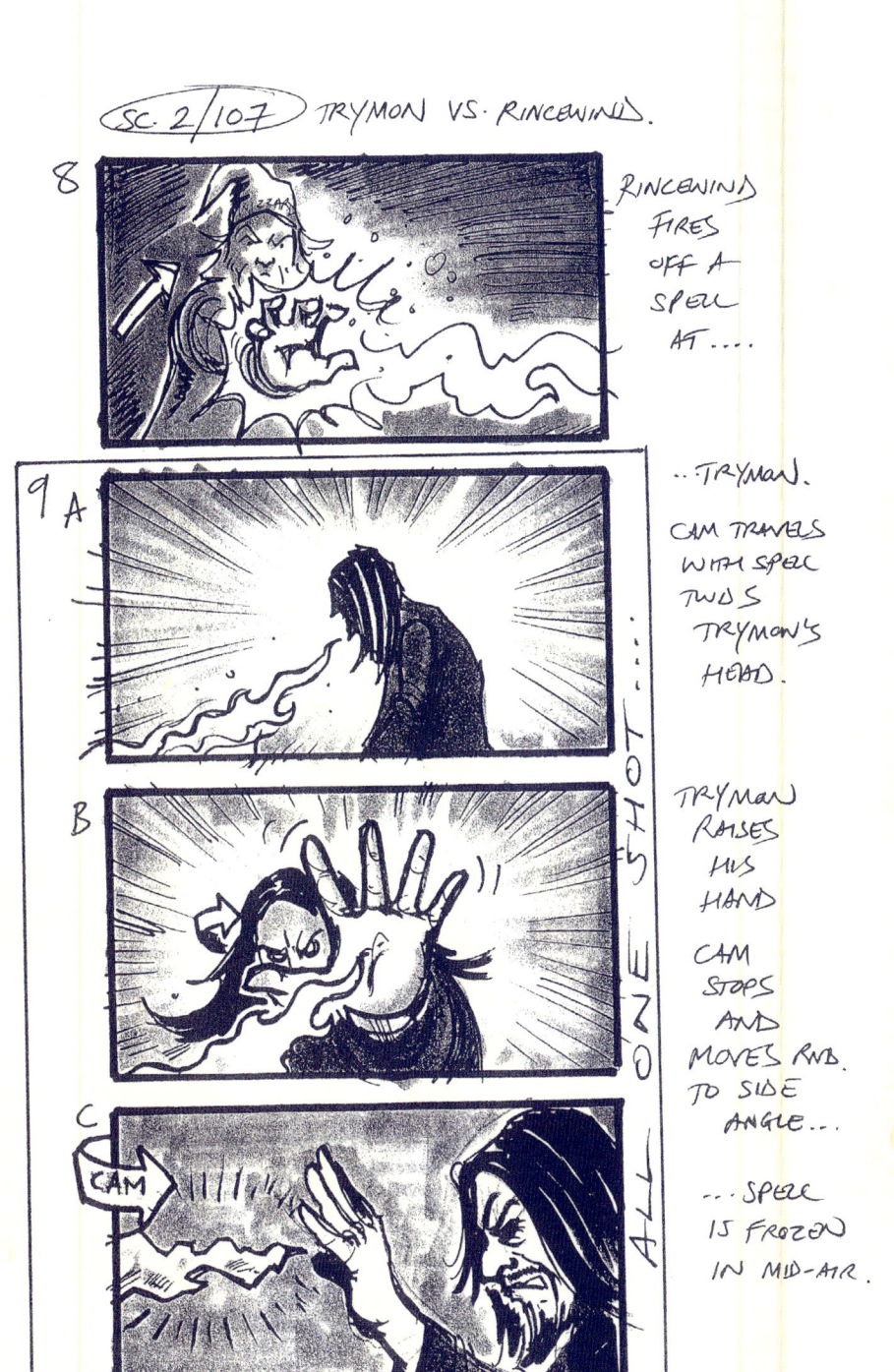

TWOFLOWER
Rincewind, where's the sword? I'll get it.

Rincewind struggles to his feet and lifts the Octavo above his head, ready to crush Trymon. But before he can drop the book he overbalances and topples backwards.

Trymon stands menacingly and walks slowly towards him.

Though flat on his back Rincewind raises his arms in the traditional spell-casting pose.

RINCEWIND
I have to warn you that . . . I'm a real wizard now.

Trymon snorts.

TRYMON
Then join your fellow wizards, you turgid little worm. I have no need of you now.

Rincewind, in terrified rage, starts to send a spell. He scrunches up his eyes, but nothing comes out.

TWOFLOWER
(finding the sword)
There it is.

TRYMON
Come. The little spell . . . unto me.

Trymon smiles a vicious smile, raises his arms and summons the spell, which begins to escape from Rincewind's eyes and make its way to Trymon.

RINCEWIND
(to Twoflower)
Now!

TWOFLOWER
Now what? Oh right.

Trymon sees Twoflower, with his eyes shut, prepared to strike and launches the Royal Fireworks of spells towards him.

Trymon casts another spell whizzing towards Rincewind who in complete panic looks down at the Octavo in his hands and instinctively raises it in front of his face.

The spell fizzes towards him, hits the Octavo and . . .

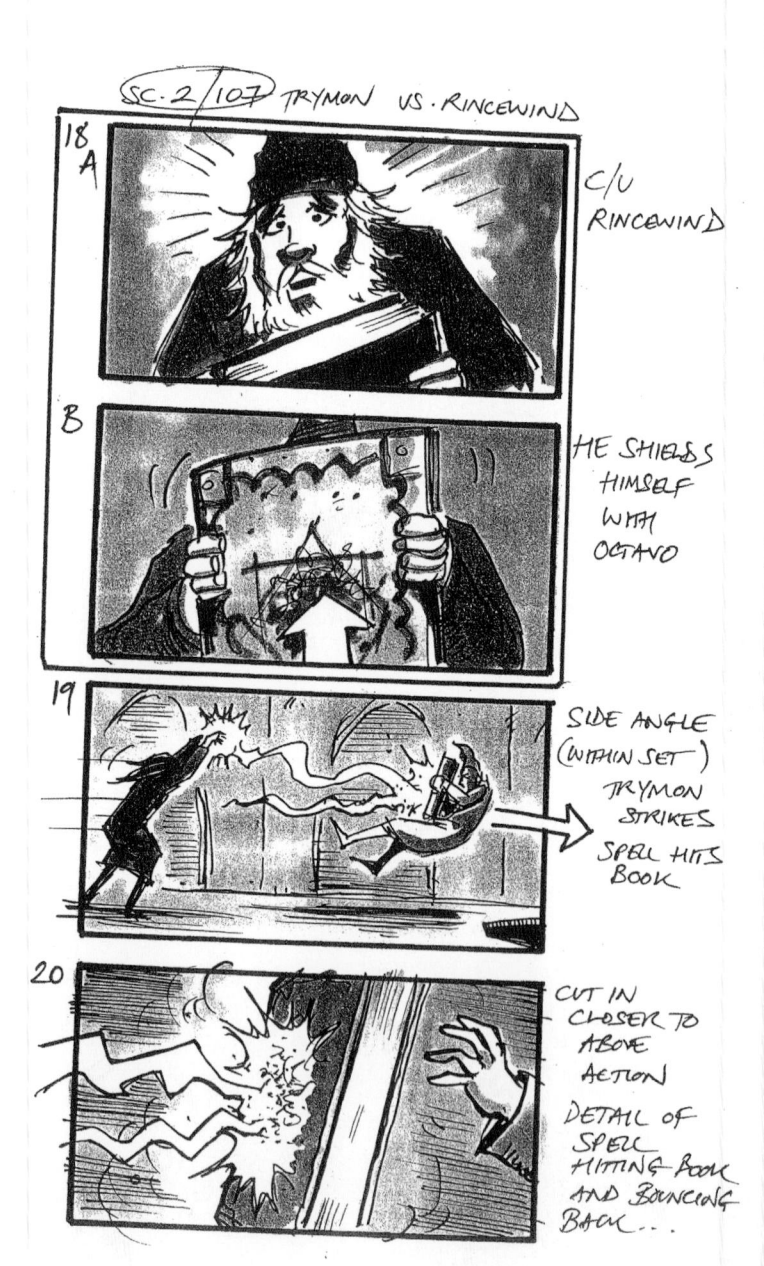

SC. 2/107 TRYMON VS. RINCEWIND

18A — C/U RINCEWIND

B — HE SHIELDS HIMSELF WITH OCTAVO

19 — SIDE ANGLE (WITHIN SET) TRYMON STRIKES SPELL HITS BOOK

20 — CUT IN CLOSER TO ABOVE ACTION DETAIL OF SPELL HITTING BOOK AND BOUNCING BACK...

. . . bounces back in the direction it came from, knocking Rincewind off his feet and reeling across the tower.

The spell whirls towards Trymon who nonchalantly raises a hand, sending it hurtling vertically into the air like a firework rocket. He strides towards the prostrate Rincewind, raises his hands, and suddenly slips. His legs fly in the air and he lands flat on his back.

Lying by Trymon's feet is . . . a BANANA SKIN.

Trymon looks up to see that his spell has reached its apex and is now falling back down towards him.

From the spell's POV we hurtle down towards Trymon's face which turns from victorious smugness to abject horror as it begins to freeze and become a stony grey colour.

Twoflower advances towards Trymon with his eyes closed and swings the sword inexpertly.

CLANG. He opens his eyes and turns slowly to look at his target.

Trymon has turned to stone.

EXT. UNSEEN UNIVERSITY/TOP OF TOWER OF ART - NIGHT

Twoflower is alone. It is eerily quiet. He sits bewildered.

Then seven fireballs rise out of the blackness and plunge into the discarded Octavo, which suddenly looks its old self.

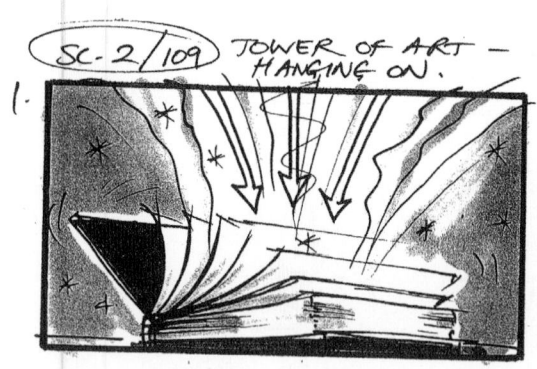

[Storyboard panel 1: SC-2/109 TOWER OF ART - HANGING ON. C/U OCTAVO. THE SPELLS RUSH BACK INTO THE BOOK AND PAGES FLUTTER.]

    TWOFLOWER
I suppose they're the spells.

    RINCEWIND (O.C.)
Twoflower.

The voice is echoing and just recognisable as Rincewind's.

Twoflower stops with his hand halfway to the book.

    TWOFLOWER
Yes? Is that . . . is that you, Rincewind?

Twoflower bends over the Octavo, speaking to it.

    RINCEWIND (O.C.)
Yes and I want you to do something very important for me, Twoflower.

Twoflower looks around. He pulls himself together.

    TWOFLOWER
    (with pride)
Yes, I'll . . . I'm ready. What is it you want me to do?

Rincewind's voice rises from the depths of the stairwell.

    RINCEWIND (O.C.)
I want you to come over here and help me up before my hand slips off this stone.

The Octavo snaps itself shut.

Twoflower opens his mouth, then shuts it quickly. He runs to the square hole and peers down.

By the ruddy light of the star he can just make out Rincewind's eyes looking up at him.

[Storyboard panel 2: WIDE ANGLE LOOKING STRAIGHT DOWN SPIRAL STAIRCASE. TWFL. HOLDS ONTO RINCEWIND. [+ TIGHTER OF THE SAME]]

[Storyboard panel 3: REVERSE - LOW ANGLE UP TO STRUGGLING TWOFL. (CGI SKY ABOVE)]

Twoflower lies on his stomach and reaches out.

Rincewind's hand grips his wrist.

> TWOFLOWER
> I'm glad you're alive.

> RINCEWIND
> Yes, so am I. Here, could you . . . could you now help me up?

He hangs around in the darkness for a bit.

> TWOFLOWER
> That might be a little difficult.

> RINCEWIND
> Why, what are you holding onto?

> TWOFLOWER
> To you.

> RINCEWIND
> Besides me.

> TWOFLOWER
> What do you mean besides you?

> RINCEWIND
> Uh, oh, bugger.

Rincewind grunts.

There is a flare of light far below, and shouting.

                RINCEWIND
    I don't know why it is, but ever
    since I've met you, I've spent a
    lot of my time hanging on by my
    fingertips over certain depths.
    Have you noticed that?

Twoflower wedges his toes into a gap in the flagstones and tries to make himself immobile by sheer force of will.

Rincewind looks up.

Standing over Twoflower looking down at him is DEATH.

Twoflower looks down as the leading torch comes around the last turn of the spiral to reveal the grinning face of Cohen. Behind him, hopping awkwardly is the LUGGAGE.

                RINCEWIND
    Oh it's you. Oh no, not again.
    Aaarrrghhh!

Rincewind's hand loses his grip just as . . .

. . . DEATH raises his scythe . . .

. . . and Cohen catches Rincewind by the hood. He jerks him unceremoniously onto the stones.

                DEATH
    I THINK I'VE JUST HAD ANOTHER NEAR-
    RINCEWIND EXPERIENCE.

He stomps off in a huff.

                RINCEWIND
    A little bit earlier would've been
    nice.

Unsteadily, with his arms screaming at him, Rincewind lets himself be helped back onto the roof of the tower.

He regains his feet.

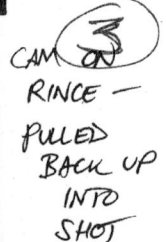

Cohen is looking at the seven senior wizards.

> **COHEN THE BARBARIAN**
> Funny place to put statues. No one can see them. Mind you, can't say they're up to much. Very poor work.

The sky is full of MOONS, huge cratered discs now ten times bigger than the Disc's tiny satellite.

Then his gaze falls on the Octavo, which is outlined in tiny flashes of octarine fire.

He hurries over to pick it up and thumbs through its pages.

They are thick with complex, swirling script that changes and reforms even as he looks at it. The last page is empty.

Rincewind takes a big breath.

> **RINCEWIND**
> This . . . this is where we say . . . goodbye.

He raises his hands over the Octavo.

> **RINCEWIND**
> Out.

From deep in the black of his pupils runes start to appear, pushing forward from the back of his head. There is a blue flash behind his eyes and the runes emerge from his eyes at speed, heading for the Octavo.

When he looks down at the page . . . it is full of runes again.

While Twoflower bustles and Cohen tries to lever the rings off the stone wizards, he opens the book at the first page and begins to read, his lips moving and his forefinger tracing each letter. As he mumbles each word it appears soundlessly in the air beside him, in bright colours that stream away in the night wind.

He turns over the page.

Other people are coming up the steps now.

           COHEN THE BARBARIAN
      What's he doing now?

The bulk of the star looms ever closer to the Disc. In the sky around it the new moons turn slowly and noiselessly.

The only sound is Rincewind's hoarse whispering as he turns page after page.

           TWOFLOWER
      Isn't all this magic exciting?!

Cohen looks at him blankly, paper halfway to his lips.

           COHEN THE BARBARIAN
      It's only lights. Hasn't even
      produced doves or billiard balls out
      of his sleeve.

There is a loud snap as Rincewind shuts the book. He stands up and looks around.

Everyone ducks instinctively, waiting for the explosion of white light or a scintillating fireball.

Nothing.

           COHEN THE BARBARIAN
      Is that it?

There is a general muttering from the crowd.

The wizard stares blearily at Cohen, and then looks blankly at the Octavo.

The book trembles in Rincewind's hands and lifts up into the air. The air around the Octavo glows. It rises sweetly, there is a sweet twanging noise and it seems to explode in a complicated silent flower of light which rushes outward, fades, and is gone.

EXT. DISCWORLD/GREAT A'TUIN – NIGHT

But something is happening much further up in the sky as . . . if it's possible for a sky turtle to change its expression, its face looks quite expectant. It stares fixedly at the eight spheres endlessly orbiting around the star, on the very beaches of space.

The spheres are CRACKING. Huge segments of rock break away and begin the long spiral down to the star. The sky fills with glittering shards.

EXT. UNSEEN UNIVERSITY/TOP OF TOWER OF ART – NIGHT

Twoflower stares raptly at the display overhead . . .

EXT. DISCWORLD/GREAT A'TUIN – NIGHT

From the wreckage of one hollow shell a very small SKY TURTLE paddles its way into the red light. It is barely bigger than an asteroid, its shell shiny with molten yolk.

240

241

COHEN THE BARBARIAN (O.C.)
Young worlds.

There are four small WORLD-ELEPHANT CALVES there, too. And on their backs is a DISCWORLD, tiny as yet, covered in smoke and volcanoes.

EXT. UNSEEN UNIVERSITY/TOP OF TOWER OF ART - NIGHT

. . . until his face changes with worry.

TWOFLOWER
Must get a picture of this. Might forget.

Sc 2/111 — TOWER OF ART / BABY TURTLES

1. C/U TWOFLOWER — STARES RAPTLY AT THE DISPLAY OVERHEAD

2. WIDE ANGLE FROM BEHIND TWOF. RINCE. COHEN BETHAN AS THEY LOOK OUT INTO SPACE — WATCHING THE FRESHLY TURTLES SWIMMING ALONG... "THE PICTURE BOX! I MUST GET A PICTURE OF THIS!"

EXT. DISCWORLD/GREAT A'TUIN - NIGHT

Great A'Tuin waits until all EIGHT baby turtles have freed themselves from their shells and are treading space and looking bewildered. Then they see A'Tuin and move closer to nuzzle it.

EXT. UNSEEN UNIVERSITY/TOP OF TOWER OF ART - NIGHT

Rincewind's face is fixed on the sky.

BETHAN
How could you ever forget? It's the most beautiful thing I've ever seen in my life.

Bethan isn't looking at him.

TWOFLOWER
Got it.

RINCEWIND
That's old Twoflower for you. He just appreciates beauty in his own way. I mean, if a poet sees a daffodil, he stares at it and then writes a long poem, but Twoflower would wander off and buy a book on botany and then, as he reads it . . . he would tread on the daffodil.

Rincewind looks out again across the Discworld.

EXT. DISCWORLD/GREAT A'TUIN - NIGHT

Carefully, the old turtle turns and with considerable relief sets out on the long swim to the blessedly cool bottomless depths of space.

The young turtles follow, orbiting their parent.

SC.2/112 - DISCWORLD/A'TUIN

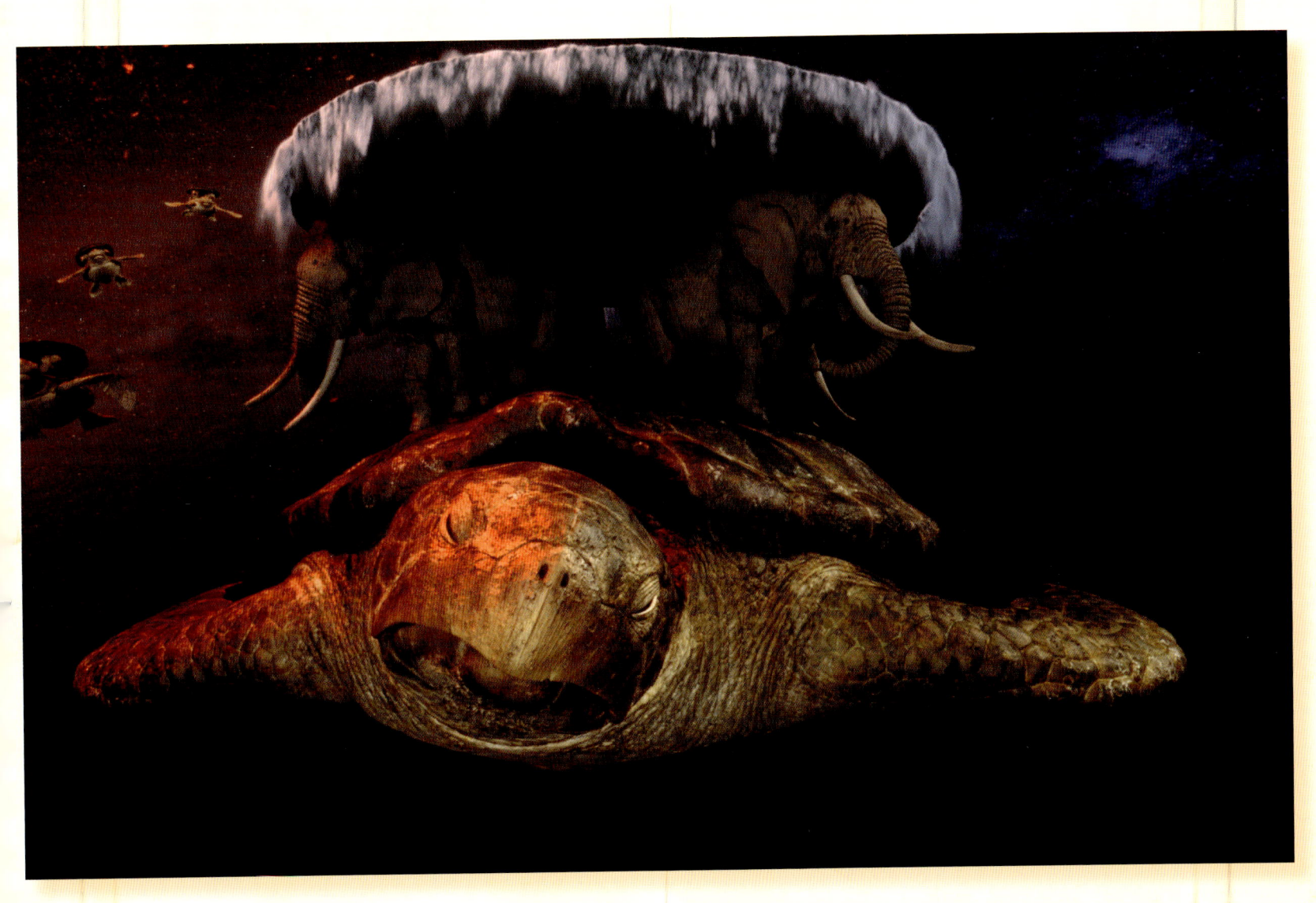

IN SPACE - GREAT A'TUIN SWIMS TWDS CAM WITH BABY TURTLES FOLLOWING CLOSE BEHIND... A'TUIN HAS A LOOK OF CONTENTMENT!

...GREAT A'TUIN GOES PAST CAM AND BABIES COME TWDS US

EXT. UNSEEN UNIVERSITY/TOP OF TOWER OF ART - NIGHT

Rincewind is vaguely aware of Twoflower's voice arguing with the picture imp.

     BETHAN
 The star. It's getting smaller.

The Disc's own sun rises. The star is already dwindling. Disc light pours across the enraptured landscape.

The ghosts of the baby turtles can just be seen, fading in the sky.

     TWOFLOWER
 It's like a sea of gold.

     RINCEWIND
 Golden syrup, more like.

Rincewind, Twoflower, Bethan, Cohen and even the Star People look out across the vista as the CAMERA pulls out.

     NARRATOR (V.O.)
 That is a nice dramatic ending. But life doesn't work like that and there are other things that have to happen.

The CAMERA passes the Octavo, which is slowly spinning in the air.

     NARRATOR (V.O.)
 There is the Octavo, for example.

As the sunlight hits it the book snaps shut and starts to fall back to the tower.

     NARRATOR (V.O.)
 And many of the observers realise that dropping towards them is the single most magical thing on the Discworld.

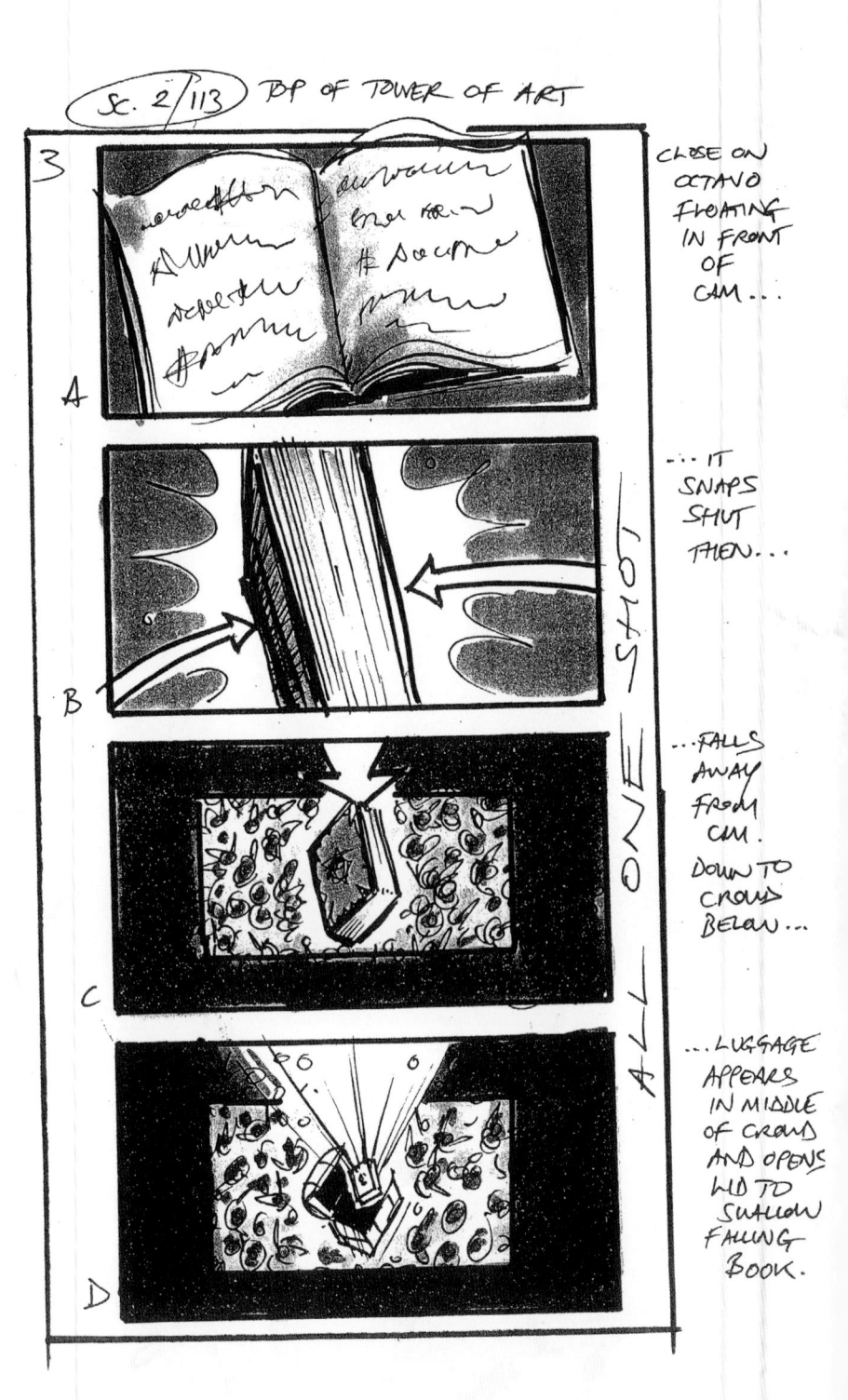

The crowd surges forward, hands outstretched.

Sc. 2/113 TOP OF TOWER OF ART

A — CLOSE ON OCTAVO FLOATING IN FRONT OF CAM...

B — ...IT SNAPS SHUT THEN...

C — ...FALLS AWAY FROM CAM. DOWN TO CROWD BELOW...

D — ...LUGGAGE APPEARS IN MIDDLE OF CROWD AND OPENS LID TO SWALLOW FALLING BOOK.

ALL ONE SHOT

The Octavo drops into the centre of the shouting mass. There is the snap of the Luggage's lid closing firmly.

                RINCEWIND
  Okay, right, come on. Oh dear. No, it's better off in there anyway. Come on.

Rincewind leads Twoflower firmly away.

                NARRATOR (V.O.)
  Later, Twoflower did ask the Luggage what it had done with the Octavo, but its expression could only be described as . . .

                TWOFLOWER
  What are they doing now?

He tries to see over the heads of the throng.

                NARRATOR (V.O.)
  Wooden.

                RINCEWIND
  They're trying to open the Luggage. Come on.

EXT. UNSEEN UNIVERSITY/BASE OF TOWER OF ART - DAY

Rincewind and Twoflower are walking away from the University gates.

          RINCEWIND
Ah. It's a nice day. Air like wine.

          TWOFLOWER
Rincewind, I've decided that I'm—

          RINCEWIND
You know, I think I might re-enroll. I think I could make a good go of this magic thing and graduate very well 'cause they do say that if it's summa cum laude, then the living is easy.

          TWOFLOWER
Well that's good—

          RINCEWIND
And of course there's plenty of room up top now that the big boys are on doorstep duty.

Rincewind looks over at a team of workmen who have rigged up a gantry on the roof and are lowering the STONE WIZARDS to the ground. The Head Librarian looks over to them.

          TWOFLOWER
Will they be able to be turned back?

Rincewind looks around.

The rope holding the statue slips on the gantry a little. The statue teeters and crashes to the ground, shattering.

                RINCEWIND
Probably not.

                TWOFLOWER
Will they be able to do something with Trymon?

                RINCEWIND
Yes . . . he'll make a very nice rockery.

Rincewind turns and waves at the workmen. He indicates the Librarian, who tries to hold his hand, and starts organising things. Rincewind takes a banana out of his pocket.

                RINCEWIND
Go on. You go and sort this all out. I think I could do very well with this magic lark . . .

They carry on walking.

                TWOFLOWER
The thing is, Rincewind, I'm going home.

                RINCEWIND
. . . and a sharp lad who's had some experience of the world could quite easily . . . sorry, what did you say?

                TWOFLOWER
I said I'm going home.

                RINCEWIND
                (astonished)
What home?

                TWOFLOWER
Home home. Back across the sea where I live, you know.

                RINCEWIND
Oh.

There is a pause.

                TWOFLOWER
You see, it occurred to me last night. All this travelling and seeing things is fine, but there's a lot of fun to be had in having been. You know, I'm . . . putting your pictures in a book and remembering things . . .

                RINCEWIND
There is?

                TWOFLOWER
Oh yeah, and the important thing about having a lot of things to remember is that you have to have some place to go afterwards where you can remember them. You see, you haven't really been anywhere until you've got back home.

TWOFLOWER
Well, that settles it then. He'll drop me at the Brown Islands and I can easily get a ship from there.

RINCEWIND
Oh, well, great.

At that moment Cohen and Bethan arrive at the quay. Bethan is in her wedding dress.

RINCEWIND
Oh, you found a priest then.

BETHAN
Yes and Cohen didn't even try to kill him for his valuables.

TWOFLOWER
It's a great dress.

Rincewind runs the sentence across his mind again.

RINCEWIND
Oh, good. Well, if that's the way you see it . . . when are you going?

TWOFLOWER
Today, I think. There's bound to be a ship going part of the way.

RINCEWIND
Yes, I . . . I expect so.

Rincewind looks at his feet.

EXT. ANKH-MORPORK/QUAYSIDE - DAY

Twoflower is stood with a ship's captain by his vessel.

Rincewind waits on the quayside until Twoflower has finished paying.

COHEN THE BARBARIAN
                Thank you. I stole it myself.

Twoflower looks thoughtful for a moment.
Then he opens the Luggage and pulls out
a box.

                    TWOFLOWER
                Look . . . this is for you two.

Twoflower hands them the box. It is full
of GOLD RHINU.

                    COHEN THE BARBARIAN
                Oh.

                    TWOFLOWER
                I know it can be expensive setting
                up home for the first time.

Rincewind looks inside the box.

                    RINCEWIND
                Or a small kingdom, even.

Bethan can't believe it. While Cohen
looks in the box she gives Twoflower a
hug and a kiss on the cheek.

Twoflower flushes and then turns to
Rincewind.

                    TWOFLOWER
                I've also thought about something I
                can give you.

                    RINCEWIND
                Oh, please, really no, you don't
                have to—

Twoflower rummages in the Luggage and
produces a large sack.

                    TWOFLOWER
                It's all yours. I don't need it any
                more and it won't really fit on my
                wardrobe.

He shuts the Luggage's lid.

                    RINCEWIND
                What?

                    TWOFLOWER
                The Luggage. Don't you want it?

A member of the crew comes and relieves
Twoflower of his sack.

                    RINCEWIND
                Oh. Luggage. Aha, ahh. Yes, I . . .
                I . . . but it's yours, yours, it
                follows you, it won't follow me.

                    TWOFLOWER
                Ah. Luggage. This is Rincewind.
                You're his now, right?

The Luggage slowly extends its legs,
turns very deliberately and looks at
Rincewind.

                    TWOFLOWER
                It doesn't really belong to anyone
                but itself really.

                    RINCEWIND
                        (uncertainly)
                Yes.

                    TWOFLOWER
                Well . . . I guess this is it.

Twoflower holds out his hand.

                    RINCEWIND
Yes.

                    TWOFLOWER
Goodbye, Rincewind. When I get
home, I'll send you a postcard or
something.

Rincewind holds out his hand. They both
check palms and then . . .

                    RINCEWIND
Oh come here.

Rincewind hugs Twoflower.

                    RINCEWIND
And . . . any time you're
passing . . . someone here is bound
to know where I am.

                    TWOFLOWER
Yeah.

                    TWOFLOWER
Well . . . I guess that's about it
then.

                    RINCEWIND
Yes, that's about it right enough.

                    TWOFLOWER
Right. Yeah.

                    RINCEWIND
Right.

Twoflower walks up the gangplank, which
the crew haul up behind him.

Rincewind, Cohen and Bethan all wave him
goodbye.

Rincewind looks over his shoulder and
starts.

The PATRICIAN, in a sedan chair, is
watching. He sees Twoflower aboard the
ship and gives Rincewind the smallest of
nods, before being carried away.

Rincewind watches him leave and then he
looks down at the Luggage.

It stares back at him.

                    RINCEWIND
No, no, no, no. I don't want you.
I give you to yourself. Do you
understand?

He turns his back on it and stalks away.
After a few seconds he is aware of the
footsteps behind him and spins.

                    RINCEWIND
I said I don't want you. Go on. Go
away.

They pad along the quay and into the city, two dots on a dwindling landscape which, as the CAMERA CRANES up and the perspective broadens to watch the ship sets sail and be propelled slowly out onto the turbid waters of the Ankh, where it catches the tide and turns towards the open sea, Twoflower standing proudly at the prow, watching the horizon, and Bethan and Cohen watching him go.

THE END

EXT. AMPHIHEATRE/KRULL/ARCH-ASTRONOMER'S TOWER – DAY

> **DIM STUDENT**
> So . . . does that mean the star turtle's female then?
>
> **ASTROZOOLOGIST 2**
> Well . . . in my opinion it's all a question of perspective.

He kicks the Luggage.

The Luggage sags.

Rincewind stalks away. After he has gone a few yards he stops and listens. There is no sound. He turns.

The Luggage is where he left it. It looks sort of huddled.

Rincewind thinks for a while.

> **RINCEWIND**
> All right. Come on.

He turns his back and strides off towards the University.

The Luggage waits for a few moments then . . . extends its legs again and pads after him.

AFTERWORD
By Ian Sharples and Rod Brown

WE HAVE to say how thrilled we were, after *Hogfather*, that Sky One and RHI Entertainment commissioned us to produce a further Discworld adaptation, in the form of *The Colour of Magic*. So the very first and biggest thanks must go to Sophie Turner Laing, Richard 'The Alchemist' Woolfe, Elaine Pyke, Sarah Conroy and Huw Kennair-Jones at Sky, and Robert Halmi Sr. and Robert Halmi Jr. at RHI Entertainment, for agreeing to another journey through the Discworld, for investing their enthusiasm and experience and for backing us to deliver a project that was even more ambitious than the last.

Standing on the *Hogfather* set one day with Terry Pratchett, watching some wizardly action being filmed, we were talking about all the hard work that goes in to making a show like ours. It was suggested to Terry that it might all be much easier if there were a filmmaking spell we could use. 'Ah yes, that's very simple,' he said. 'All you need is a good story, a big pot of money, a few hundred people and several months; that's a filmmaking spell.' That's a wonderful Terry line, with all his usual wit, well-observed humour, understatement – and a large dollop of tongue-in-cheek truth.

Those few simple ingredients really are all that is needed. As producers, we would like to think that we provide these ingredients, but for the spell to turn out well, really well, as *The Colour of Magic* has done, there needs to be the magic itself: that certain something that you can't quantify, that you can't always see at first, and that you can't take for granted. That magic – that spark – comes from the cast and crew, every day on set, and throughout the whole process, each adding their own touches through talent, perseverance and dedication. So here is our opportunity to thank some of those who helped make the spell work so very well, and produce such a great end result. We are extremely proud of it, and we hope all of you are too.

To all our fabulous cast, for making the journey so enjoyable: the incomparable Sir David Jason, who insisted on doing all his own stunts (well, nearly all!), and Sean Astin, who encouraged him. Both of them were big fans of Terry's work before they joined the project – David had been wanting to play Rincewind for many years, and Sean once queued up at a book signing in New Zealand whilst working there on a previous series of movies you might have seen him in. Tim Curry was a fabulous Trymon, and who other than Jeremy Irons could have played the Patrician? Our casting director Emma Style never flinched from approaching actors who we thought we might not be able to get, but somehow nearly always did.

Behind the cameras we used many of the same team who worked so well together on *Hogfather*. Our BAFTA Award-winning VFX supervisor Simon Thomas, having previously made pigs fly, now had to produce dragons and trolls, with the help of MPC, Fluid Pictures and Mac Guff. Our production designer Ricky Eyres and his team, with their usual flair and ingenuity, had to wrestle with the challenges of blowing up the Broken Drum right after they had finished building it, not to mention working out what a Dragon Home really looks like. Jane Spicer, our costume designer, had to cope with the rare problem of upside-down sword fighting – just how do wizards' robes behave when you hang them upside down during a (talking) sword fight? Our make-up and hair designer Clare Juhasz did brilliant work with a huge variety of wigs and other facial hair (real, artificial – and orang-utan).

Gavin Finney BSC, our BAFTA-nominated (for *Hogfather* . . . he was robbed!) director of photography always seemed to be in three places at the same time, and of course he had the ultimate challenge of bringing the very colour of magic itself to the screen – no pressure there, then!

For keeping it all together for us on a daily basis we have to thank Peter Freeman, our first assistant director, who has undoubtedly read more Discworld books than anyone else on the crew, and our line producer, Sean Glynn, for making sure the ten thousand small and not-so-small things that needed doing each day just got done, and with the assistance of our production manager Sophie Inman, made sure that the drama stayed in front of the camera and not behind it. Our production accountant Dan Liddiard was patient and dedicated throughout the project, keeping tabs on the pot of money.

Our editing duo of Joe McNally and Liz Webber worked tirelessly to complete the film on a very tight deadline, without loosing the essence of Terry's story, its pacing, action and comic timing and, most of all, the inherent sense of fun.

The pictures, of course, are only part of the story, and sound recordist Henry Milliner and sound supervisor Dan Green delivered a mix worthy of any big budget movie, with fabulous sound effects and atmospherics, driven along by our terrific original score from David A. Hughes and Paul E. Francis. How do you do it, fellas?

A special thanks is due here to David Allcock, for generating the very detailed production storyboards, only a tiny selection of which is included in this book, and of course to Bill Kaye our unit stills photographer for his outstanding on set photographs that have brought the last two hundred and fifty pages to life.

As the man with the most job titles, a big thanks to Vadim Jean, our writer, director and business partner, for his boundless energy and enthusiasm as a filmmaker, and for turning up every day to squeeze everything possible from the resources at his disposal, and for delivering a show that is so very different to *Hogfather*.

We need to thank all of our fellow Mobsters, and in particular John Brocklehurst, our fourth partner, for his support, and although they are not on the crew list, we also owe a big debt of gratitude and lots of love to our wives, Pauline and Kate, for putting up with us calling each other on the phone day and night for long conversations about all manner of things – we really couldn't do it without you.

To all the other providers of magic on the cast and crew a great many thanks: we know who you all are and what you contributed to this particular filmmaking spell, even though we haven't the space to mention you all by name here. We hope you enjoyed the journey to Krull and back as much as we did.

And finally, to Terry Pratchett himself, without whom there simply would be no spell at all. He has always been interested in everything we've done, and made himself available to offer suggestions and advice about a whole host of details, from costumes to picture boxes to swords, and in particular on the script, re-writing lines for the Patrician once he was cast, and even providing the rather simplistic hook for this afterword. He once again trusted us with his Discworld, to play with his creation and characters, and we hope we didn't disappoint.

Ian Sharples and Rod Brown
Producers
London 2008

CAST

Rincewind	David Jason
Twoflower	Sean Astin
Trymon	Tim Curry
Patrician	Jeremy Irons
Narrator	Brian Cox
Galder Weatherwax	James Cosmo
Voice of Death	Christopher Lee
Ninereeds	Janet Suzman
Cohen the Barbarian	David Bradley
Arch-Astronomer	Nigel Planer
Broadman	Stephen Marcus
Bethan	Laura Haddock
Herrena	Liz May Brice
Liessa	Karen David
Picture Imp	Geoffrey Hutchings
Death	Marnix Van Den Broeke
Head Librarian	Nicolas Tennant
Jiglad Wert	Michael Mears
Lumuel Panter	Roger Aston Griffiths
Ganmack Treehallett	Will Keen
Spold	Peter Copley
Wizard Leader	Ian Puleston-Davies
Narrowbolt	James Greene
Ymor	Ian Burfield
Rerpf	Arthur White
Zlorf	Miles Richardson
Luggage	Richard Da Costa
Third Rank Wizard/Spell Voice 2/Kring	Andy Robb
Master Launchcontroller	Adam Ewan
Astrozoologist 1/Rabble-rouser	Phillip Philmar
Astrozoologist 2	Terry Pratchett
Dim Student	Thomas Morrison
Brother of the Order	Brian Hammond
Blind Hugh	Paul M Meston
Gancia	Christopher Willoughby
Weems	Pia Mechler
Barbarian Chieftain	Shend
Barbarian 1	Ray Newe
Marchessa	Noma Dumezweni
Big Star Man/Star Refugee	Joe Sims
Book Burner Woman	Bridget Turner
Lackjaw	Rusty Goffe
Alchemist	Richard Woolfe
Spell Voice 1	Eloise Joseph

ARCH ASTRONOMER'S TOWER.

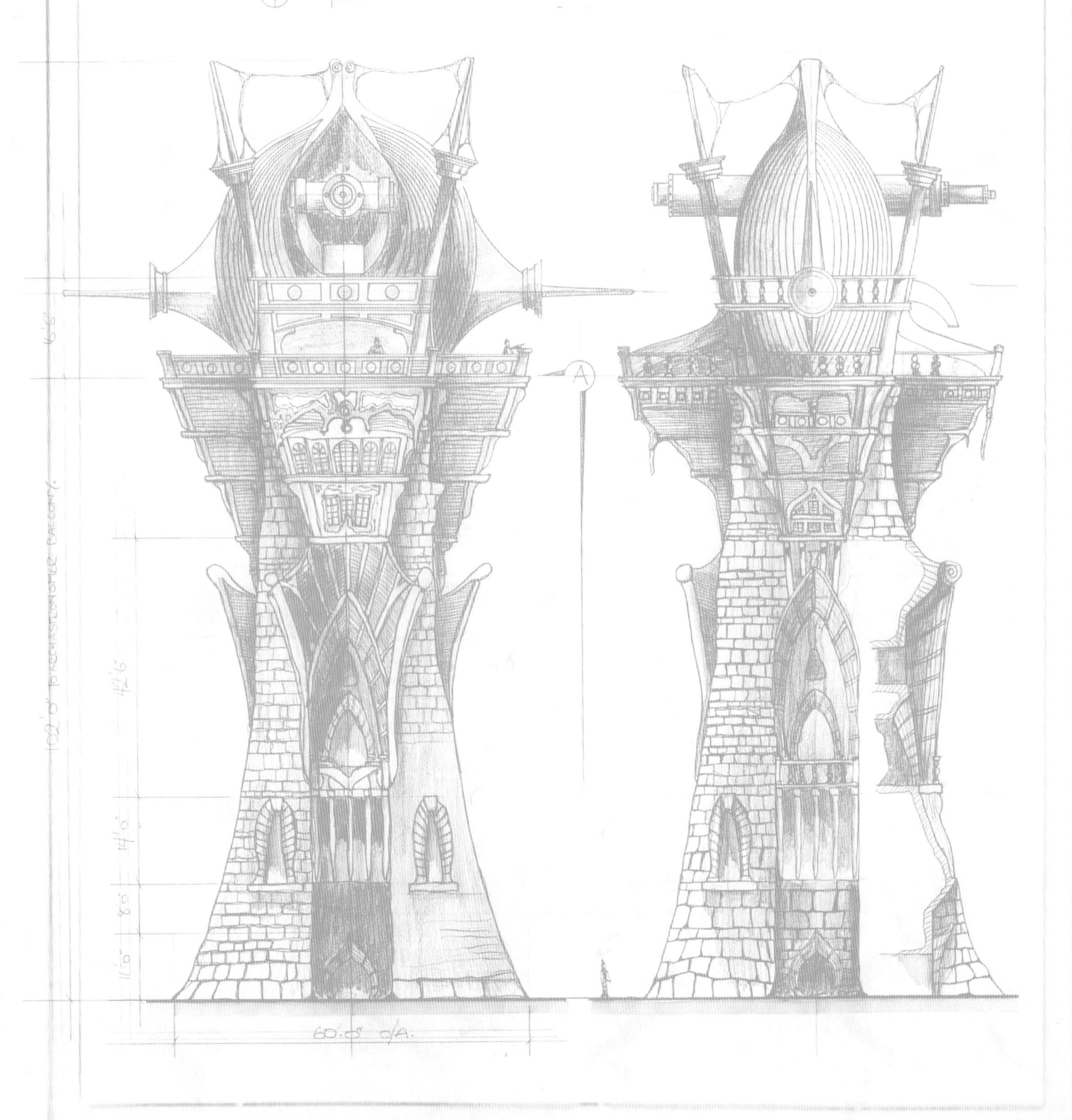